SK 2/2017 very good!!!

S0-BZO-387

MURDER
LIST

*Also by Julie Garwood
in Large Print:*

Castles
Killjoy

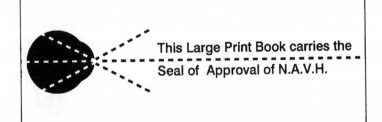

This Large Print Book carries the
Seal of Approval of N.A.V.H.

MURDER LIST

Julie Garwood

Thorndike Press • Waterville, Maine

Copyright © 2004 by Julie Garwood

All rights reserved.

Published in 2005 by arrangement with The Ballantine
Publishing Group, a division of Random House, Inc.

Thorndike Press® Large Print Basic.

The tree indicium is a trademark of Thorndike Press.

The text of this Large Print edition is unabridged.
Other aspects of the book may vary from the original edition.

Set in 16 pt. Plantin by Minnie B. Raven.

Printed in the United States on permanent paper.

Library of Congress Cataloging-in-Publication Data

Garwood, Julie.
    Murder list / Julie Garwood.
        p. cm.
    ISBN 0-7862-6514-0 (lg. print : hc : alk. paper)
    1. Large type books.   I. Title.
                                                2004062107

MURDER LIST

National Association for Visually Handicapped
---------------------- *serving the partially seeing*

As the Founder/CEO of NAVH, the only national health agency solely devoted to those who, although not totally blind, have an eye disease which could lead to serious visual impairment, I am pleased to recognize Thorndike Press★ as one of the leading publishers in the large print field.

Founded in 1954 in San Francisco to prepare large print textbooks for partially seeing children, NAVH became the pioneer and standard setting agency in the preparation of large type.

Today, those publishers who meet our standards carry the prestigious "Seal of Approval" indicating high quality large print. We are delighted that Thorndike Press is one of the publishers whose titles meet these standards. We are also pleased to recognize the significant contribution Thorndike Press is making in this important and growing field.

Lorraine H. Marchi, L.H.D.
Founder/CEO
NAVH

★ Thorndike Press encompasses the following imprints: Thorndike, Wheeler, Walker and Large Print Press.

Prologue

The first day of kindergarten at the exclusive Briarwood School was the worst day of Regan Hamilton Madison's life. It was such a disaster she made up her mind never to go back.

She had started out the day believing the new school would be wonderful. And why not? She'd been told so by her brothers and her mother, and she had no reason to doubt them. Seated in the back of her family's limo for the ride to Briarwood, she proudly wore her new school uniform, a navy blue and gray plaid pleated skirt; a white blouse with mandatory pointed collar; a navy blue tie, knotted just like a man's tie; and a matching gray blazer with a pretty gold emblem of the school's initials on the breast pocket. Her curly hair was pinned back with school-approved, navy blue barrettes. Everything she wore was brand-new, including her white knee-high socks and navy blue loafers.

Regan had thought school would be fun. For the past two years, she and nine classmates at her posh preschool had been pampered and told how wonderful they were by teachers who never lost their smiles. She fully expected her first day at Briarwood to be about the same. Maybe even better.

Her mother was supposed to ride with her to the new school, just like all the other mothers — and sometimes even fathers — of new students did, but due to circumstances she assured her she couldn't control, her mother had to stay in London with her new boyfriend and couldn't get back to Chicago in time.

Grandmother Hamilton would have been happy to go with her, but she, too, was out of the country, visiting friends, and wouldn't be home for two more weeks.

When Regan had spoken to her mother over the phone the day before, she'd told her she didn't need Mrs. Tyler, the housekeeper, to take her to school. Her mother had then suggested Aiden. Regan knew that if she had asked her oldest brother, he would have done it. He was seventeen and wouldn't like going with her, but he would have . . . if she had asked. He would do anything for her, just like her other brothers, Spencer and Walker.

Regan decided she didn't want anyone to walk her to her classroom. She was a big girl now. The uniform she wore proved it, and if she got lost, she would simply ask for help from one of the smiling teachers.

School, as it turned out, wasn't at all what she had imagined. No one had told her kindergarten at Briarwood lasted all day. She hadn't been warned about the huge number of children attending the school, either, and she certainly hadn't been warned about the bullies. They were everywhere. But she was most concerned about one older girl in particular who liked to torment kindergartners when the teachers weren't looking.

By the time the school bell rang to dismiss the students at three o'clock that afternoon, Regan was so distraught and worn out she had to bite her lower lip to keep from crying.

There were cars and limos lined up in the circular drive. Evan, her driver, got out of the car and started toward her.

Regan spotted him but was too tired to run to him, so he hurried toward her, alarmed at her appearance. Her barrettes were dangling on strands in her face; her necktie was undone; her shirttail was out, and one of her knee-high socks was down around her ankle. The five-year-old looked as if she'd gone through a tumble cycle in the clothes dryer. Evan opened the back door for her as he inquired, "Everything all right, Regan?"

Head down she responded, "Yes."

"How was school today?"

She dove into the car. "I don't want to talk about it."

That specific question was asked again by the housekeeper when she opened the front door for her. "I don't want to talk about it," Regan repeated.

The housekeeper took her book bag. "Thank you," Regan said. She ran up the circular staircase and down the south hallway to her bedroom, slammed the door shut, and promptly burst into tears.

Regan knew she was a disappointment to her mother because, try though she did, she couldn't keep her emotions under control. If she fell and scraped her knee and it stung, she just had to cry, no matter where she was or who was around to observe her behavior.

When she was unhappy, she broke all the rules her mother had tried to teach her. Regan had been told time and again to be ladylike, but she wasn't sure what that entailed, except, of course, to keep her knees together when seated in a chair. She didn't like to suffer in silence, no matter how golden that rule was in the Madison household. She didn't particularly care about being brave either, and if she was miserable, then her family needed to hear all about it.

Unfortunately, the only family member home at the moment was Aiden. He was the least sympathetic, probably because he was the oldest, and couldn't be bothered with the worries of a five-year-old. He hated it when she cried, but that didn't stop her.

She blew her nose, washed her face, and changed her clothes. After she removed her uniform, she carefully folded it and then dropped it into the wastebasket. Since she wasn't going back to that terrible school, she wouldn't need those ugly clothes ever again. She put on shorts with a matching top and broke another rule by running barefoot down the hall to her brother's room.

She timidly knocked on the door. "Could I come in?"

She didn't wait for an answer but opened the door, ran across the room to his bed, and jumped up on the soft comforter he always tossed on the floor when he slept. Folding her legs underneath her, she pulled the dangling, school-approved barrettes from her hair and dropped them in her lap.

Aiden looked irritated. Dressed in his rugby clothes, he was sitting at his desk, surrounded by textbooks. She didn't notice he was on the phone until he said good-bye and hung up.

"You're supposed to wait until I say it's okay for you to come in my room," he said. "You don't just barge in." Then, when she didn't respond, he leaned back in his chair, studied her face, and asked, "Have you been crying?"

She thought about it and decided to break another rule. She lied. "No," she said, her gaze glued to the floor.

He knew she wasn't telling the truth but decided not to press the honesty issue now. His little sister was clearly distraught. "Is something wrong?" he asked, knowing full well there was.

She wouldn't look at him. "Nooo . . ." she said, drawing the word out.

He let out a loud sigh. "I don't have time to guess what the problem is, Regan. I'm going to have to leave for practice in a couple of minutes. Tell me what's wrong."

She lifted her shoulders in a shrug. "Nothing's wrong. Honest."

She was making circles with her fingertips on top of the comforter. Aiden gave up trying to find out what was worrying her. He bent down and put on his shoes. He suddenly remembered that today was Regan's first day at Briarwood and casually asked, "How was school?"

He was totally unprepared for her response. She burst into tears and threw herself down, burying her face in his comforter and conveniently wiping her eyes and her nose on his duvet. She told him everything she'd been saving up since recess. The problem was, she didn't make a lick of sense.

It all came out in one long, rambling, barely coherent, sentence. "I hate school and I'm never going back, not ever, 'cause they didn't let us have snacks and I had to sit still for too long and there was this girl and the other big girl made her cry and the big girl said if we told teacher, she'd get us too and I didn't know what to do so I went by the building with the girl at recess and I helped her cry and now I'm never going back to that bad school again 'cause tomorrow the big girl said she was going to get the girl again."

Aiden was astonished. Regan was wailing for all she was worth. Had she not been so miserable, he would have laughed. Such drama. She got that trait from the Hamilton side of the family. All the Hamiltons wore their emotions on their sleeves. He and Spencer and Walker fortunately took after the Madison side. They were far more reserved.

Regan was making so much noise Aiden didn't hear the knock on the door. Spencer and Walker came rushing inside. Both brothers were tall, lanky, and dark-haired like Aiden. Spencer was fifteen, and of the three brothers, he had the softest heart. Walker had just turned fourteen. He was the daredevil in the family and the most reckless. He looked as if he'd been through a war. His arms and face were covered with bruises. Two days before, he'd climbed up on the roof to retrieve a football, had lost his footing, and surely would have broken his neck if he hadn't grabbed hold of a tree branch to slow his descent. His friend Ryan hadn't been as fortunate. Walker landed on him and broke his arm. Ryan had been the junior varsity quarterback but now would have to sit out the season. Walker didn't feel much guilt about the accident. He blamed the mishap on the branch that had trapped Ryan making it impossible for him to get out of Walker's way.

Walker now was looking for bruises on Regan. None were visible, so why then was she crying? "What'd you do to her?" he asked Aiden.

"I didn't do anything," Aiden answered.

"Then what's wrong with her?" Walker asked. He leaned over the bed and inspected his little sister, unsure what to do.

Spencer nudged him out of his way, sat down next to Regan, and began to awkwardly pat her shoulders.

She was finally calming down. Aiden let out another loud sigh. Maybe the storm was over. He finished tying his shoes as he said, "There, she's feeling better. Just don't ask her about —"

"So how was school?" Walker asked at the same time.

The wailing started all over again. "—school," Aiden finished. He lowered his head and turned toward the desk so his sister wouldn't see him smile. He didn't want to hurt her tender feelings, but Lord, was she loud. Considering her size, the noise she made was downright impressive.

"She had a bad day," he told his brothers.

"You think?" Spencer responded.

Regan stopped crying long enough to say, "I'm not ever going back there."

"What happened?" Walker asked.

Regan recited her litany of complaints in between her sobs.

"You have to go back," Spencer said.

It was the wrong thing to say. "No, I don't."

"Yes, you do," Spencer said.

"Daddy wouldn't make me go."

"How do you know what he would do? He died when you were still a baby. You can't possibly remember him."

"Yes, I can. I remember him good."

"Your grammar is appalling," Aiden remarked.

"Which is why you need to go to school," Spencer pointed out. He had to raise his voice to be heard because his sister was once again crying.

"Damn, she's loud," Aiden muttered. He shook his head and added, "Okay. I'm going to be late for practice if I don't leave soon, so let's get to the bottom of this. Regan, stop wiping your nose on my sheets and sit up."

He tried to make his voice stern. Neither his order nor his tone made any difference to her. She wasn't going to stop crying until she was good and ready.

"Listen, Regan. You need to calm down and tell us what happened," Walker said.

"What exactly did the big kid do?"

Spencer dug into his pocket and pulled out a crumpled Kleenex. "Here," he said. "Wipe your nose and sit up. Come on. We can't fix this problem for you until we know exactly what the big kid did, okay?"

Aiden was shaking his head. "Regan's going to fix the problem," he said.

She bolted upright. "No, I'm not, 'cause I'm not going back to that bad school."

"Running away isn't the answer," Aiden said.

"I don't care. I'm staying home."

"Hold on, Aiden. If some big bully is picking on our sister, then by God, we ought to . . ." Walker began.

Aiden raised his hand for silence. "Let's get all the facts straight before we do anything, Walker. Now, Regan," he said, his voice soothing, "how old was this big girl?"

"I don't know."

"Okay. Do you know what grade she's in?"

"How would she know that?" Spencer asked. "Regan's just a kindergartner."

"I do too know," Regan said. "She's in second grade, and her name's Morgan, and she's mean."

"We've established that she's mean," Aiden said impatiently. He checked the time before continuing. "So now we're getting somewhere."

Walker and Spencer were both smiling. Fortunately, Regan didn't see.

"You said that the second grader made another girl cry?" Aiden asked.

Regan nodded. "She made her cry, all right."

"What did she do to make her cry?" Walker asked. "Did she hit her?"

"No."

"Then what?" Now Walker sounded as frustrated as Aiden did.

Tears welled up in Regan's eyes again. "She made the girl give her her barrettes."

"Was the girl in kindergarten?" Aiden asked.

"She's a very nice girl too. She sits beside me at the round table. Her name's Cordelia, but she said everybody calls her Cordie and I should call her Cordie too."

"Do you like this Cordelia?" Spencer asked.

"Yes," she said. "And there's another girl I like too. Her name's Sophie, and she sits at the same table with me and Cordie."

"There you go," Aiden said. "You've only been at the new school for one day, and you've already made two new friends."

Believing the trauma was over, he

grabbed his car keys and headed for the door. Walker stopped him. "Wait a minute, Aiden. You can't leave until we figure out what to do about the bully."

Aiden paused at the door. "You've got to be kidding. The bully is a second grader."

"We still need to do something to protect Regan," he insisted.

"Like what?" Aiden demanded. "You think maybe all three of us should go to school tomorrow and terrorize the kid?"

Regan perked up. "That'd be good," she said. "Make her leave Cordie and Sophie and me alone."

"Or," Aiden said, "you could handle the problem on your own. You could stand up to the bully. Tell her you aren't going to give her anything and to leave you and your friends alone."

"I want the first one."

Aiden blinked. "The first one?"

"The one where you and Spencer and Walker come to school with me and scare her. That's the one I choose. You could stay all day with me if you want."

"This isn't a multiple choice . . ." Aiden began.

"Hold on. Didn't you say the bully . . . what's her name?" Walker asked.

"Morgan."

19

"Okay. Didn't you say that Morgan was going to torment Cordelia again tomorrow?"

Regan sniffed, and her eyes widened.

"So why are you worried? She's not coming after you," Walker said.

She looked so serious. "Because she's my friend, Walker."

Aiden smiled. "How do you think she'll feel if you don't show up tomorrow?"

"Cordie isn't going back to that school either. She told me so."

"Yeah, well, I'm sure her parents will make her go," Aiden said. "You know, Regan, there are two kinds of people in the world. Those who run from bullies and those who face them."

She wiped the tears away from her face. "What kind am I?"

"You're a Madison. You face trouble. You don't run from anyone."

She didn't like hearing that but knew from the set of her brother's jaw that he wasn't going to change his mind, no matter how much she argued. She at least felt better because she had shared her fears.

The next morning when Mrs. Tyler was brushing Regan's hair, she thought about not wearing the barrettes, but she wore them anyway, just in case Cordelia needed extra ones.

By the time she arrived at Briarwood, she was sick to her stomach. She spotted Cordie waiting by the school doors.

"I thought you weren't coming back to this school," Regan said when she reached her.

"Daddy made me," Cordie answered dejectedly.

"My brother made me."

Sophie called out to them. She had just gotten out of her car and was struggling to get her book bag straps over her shoulders.

When she saw Cordie and Regan together, she ran to them, her long golden hair flying out behind her. Regan thought Sophie looked just like a princess. Her hair was such a light color, it looked almost white, and her eyes were the prettiest shade of green.

"I know what we can do," Sophie announced the second she'd caught up with them. "We can hide behind the fifth graders on the jungle gym during recess, and then, Regan, you can sneak up on Morgan and get Cordie's barrettes back."

"How?" Regan asked.

"How what?" Sophie said.

"How do I get the barrettes back?"

"I don't know, but maybe you can think of something."

"Daddy says I have to tell the teacher about Morgan, but I'm not going to," Cordie said. She brushed her dark curls over her shoulder and added, "Telling will only make Morgan madder."

Regan was suddenly feeling very adult. "We have to tell her to leave us alone. Aiden said so."

"Who's Aiden?" Sophie asked.

"My brother."

"But Morgan's only bothering *me*," Cordie said. "Not you or Sophie. You should run and hide from her."

"You could hide with us," Sophie suggested.

"Teacher will make us go outside for recess," Cordie said. "Morgan will find me then."

"We'll stay together, and when she tries to make you give her things and tries to scare you, we'll tell her to go away. Maybe because there's three of us, we could scare her good."

"Maybe," Cordie allowed, but her voice lacked enthusiasm, and Regan knew she didn't really believe it.

"By recess I can come up with a good plan," Sophie said.

She sounded so sure of herself, so confident. Regan wished she could be more like

Sophie. Her new friend didn't seem to fret about anything. Regan, on the other hand, was a worrier. And obviously so was Cordie. The two of them worried all morning about Morgan.

Because it was sprinkling outside, they had their first recess in their room, but by lunchtime and general recess, when the kindergartners mingled with the rest of the school, it was sunny, and they were forced to go to the playground.

Too late, Regan realized she shouldn't have eaten lunch. The milk in her stomach was rapidly turning sour, and she felt as though she'd swallowed a rock.

Morgan was waiting for them by the swing sets reserved for the kindergarten and first grade. Fortunately, Sophie had her new plan in mind.

"As soon as Morgan sees Cordie and starts walking over to her, I'll run inside school and get Mrs. Grant."

"Are you going to tell teacher what Morgan's doing to Cordie?"

"No."

"How come?" Regan asked.

"I don't want people to call me a snitch. My dad says being a snitch is the worst thing you can be."

"Then what are you going to do?" Regan

asked. She was watching Morgan out of the corner of her eye. So far, the bully hadn't spotted them.

"I don't know yet what I'll tell teacher, but I'll get her to come outside, and then I'll get her to get close enough to hear Morgan scare Cordie. Maybe she will see Morgan making Cordie give her her barrettes."

"Sophie, you're so smart," Cordie said.

It was a great plan, Regan thought. Sophie disappeared inside the school just as Morgan, looking every bit like the giant Regan likened her to, came stomping toward them.

The two girls took an involuntary step back. Morgan stepped forward. Regan frantically looked for Sophie and Mrs. Grant but couldn't find either one of them. She was terrified. She stared at Morgan's feet, thinking they looked as big as Aiden's, and then timidly looked up into her beady, brown eyes. She felt nauseated.

Now Regan had two horrible worries. Suffering Morgan's wrath, and puking in front of the entire school.

The bully put her hand out, palm up, and glared at Cordie. "Give them here," she said, wiggling her fingers. Cordie immediately reached up to remove the barrettes, but Regan grabbed her hand and stopped her.

"No," she said as she stepped in front of Cordie. "You leave her alone."

It was the bravest thing she had ever done, and she felt faint and giddy and sick all at the same time. Bile was burning a path up into her throat now, and she couldn't quite swallow, but she didn't care how miserable she was. She was being brave, and she couldn't wait to tell Aiden all about it.

Morgan poked her in the chest. Regan staggered back and almost fell down, but she quickly righted herself and defiantly planted her feet. "You leave Cordie alone," she repeated. The bile in her throat made her voice weak, and so she swallowed hard and then shouted the order again.

Uh-oh. Her stomach lurched, and she knew she was never going to make it to the girls' restroom in time.

"Okay," Morgan said. She took another threatening step forward and poked Regan again. "Then *you* give me something."

Regan's gurgling stomach was happy to oblige.

Chapter One

The demon wanted out.

The man wasn't surprised or alarmed. The beast always began to stir at the end of the day when his mind wasn't consumed with his job, and his body so desperately needed to relax.

For a long time, nearly a full year, the demon had hidden from him, and he hadn't known it was there. And so he'd naively believed that he was having panic attacks, or spells, as he liked to think of them, because that somehow made them less threatening. They started with a yearning deep in his belly. It wasn't altogether unpleasant. He likened the sensation to wrapping his arms around a hot stone to warm his freezing body, but as the day progressed, the stone began to get hotter and hotter, until it radiated unbearable heat. Anxiety would come over him then, horrific anxiety that would make his skin crawl and his lungs burn with the need to scream and scream and scream, and in desperation he would think about taking one of his special pills the doctor

26

had prescribed, but he never did take anything, not even an aspirin, for fear the medication would weaken him.

He believed he was a good man. He paid his taxes, went to church on Sundays, and held down a full-time job. It was a stressful, had-to-stay-on-his-toes kind of job, requiring his full concentration, and there wasn't time to think or worry about the heavy burden waiting for him at home. He didn't mind the long hours. In fact, there were times he was grateful for them. He never ran from his responsibilities in his professional or his personal life. He took care of his invalid wife, Nina. At her insistence they had moved to Chicago for a new start after the accident. He'd found employment within two weeks of his arrival and had felt that was a good omen. It was a hectic but joyful time. He and Nina decided to use a small portion of the settlement money to purchase a spacious story-and-a-half house on the outskirts of the city, and once they were unpacked, he spent the summer evenings putting in ramps and modifying the first floor so that Nina wouldn't have any trouble getting around in her new state-of-the-art, featherweight wheelchair. Nina's legs had been mangled in the accident, and she would, of course, never walk again. He accepted what fate had dealt them and moved forward. He was relieved when his wife slowly regained her strength and learned to do for herself during the day.

When he was home, he insisted on pampering her. He prepared their dinner every night and did the dishes, then spent the rest of the evening with her watching their favorite television shows.

They'd been married ten years, and in all that time their love hadn't diminished. If anything, the terrible accident had removed any possibility of their falling into complacency or taking each other for granted. And no wonder. His sweet, gentle Nina had died on that operating table, and then, miracle of miracles, had come back to him. The surgeons had worked through the night to save her. When he heard the news that she would recover, he got down on his knees in the hospital chapel and vowed to spend the rest of his life making her happy.

He lived a rich, full life . . . with one little exception.

Awareness of the demon hadn't been gradual. No, enlightenment had come all at once.

It was the middle of the night. He hadn't

been able to sleep, and rather than toss and turn and possibly wake Nina, he went to the kitchen on the opposite end of the house and paced about. He thought a glass of warm milk might help calm his jitters and make him sleepy, but it really didn't do much good. He was putting the empty glass in the sink when it slipped out of his hand and shattered in the basin. The sound seemed to reverberate throughout the house. He rushed to the bedroom door and stood outside, waiting and listening. The noise hadn't awakened his wife, and he felt a moment of relief as he padded back to the kitchen.

His anxiety was building. Was he losing his mind? No, no. He was having one of his spells. That was all. And this one wasn't so terrible. He could handle it.

The newspaper was on the counter where he'd left it. He picked it up and carried it to the table. He decided he would read every single page, or until he was so sleepy he couldn't keep his eyes open.

He started with the sports section, read every word, and then moved on to the metropolitan news. He scanned an article about the dedication of a new park and jogging path, spread the paper wide and immediately saw the photo of a beautiful young woman standing in front of a group of men. She was posed with scissors ready to cut a ribbon draped from one stake to another across the path. And she was smiling at him.

He couldn't take his eyes off her.

He was reading the names under the photo when it happened. He suddenly felt a crushing tightness, and he couldn't catch his breath. A jolt very much like lightning raced through his heart causing excruciating pain. Was he having a heart attack, or was it another panic attack?

Try to calm down, he told himself. Just calm down. Take deep breaths.

The anxiety was growing even stronger, and with it came the horrific yet familiar terror. Then his skin began to burn and itch, and he frantically scratched his arms and legs as he jumped up and paced around the kitchen island. What was happening to him?

He realized he was running and forced himself to stop. Looking down, he saw the long, jagged scratches. There were bloody streaks on his arms and legs, some cuts so deep, blood dripped on the floor. He was close to exploding. He tore at his hair and whimpered, but the terror was taunting him now. Then, like a blinding light, the epiphany came. He suddenly realized he no longer had control over his own body. He couldn't even make himself breathe.

With startling clarity he saw and understood. Someone else was breathing for him.

He awakened the following morning curled up in the fetal position on the kitchen floor. Had he fainted? He thought maybe he had. He staggered to his feet and braced his hands on the island to steady himself. Closing his eyes, he took several deep breaths and slowly straightened. He spotted the scissors on top of the folded newspaper. Had he placed them there? He couldn't remember. He put the scissors back in the drawer where they belonged and picked up the newspaper to throw it into the recycle bin in the garage. He saw the clipping from the newspaper then. Both the article and the photo of the smiling woman were there in the center of his table, waiting for him. He knew who had placed them there. And he knew why.

The demon wanted her.

He buried his face in his hands and wept.

He knew that he must find another way to placate the beast. Physical activity seemed to help. He went to the gym and began to work out like a man obsessed. One of his favorite routines was to put on boxing gloves and pound the bag as hard as he could for as long as he could. He would lose track of time and stop only when he couldn't raise his arms without suffering unbearable pain.

For days he'd kept his body in the state of perpetual exhaustion. Then, even that wasn't enough.

Time was running out. The demon was consuming him. Ironically, it was his wife who gave him the idea. One evening, while she kept him company as he did the dishes, she suggested that he should have a night out. A night, she insisted, when he could enjoy himself and have some fun with his friends.

He put up quite an argument. There were already too many nights when he had to be away from her because of pressing commitments at work. And what about all the time he left to go running or to work out at the gym? Surely that was enough alone time.

She was more stubborn than he was and wouldn't stop cajoling. He finally agreed, only to make her happy.

And so, tonight would be his first night out. He could already feel the adrenaline pumping. He was as nervous and excited as he had been when he had gone on his first date.

Before leaving home, he told Nina he would be heading into the city after work to meet some friends at Sully's, a popular bar and grill, but she wasn't to worry; if he had more than one drink, he wouldn't drive home. He'd take a cab.

All of it was a lie.

No, he wasn't going to the city to relax. He was going there to hunt.

Chapter Two

Regan Madison had spent three miserable days and nights surrounded by sleazebags. They seemed to be everywhere — in the airports, at the hotel, and on the streets of Rome as well. A sleazebag, as she defined him, was a lecherous but rich old man with a mistress less than half his age hanging on his arm. Regan had never really paid any attention to such couples before her stepfather, Emerson, married Cindy, his child bride. Regan understood the appeal. Cindy had the body of a stripper. She also had the IQ of plywood. And that made her perfect for him.

Fortunately for Regan, the deliriously happy and definitely dysfunctional couple stayed on in Rome while she flew home to Chicago. Exhausted from her long flight, she went to bed early and slept a full eight hours thinking that tomorrow would be a better day.

She was wrong about that.

She awakened at six o'clock the following morning feeling as though a thousand rubber bands were wrapped around her left knee, cutting off her circulation.

She had banged it on her dresser the night before and hadn't taken the time to ice it. The pain was nearly unbearable. Throwing her covers back, she sat up and rubbed her knee until the throbbing subsided.

Her bad knee was the result of an injury in a charity baseball game. She had been playing first base, doing a creditable job too, until she pivoted the wrong way and tore her meniscal cartilage. The orthopedic surgeon she'd consulted advised surgery and assured her she'd be back in action in just a few days, but Regan kept putting the procedure off.

She swung her feet off the bed and leaned forward to stand, cautiously putting her weight on the sore knee. Then, as if she weren't miserable enough, she started sneezing, and her eyes began to water.

Regan had a love/hate relationship with her hometown. She loved the galleries and the museums, thought the shopping was every bit as wonderful as it was in New York — an opinion her two best friends, Sophie and Cordelia, vehemently disagreed with — and she believed that at least eighty percent of the inhabitants were good, decent, law-abiding citizens. Most smiled when she passed them on the street; some even said hello. Like the majority of

Midwesterners, they were friendly and polite, but not intrusive. They were hardy souls, even though they loved to complain about the weather, especially in the winter months when the wind really did feel like knives slicing through your back or chest, depending on whether you were walking away from Lake Michigan or toward it.

For Regan, however, spring was a real nuisance. She suffered from allergies, and each spring, while ragweed and mold flourished, she turned into a walking pharmacy. Yet, she refused to let it slow her down. On the days when the air was heavy or the pollen count was sky high, she stuffed packets of tissues, aspirin, antihistamines, decongestants, and eyedrops into her purse and kept on going.

She had a full day scheduled and knew she should get cracking, but all she wanted to do was crawl under the soft down comforter in her soft warm bed. It was so good to be home.

Home for Regan was a suite at The Hamilton, one of the five-star hotels owned and operated by her family. It was located in the fashionable Water Tower district of Chicago and boasted a reputation for elegance, sophistication, and comfort. For the time being, she was satisfied with her living arrangements. She had everything she needed at the hotel. The corporate offices were there, and so her work was conveniently an elevator ride away. Besides, she had known most of the staff her entire life and thought of them as family.

As much as she wanted to go back to bed, she didn't give in to the urge. Shoving her hair out of her eyes, she staggered into the bathroom, washed her face and brushed her teeth, then put on her workout clothes, clipped her hair in a ponytail, and took the elevator up to the eighteenth floor to do two miles on the new, indoor track. She wasn't about to let a little bout of hay fever or any aches and pains in her knee set her back. Two miles every day, no matter what.

By seven-thirty she was back in her room and had showered, dressed, and eaten her standard breakfast of wheat toast, grapefruit, and hot tea.

Regan had just sat down at the desk in the parlor suite to go over her notes when the phone rang.

Cordelia was calling to check in. "How was Rome?"

"Okay."

"Was your stepfather there?"

"Yes, he was."

"So how could the trip have been okay? Come on, Regan. You're talking to me, Cordie."

Regan sighed. "It was awful," she admitted. "Just awful."

"I take it stepdaddy had his new bride with him?"

"Oh, yes, she was there."

"Is she still hanging out of everything Escada?"

Regan smiled. Cordie did have a way of making the most horrid situations amusing. She knew what her friend was doing — trying to lighten the mood. It worked too. "Not Escada," she corrected. "Versace. And yes, she's still spilling out of everything Versace."

Cordie snorted. "I can just picture it. Were your brothers there?"

"Aiden was, of course. The hotel in Rome was his pet project, and he was his usually serious self. I don't think I've seen him smile in years. Guess that goes with being the oldest."

"What about Spencer and Walker?"

"Spencer had to stay in Melbourne. Some last-minute problems developed with the design for the new hotel. Walker was there, but only for the reception. He wanted to rest up before the race."

"So did you speak to him?"

"Yes, I did."

"Good for you. You've finally forgiven him then, haven't you?"

"I guess I have. He was only doing what he thought was right. Time has given me some perspective, as you predicted, so go ahead and gloat. Besides, I'd feel terrible if he used up all of his lives before I let him know I'd forgiven him. He wrecked another car last month," she added.

"And walked away without a scratch on him, right?"

"That's right."

"I'm glad you aren't mad at him anymore."

"I just wish he wouldn't jump the gun the way he does. He's so impulsive. I have a couple of dates with a man, and he's hiring people to investigate him."

"Excuse me. You had more than a couple of dates with Dennis."

"Yes, well . . ."

"At least you didn't let him break your heart. I know for a fact you didn't love him."

"How did you know?"

"When you broke up, you didn't shed a tear. Face it, Regan, you cry at Puppy Chow commercials. If you didn't cry over

Dennis, your heart wasn't really in it. And just for the record, I'm thrilled you dumped him. He was all wrong for you."

"At the time I didn't think he was all wrong. I thought he was close to perfect. We had so much in common. He loved the theater, the ballet, and the opera, and he didn't mind attending all those fund-raisers. I thought we had the same values —"

"But that wasn't the real Dennis, was it? He was after your money, Regan, and you've got too much going for you to put up with that nonsense."

"You aren't going to give me another pep talk about how pretty and smart I am, are you?"

"No, I don't have time to do the pep talk now. I've got to get back to the lab before one of my students blows it up. I'm calling to make sure you got home okay and to ask if you want to have dinner tonight. I'm starting my grapefruit diet tomorrow."

"I wish I could, but I'm swamped with work. I'm going to be playing catch-up for a week," she said.

"Okay, then plan on Friday, and I'll start the diet on Saturday. We both need to have some fun," Cordie protested. "Last week was awful for me. Monday one of the kids dropped a box of supplies, and every one of the new beakers broke. Then Tuesday I found out my budget for next year has been cut in half. In half," she stressed. "Oh, and on Wednesday Sophie called and asked me to do an errand for her, and that turned out to be pretty awful too."

"What was the errand?"

"She made me go to the police station to check on something."

"What something?"

"You'll have to wait to hear the gory details. Sophie made me promise not to say anything. She wants to explain it to you."

"She's cooking up another scheme, isn't she?"

"Maybe," she answered. "Uh-oh. One of my students is frantically waving to me. Gotta go."

She hung up before Regan could say good-bye. Five minutes later Sophie called. She didn't waste time on pleasantries.

"I need a favor. A big one."

"Rome was fine. Thank you for asking. What kind of favor?"

"Say yes first."

Regan laughed. "I haven't fallen for that ploy since kindergarten."

"Then meet me for lunch. Not today," she hurried to add. "I know you're probably swamped with work, and I've got two meetings back to back I can't miss. Maybe we could do it tomorrow or the day after. I'll need a couple of hours."

"A couple of hours for lunch?"

"Lunch and a favor," she corrected. "We could meet at The Palms at twelve-thirty on Friday. Cordie's through at noon, and she could join us. Can you do Friday?"

"I'm not sure I —"

"I really need your help."

She sounded pitiful. Regan knew it was deliberate manipulation, but she decided to let her get away with it.

"If it's that important . . . ," she began.

"It is."

"Okay, I'll make it work."

"I knew I could count on you. Oh, by the way, I checked with Henry to make sure your calendar was clear next weekend, and I told him to pencil me in."

"For the entire weekend? Sophie, what's going on?"

"I'll explain it to you at lunch, and you'll have a whole week to think about it."

"I can't —"

"I loved the picture in the newspaper. Your hair looked great."

"Sophie, I want to know —"

"I've got to get going. I'll see you Friday at twelve-thirty at The Palms."

Regan wanted to argue, but it was point-less since Sophie had already hung up the phone. She checked the time, then grabbed her PDA and rushed out the door. Paul Greenfield, a senior staff member and a dear friend, was waiting in the lobby. Regan had known Paul since she was a teenager. She'd worked as his intern during the summer months of her junior year in high school, and for those three months she'd been madly in love with him. Paul had known about her infatuation — she'd been ridiculously obvious about what her mother called a bad crush — but he was very sweet about it. Married now with four children of his own who ran him ragged, he always had a ready smile for her. Paul's hair was graying at the temples and he wore bottle-thick glasses, but Regan still thought he was extremely hand-some. He was holding what looked like a five-hundred-page printout in his arms.

"Good morning, Paul. Looks like you've got your hands full."

"Good morning," he replied. "Actually, these are for you."

"Oh?" she took a step back.

He grinned. "Sorry, but about an hour ago I got an e-mail from your brother Aiden."

"Yes?" she asked when he hesitated.

"He was wondering why he hasn't heard from you."

He tried to hand the stack of papers to her. She took another step back and smiled. "What exactly does Aiden want to hear?"

"Your opinion of his report."

"He wrote all that? When in heaven's name did he have time to write a five-hundred-page report?"

"Two hundred and ten pages," he corrected.

"Okay. When did he have time to write a two-hundred-and-ten-page report?"

"You know your brother doesn't sleep."

Or have a life, she thought but didn't dare say because it would have been disloyal. "Apparently not," she said. "What kind of report is it?"

Paul smiled. She was looking at the pages as though she expected a jack-in-the-box to jump out at her. "Aiden's plans for expansion," he said. "He needs to know what you think before he can go forward. All the numbers are there. Spencer and Walker have already gotten on board."

"Bet they didn't have to read the thing."

"Actually, no, they didn't."

She could see the guilty look on his face

as he transferred the pages into her arms. She balanced the PDA on top.

"Aiden didn't even mention this when we were in Rome. He now thinks I should have already read it?"

"There's obviously been a mix-up. This is the second time I've had to have the pages printed for you. The first copy seems to have disappeared. I gave it to Emily," he said, referring to Aiden's assistant. "She insists she gave it to Henry to pass on to you."

"If she had given the report to Henry, he would have given it to me."

Paul was always diplomatic. "It's a puzzle, but I don't believe either one of us should waste time or energy trying to figure it out."

"Yes, right. A puzzle." She couldn't keep the irritation out of her voice. "We both know that Emily —"

He didn't let her continue. "We shouldn't speculate. However, your brother is waiting to hear from you, hopefully by noon today."

"Noon?"

"He told me to tell you not to worry about the time difference."

She gritted her teeth. "Okay. I'll read it this morning."

His smile indicated he was pleased with her decision. "If you have any questions, I'll be in my office until eleven. Then I'm on my way to Miami."

He was walking away when she called out, "You knew I'd cave, didn't you?"

His laughter was her answer. Regan checked the time, groaned, and then straightened her shoulders and headed to her office.

Chapter Three

The murder was a mistake.

He stood in the shadows of a building near the Water Tower district watching the entrance, waiting for the chosen one to appear. The damp, cool night air settled in his bones. He was miserable but didn't dare give up, and so he continued to hide there waiting and hoping for over two hours. Then he finally accepted that he had failed.

Defeated, he climbed back into his Jeep and headed home. Tears came into his eyes, so severe was his disappointment and shame. He heard someone sob, realized that he had made the sound, and impatiently wiped the tears from his cheeks.

He couldn't stop shaking. He had failed. What would the demon do to him now? He sobbed again.

And then, just as he was about to scream with the despair, the answer came. He saw the entrance to Conrad Park and suddenly knew the demon had guided him to where he needed to go. The jogging trail circled the university and the park in a perfect figure eight. He remembered seeing the diagram in the newspaper along with a long article about a festival. The proceeds would go to some sort of charity, but he couldn't remember which one.

You'll find her here, the demon whispered.

He was suddenly relieved. He found a perfect parking spot along the street next to the university. He pulled up beside a telephone pole. There was a poster for a coming race north of the city nailed to it. The poster showed a pretty young woman crossing a finish line.

He started to open the door and then froze. He wasn't dressed properly. He'd worn his cheap but serviceable black suit with a white shirt and pinstriped tie because he thought he'd find her down by the Water Tower district, and he wanted to blend in with the other businessmen going home from work. He had stuffed a baseball cap in his pocket and planned to put it on once he started following her so that no one else on the street would be able to identify him after the fact.

What should he do?

Make the best of it, the demon hissed.

He grabbed his briefcase and decided to act as though he were a professor at the university, walking in a hurry. It wasn't such a stretch. Yes, he could pull it off.

The weather had turned foul again. It had rained hard every day for the past four days, but it was supposed to be clear tonight. The weatherman had obviously been wrong. Damn, he should have thought to bring his umbrella along. It was too late to get one now.

Gripping the vinyl handle of the briefcase in his left hand, he walked quickly along the trail, trying to act as though he knew where he was headed. He walked for almost a mile, a fine mist covering his clothes, the urgency building inside him as he searched for the perfect spot. There weren't many wooded areas, and he knew the specimen would be more cautious and watchful there.

He wasn't too concerned that the mist would keep her away. Runners run, no matter the weather. And there was an important race to get ready for, he thought. Oh, yes, he would find her there.

But where should he hide? He kept walking, looking for a good spot. New lights designed to look like old-fashioned gas lamps were spaced along the path about twenty feet apart, some even closer together near the back of a building he was approaching. A sign with an arrow pointing to the building indicated it was a lecture hall. "Won't do, won't do," he muttered. Too much light for what he intended.

His suit was soaked through, and still he continued on. What was that against the wall? He walked closer, stepped off the path, and then stopped. A shovel? Yes, that's what it was.

There were three large holes along the side of the stone building where shrubs had been pulled out to make room for new ones. One of the workmen had obviously left the shovel behind. And a few other items as well. On the ground next to the shovel was an orange tarp folded haphazardly, and sticking out from one edge was a hammer, rusty but adequate. He seized it, measured the weight and grip in his hand, and held it close to his side. He hadn't thought to bring a weapon. He was strong, terribly strong, and he believed he could subdue any woman, no matter her size, with his bare hands. The hammer might make it easier to convince her not to struggle. Better safe than sorry, he thought.

He walked around the curve in the path and gasped with excitement. A renovation was in progress. There was a pyramid of dead shrubs and trees, the roots like dried-up octopus tentacles reaching into the path. The trash was waiting to be carted away. He looked around for signs of anyone who could see or hear, then picked up a rock, and with his first pitch, broke the lamplight nearest the pile. Still too bright, he decided and threw another rock to break a second lamp.

"Perfect," he whispered. A perfect little nest.

He kept thinking about those big, deep holes someone had thoughtfully left for him. A couple of them were on the south side of the building, but there were two more adjacent to the path with neon orange cones around them. Although he was wearing gloves, he still brushed his palms against his pants as he hunkered down behind the stack of foul-smelling, decomposing rot. His loafers sank into the mud. He gingerly placed the cheap attaché case on the ground next to him and took a deep, calming breath.

His senses were heightened by adrenaline, and he was more attuned to his surroundings. He could hear every little sound, smell every musty scent.

He heard the pounding of feet against the pavement as a runner approached. He smiled with satisfaction. Runners run, no matter what. He scrunched down lower still and squinted through the triangular opening he'd made between the branches. He watched the spot under a bright light he knew the runner would have to pass.

"Yes." The runner was indeed a woman. But was she the right woman? Was she the perfect chosen one? He couldn't see her face — she was looking down at the path as she sped along. He could see her slim, athletic body, though, and her thick, dark hair pulled back in a ponytail. She had to be the one. He stared at her long, luscious, incredibly perfect legs.

Clutching the hammer like a baseball bat, he prepared to spring.

He didn't mean to kill her. He wanted only to daze her. Too late, he discovered his timing was off. He should have let her get past him and then struck her from behind, at the base of her skull, but he was too eager and too inexperienced. She was a fighter, clawing at his face as he struggled to take her down.

He dodged her hands, and when he was finally able to get a good look at her face, he realized she was seeing him clearly. Panic set in, and then fury.

She was pulling pepper spray from her

pocket and screaming at the top of her lungs. He struck her hard — one blow from the hammer — and she collapsed. The demon wouldn't let it end there. Again and again he struck her legs, pounding her knees and her thighs and her ankles.

There was blood everywhere.

Luck stayed on his side, for the mist had turned into a hard rain. He turned his face up to the sky and let the cold rainwater wash the blood away. The crimson stream flowed under his shirt collar giving him goose bumps. He closed his eyes to rest.

He suddenly bolted upright. How long had he been squatting next to her body, stupidly looking up at the black sky while anyone and his uncle could have wandered by?

He shook his head. He had to hide the body.

The holes. Those beautiful, big holes on the side of the building. Dare he risk carrying her all that way? Or should he use the shovel and dig a better hole underneath all the dead shrubs. Yes, that's what he would do. But not yet. He quickly hid her under some branches, then found a spot near the shovel to hunker down and wait. After midnight, when he was sure no one would disturb him, he moved the dead branches and dug a pit for her. He made sure it was deep enough to cover her folded body. As he dragged her to the hole, both shoes and one of her socks came off, so he threw them in. He stuffed her into the hole butt first, shoveled dirt on top of her and patted it down, and then dragged the rotting branches and dead shrubs over his work.

After he covered his footprints as best he could, he stood off to the side of the path to survey his handiwork. He was relieved to see that the rain had already washed the blood away from the walk.

The shaking started when he got back in his Jeep. He could barely get the key into the ignition, so undone was he by what had just happened. By the time he got home, an overwhelming sensation of peace and tranquility eased through his limbs, and he was feeling just like he used to after sex. Satisfied, content, relaxed.

And guilt free. That surprised him a little. He really didn't feel any guilt at all. But then, why should he? The woman had tricked him, and for that reason alone she deserved to die.

Two other runners had passed by while he'd waited to bury the body, and either one of them, both males, might have noticed the bloodstains the rain hadn't completely washed away yet. Yes, he'd taken quite a risk tonight.

He flipped the car lights off before he turned the corner so the nosy bitch neighbor wouldn't see him pulling into his drive. Several weeks before, he'd removed the garage door light. As he approached his house, he drove at a snail's pace. There she was, standing at her kitchen window, staring out. She was always checking on the neighbors.

She disappeared just as the garage door went up. Her name was Carolyn, and she was becoming more than just a pain in the ass. Too bad Carolyn didn't live alone. She took care of her mother. One would think that the old woman would keep her occupied, but apparently that wasn't so. Carolyn was a busybody and intrusive, always wondering when she could stop by to meet Nina. If she kept it up, he would have to do something about her.

After he parked in his garage, he pulled a wooden crate from a shelf and laid the bloody hammer in the bottom. Then he emptied his pockets. The pepper spray and driver's license he'd impulsively taken from the woman went into the box next. He shoved the crate and the attaché case into a corner. After that, he stripped and put his muddy clothes and shoes in a trash bag.

He had to be quiet. He didn't want to awaken Nina, and so he decided he'd sleep in the guest room. He silently crossed the house and climbed the stairs. When he saw his face in the bathroom mirror, he gasped and recoiled in horror. What had the woman done to him? His face looked like raw hamburger. He quickly turned on the faucet and used a cloth to gently wash the blood away. Her nails had ripped long tears in his skin on both sides of his face. There was even one long scratch down the side of his neck. He raged against her as he stepped into the shower and turned the water on. His arms were a mess, too.

My God, what if someone had seen him on the drive home? How many times had he sat at stoplights looking left and right. Maybe one of the other drivers had already called the police and given them his license plate number.

He began to bang his head against the tile. They'll catch me; they'll catch me. What will I do? Oh, God, what will happen to Nina? Who will take care of her? Will she be forced to watch me being dragged away in handcuffs? That humiliation was too appalling to think about, and so he did what he had trained himself to do while Nina was in the critical care unit at the hospital. He forced himself to block the image until it disappeared.

He stayed inside his house all weekend, glued to the television set, waiting to hear the newscasters talk about the murder. As time went by, he became strangely detached because the woman hadn't been discovered. By Tuesday, he counted himself lucky and was feeling quite confident.

Not bad, he told himself. Not bad at all for a dress rehearsal.

He'd even come up with the perfect explanation for his scratches. The rain had made the ground slick and he'd slipped and fallen into some thorny bushes.

His department head, a pissant of a man, called him into his office on Wednesday at four to tell him that everyone had noticed how hard he was working and how cheerful he had been these past three days. Why, one of his colleagues had mentioned that he'd even told a joke. The pissant hoped that he would continue with this bright, fresh, wonderful attitude.

As he was leaving his boss's office, he was asked a question. What had caused this transformation? Spring, he'd told him. He was ignoring the foul weather and relandscaping his entire backyard. He was having a delightful time, but he wasn't doing any planting yet. The ground was warm now, and he was tearing up everything. Out with the old and in with the new. He was even thinking about building a gazebo.

"Do be careful pulling out those shrubs," the pissant cautioned. "You don't want to fall into any more thorny bushes and get hurt again. You're lucky the scratches didn't become infected."

Indeed. He most certainly didn't want any more scratches, and yes, he was a very lucky man.

Chapter Four

The week went by in a blur. By Friday, Regan was in a much better mood. She'd caught up on all of her paperwork, and she was able to get back to what she loved to do.

Even running into Aiden's assistant didn't dampen her spirits. Regan had been hurrying down the hall to her office when Emily Milan called out. She turned and waited for Emily to catch up to her. The woman was at least three, maybe four, inches taller than Regan and towered over her when she wore high heels. Her blond hair was cropped short with jagged wisps framing her striking features. Everything about Emily was trendy, from her short, tight skirt to her bold, colorful jewelry.

Regan didn't like Emily, but she tried her best not to let her personal feelings interfere with work. For some reason, Emily had taken a real dislike to Regan too. Emily's animosity had been building over the past couple of months, and she was becoming more openly hostile.

"Aiden would like me to take over the meeting you were scheduled to run this morning. I'm sure he wanted to make certain it ran smoothly."

It was an insult, and not even a veiled one. Regan had to remind herself why she put up with the woman. As unpleasant as she was, she did ease Aiden's workload, and that was all that mattered.

"That's fine," she said.

"I'll need the notes Aiden e-mailed you. Print them out and have your assistant bring them to me."

No *please* or *thank you*, of course. She simply turned and walked away. Regan took a breath and decided she wasn't going to let Emily ruin her morning. Think of something good, she told herself. It took a minute, but she finally came up with something. She didn't have to work with Emily. That was definitely good.

Most days, Regan believed she had a dream job because she got to give away money. She was the administrator of the Hamilton Foundation. Her grandmother Hamilton had begun the philanthropic program, and when she had a fatal stroke a couple of years ago, Regan, who was already being trained for the position, stepped in and took over. It wasn't yet the multimillion-dollar foundation Regan hoped for, but it was successful and had provided money and supplies to many struggling schools and community centers. Now all she needed to do was convince her brothers to increase the funding. And that was no easy task, especially with Aiden, whose entire focus was on expanding the hotel chain.

The Chicago Hamilton was just one of Aiden's babies, but he used it as the model for other ventures. Customer service was the number one priority, and because of the staff's attention to detail, the hotel had won every prestigious award possible since the year it had opened. The operation of all the hotels ran very smoothly because Aiden took pains to hire people who shared his commitment.

Henry Portman was waiting for Regan when she entered her office. Her young assistant worked part-time while he attended college. The young African-American man had the body of a lineman, the heart of a lion, and the mind of a young Bill Gates.

"The dragon's looking for you," he said in greeting.

She laughed. "I ran into Emily in the hall. She's going to take over the ten o'clock meeting. Anything else going on I need to know about?"

"I've got good news and bad news."

"Give me the good news first."

"The supplies are on the way to two more schools for their art programs, and there are sixteen more letters waiting for your signature." Grinning from ear to ear, he added, "Sixteen very worthy high school seniors are going to go to college now, all expenses paid."

She smiled. "That is good news. On days like this, I do love my job."

"Me too," he said. "Most of the time anyway."

"Which leads you to the bad news?"

She sat down behind her desk and began to sign the letters. As she finished each one, she handed it to Henry, who folded it and put it in an envelope. "There was a problem this morning. Well . . . actually, the problem's been ongoing for about a month, but I thought I could handle it. Now, I'm not so sure. Do you remember a guy named Morris? Peter Morris?"

She shook her head. "What about him?"

"You turned him down for a second grant about a month ago. When he received the denial letter, he immediately reapplied. He thought it was some kind of clerical error or that he hadn't dotted all his *i*'s or left a line blank or something on what he called the automatic-renewal application, and that's why he filled out another one. Anyway, he called several weeks ago and asked when he could expect the money. He had this crazy notion that, once he'd been approved for the first grant, it was gravy from then on. I straightened him out on that score," Henry said. He shook his head as he continued. "Then he calls me again and tell me he doesn't think I understand what an automatic renewal means."

"He sounds tenacious."

"He's a pain in the . . . you know. I didn't want to bother you about it, but the guy just won't go away. Since you left for Rome, he's increased his calls. It's like he's got this campaign going. Maybe he thinks that if he keeps bugging me, I'll give in just to get rid of him."

"If he's that much of a nuisance, I should talk to him. Would you pull his paperwork? I must have had a good reason for turning him down."

"I already pulled it," he told her, pointing to a file on the edge of her desk. "But I can save you some time and tell you why you denied his request. He misused the money from the first grant. The grant was specifically targeted for the purchase of new supplies for the community center."

"Oh, yes, I do remember him now."

"Morris told me he *had* purchased new materials. He just misplaced the receipts."

"And what did you say to that?"

Henry laughed. "I said, okay, that's good to know, and then I asked him when it would be convenient for you and me to swing by and see for ourselves. He did some fancy dancing then. You should have heard him stammering and sputtering."

She shook her head. "In other words, no new supplies for show-and-tell."

"That's right. I don't think he has any idea how much trouble he's in. When his employers find out he misused the grant money, they'll want to prosecute. I would." He added, "I didn't tell him that, though."

"How did you end the call?"

"We're not best friends, if that's what you were wondering," he said. "It was hard being polite to the jerk, but I managed. He wants to come down and talk to you personally. Before he hung up, he assured me that he could get you to change your mind."

"Fat chance."

"My thought exactly. It was odd, though. He acted like he had some kind of personal connection to you. I think he's a worry. He's got this edge about him. I don't know how he got past the initial screening the accountants did for all the applicants, but he somehow managed. I really don't think you should waste your time talking to him. But if you insist, and he threatens you, I think you ought to tell Aiden about him."

It was the wrong thing to say. The look she gave him made her six-foot-three assistant wince.

"I'm not going to involve any of my brothers, Henry. Are we clear on that?"

"Yes, ma'am. We're clear."

"If Morris becomes a threat, I'll notify security, and I'll call the police. Now enough about him. I've signed the last letter. They're ready to mail."

Henry scooped up the envelopes and turned to leave. "One more thing," she said. "Will you print out Aiden's e-mail. There are notes for the meeting Emily's going to handle."

"You want me to take the printout down to her?" he asked. His expression was pathetic.

She laughed. "You'll survive."

He cleared his throat and took a step back inside. "About Aiden . . ."

"Yes?"

"I'm not supposed to tell you, but the

way I see it, I work for you, not your brother. Right?"

She looked up. "That's right."

"A couple of weeks ago he stopped in. You weren't here, and he told me that if there was ever any problem, I was supposed to call him."

She tried not to get angry. "Aiden's got a father complex."

"I told him there weren't any big problems and that we're doing great. We *are* doing great, don't you think? And we're making a difference."

"That's right. We are."

He was pulling the door closed when he remembered one other bit of news. "I forgot to mention it, but last week I found the dragon in here."

"In my office? What was she doing?"

"She said she put some papers on your desk, but after she left, I looked and I didn't see anything new. I think she was snooping. I also think she messed with your computer."

"Are you sure about that?" she asked, wondering what Emily had been searching for. The longer Regan thought about it, the angrier she became.

"I'm pretty sure. You always turn your computer off when you leave for the night, and I had only just gotten to work when I walked in and found her in your office. She's got some gall, doesn't she?" That was an understatement. Before Regan could respond, Henry said, "I think we should start locking this door so the dragon can't get in."

"You've got to stop calling her dragon. One of these days it will slip out in front of her."

He shrugged, letting her know without words that he really didn't care.

Regan worked until eleven-thirty, then ran upstairs to her suite to freshen up.

Since it was only seven short blocks to The Palms, Regan decided to walk. On the way back, she would drop off the grant reports at the attorney's office, and she wanted to stop by Dickerson's Bath Shop to buy a bottle of Sophie's favorite body lotion. Her friend's birthday was just around the corner. Regan had already purchased a gorgeous Prada bag Sophie had admired, and she was going to fill it with all the things her friend loved. If there was time, she would also stop in Nieman Marcus and buy a bottle of Vera Wang's perfume. It was all Sophie wore these days.

Regan decided walking would do her

good. The exercise would hopefully help her get rid of her bad mood. Finding out that Emily had been snooping around her office was infuriating, and she wasn't able to get past it yet.

She was thinking about the invasion of her privacy as she crossed the lobby. She spotted Emily heading toward the concierge and decided to confront her.

"Emily, have you got a minute? I'd like to speak to you."

Emily turned, a look of irritation on her face, and said, "Yes, of course."

"Henry mentioned that he found you in my office last week."

Regan expected a denial and was shocked when Emily said, "Yes, that's correct."

"What exactly were you doing?"

"I placed some papers on your desk."

"Why didn't you give them to Henry or leave them on his desk?"

"I didn't want them to get misplaced." Emily was looking over Regan's shoulder instead of directly at her, letting her know how unimportant the conversation was.

"Henry doesn't misplace things." She was going to launch into a litany of praise for her assistant, but Emily didn't stay around long enough to listen.

She walked away and without a backward glance said, "Henry misplaced Aiden's report, didn't he?"

"No, he did not," she said emphatically.

"Then I must assume you did."

Emily kept going. Regan wasn't about to get into a shouting match with the woman or go chasing after her, but trying to get along with her was becoming more and more impossible. Something had to be done, and soon. Count to ten and concentrate on something good, she told herself. Something positive.

She stepped outside of the hotel and immediately noticed what a beautiful, clear day it was. The gray haze had already burned off the city, and the sun was shining brightly. The sky was a perfect shade of powder blue. Spring flowers were budding out of giant earthen pots along the street. She took another deep breath and promptly started sneezing. The pollen count must not be too bad today, she thought. Her eyes weren't burning and she only sneezed six or seven times.

Things were looking up. She was staying positive. Mind over matter, she told herself.

Then she encountered her first sleazebag of the day on the corner of Michigan and

Superior while she was waiting for the light to change. A late-to-middle-aged man, who didn't seem to care how many people watched, groped a petite redhead Regan estimated to be around eighteen years old. The silly girl obviously loved the attention. Her squeaky laughter could have broken glass. Regan gripped the leather strap of her purse and strode past the lovey-dovey couple, forcing herself not to say anything judgmental out loud.

She ran into another early May–late December couple as she was striding past Nieman Marcus, and by the time she reached the restaurant, she was hopping mad and nauseated.

Kevin was on duty today. Tall, lanky, and painfully thin, the twenty-year-old had spiked black hair and almond-shaped eyes. He was Henry's best friend. His smile put her in a much better mood.

"Looking awful good today, Regan," he said after giving her a quick once-over. "That fitted suit sure accents your . . ."

She raised an eyebrow. "My what?"

"Curves," he whispered, and had the good grace to blush.

Before she could answer, he leaned over the podium to look at her shoes. "Hey, are those Jimmy Choo?"

She laughed. "What do you know about Jimmy Choo shoes?"

"Not from nothing," he admitted. "But my girlfriend lusts after them, so I figured, you being so classy and all, you'd have a couple hundred pair."

"Kevin, I don't have a couple hundred anything, and no, these aren't Jimmy Choo shoes. Is that a new earring?"

He nodded. "Carrie gave it to me for our six-month anniversary. Dad hates it, but he's so happy about my grades he isn't making a big deal about it. Carrie's trying to talk Henry into getting one too."

Kevin noticed Mr. Laggia, the owner, heading their way. "Uh-oh," he whispered. "Here comes Laggia. Be sure to rave about the ferns. The guy's obsessing about them."

Regan smiled as the owner approached. "I love what you've done with the place, Mr. Laggia. Those ferns are wonderful."

He beamed with pleasure. "You noticed?"

How could she not notice? They were everywhere. "Oh, yes," she said.

"You don't think it's too . . . jungle?"

"No, no, of course not."

The restaurant did have a bit of a jungle theme going, but it wasn't overwhelming, and the ferns above each booth gave the customers the feeling of being in a private room.

"How many today?" Kevin asked.

"Three," she answered. "Sophie made the reservation for twelve-thirty. I'm a little early."

"Show her to section four," Laggia said. "I've just put in some ficus. They're quite robust."

Kevin stood behind the squat man, rolling his eyes and grinning. He showed her to a booth that was completely surrounded by ficus and palms and ferns. Cordie and Sophie were both late. Regan sipped Sprite, hoping to settle her stomach, and she was actually beginning to relax when, lo and behold, in walked another disgusting couple. Regan tried to think positive. Maybe the gray-haired gentleman was the girl's father or grandfather. When Kevin led them past her booth, she noticed the old man's hand moved down the girl's spine. Was he fondling her or guiding her?

Regan knew she was obsessing now but didn't care. She was determined to find out if the overly endowed girl was the man's grandchild or girlfriend. She leaned out ever so slightly and tracked them as they turned the corner. She tilted farther and farther to watch them. She lost her balance and would have landed on the floor if she hadn't grabbed hold of the edge of the table.

She felt like a fool. She sat up straight, adjusted the white tablecloth she'd nearly ripped off the table, and sat back. Let it go, she told herself. Just let it go.

She could just see the top of the man's head. She had to know, and so she got up on one knee to watch the pair, but the leafy plants that lined the top of the booth were in her way. She parted the springy leaves. One got loose and smacked her in the face. She wasn't deterred. She spotted the girl sliding into a booth on the far side of the restaurant. The old man didn't sit across from her. Regan pushed the leaves farther apart just in time to see him slip into the booth next to the girl. Kevin handed each one a menu. He hadn't even turned to go back to his station before the old man put his arm around the girl's shoulders, leaned down, and kissed her.

"Lecher," she whispered.

"Doing a little gardening?"

Regan jumped at the sound of Sophie's voice. She hastily let go of the fern, dodged another leafy ficus branch, and sat down.

"You're late."

Sophie ignored the criticism. "What were you doing? Looking at a gorgeous man, I hope."

"Sorry, no. I was watching another sleazebag."

"So you're still doing that, huh?"

Regan nodded. "I can't seem to help myself. Honest to heaven, they're everywhere."

Sophie laughed. Regan thought she looked like a young teenager. Her hair was up in a ponytail, and her cheeks were flushed from running. Sophie ran everywhere because she was usually late. She looked lovely today, but then she always did. "Is that a new blouse? I like it."

"I wear too much pink," Sophie said. "But I saw this and I just had to have it."

The waiter appeared at the table and took Sophie's drink order.

Regan turned toward the entrance of the restaurant and said, "I can't believe you beat Cordie here. I wonder what's keeping her. She's never late."

"I told her she didn't need to be here until one or a quarter of," she said.

The waiter had returned with a tall glass of iced tea. Sophie immediately grabbed three sugar packets and dumped the contents into the glass.

"Why did you tell her —"

"She already knows what I want to talk to you about. I dragged her into this a good month ago, but I didn't want to bother you because you were doing so much traveling back then."

"I just went to Rome."

"Excuse me. Before Rome you were in Houston and Miami and . . ."

"L.A.," she supplied. "I guess I have done a lot of traveling in the last two months. So tell me. What's the 'this' you dragged Cordie into?"

"The plan."

She'd used the word with relish, and Regan saw a gleam in her eyes.

"You're sounding awfully earnest, Sophie. So, tell me about *the plan*," she added, exaggerating the words.

"Don't mock me."

Regan put a hand up. "I'm not mocking you. I swear it on your iced tea."

The waiter had heard "iced tea," and a few seconds later a tall glass was placed before Regan. She didn't tell the eager man she didn't want it. She thanked him instead.

Sophie folded her hands. "To begin with, the plans have changed for this evening."

"We aren't going to dinner?"

"Yes, of course we're going to dinner. Cordie already made the reservations. We're going to a reception first." She turned to her purse and pulled out a wad of folded papers and placed them on the table.

"What are those?"

"I'll explain in a minute."

"Okay. Then tell me about the reception."

Sophie was frowning at a group of businessmen seated at a long table adjacent to them.

"What's wrong?"

"Those men are staring at you."

"They aren't staring at me. They're staring at you," Regan said. "Just ignore them."

"The one on the end is really quite cute."

Regan didn't look. "Tell me about the reception."

Sophie finally gave Regan her full attention. "It's for the men and women who register early for the weekend seminar we're all going to attend."

She'd blurted it all out and then gave Regan her brightest smile. It didn't work.

"Can't do it."

"Sure you can. You're all stressed out

from the trip to Rome, and having to be in the same room with your sleazebag stepfather — to borrow your opinion of the man. This is something completely different and . . . noble. Yes, what we're going to do is noble."

"How noble?"

Sophie leaned forward. In a whisper she said, "We're going to catch a murderer."

Chapter Five

Regan hadn't been shocked by Sophie's announcement. After all, she'd grown up with her and was certainly used to her dramatic ways. " 'We're going to catch a murderer'? Is that what you just said?" Regan asked.

"Yes, that's exactly what we're going to do."

"Okay," she said. "And how exactly are we going to do that?"

"I'm serious, Regan. I really want to get this bastard."

Regan raised an eyebrow. It wasn't like Sophie to ever curse. "Who are we talking about?"

"Dr. Lawrence Shields," she said. "He's a doctor of psychology who uses his mail-order credentials to fleece rich but lonely, vulnerable women, both young and old."

Regan was nodding. "Have you heard of him?" Sophie asked.

"I've read a couple of articles about him in the newspaper."

Sophie took a drink of her tea and then said, "His self-help, let-me-show-you-how-to-turn-your-miserable-life-around seminars draw hundreds of unsuspecting men and women. It's so sad, really. The young are looking for a guru for guidance in figuring out what they should do with their futures, and the older men and women are looking for ways to change the paths they've taken."

"I remember reading that Dr. Shields is considered to be a miracle worker."

"He most certainly is not. Those articles and interviews are paid advertisements. Shields spends a considerable amount of money promoting his seminars. He does two a year here in Chicago."

Sophie was getting all worked up. The spots of color on her cheeks had spread.

"I imagine he makes quite a lot of money on those seminars," Regan said, wondering how much the man charged for a weekend of group therapy. It was probably exorbitant.

Her friend picked up the stack of folded papers and handed them to Regan. "These are photocopies of a diary written by a woman named Mary Coolidge. She's one of the women Shields conned."

"I'll read this later," she promised. "Just give me the highlights now."

Sophie agreed with a nod. "Mary Coolidge's husband died two years ago, and after that, she moved around in a fog of depression. Her daughter, Christine, tried to help, but Mary refused to go to counseling or take medication."

"After you lose someone you love, it's natural to mourn," Regan said. "It's still hard for me to deal with my mother's death, and she's been gone almost a full year."

"Yes, it's natural to mourn, but it took Mary two years before she'd even leave her house."

"So what did she do?" Regan asked. She watched Sophie add yet another packet of sugar to her drink and was a little amazed she could stand the taste.

"Mary heard about the seminars Shields held, and without telling her daughter or any of her friends, she paid the thousand-dollar fee and attended the two-day workshop."

"A thousand dollars? How many people attend these workshops?"

"Three or four hundred. Why?"

"Do you realize how much money he's taking in?" She leaned back against the padded booth and said, "I'm sorry. I didn't mean to interrupt. Please continue."

"Shields was as good as his promise. He did change Mary's life. The charismatic fraud pounced on her loneliness, methodically weaseled his way into her heart, and then took every dollar her husband had left her, which, as it turned out, was well over two million dollars. Shields is a snake," she added. "But a clever snake. Everything he did was legal. Mary willingly turned her assets over to him."

"And this is all in her diary?" Regan asked.

Sophie nodded. "Had her daughter not found the thing, she never would have known all the details of what had happened. Mary had written all about her whirlwind romance. Just three short months after meeting Shields, he asked her to marry him and she agreed. He insisted she keep their engagement their little secret until he had the time — and the money — to buy her a proper engagement ring."

"What do you mean, until he had the money? If he was charging —"

Sophie cut her off. "It was a con, of course. He told her he was experiencing 'temporary' money problems, and she, wanting to prove her love and trust, willingly transferred her savings over to him."

"How could she have been so gullible?"

"Loneliness," she said. "You know what

happened next, don't you?"

"He changed his mind."

"Exactly," she said. "He told her he'd had a change of heart. Not only didn't he want to marry her, he didn't want to give her the money back. He also pointed out that there really wasn't anything she could do about it."

"That poor woman."

The waiter interrupted to take their lunch orders.

"I think we should go ahead," Sophie said. "I can't take a long lunch today."

Regan checked the time. It wasn't quite one yet. "I'll wait for Cordie, but you go ahead."

Sophie ordered a salad and a refill on her iced tea. The second the waiter left, Regan asked, "What happened to Mary?"

"She killed herself. At least that's what everyone believes."

"Everyone but you?"

She nodded. She put her napkin down and excused herself. "I'll explain when I come back."

Sophie headed for the ladies' room, leaving Regan hanging. Regan noticed the men at the table were all watching her friend pass by. Sophie knew it too, which was why she was walking with such an exaggerated stride. It's all in the hips, she used to tell Cordie and Regan. If you wanted to get a man's attention, move the hips. And heavens, was she moving them now. It certainly worked for her, Regan thought. She picked up the papers to look them over and happened to glance toward the entrance just as Cordie walked in.

Everything about Cordie was a contradiction. Men found her quite sexy because she had an hourglass shape, long dark hair, and moved with the grace of a feline, but she was totally oblivious of any stares of admiration — the men at the table were now gawking at her — and she was far more comfortable underneath a car than inside it. Like Sophie, she was an only child and had lost her mother at an early age. Her father owned an extremely lucrative chain of auto repair shops all through the Midwest. Though he'd become a very wealthy man, in his heart he was still a mechanic, and as a way of bonding with his daughter, had taught her everything he knew about cars. He'd given her an old Ford a couple of years ago, and since then, she had rebuilt the engine and replaced everything but the muffler and the windshield. One night a week Cordie taught an auto mechanics class. She also taught chemistry at a local high school and at the same time was working on her PhD at the university. If she stayed on schedule, she'd be finished with her dissertation in another year.

She was dressed in a black suit and a pale silk blouse. She looked quite chic. If Cordie had any flaws, it was her terrible taste in men.

Sophie bumped into her on her way back from the ladies' room. They both stopped to talk to Kevin.

Regan watched them, smiling. Sophie was waving her hands around as she explained something. Kevin looked enraptured by whatever she was telling him, while Cordie stood there with her arms folded, nodding every so often.

Sophie had the most energy of the three friends. Taller than Regan and Cordie, and almost a full year older than the two of them, she believed that since she was the oldest, she should always be in charge. In high school she was labeled a troublemaker — a title she worked hard to earn — and because she dragged Regan and Cordie into her schemes, they landed in detention on a regular basis. Sophie was still bossy, but nowadays, Cordie and Regan rarely went along with any of her plans.

Regan had a feeling that this weekend might turn out to be an exception.

Cordie gave a quick wave as she walked down the aisle and slid into the booth across from Regan. Sophie was still talking to Kevin. His boss, Mr. Laggia, had joined the conversation.

"I'm starving," Cordie said. "And no wonder. It's one o'clock. Are you ready to order? Sophie said she already did."

"I'm ready. What's she talking to Kevin and Mr. Laggia about?"

"She thinks it would be a nice idea to feature the restaurant again and is going to talk to the food editor about it."

Cordie motioned to the waiter, and after the two of them had ordered their lunch, she nodded to the folded papers. "Are those copies of Mary Coolidge's diary?"

"Yes," Regan answered. "You've read it?"

"I have. It's heartbreaking."

"Why didn't you mention any of this when you called?"

"I knew Sophie would want to tell you. It's her plan after all."

"I haven't heard the plan yet."

Cordie smiled. "You will," she said. "Besides, she already made me promise I'd attend the reception and the weekend seminar, and I knew she was going to rope you into going too. She's had some hare-brained ideas in the past, but this one is for a good cause."

The waiter placed the Diet Coke she'd ordered on the table with a bread basket.

Cordie immediately took a wheat roll and was tearing it apart when Regan said, "If what Sophie has told me about Mary Coolidge is accurate, then Shields should be in prison. Why isn't he?"

"He's as slick as an eel, that's why," she said. "I've filed a complaint with the state board hoping they'll yank his license, and I'm sure others have done the same. Something needs to be done to stop him from preying on other vulnerable women."

"I don't understand. He's making a fortune with his seminars," she said. "Why would he . . ."

She was searching for the right word. Cordie supplied it. "Fleece? Rob? Steal?"

". . . fleece lonely women? He doesn't need the money."

"I don't think it's a question of need with him," she said. "I think he does it for the power it gives him. I think he gets off on it."

"Who's getting off on what?" Sophie asked as she sat down next to Cordie.

"Hand me my iced tea, please."

"We're talking about why Shields goes after rich, unhappy women," Cordie said. She handed Sophie her drink as she added, "And I was saying it isn't about the money."

"I disagree," Sophie said. "I think it's all about the money."

"The risk of someone going to the police . . ." Regan began.

"He thinks he's invincible," Sophie said. "And the risk? Must be worth it to him. Mary Coolidge handed over a little more than two million. And that's a whole lot of money, ladies."

"Definitely worth the risk," Cordie said. "When you're as greedy as he is."

Regan looked at Sophie. "How did you get hold of this diary?"

"I told you Mary's daughter found the diary after the funeral . . . when she was packing her mother's things."

"Yes."

"She immediately went to the police and got nowhere. She also hired an attorney to get her mother's money back, but after reviewing the paperwork Mary had signed, the attorney told the daughter that what Shields had done was reprehensible, but legally he hadn't broken any laws."

"And?" Regan asked when Sophie didn't continue.

"Christine — that's the daughter's name — had to return to Battle Creek, where she and her husband live, but before she left, she mailed copies of the diary to the *Tribune*. The reporter who got the envelope made a few phone calls, but he had more pressing work to get done, and he didn't have the time to devote to what he considered to be a lost cause. The letter and the photocopies ended up in his trash can.

"I heard him telling another reporter about the gullibility of the woman, and, of course, I became curious, so after he left, I took the copies out of the trash and read them."

"You know what a sucker Sophie is for lost causes," Cordie said. "And since she needed help, she coerced me into reading the diary . . ."

"And she promptly got on board," Sophie added.

"When did all this happen?" Regan asked.

Sophie answered. "You were in L.A. when Cordie went to the police to find out what she could."

"She made me go," Cordie said. "And I'll admit that I was initially encouraged to learn that the police did, in fact, have an active file on the man. My excitement didn't last long, though. Lieutenant Lewis is a silver-haired charmer and a bad flirt. He oozed sympathy and understanding," she added. "And it took me all of two minutes to figure out he wasn't the least bit sincere."

Sophie had forgotten to tell the waiter to bring her salad as soon as it was ready. All three lunches arrived together. In a hurry now to get back to the office, she picked up her fork and attacked her salad with gusto. Cordie poured ketchup all over her cheeseburger, slapped the top bun on, and picked it up.

"Have there been any other complaints against Shields?" Regan asked.

Cordie put the cheeseburger back on her plate before answering. "Yes, it looks like there were other women, but no hard evidence had been collected. The lieutenant insisted he was working on it. I'm not sure what that's supposed to mean. Anyway, another month went by and still no arrest had been made. I found out that Lewis had shuffled the investigation over to one of his more lackluster detectives named Sweeney."

She picked up the cheeseburger again

and was about to take a bite when Regan asked, "And how long did you say you've been working on this?"

"Not that long," Cordie said.

Regan deliberately waited until Cordie was about to take a bite of her sandwich and then said, "One more question . . ."

Cordie put the sandwich down again. "You're doing that on purpose, aren't you? Asking me questions just as I . . . Sophie, leave my french fries alone."

"They're not good for you. I'm just helping you eat them because I care about your health. That's the kind of friend I am."

Cordie rolled her eyes at Sophie and then turned back as Regan was asking, "I do have a serious question. Do you think Mary Coolidge committed suicide, or do you believe what Sophie believes?"

"That she was murdered?" Cordie whispered. "I'm not sure. It's possible."

Regan dropped her fork and leaned forward. "Are you serious?"

"How come you didn't act shocked when *I* told you my opinion?" Sophie asked.

Regan didn't mince words. "Because you're a drama queen. Cordie's more practical, and if she thinks it's possible, then . . ."

"Then what?" Sophie asked, frowning now.

"Then it's possible."

"I'm not a drama queen."

"Tell me why you think it's possible," Regan asked Cordie, ignoring Sophie's comment.

"Read the diary."

"I will, but tell me now."

"Okay. You'll see toward the end, Mary was scared of Shields. He had threatened her. If you read the last entry, you'll see that her handwriting is all over the page, which tells me the drugs were in her system and making her loopy. Maybe that's why she wrote what she wrote . . . but then again, maybe it was really happening."

Regan picked up the papers, pulled the last page out, and read. There were only four words.

Too late. They're coming.

Chapter Six

The alley smelled like wet dog hair and puke. The overflowing Dumpster that Detective Alec Buchanan had spent most of the night behind smelled much, much worse.

In all, there were now seven detectives working the case. Alec had drawn the short straw and was relegated to doing backup for another detective named Mike Tanner, who was inside the dry and most likely warm warehouse, waiting to make the deal.

Undercover detectives Dutton and Nellis were across the street, watching the entrance to the warehouse from different angles.

Two other detectives were across town at a restaurant, looking as young and clean-cut as high school honor-roll students dressed in the uniform of all the teenagers in the city — Old Navy T-shirts, Gap loose-fit jeans, and scuffed white Nikes. They were impatiently waiting for a fresh supply intended for the streets of suburbia.

The seventh detective was following the money.

Detective Dutton was officially running

the show, but Tanner thought *he* was in charge. Alec had worked with Tanner for only a couple of days, and so he tried not to make any snap judgments about the man. He'd adopted a wait-and-see attitude. Though, admittedly, what he had seen so far hadn't impressed him. Tanner had a short fuse and let his temper get the upper hand. Not good, Alec thought, in a situation like this. Not good at all.

Tanner had already caused problems. He'd refused to wear a wire and wouldn't let the techs put a couple of bugs inside the warehouse. Tanner was worried the mikes would be discovered, and since he was the only one who had worked with the twins, the others had to acquiesce.

Alec had been told to expect the deal to go down around three or four in the morning, when the scum crawled out from under their rocks to buy and sell anything and everything. These two lawyers were a different breed, though. They apparently started their workday around noon.

The attorneys, Lyle and Lester Sisley, were identical twins who had migrated to Chicago from a 7-Eleven-sized town in Georgia. They sounded and acted like good ol', down-home, country boys who pledged allegiance to the flag and to Elvis every morning, and who liked to go out on the town and kick up their boots every now and then, but who would never ever get into any real trouble. Casual acquaintances considered the twins a little slow-witted, but sweet, terribly sweet.

The opposite was the case. There was nothing sweet or slow-witted about them. Their IQs were identical and hovered just one point above genius. It was reported that they had partied their way through law school and still had managed to graduate at the top of their class.

The twins had been in Chicago for a little over a year when they came to the conclusion that they were working too much and making too little. They decided then that they needed to branch out.

Five years later, they were taking in millions, and it sure as certain wasn't from their legal fees. They continued to practice law and maintained offices on Elm Street, but they had very few clients. The two shared an impressive title, yet neither dared print it on the glass of their office door. They were quite simply known as the premier drug lords of Chicago.

And more. Much, much more. It was estimated that in the past twelve months, Lyle and Lester had sold more drugs than

Pfizer Pharmaceuticals. There wasn't a pill they didn't push or a drug they didn't lace with other, more addictive substances.

Needless to say, the undercover detectives had been trying to nail their sorry asses for a long, long time. Today would hopefully be the end for Lyle and Lester, if all went as planned. It had taken months of hard work to entice the twins into taking the risk of actually transferring the money personally. Greed had been a powerful motivator, and Tanner, who had set up this latest venture, believed he had successfully penetrated their inner circle.

Most of their illegal business transactions were conducted in the warehouse where Tanner was waiting.

The twins were the odd couple. They did almost everything together. They worked together, played together, and lived together in a high-rise apartment on Lake Shore Drive. They would even occasionally dress alike in cowboy attire.

There were a few differences. Lyle had a thing for buxom women. He consumed them like a baseball player chewing on sunflower seeds and spitting out the shells when the taste was gone. Yet, the women he so casually discarded couldn't say enough nice things about him. After he finished with them, he lavished them with expensive "parting" gifts. The women called Lyle the ultimate gentleman.

Lester had a thing for cars, Rolls-Royces to be specific. He had over fifteen of them stored in his warehouse now and had just purchased another one. The cost was a mere one hundred fifty-three thousand, but that was chump change to the drug lord.

Lester never drove the cars. Every Friday he liked to walk around the warehouse and look at them. He was overheard telling a friend that he was saving the cars and needed to keep them in mint condition, but he didn't explain exactly what he was saving them for.

"Heads up."

The whisper came through Alec's earpiece. Dutton, from his position across the street, had spotted the twins.

Alec dropped into the Dumpster and squeezed down in the garbage. Something crawled up his neck, and he fought the urge to slap it away as he turned ever so slightly and peered out the hole he'd drilled in the metal. The lousy hiding place had been Tanner's idea. Alec had wanted to find a spot in the loft of the warehouse where he could watch and listen, but

Tanner wouldn't hear of it. He was sure the twins would know if anyone was hiding inside, and since Tanner had set the meeting up, Alec didn't argue.

Alec told Dutton he had no intention of waiting in the damn Dumpster. Dutton agreed. Tanner's determination to be a superstar cop and make a name for himself was jeopardizing the operation. Dutton gave the order that as soon as Lyle and Lester went to the door, Alec was to climb up the fire escape and go in through a window he'd already scoped out for trip wires.

Alec kept watching the street. No one there yet.

"We've got a problem." The voice belonged to Detective Nellis. "There's a uniform talking to the twins. Ah, hell, he's gonna give them a ticket. They parked in a tow-away zone."

"No," Dutton said. "He's not writing a ticket. They're all walking toward the warehouse now. The uniform's between them."

"Is he willingly going with them?"

"Can't tell," Dutton said.

"What about a gun? Does Lyle or Lester have a gun on him?" Nellis was angry. "Can you see, Dutton?"

"I can't tell about the gun," he whispered. "Alec, you've got time to get inside and warn Tanner. I'll be right behind you."

"Tell Tanner to abort," Nellis whispered.

"He won't, he won't," Dutton argued. "Alec, go. They've stopped in front of the main entrance, so they're not gonna use the side door. They're looking up and down the street. Not another soul around. Lester's unlocking the door now. The uniform looks worried."

Alec was already moving. He swung out of the Dumpster, raced across the alley, and climbed up the fire escape. The window was just out of reach. He jumped, grabbed the ledge, and then lifted himself through the window.

Dutton was right behind him. The detective wasn't as big or as muscular as Alec, but he was just as nimble and didn't make a sound.

There were boxes of auto parts stacked six feet high all over the loft and video cameras attached to the rafters. The twins didn't have an alarm system. They took care of their own problems, and anyone who was crazy enough to rob or vandalize any of their property simply disappeared.

Dutton was slowly crawling toward the rail. Alec held up a hand to stop him and pointed to one of the cameras.

They could hear voices. The twins were talking to each other as they walked toward the office, which was directly below the loft. Tanner must have been waiting for them in the doorway of the office, because they heard him shout, "What the hell is this?"

Another voice — it had to be the young cop — answered, "What are you . . ."

And then there was a second of dead silence.

Dutton whispered, "They know."

Alec nodded. He motioned to Dutton to cover the steps while he slowly edged closer to the railing so he could see what was happening.

Tanner was losing it, pacing back and forth, defensively throwing accusations at the twins. Lyle shoved the cop toward Tanner and pulled a gun.

It all went to hell then.

Chapter Seven

"So are you in, Regan?" Sophie asked.

"Of course I am."

"I knew you would be," she said. "You're always telling me I'm a sucker for lost causes . . ."

"Actually, that's what Cordie tells you."

"Yes, but you're a sucker too."

"Is that supposed to be a compliment?" Regan asked.

Cordie was just finishing her cheeseburger. She waved a fry in Sophie's direction and said, "You're going to be late. Didn't you tell me you had a meeting at one-forty-five?"

"I need to talk to Regan first," Sophie said. She turned her full attention on her friend and said, "I need you to read the diary as soon as possible, but definitely before tonight. It won't take long. Mary didn't write in it every night. I think it's only forty-some pages. You know what? Maybe you could read it after Cordie and I leave. And then . . ."

"Yes?"

She took a breath and blurted out, "I

need another favor. I need you to go to the police station and find out if anything has been done with the investigation. Cordie went last time, so it's your turn."

"My turn? I just joined in this —"

"It's still your turn," Sophie pointed out.

"Why can't *you* go to the police station?" Regan asked.

"Are you serious? I'm a reporter. They won't tell me anything."

Before Regan could say a word, Sophie said, "Okay, I know what you're thinking. You too, Cordie. So I'm not a full-fledged investigative reporter yet, and, yes, I know you know I haven't written any big exposés yet, and I've been working my butt off on the advice column at the paper for almost five frickin' years, but honestly, Regan, you should have more faith in me. You too, Cordie," she said again. "Everything's going to change soon. You'll see."

"I have complete faith in you," Regan protested. "And I wasn't thinking . . ." She suddenly stopped arguing and laughed. "You're really good, Soph, with the guilt thing."

"She's a pro all right," Cordie said.

"I *was* trying to guilt you, wasn't I? Old habits die hard, I suppose. But I still can't go to the police station because there are always reporters hanging around in case something big happens, and one of them will surely recognize me and want to know what I'm doing there. I know how busy you are . . ."

"I can make the time," Regan promised.

Sophie was thrilled. "You do understand why I don't want any other reporter snooping around, don't you? This is my investigation. I want to be the one to nail Shields and get justice for Mary Coolidge."

"And maybe get yourself a Pulitzer?" Cordie asked.

Sophie smiled. "That's a one-in-a-billion possibility, but one can always hope. That's not why I'm doing it, though."

"We know," Cordie said. "Shouldn't you get going, Soph?"

Sophie looked at her watch and groaned. "I'm gonna be late. I've got to get out of here," she said as she grabbed her purse. "Will one of you pay for my lunch? I'll pay for dinner tonight."

"Sounds like a plan to me," Cordie said.

"What time are you picking me up?" Sophie asked. "And who's driving?"

While Cordie was answering, the sleaze-bag and his babycakes girlfriend caught Regan's eye as they strolled out of the restaurant. Cordie noticed the change in her friend's expression and asked, "What's wrong?"

"That creepy old man hanging all over that twelve-year-old."

Cordie turned and spotted the couple. "She isn't twelve. She's got to be at least eighteen. Otherwise he could get busted."

"And he's what? Sixty?"

"He could be," she said. "And the age difference bothers you because . . ."

"It's disgusting."

"And?"

"You're sounding like a therapist."

"I just think you ought to admit why you're so disgusted. The couple remind you of your creepy stepfather and his sleazy bride."

"Of course they do."

"Oh."

"Oh, what?"

"I thought I was helping you make a breakthrough." She smiled then. "You really need to lighten up a little. It's time."

Regan nodded. She knew Cordie was right. She just wasn't sure how to go about it.

"I've had the most horrible morning. Have you got time for me to do some whining?"

"How much whining?"

"A bunch."

Cordie laughed. "I can give you ten minutes. Then I've got to leave."

Regan immediately launched into her complaints about her job, her brother Aiden's constant interference, and her run-in with his assistant, Emily. When she told Cordie that Henry had caught Emily snooping in her office, Cordie was incensed and said, "You need to fire her ass."

Regan's eyes widened. Cordie laughed. "I'm starting to sound like my students. You do need to fire her, though."

"I can't. She's Aiden's assistant. He has to fire her," she said. "But knowing you're as outraged as I am makes me feel better. I've done enough whining for now. I think I'll order another iced tea and read this diary. Then I'll walk over to the police station. I'm going to stay positive," she added.

"How are you going to do that?"

"I'm going to believe that the day is going to get better."

"I wouldn't count on it. And good luck with Detective Sweeney." Before Regan could ask why, she added, "He's the man you'll have to talk to about the investigation. He's a real piece of work."

"I'm not worried. How bad can he be?"

Chapter Eight

Detective Benjamin Sweeney, known by his initials, B.S., to all the other detectives in the department, was having a worse than usual bad day. It started at five-thirty a.m., when he woke up with a hangover that felt like a jackhammer drilling behind his eyeballs. The only medicine that would take away the hallucination and stop the pain was what had caused it in the first place, another stiff drink of bourbon, which he downed in two thirsty gulps. It burned his throat and took the hair off his tongue. Bleary-eyed, he gargled Listerine to hide the smell of the booze, got dressed, and went to the dentist. At seven he had a bad root canal. By nine the shot of novocaine had worn off, and he was in agony. Then, at ten, the sun vanished, heavy dark clouds moved in, and he got soaked running from his car into a roach-infested apartment building with his partner, Lou Dupre. They climbed four flights to stare down at the decomposing body of a young twentysomething female. There were empty crack vials littering the room. Sweeney figured one druggie had offed another. No real loss that he could see.

He also knew there wouldn't be any identification on the victim — that would have been too easy — and of course he was right. There wasn't. Usually he could complain enough to make Dupre do all the paperwork and the running around in circles before the file was put in the "still pending" drawer, which Sweeney had secretly labeled "who gives a damn."

Today, however, Dupre wasn't cooperating. He called Sweeney an asshole, told him he was sick and tired of his constant bitching, and insisted he was going to have to get off his lazy fat ass and start pulling his own weight.

In all the movies about cops and robbers that Sweeney had watched on television while he was drinking himself into oblivion, the detectives were like brothers with their partners. One would take a bullet — and inevitably did before the movie was over — for the partner. A frickin' love affair in the movies. A fairy tale. In Sweeney's miserable world — the real world — he and his partner, Dupre, hated each other's guts. There were times when Sweeney would fantasize about a good old-fashioned shootout where he could get behind his partner and blow his brains out.

He knew the feeling was mutual. Hell, these days everyone in the department was avoiding him as if he had the clap. They knew he was under investigation, unofficial though it was, and they had decided to condemn him before any of the facts were in. Sweeney wasn't worried about Internal Affairs. Yes, he was guilty of taking the money to look the other way while a drug dealer was killed, but the men who paid him to close his eyes weren't in any position to rat on him. And the money, ten thousand dollars, was clean. Squeaky clean. Sweeney had been real careful. Let the task force listen to all the rumors from the out-of-work whores the murdered dealer had been running. It didn't matter to Sweeney. If they had anything concrete, he would already have been suspended.

Sweeney had two years and three months to go before he could retire, but there were days, like today, when he knew he wasn't going to make it. He could understand what happened inside a madman's head just seconds before he opened fire on his coworkers, and sometimes he got a hard-on just thinking about Dupre's blood and guts splattered all over the walls.

Before she'd run off with their boy, his wife had told him that he'd turned as mean as a rabid rottweiler and that the booze had corroded his brain. His response hadn't been very clever, but he'd gotten his point across. He'd backhanded her and ordered her to get his supper on the table. Later that night, while he was watching some brotherly love movie on TV, she'd packed up some suitcases and sneaked out the back door with the kid, but he'd caught up with her as she was starting her old Honda Civic. He'd reached in through the window she was frantically trying to roll up, ignoring the kid screaming in the backseat, grabbed her by the throat, and told her it would be fine and dandy with him if he never laid eyes on her or the brat again. He leaned in real close to her face then and told her that if she ever tried to get so much as a dime in alimony or child support he would come after her with an ax.

She must have known from the look in his eyes he wasn't bluffing. He never heard from her again, and as the days and nights dragged on, he became convinced that he was better off living alone.

No matter what the gossip in the department said, he wasn't a drunk. Not yet anyway. He was just tired of having to deal with all the scum on the streets. Chicago had turned into a cesspool where only degenerates knew how to survive and thrive. Like bacteria, they multiplied and flourished in the filth.

He was afraid the bacteria had already invaded his body and that he was slowly turning into one of them. And when he got real scared and the booze wouldn't dull the night terrors, he'd fantasize about taking early retirement. All he needed was one big score, and he could walk away. Screw the pension. If he hit it big, he could buy a boat and sail to the Bahamas. He'd never even been on a boat, and he'd never been to the islands, but the brochures he kept tacked up on the wall above his bureau had lots of photos showing how clean the place was.

He wanted to walk down a clean street, breathe clean, unpolluted air, look up and see a clean blue sky without a trace of gray haze, but most of all, he wanted to *feel* clean again.

Whenever any dark fantasies got in the way of his concentration, he would buy a bottle of bourbon, take a sick day, and go on a little binge. The way he figured it, he was doing the taxpayers a favor. If he stayed holed up at home and got roaring drunk, he was protecting the law-abiding citizens of Chicago by not killing them.

He knew he had to hang on and stay sane until he either hit the big score or until his pension kicked in, and so he tried to find a little happiness in the day-to-day things. Tonight, for example, was going to make him very happy. His shift would be over in just twenty minutes, and unlike his kiss-ass partner, he wasn't going to stay a minute longer. He'd gotten his paycheck today, and so tonight he was going to treat himself to an expensive porterhouse steak, then drive across town to Lori's School of Beauty, which fronted for a thriving whorehouse, and get himself a free haircut and blow job from one of the hookers who was too afraid of him to turn him down. He planned to cap off his romantic evening with an old friend, Jack Daniel's Black Label.

Time was creeping by. He must have checked his watch twice in the last minute. Nineteen more to go. God, he hated this place. His desk was on the far right of an ugly oblong room. The side of his desk butted up against a pea green wall. Some mornings, as he was climbing the stairs to the second floor of the station, he would feel as if he were going into a sweatshop, so crowded and dismal was the place. There was talk of remodeling, but, thus far, only one room had new paint.

He leaned back in his chair and looked around. There was a handful of detectives working at their cluttered desks, most on their phones, but none of them were paying any attention to him. Sweeney thought he could get away with leaving early and not be missed.

That possibility was quickly squelched when the new prick boss came up the stairs. Lieutenant Lewis had only been in charge for five weeks, but it was long enough for Sweeney to decide he hated him. The lieutenant didn't like problems, and after I.A. had a little chat with him about their unofficial investigation, Lewis had turned against Sweeney. Well, screw him. The prick didn't want any of Sweeney's dirt to rub off on him. Too late, Sweeney thought with a snicker.

Lewis wasn't so pristine either. Sweeney watched him saunter into his glassed office at the back of the room. He'd gotten wind that Lewis was screwing around on his rich, high-society wife. Every man had secrets he didn't want anyone else to know about, and if the lieutenant kept breathing down his neck, Sweeney had made up his mind to do a little investigative work of his own. It'd be easy for him to find out who the whore servicing Lewis was and take a few photos for the little missus. He'd do it anonymously, of course. How would Lewis live without his rich-bitch wife paying all the bills? Maybe Sweeney ought to buy one of those digital cameras and send the wife some explicit eight-by-ten photos. Hell, he might as well have some real fun and post them on the Internet too. He caught himself before he laughed out loud over the possibility. Serve the prick right if the missus took a scissors to his expensive suits, smashed that Rolex he always made sure everyone noticed, and kicked him out on his bony ass.

Tit for tat. He knew Lewis was keeping a notebook on him, listing all the little infractions, so he could weed him out without getting into trouble with the union, but as long as Sweeney stayed careful, Lewis couldn't fire him.

Only three lousy minutes had passed. He shuffled some papers around on his desk and looked over his shoulder again. Crap. Lewis was watching him. He hastily turned back to his papers and opened a file, pretending to be engrossed.

Alec Buchanan came rushing up the stairs. The undercover detective looked like a drugged-out gang leader with his long, dark hair, bloodshot eyes, and scraggly beard. Buchanan hadn't been in this division long. He'd transferred over a short time ago, and before that he'd been strictly vice. Sweeney had never spoken to him, but he knew him by reputation. You didn't want to get on his bad side.

A young street cop in blue chased after Buchanan. His expression was pained, and he was sweating profusely. Sweeney pretended to be engrossed in his paperwork until the two men went into the lieutenant's office. Then he picked up the phone, punched the hold button, and with the receiver to his ear, turned in his chair to see what was going on.

Lewis didn't waste any time throwing a tantrum. His anger was directed at the kid cop. Sweeney tried not to smile as he watched the lieutenant lose it. He kept stabbing the air with one long, bony finger as he railed.

Sweeney had heard what had happened. The street cop had ruined God-only-knew how many months of undercover work. It had been a bad scene. He'd heard a couple of detectives talking about it in the coffee room that afternoon. From what he'd overheard, Buchanan had turned into a frickin' superhero. He'd gotten the cop out of the drug hole while the guns were blazing. Buchanan would probably get another commendation, but from the look on his face, he wanted someone's blood, not medals. Sweeney assumed Buchanan was out to get the stupid kid cop, but after watching for a long minute, he realized the detective's anger was directed at Lieutenant Lewis. Maybe it was because he'd been assigned with Tanner, who everyone in the department knew was a loose cannon.

Speaking of the devil. Tanner came flying through the room, a look of pure hate in his eyes as he shoved a detective out of his way and barged into the lieutenant's office. He was shouting before he'd shut the door.

This was better than one of those old movies on television. All he needed now was a beer and some popcorn.

"What's going on?" a detective across the room called out.

Another detective answered. "Buchanan's trying to save the kid's ass. Tanner wants him hung out to dry."

Sweeney rolled his eyes. Frickin' saint, that's what Buchanan was. Sweeney enjoyed watching Lewis get all bent out of shape. His face was bright red. Maybe he was gonna have himself a stroke. Wouldn't that be nice?

He checked the time again. Fifteen minutes to go. Damn, he was thirsty. He needed to get the hell out of here so he could start drinking. The lieutenant sure wasn't paying any attention to him now. Sweeney turned to his computer, shoved the papers back into the file, and stuffed the folder into his "who gives a damn" drawer. He was pushing his chair back when he happened to look up. A sweet young thing was coming up the stairs. He couldn't take his eyes off her. By the time she reached the reception area, he was salivating. He wasn't the only one. The noise had subsided in the room, and Sweeney guessed the other detectives were looking her over too.

A kiss-ass detective on the opposite side of the room all but pole-vaulted over his desk to get to the woman and offer her assistance, blocking Sweeney's view. He glanced behind him. The men inside the lieutenant's office were all still engrossed in their argument.

The detective trying to sweet-talk the woman reluctantly pointed to Sweeney. The woman began to make her way around the cluttered desks to get to him.

Sweeney hastily adjusted his tie to hide the ketchup stain, sucked in his gut, and pulled a folder out of his drawer so he would look busy.

She was a knockout with those full, luscious lips. To say nothing about the soft curves and long legs. Maybe she was one of those-thousand-dollar-a-night whores he'd heard about but had never actually seen. Wouldn't that be a piece of luck? He thought he was smart enough to figure out a way to make her put out for him. That would certainly be something to remember on long, lonely nights. He could just picture her down on her knees, her long curly hair brushing against his thighs . . .

He forced himself to stop the budding fantasy before he got too horny. His chair groaned as he leaned back and watched her walk closer. Classy bitch, he thought. Too classy to be a high-priced whore. He spotted the sapphire ring and knew it had to be the real deal. No phony stones for this broad. No ring on the left hand, though, so the sapphire hadn't come from a rich husband. She either had a wealthy father or a sugar daddy paying all her bills, and Sweeney, cynical to the bone, opted for the second possibility. Pretty-girl reeked of money. He could almost smell it on her, and his mind raced for a way to get some of it.

Maybe she would turn out to be his one big score. Everyone had secrets, even classy ladies like her. He licked his lips in anticipation, but caution set in quickly. Stop being a fool, he told himself. His eyes narrowed as he watched her. Deep inside he knew she was out of his league. Resented it too. She had that rich, well-scrubbed look he rarely saw these days. Pretty-girl had striking blue eyes, a shade lighter than the stone on her finger. Rich and beautiful. Out of his reach, all right.

She stopped in front of his desk. Before she could speak, he said, "Can I help you?" He knew he sounded surly. He didn't care.

"Detective Sweeney?"

He pointed to the nameplate with his cigarette-stained finger, then realized his name was facing him, not her. He leaned forward, turned the nameplate around, and in the process spilled half a cup of cold coffee on his keypad. Muttering a foul word, he grabbed a sheet of paper and wiped up the liquid.

"That's me, sweetheart. I'm Detective Sweeney."

He could tell she didn't like being called sweetheart. Her eyes narrowed ever so slightly. Tough, he thought. He didn't care if he pissed her off or not. Since he'd already figured out he didn't stand a chance with her, why bother to be politically correct? Besides, his good friend Jack Daniel's was waiting for him.

"My name is Regan Madison," she said as she placed her briefcase on the vinyl chair facing his desk and stood next to it.

"Are you here to report a crime?"

"No. My friend, Cordelia Kane, asked me to stop by and find out what developments have been made regarding her complaint against a psychologist named Dr. Lawrence Shields."

He didn't pretend to know whom she was talking about. "Who?"

She repeated word for word what she'd just said. He still didn't know who or what she was talking about. He hemmed and hawed, trying to bluff his way with the catchall phrase he used on nearly every inquiry he received over the phone. "Oh, yes . . . that's still an ongoing investigation."

"What exactly has been done?"

"Look . . . you're gonna have to refresh my memory. I've got so many cases to oversee . . ."

He left the sentence hanging and let out

a loud yawn. What a colossal waste of time, Regan thought. Cordie was right. Sweeney was obnoxious and obviously incompetent. His I-don't-give-a-damn attitude infuriated her.

He was also a lecher. He was too busy ogling her chest to look into her eyes. With effort, she held her patience as she explained who Dr. Shields was and what he had done to Mary Coolidge. Sweeney was still looking clueless when she finished.

"Your friend . . . what's her name?"

"Cordelia Kane."

"What's your connection to her?"

"Excuse me?"

"I said, what's your connection to her?"

"Cordelia's my friend."

"No, not her. The other woman. The one who killed herself."

"Her name was Mary Coolidge."

"I see."

He was making sure she knew he wasn't really interested in anything she had to say. His eyes were half closed, and he was rudely yawning every other second now. God, he was such a jerk. If he leaned back any farther in his chair, he'd land on his backside, and she began to hope that he would.

"I'd like to talk about the investigation,

Detective. Do you have any idea . . ."

He waved his hand to stop her. "It's all coming back to me now. Like I was telling you, I've got so many cases it's hard to keep track of all of them. I remember now. Your friend was really angry with this Dr. Shields. Told me she was sure he was responsible for the old lady killing herself. My investigation is in my pending file," he added with a straight face as he pointed to his desk drawer.

"What progress has been made with the investigation?"

"Well, the truth is . . ."

"Yes?"

He shrugged. "I'm working on it."

She wanted to scream. She took a breath instead. Antagonizing him wouldn't help her get any straight answers. "I see. Could you tell me —"

It was as far as he would let her get. "I'm going off duty now. Why don't you come back tomorrow and inquire?"

Regan's temper was near the boiling point. "I'm afraid that won't be possible. Is Lieutenant Lewis available?"

Pretty-girl was becoming a pain in the ass. Sweeney's resentment turned into hostility. How dare she try to intimidate him by pulling rank on him.

"The lieutenant's busy," he said, nodding his head to the office behind him. "Besides, he will only bounce you back to me, and I've got nothing to report."

"Has anything been done? Has anyone talked to her neighbors or —"

"The way it looks, this Shields guy didn't do anything illegal. I know that's hard to swallow, but that's the way it is. The woman willingly gave him all her money and then committed suicide. Simple as that. Case closed."

"So the investigation isn't really pending, is it?"

She was furious. Her face was bright pink, but he didn't care. Shrugging, he said, "Sure it's pending. Pending on getting some real evidence."

Regan glanced around the room for help. She looked at the four men inside the glassed-in office at the back of the station. The man standing behind the desk was evidently the lieutenant. He was shouting and waving his hands around.

One of the other men drew her attention then. Dressed in filthy clothes and leaning against the window, he said something that infuriated the lieutenant, who was now pounding the desk and shouting. The tantrum didn't seem to faze the man.

The lieutenant turned his wrath on the uniformed policeman. Even with the door closed she could hear a few of the vile insults and threats the lieutenant was making. The man leaning against the window came to the policeman's aid. He got in front of him and said something to the lieutenant that sent him into a rage.

Regan wasn't about to interrupt. She didn't want to have anything to do with this lieutenant, and she certainly wasn't going to ask him for help.

Deciding that she'd done all she could, she picked up her briefcase and left the station. The second she reached the sidewalk, she pulled out her cell phone and called Sophie.

"I talked to Detective Sweeney."

"And?"

"The man's a mess."

"That's what Cordie said about him," she said. "But was he useful? Did he give you any information that might be helpful?"

"No, nothing," she said. "I don't think anything's been done. He couldn't have cared less about poor Mary Coolidge."

"You read the journal didn't you?"

"Yes, I did. Dr. Shields needs to be stopped."

"Which is why you went to the police station to find out —"

"Sophie, there is no investigation under way."

"Did you talk to Lieutenant Lewis?"

"No," she said. "He won't help. He's worse than Sweeney, if such a thing is possible."

"I thought you didn't talk to him."

"I saw him in action," she said. "He was screaming and carrying on."

"Exactly what did Sweeney tell you?"

Regan walked along as she related the conversation she'd had with the obnoxious detective. "I'm telling you, it was a complete waste of time."

She ended the call just as she turned the corner. She thought she heard someone shout and instinctively turned around.

The crash was inevitable.

Chapter Nine

Alec Buchanan was in a hurry to get to his car and drive home so that he could get out of the filthy clothes he was wearing. He felt as if he had bugs crawling all over him, and all he wanted to do was take a long, hot shower. He was all but running as he turned the corner and damn near rolled over the woman standing there.

He hit her hard. Her briefcase went flying in one direction, and she went flying in the other. He caught her around the waist and lifted her just as she was about to go headfirst into the brick building.

Alec held on to steady her. Damn, she was pretty. Smelled nice too. Surprising that he could smell anything today after his night in the garbage.

He released his hold, picked up her briefcase, handed it to her, and then stepped back. "Sorry about that."

She nodded to let him know she'd heard his apology. She couldn't speak. She looked into his eyes, tried to smile, then turned and walked away as fast as she could. She took deep, gulping breaths, trying not to gag. Dear God, the stench radiating from him made her eyes tear.

She burst out laughing. When she looked back, he was still watching her. She smiled but turned the corner and began laughing again. The man with the beautiful white teeth reminded her of a childhood trip to the zoo. Her brother Aiden had taken her when she was seven or eight years old. She remembered they'd gone inside a big, gray stone building. It was crowded and musty inside, but at the end of a long aisle was the new gorilla habitat. The finishing touches hadn't been put on the gorilla's new home. There was a double set of bars separating the gorilla from the crowd, but a thick, unbreakable Plexiglas pane hadn't been installed yet. Regan pulled away from Aiden and ran, darting in and out of the crowd to get there before anyone else noticed there was room right in front of his cage. She made it all the way to the first set of bars before the smell knocked her to her knees. The stench was overpowering, and she began to gag. Aiden had to pick her up and carry her outside to fresh air.

She still remembered the horrible odor from the gorilla's cage. The man she'd just run into smelled much worse.

Laughing about the old memory put her in a much better frame of mind. Unfortunately, her good mood didn't last long.

She had just left Neiman Marcus and was hurrying down a side street with her briefcase and shopping bag in one hand and her purse in the other when a man twice her size bumped into her. What am I? Invisible? she thought. Twice in one day men had tried to walk through her.

This one didn't bother to apologize. In fact, he seemed to deliberately step on her foot. He never looked back as he hurried down the street. Her toe stung where he'd stomped on it, and she walked at a slower pace toward Dickerson's Bath Shop. The day was only half over and things could improve, she told herself. What good were negative thoughts?

Then she walked into Dickerson's, and staying positive just wasn't possible. The salesclerk, a woman wearing the name tag, "Ms. Patsy," was leaning against the cash register and talking on the phone. She had the receiver cradled in the crook of her shoulder while she filed one of her fingernails.

Ms. Patsy's face was such a bright red she was obviously worked up about something. She spotted Regan, impatiently waved at her to wait, and continued her conversation. The woman was in her late fifties or early sixties, but she was babbling on the phone like a teenager. She was apparently talking to a friend, filling her in on the latest gossip she'd heard about another woman named Jennifer. Regan wasn't trying to listen in, but she couldn't help overhearing a little of what she was saying, and she was appalled by the woman's cruel remarks.

Regan moved down to the end of the glass counter so she wouldn't have to listen, and after waiting for several minutes, she picked up the bottle of lotion and turned to go to another counter. Ms. Patsy shouted to her to wait, hung up the phone, and rang up the sale. Resentment simmered in her sour expression as she handed the package to Regan, and without a word, walked away. Regan was astonished by the woman's rudeness.

She was actually relieved to get back to the hotel and her office, but the day didn't get better. She spent the rest of the afternoon putting out one fire after another.

She worked until six, then ran up to her suite to freshen up, and was back downstairs by the door waiting for Cordie by six-fifteen. Her friend arrived by cab, which meant the old Ford was on the fritz again. Regan called for her car before going outside to greet her friend.

"What is it this time? The radiator?"

"Muffler," Cordie called out as she crossed the pavement. "I'll buy a new one tomorrow and install it this weekend."

When Regan's car was brought around, the doorman rushed to hold the door open.

"I know what you're thinking, Terry," Regan said as she slid behind the wheel of her fifteen-year-old Chevy.

The doorman grinned. "You really should think about trading it in."

"Are you kidding? It's in mint condition." Cordie had leaned across the bench to offer her comment.

Sophie wasn't waiting out in front of her apartment building when they pulled up. They had to circle the block three times before she appeared. Regan had been telling Cordie about the rest of her horrid day and how she was losing faith in her fellow man, but once Sophie got in the car, Regan didn't get in another word on the drive to Liam House, ten miles away.

The parking lot adjacent to the conference center was full, so Regan circled the park, looking for a space. The dim lighting made it difficult for her to see. Sophie was directing from the backseat. "There's one . . . no that's a driveway. Never mind. Keep going."

"Look at that idiot jogging down the middle of the street. Is he trying to get killed?" Cordie said.

"I've got to start running again," Sophie said. "I'll run with you, Regan, on the university path."

"I don't go there anymore," Regan said. "Not since the indoor track was finished at the hotel. It's much more convenient."

"I'd work out more often if I had a gym in my house," Cordie said.

"When have you ever worked out?" Sophie asked.

"I work out," Cordie countered. "I just don't do it consistently."

Sophie laughed. "If you'd only get into shape, you wouldn't have to diet all the —"

Cordie cut her off. "You were going to tell us your big plan."

"What?"

Cordie patiently repeated the reminder. "Oh, my God," Sophie said. "I forgot."

Regan looked at her in the mirror. "You forgot your big plan?"

"No, I forgot to tell you what happened today. You're not going to believe it."

"So tell us," Cordie demanded.

"Mary Coolidge's neighbor finally called me back. I've left at least ten messages for the man over the past couple of weeks and was about to give up, but as it turned out, he was out of town, and that's why he didn't call."

"And?" Cordie prodded.

"You know that Shields always has two assistants flanking his sides?"

"Yes," Regan said. "Mary wrote about them in her journal."

"They're really his goons."

"Goons? Who says 'goons' these days?" Cordie asked with a laugh.

"Mary's neighbor," Sophie said. "He called them goons. Now, pay attention. Mary told her daughter that Shields said he'd hired the two men as bodyguards. She was afraid of them and said they seemed to enjoy intimidating people. They even went so far as to wear sunglasses day *and* night."

"That's ridiculous," Regan said.

She spotted a car backing out of a parking space, put her blinker on, and pulled in.

"So what did the neighbor say?" Cordie asked. She was getting a crick in her neck looking at Sophie.

"He was letting his cat in when he saw

two men walking up Mary's drive."

Regan turned the motor off. "And you think they went to her house to threaten her?"

Sophie nodded. "This is all speculation, but . . ."

"But what?" Regan asked.

"But I think she told Shields she was going to the police, and he sent his goons to dissuade her."

"I guess that's possible," Cordie said. "But it's going to be tough to prove."

"Does the neighbor remember when the men were there?" Regan asked.

"He's pretty sure they were there the night Mary killed herself. I think they went there to terrorize her, and she thought that taking the pills was the only way out. Either that or . . ."

"Jeez, Sophie, quit making us guess," Cordie said. "Or what?"

In a near whisper, Sophie said, "Maybe they forced her to take those pills, and they stayed there until she was unconscious."

Regan shook her head. "Think about it, Sophie. What was the last entry in her journal?"

Cordie answered. "Too late. They're coming."

"And the handwriting was pretty loopy, wasn't it?"

"It was all over the page," Cordie said, "suggesting that Mary had already ingested pills."

"Unless they forced her to take some pills, then let her have a break so she could jot down a few thoughts in her journal, and then forced her to take more, I'd have to say . . ."

"Okay, that theory doesn't hold up," Sophie said. "But if Shields's men went there to threaten her . . ."

"That would be very difficult to prove," Regan said.

"If we got a photo of the bodyguards and showed it to this neighbor . . ." Cordie began.

Sophie slapped the headrest behind Cordie. "That's exactly what I was thinking. Only, the thing is . . ."

"Yes?" Regan asked.

"The neighbor isn't so sure he could recognize them," she said. "He told me he didn't get a real good look at their faces, but I still want to show him a photo just in case."

"So that's it? That's the big plan? Get a photo of the goons?" Cordie asked. "We could just drive up to the circle drive, sit in

132

the car, and when they come out, snap, snap. We've got our photos."

"No, there's more," Sophie said. "First, we go in and I pay our fees."

"You're not paying for me," Regan said.

"You're not paying my fee either," Cordie said.

"You're doing me a huge favor. You're giving up your weekend to help, so no more argument. Paying the fees is the least I can do as a thank-you. I'm going to pay in cash," she added in an attempt to deflect further argument. "I don't want Shields or his people to have access to any accounts, so I don't want to pay by check or credit card."

"Good Lord. Are you telling me you're carrying three thousand dollars in your purse?"

Sophie grinned. "There wasn't room in my bra, so, yes, it's in my purse."

"Who carries that kind of cash around?" Cordie asked Regan.

"Apparently Sophie does," she answered.

"My father carries ten times that amount in cash all the time," Sophie commented.

"Soph, how can you afford to pay three thousand dollars?" Cordie asked. "You make less than I do."

"Daddy."

"You told me last month you weren't ever going to take any more money from him, remember? You were determined to make it on your own."

"It was an early birthday present," Sophie said. "He just purchased another vacation home, and for tax purposes put that one in my name too. Daddy has enough money stashed away to last three lifetimes."

Although they had known Sophie since kindergarten and were her best friends, Regan and Cordie still didn't know what her father actually did for a living. Every time one of them asked him, he came up with a different answer. Either he was changing occupations once a month, or he was making it up as he went along. For a long time, Regan thought he was in banking, and Cordie believed he was a real estate mogul. Now that they were older and had heard all the rumors and speculation, they knew Sophie's father was into some shady dealings. He was always cooking up one scheme after another, and they now worried that it was only a matter of time before one of his schemes backfired.

Regan worried about Sophie. As sophisticated as her friend considered herself to be, she was horribly naive about her father. And extremely protective.

Cordie looked as if she wanted to continue to argue. Regan, determined to get her friends back on track, asked, "What's the plan once we're inside the conference center?"

"We join the reception and . . . look around."

Regan glanced at Cordie. "What do you mean 'look around'?" she asked.

"Yes," Cordie said. "Exactly what are we looking for?"

Sophie grabbed her purse and opened the back door. "His computer. I've done some checking and know the registrations and records are computerized. I also found out he carries a laptop computer with him and I'm hoping that sometime this weekend we can get to it."

"Uh-oh, I don't like the sound of that," Cordie said.

"You can't be thinking about breaking into his computer," Regan said, appalled at the idea.

Sophie laughed. She waited until both of her friends had gotten out of the car before answering. "No, of course not. I don't have the skill to break into his computer. Cordie will have to do it."

"No way. I'm not doing anything illegal."

"I need to get into his records," Sophie argued. "It's the only way I can find out about the other women he's scammed."

"His bodyguards aren't going to let any of us near his computer," Regan said.

"We've got all weekend to try."

"Sophie, please tell me there's more to the plan than breaking the law," Regan said.

"Of course there is," Sophie said. "We're here to investigate. We're going to talk to every person who signed up, and maybe someone knows something that will help us."

"Like what?" Cordie asked.

"Like who Shields has been seeing," she said. "We have to play this by ear."

"Sounds like we're playing it by the seat of our pants," Cordie said.

"How does she talk us into these things?" Regan asked. She was trying not to laugh.

"She always makes her plans sound . . . reasonable."

"Hello. I'm right here. I can hear every word you're saying."

Cordie and Regan ignored her. "It's a lousy way to spend the weekend," Cordie complained.

"But it's for a good cause," Sophie said. "And it's too late to back out."

Cordie looked up at the sky. "It's going to rain. Damn, my hair's going to frizz."

"Are we going to stand here all night or what?" Regan asked.

Cordie and Sophie took the lead across the dark parking lot. Regan's knee was throbbing, so she walked at a more sedate pace, trying not to limp. She cursed herself for wearing impractical shoes.

"Slow down," Cordie said. "Regan's having trouble with her knee again. When are you going to get that surgery?"

"Soon," she said. So they wouldn't nag her into doing what she wasn't ready to do, she switched subjects. "My car needs an oil change. Are you up to it, Cordie?"

"Sure. I'll do it next weekend."

Sophie rolled her eyes. "You spend more time under the hood of a car than a mechanic, Cordie. I swear, I'm never going to understand the two of you. You can afford any car you want, and yet you both drive old heaps. But then, I guess we know why Regan keeps her heap."

"Aiden." She and Cordie said his name at the same time.

"It makes him crazy, doesn't it?" Sophie said laughing. She hurried ahead and waited at the door for her friends to catch up. "Okay, ladies. Time to concentrate on the task at hand."

Liam House was an old stone building that had seen many uses in its lifetime. It now served as a facility for seminars and retreats. The interior was a pleasant surprise. Newly remodeled, the marble floors gleamed against the soft, warm beige of the walls. The registration table was on the opposite end of a rectangular foyer.

A thirtysomething woman, wearing the name tag "Debbie," sat behind a table handing out registration forms. She wore a bright periwinkle blue flannel blazer. Behind her, dangling down from the balcony, were two twelve-foot-long banners. Each had a life-size photo of Dr. Shields. In both banners, Shields wore the same periwinkle blazer and the same smile.

"Is the guy a psychologist or a realtor?" Cordie whispered.

Sophie nudged her. "Notice the laptop?"

"It's on the table right in front of me. How could I not notice? Do you want to distract her so I can grab it and run?" Cordie asked sarcastically.

"Get with the program," Sophie whispered.

All three of them filled out their registration forms. Sophie handed them to Debbie.

"The fee's a thousand dollars for each of you, hon."

"Yes, we know," Sophie said as she handed the wad of cash to the woman. Debbie took her time counting the hundred-dollar bills. Satisfied the amount was accurate, she typed their names from their registration cards into her computer, pushed a button, and the printer on the table behind her immediately spit out three receipts. "Dr. Shields is in the living room with some of the other participants. We're having a welcome reception, and you won't want to miss it. The doctor does such marvelous exercises."

"Exercises?" Regan asked.

"Challenges," Debbie corrected. "Mental challenges. That's what Dr. Shields calls them. He helps you pull out all the anger and bitterness and hostility that's eating away at your creativity, and once you've gotten all that poison out, you can move in a more positive direction. He really changed my life," she added. "And he'll change your life too if you work with him and trust him."

Regan mustered up a big smile. "Oh, I want to change. I really do. That's why I'm here."

"Me too," Sophie gushed.

Debbie eagerly nodded. "The reception is being held down the hallway and around the corner, behind a double set of doors. You don't know how lucky you are, ladies. It's a real bonus that the doctor isn't just mingling. He's already hinted that he might do a couple of exercises tonight. It wasn't printed in the program. Dr. Shields is so busy these days with all the demands on his time, but he loves to be spontaneous when he can schedule it on his calendar."

"He schedules spontaneity?" Regan asked, trying not to laugh.

Debbie was as enthusiastic as a Lakers' cheerleader. "Why, yes, he does."

Regan turned to leave. "Wait," Debbie called out. "I forgot to give you ladies your packets." She handed each of them a blue folder. "There's a notebook and pen inside the folder so you can write down the doctor's words of wisdom. No tape recorders or cameras allowed inside. Now, if you have any questions or need anything, all the personnel are dressed in identical blue blazers like the one I'm wearing. We're all here to help make this seminar a fabulous experience for you."

"I'm sure it will be," Sophie said.

Regan walked ahead down a wide

hallway, turned the corner, and came to an abrupt stop. "Good heavens," she whispered.

There, adjacent to the double doors was an impossible-to-miss, eight-foot-tall cardboard cutout of Shields. A full-color body shot had been done, and with his bright blue blazer and dazzling, obviously capped, white teeth, he really did look like an advertisement for a real estate agent who had just made the deal of a lifetime. One of Shields's eyelids was lowered ever so slightly, as though the photographer had caught him in the middle of a wink.

"Think he likes himself?" Cordie asked.

"He's an egomaniac," Sophie said.

"Do you think he's wearing colored contacts?" Cordie asked.

"Have you ever met anyone with cobalt blue eyes?" Regan responded.

"Good point."

Cordie stepped forward to open the door when Sophie stopped her. "Hold on. I have to turn my tape recorder on."

"You better sit up close to him," Regan said.

"I'm sitting in the back," Cordie said.

"Okay. Let's do it," Sophie said as she opened the door.

The living room was surprisingly large

and very crowded. There was a long, cream-colored sectional in front of the stone fireplace, and easy chairs were grouped in pairs around the room. Folding chairs lined the back walls.

At least eighty percent of the participants were women, but there wasn't one age group that was more prominent than another. Regan had assumed most of the registrants would be men and women going through some kind of midlife crisis, but she was wrong about that. There were just as many twentysomething women and several who were well over sixty.

Sophie headed to the front and squeezed in between two men on the sofa facing the fireplace. Both men were happy to accommodate her.

Cordie spotted two empty folding chairs in the corner against the back wall. She nudged Regan. "Follow me."

Regan hurried after her friend, took her seat, and then gave Shields her full attention. The psychologist stood in front of the massive stone fireplace. He was an imposing figure. Tall, tanned . . . or was that makeup he was wearing? His bodyguards were easy to spot. They stood like robots at opposite ends of the hearth. They weren't wearing sunglasses, and their eyes were constantly scanning the audience.

"They're creepy," she whispered.

"The bodyguards?" Cordie asked.

"Yes."

"So is Shields. Is he wearing makeup?"

"I think so."

The psychologist didn't look like a monster, just a vain, fiftyish con artist trying to be twenty again. Mary Coolidge had written that he was the most charismatic man she had ever known. Maybe it was because Regan was predisposed to disliking him, but she couldn't find anything charismatic about him.

Cordie nudged her. "You know who he kind of reminds me of?"

"Who?"

"Your stepfather."

"Another reason not to like him," Regan replied.

Shields did have a dazzling smile. He had moved to a corner of the room and was surrounded by adoring women. He suddenly motioned for the women to take their seats. He waited until they had found spots, then strode back to the center of the fireplace. A hush fell over the group.

"Showtime," Regan whispered.

Chapter Ten

Shields began his greeting. He had a crooning, hypnotic voice that was a cross between Barry White and Mr. Rogers.

Cordie nudged Regan. "One of the bodyguards, the guy on the left, has been staring at you since you walked in. What's his problem?"

"Ignore him," Regan said.

Shields clapped his hands. "The early bird gets the worm, as my grandmother used to say. Tomorrow there will be five hundred people in the auditorium. Space is at a premium here, so I had to limit the number at this conference, but because you men and women came early and paid your fee, I decided to have this little get-together. If more show up tonight, we'll open those doors and expand. Now then, let me tell you what you'll learn during this weekend."

He was droning on and on, so Regan tuned him out. She pulled his photo from the pocket of the folder and compared the likeness. Close, she thought. Her mind began to wander and then it turned to more practical matters, and she flipped the photo over to jot down some reminders for herself. *"Call security and talk to them about Peter Morris,"* she wrote. Then, *"Talk to Aiden about the Emily Milan problem."* Regan looked up and scanned the audience. Shields certainly had a way with the participants. Most of the women seemed captivated by what he was telling them. Some were actually leaning forward in their chairs as though subconsciously trying to get closer to him. She turned her attention once again to Shields, and after listening for ten minutes, concluded his extemporaneous speech consisted of two themes, fear and greed. Yes, Shields insisted, they really could have it all. They deserved to have it all. But first they needed to rid themselves of the poison inside them.

A hand shot up. Shields took a step forward, paused to flash a smile, and then said, "Yes?"

A woman bolted to her feet. While she was tugging at her ill-fitting skirt, she asked, "I . . . I'm not sure I understand. I know you said we had to open our minds to new opportunities and that we must first get rid of the poison inside . . ."

When she hesitated, Shields said, "Yes, that's right."

"Well . . . the thing is . . . I didn't know I had poison inside."

Shields dramatically waved his hands. "Everyone in this room has poison inside them."

"But that's just it," the woman said, still tugging at her skirt. "What do you mean by poison?"

He obviously expected the question. Clasping his hands behind his back, he took another step forward.

"Look how close he is to Sophie," Cordie whispered. "Her tape recorder must be getting every word."

"I think the woman who just asked the question is a plant. What do you think?"

"Maybe so," Cordie agreed.

"Have you ever been hurt by anyone," Shields asked the woman. "Hurt deeply?"

Who hadn't? Regan thought about Dennis and was suddenly interested in what Shields had to say. The woman who'd asked the question lowered her gaze, and a faint blush covered her cheeks. "Yes . . . I'll bet most of us in this room have been hurt deeply," she said as she nervously glanced around. "My boyfriend . . . he cheated on me, and he didn't care how much he hurt me. He . . . used me."

"And you took that hurt and buried it

deep inside, didn't you?" Shields nodded sagely and looked over his audience. "How many of you have been in hurtful relationships over the years? How many have endured betrayals from family and those you believed were your friends? How many of you have been overlooked for promotions time and again at work when you know in your heart you earned them?"

Hands were shooting up all over the room. "Shields has them eating out of the palm of his hand," Cordie whispered. "Uh-oh. That bodyguard is still staring. Put your hand up."

Regan dutifully put her hand up. A shiver ran down her spine the longer she watched Shields. He was smiling like a benevolent Yoda now.

"I believe that all those painful experiences have turned into drops of poison inside you, eating away at your potential, your creativity, your passion for life."

"But how do we get rid of this poison?" another woman called out.

"I'll show you," he said. "By the time this seminar is over Sunday evening, you'll be cleansed and ready to take on the world. I guarantee it."

He paused again, and then in a voice as smooth as Häagen-Dazs said, "Why don't we do a little exercise? Everyone, take out your notepad and pen. You'll find both inside your folder. We're going to make a list."

He motioned to the bodyguard on his right. The muscleman immediately knelt in front of the fireplace and turned the gas jets on. Seconds later a roaring fire was heating up the already warm room.

"Better get our notepads out and look eager," Cordie said. "It's hot in here," she added. "I should have worn my hair up. It's definitely gonna frizz."

Regan was used to Cordie obsessing about her hair and ignored her comments.

"Ready?" Shields called out. "Now, here's what I want you to think about. How can you make the world a better place for you? Would you be happier, more fulfilled, more joyful, if the people who have hurt you no longer existed? What if you could wave a magic wand and poof," he said, snapping his fingers for drama, "they're gone . . . forever. Would you be better off without them? If you could get rid of the poison inside you, would you be happier? If you believe you would, write down the names of those people you want to vanish."

Regan couldn't believe what she was

hearing. She wasn't the only one. A timid hand went up. "Excuse me, Dr. Shields. Did I hear correctly? You want us to —"

Another woman stood, clutching the notepad to her chest. "You want us to make a . . . murder list?"

"That's not what he said," a young man shouted.

Shields put his hands up. "You can call it whatever you want. Those of you who are a bit squeamish, think of it as a list of the people you simply wish to never see again."

The woman clutching the notepad couldn't seem to compute what he was telling her to do. "Okay. So you want us to write down the names of people we wish were . . . dead."

"Yes, that's exactly what I want you to do. If those people who have injured you no longer existed, then wouldn't you be able to get rid of the poison inside you?"

"Yes . . . I guess . . . but . . ."

Another man shouted, "I'm gonna need more paper."

Nervous laughter followed his comment. "Is there a limit on the names?" he asked.

"Write down as many names as you want. I do think for this exercise we'll have a time limit. Ten minutes," he said. "Shall we get started?"

He stretched his arm, stared down at his watch, and said, "You may begin."

A man sitting in front of Regan whispered, "This is going to be fun. I'm going to start with my wife."

"You mean your ex-wife," the woman sitting next to him said.

"Oh, that's good. I'll put her on my list too."

Cordie looked appalled. "Can you believe this? Shields has turned the group into ghouls."

"Hush," Regan whispered. "We better act like we're with the program. Start writing."

"No matter how obscene this exercise is?"

"No matter."

"Well, then . . ."

"Well, then what?"

Cordie smiled. "Might as well have a little fun."

They both pulled out their notepads. Regan wrote across the top of the paper, "Murder List" and underlined the words twice. Underneath she wrote, "People I Want Dead." Now what? Stalling for time, she tapped her pen against the folder until the man in front of her turned and frowned.

"Do you mind? You're distracting me."

"Sorry," she whispered.

She had a feeling the bodyguard was still watching her. Maybe she was being paranoid. She brushed her hair out of her eyes and looked up, then quickly lowered her head. Nope. Not paranoid. The creep was still staring. What was his problem?

Cordie was sniffling and digging through her purse. Regan handed her a tissue.

"Five more minutes," Shields called out. "And then I'll circle the room and I want everyone to hold up their notepads so I can see the number of names."

Uh-oh. Regan began to write. Shields, bodyguard one, and bodyguard two all made her list. Who else? Ms. Patsy, that rude saleslady from Dickerson's. Oh, yes, she mustn't forget that horrible Detective Sweeney. The world would definitely be a better place without him. She was about to add Lieutenant Lewis to her list because he'd been so vicious to that young man, but time was up.

She'd had no idea she was so bloodthirsty. Shields clapped his hands. "Pens down. Everyone hold up your notepad so I can see them. That's right. Good. Good," he praised. "Everyone participated. Now here's what I'd like you to do. One by one come up to the fireplace. Tear the paper out of the notepad and shred it. Then you'll throw it in the fire and watch the flames devour the names. Shall we begin?"

"Will that get rid of the hurt and the poison?" a woman asked.

"It's a symbolic gesture," Shields explained. "Meant to open your mind to all the possibilities."

"What's that supposed to mean?" Cordie asked.

"We get to open our minds to the possibility that we could kill all of our enemies," Regan explained with mock enthusiasm.

"Shall we begin?" Shields called out.

Sophie was the first in line. She was smiling at Shields as she walked past.

"Un-oh, Sophie's flirting," Cordie whispered. "And Shields is loving the attention."

"How can she? He's so . . . repulsive."

"This is b.s. Can you believe he actually charges money for this?"

"Shields said there were five hundred people signed up for this seminar. Multiply that number by the thousand dollars each paid, and . . ."

"He's making a bloody fortune."

"I can't believe we've committed an entire weekend to this."

"Let's get in line and then get out of here. I'm starving."

Regan had just picked up her purse when her cell phone rang. The sound earned her a glare from both bodyguards.

She answered the phone, quickly gathered up her things, and went out into the hallway while Cordie got in line to toss her list in the fire.

Emily Milan was on the line. She was in one of her moods again and didn't waste words.

"You didn't give me Aiden's latest notes," she snapped. "And as a result, the last meeting was a complete disaster. I'm not going to be able to do my job if you continue to play these childish games, Regan."

"I'm certain Henry printed out everything that was e-mailed," she said. "I didn't erase it, and I'll be happy to check again when I get back to the hotel, but —"

"I expect those papers on my desk tomorrow."

"I'm sure everything my brother sent was printed," she repeated.

"Do I have to talk to Aiden about this?"

Regan counted to five. It didn't help. "Please do."

She snapped the phone shut and stood

there glaring at it. "Oh, you are so going on my list," she muttered.

She wished she could have fired Emily right then and there, over the phone. She couldn't, though. She didn't have the authority. Thunder rumbled close by, interrupting her mental tirade. She shoved the phone into her purse and went back inside to find Cordie and Sophie so she could get out of there before her mood completely soured. She was pulling the heavy door closed behind her when she noticed one of the bodyguards was down on his knees in front of the hearth turning the gas jets off. She guessed she'd missed the fire cleansing ritual.

She couldn't find Sophie, but Cordie was where she'd left her, still sitting in the uncomfortable folding chair against the back wall. She sat down beside her and whispered, "Could we leave now?"

"In a minute," Cordie said. "Shields is telling us what he thinks is a super-inspirational story about one of his students."

"Students? He teaches a class?"

Cordie shook her head. "He's calling us his students. All the people who have attended his past seminars are former students. How can anyone with half a brain fall for his act? He's such a fraud."

"Look around," Regan whispered. "The room's full of unhappy people desperately wanting to change their lives. He's telling them what they want to hear."

"He also gives them someone to blame instead of taking responsibility for their own behavior. Sophie was right. He does prey on the vulnerable."

"I'm going to ask Aiden to fire Emily," Regan said.

Cordie bolted upright. "Really." She looked thrilled.

Regan repeated the conversation she'd had with the obnoxious woman. "What would you do?"

"Make Aiden fire her skinny little ass," she whispered. "You should hire his next assistant. He's obviously looking for the wrong type."

"What type is that?"

"Young, beautiful, blond, thin . . ."

"What do you care what she looks like?"

Cordie shrugged. "I don't care," she said quickly. "You're the one complaining."

Regan sighed. "I can't fire her. She doesn't work for me. Besides, Aiden needs help . . ."

"So? Get someone else to help him."

Shields's volume increased as he finished

his story. Applause followed. He waited for the noise to die down, then announced that the spontaneous session was over and to please mingle. Within seconds the psychologist was surrounded by women fighting for his attention.

"Is it raining?" Cordie asked. She lifted a strand of her long hair, sighed, and shoved it back behind her ear. "It's raining, all right. My hair's frizzing already."

"Nonsense," Regan said. "Your hair doesn't frizz. It curls."

Cordie dug through her purse, found a hair clip, and went to work pulling her hair into a twist.

"I'll go get the car and pull up under the overhang. You find Sophie and drag her outside if you have to," Regan said.

She gathered up her things, tucked the folder under her arm, and headed out. The mood in the room was still jovial, many of the participants laughing nervously and talking with one another. Such eagerness, such hope, she thought. She was sure she heard Sophie's distinctive laughter. How in heaven's name could she stomach being so close to Shields?

Regan seemed to be the only person in a hurry to leave. The lighting on the porch and around the building was abysmal. She could barely see her hand in front of her face.

If she had been a pessimist, she would have thought the rain had been waiting for her, because the second she stepped out from under the overhang, the soft drizzle turned into a downpour.

She sprinted across the parking lot, the rain pelting her face. Since she hadn't thought to bring an umbrella, she used the blue folder to try to block the raindrops so she could see where she was going.

By the time she reached the park, her knee was throbbing. She considered stopping and taking off her new, impossible-to-resist, sling-back heels, but it was only about fifty yards to the car, and she didn't want to stop. She already had her car key out. It was attached to a bracelet chain. Regan had slipped the chain over her wrist so she could grip her purse as she ran.

She could have taken a shortcut through the grass, but then her beautiful, soft, buttery leather shoes would have been completely ruined. God, what an idiot she'd been to wear such high heels.

She was about twenty-five, maybe thirty, yards from her car when she thought she heard someone shout her name. Regan automatically pivoted toward the sound. Her left knee buckled, and she went down hard. Crying out in pain, she let go of her purse and the folder to brace against the fall. She was used to having her knee go out — it happened at least once a month — but the pain usually went away after a couple of seconds. This time was different. It was sharp and close to unbearable.

Half the contents of her purse scattered on the sidewalk. She knelt on one knee as she scooped up her lipstick and billfold. Someone shouted at her again. It was a high-pitched voice, or was that the wind playing tricks on her? She strained to listen for the sound as she stuffed the billfold back into her purse and staggered to her feet.

Nothing. Just her imagination, she decided. All she wanted to think about was getting out of the rain.

She heard him coming before she saw him.

Chapter Eleven

A week had passed since the incident with the runner, and the police hadn't pounded down his door and dragged him away. For seven days and nights he'd vacillated between stark terror and sheer joy. He'd wake up during the night and think, oh, God, what have I done? and he would hear the demon whisper.

We've gotten away with murder.

It was Friday, and the beast was stirring. He had to go hunting again. His last venture out had nearly ended in disaster, but he hoped he had learned from his mistakes and would do better this time, for he couldn't afford to fail again. Yes, he would be better prepared tonight. In anticipation, he'd packed dark jogging clothes, a new baseball cap — he'd had to throw away the old one because of all the blood on it — and black running shoes. He'd stored the gear under the seat in the back of his car, along with thick, nonprescription, horn-rimmed glasses, a dark brown wig — shoulder-length and tied in a ponytail with a red-and-white bandana like a biker would wear — and the essential pair of new black gloves. He'd even purchased glue and a beard at a novelty store, trimming it just right, so that he wouldn't look too much like Charles Manson.

He still felt he could subdue any woman, but he slipped a knife into his pocket just in case. He spent hours figuring out his approach, trying to cover every possible angle. When he was finally dressed and ready to leave, he took a minute to stand in front of the mirror in the upstairs bathroom and look at himself. He was pleased with what he saw. Why, his own mother wouldn't recognize him.

The demon would be pleased too.

One thing was certain. He couldn't return home with more scratches on his face and arms. He could lie well when he had to, but the scratches had drawn attention to him and that was inexcusable. He simply had to be more careful. Whenever he thought about that first deadly encounter, he broke out in a cold sweat. He had come so close to getting caught, so very close.

Tonight would be different. He had been lucky the last time, but he wasn't about to rely on good fortune coming to his aid again. He had most assuredly learned from his mistakes. Blend in. That was number one on his list. And so tonight he was pretending to be a jogger. He was in wonderful shape, of course. All those nights at the gym — had he been preparing for this and not realized it? He had become a bit obsessive, but now he could see he had started his training when he'd lifted that first ten-pound weight.

Finding the chosen one turned out to be surprisingly easy. She practically strolled up to his car and tapped on his window. That's how close she was. She walked out the door of the hotel with a friend just as his car turned the corner. And, oh, what a sight. "Perfect," he whispered. "Absolutely perfect."

A car backed out of the alley across the street, so he was able to stop and stare at her without drawing attention. He even rolled his window down in hopes of getting a whiff of her perfume.

He was going to follow her and wait for his opportunity, but once again, he got lucky. He heard one of the attendants shout to another, asking if he knew the quickest way to get to Liam House. Her car pulled away, and he tried to tail her, but he lost her when she turned off Michigan Avenue. He drove on to Liam House, found a parking spot a quarter of a mile away, and then jogged back to the conference center.

Adjusting his cap over his wig, he circled the building twice, taking his time as he surreptitiously checked out the area. He'd hoped there would be a jogging path close by so he could pretend he was headed toward it, but there wasn't. Just streets, parking lots, and a little park in between.

The lighting outside the conference center was quite poor, which he found to his liking, but light did spill out from several windows and the front door as men and women hurried inside. He hung back in the shadows of the trees. He was afraid his chosen one might have gone inside while he was circling.

He waited another half hour or so and then he got nervous. Was she there? He backtracked once again, ran through the parking lot, and finally found her car on the opposite side of the park.

"Yes," he whispered, weak with relief. It was okay. She was inside.

He didn't have to wait much longer. He was looking for a better spot to watch the entrance of the building when, lo and behold, he glanced up, and there she was. Before the door shut behind her, she was surrounded by a halo of light. He actually gasped at her sheer beauty. He blinked, and for a second her face magically changed, and he saw his beloved Nina. He blinked again and saw now only the woman. What had caused his mind to play such a trick? Perhaps it was her dark hair. Perhaps, too, it was because she was the one, the perfect chosen one.

He felt the tightness gathering in his chest. Suddenly, he heard a sound behind him. He was clearly visible where he stood, and so he quickly knelt on one knee, pretending to tie his shoes, while the stranger, carrying a sack of groceries, passed him. He kept his face averted until the man disappeared. A clap of thunder ripped the sky. He knew he had to act fast. The wind had picked up and was howling. He pulled his baseball cap down farther and took a deep breath just as the clouds opened.

She was ahead of him now, her long-legged stride a sight to behold. He stepped out of his hiding place, oblivious of the wet slap of the rain against his cheeks, and watched her. Appreciated her. Her skirt was short, but not trashy short. In the misty light from the streetlamps her skin looked golden.

A golden girl, that's what she was to him,

the prize he would snatch in just seconds. He tried to savor every little detail about her. He wanted to remember everything, the way she held herself, the way she smelled, the way she felt when he grabbed her.

She had such beautiful strong legs. She was so like his Nina before the accident. Yes, just like her. Like his wife, she moved with elegant grace, her head held high, her hips gently swaying.

His mind rebelled against making the comparison, or was that the demon cautioning him not to think such dangerous thoughts? No, she couldn't possibly compare to his Nina. There was business to be done. Quid pro quo. With that singular thought in mind, his hand slipped into his pocket, his fingers coiling around his new knife . . . just in case.

He took that first step toward her and shouted, "Wait!" She didn't slow down, and so he ran at her and shouted again. This time he heard the fury in his voice.

She turned, her gaze catching him as she pivoted.

He stopped so suddenly he actually rocked on the balls of his feet. In horror, he watched her fall. Her left leg simply folded underneath her, as though her bone had melted. She crashed to the pavement and cried out in pain. He put his hands over his ears to block the sound. It all seemed to transpire in slow motion, just like the car accident of years past. Exactly like that. The tortured look on her beautiful face before the metal imploded on her legs.

His mind couldn't take it in. What had just happened? He staggered back, then stopped. The poor thing. She was in pain, her leg useless now, and, oh, she was so like his Nina.

He should help her, shouldn't he? He knew he wasn't making any sense. Why did he have this nearly overwhelming desire to help someone he was determined to destroy?

He didn't know what to do. He stood there looking at her. He backed farther away but continued to watch her struggle to get up. Twice she almost made it before she collapsed again. Poor, poor thing. He thought she might be crying, but the wind snatched the sound before it reached him.

He couldn't stop staring at her, and she kept her eyes locked on him while she tried to get back on her feet. There was a connection between them. He felt it in his heart and in his soul where the demon lived.

She broke eye contact first, turned, and limped away like a wounded animal, her open purse dangling from her arm.

She was headed to her car. He could hear the demon's voice chanting in his ear. *Get her. Get her. Get her.* He bolted after her. He could hear himself panting as he closed the distance.

He was almost on top of her when he was suddenly blinded by bright lights. What the . . . ? Ducking his head down, he turned, desperate to find the darkness again.

He hit something slick, went flying, and crashed into a tree, his right shoulder bearing the brunt. Cursing his own clumsiness, he looked down and saw what he had slipped on. It was a folder with papers spilling out. He bent down, hurriedly shoved the papers back inside, thinking he could use the folder to lure her out of her car.

He picked it up and shouted to her again, but she wouldn't stop. Too late. He was too late. She was already backing her car out of the parking space.

Filth spewed from his mouth, obscene words he hadn't even known were part of his vocabulary and he had certainly never uttered before. He found it impossible to stop the foul litany. He was losing control of himself, could feel himself slipping away, acquiescing to the demon.

Concentration was difficult, and he tried with all his might to focus. The car that had blinded him had its blinker on, obviously waiting for her parking space. His beautiful, golden prey had stopped. Why wasn't she leaving? What was she doing?

He ran across the lot keeping her car in sight. The lights made him squint. He reached up to pull the bill of his baseball cap down lower. The cap was gone.

Could she see him through his disguise? Could she see his hatred? She wasn't moving. What could she be doing? Oh, God, a cell phone. She probably had a cell phone and was using it right this second. She was calling 911. That's what she was doing.

He panicked. He actually ran around in a circle while he tried to think what he should do. If she was calling the police, how long would it take them to get here?

Stupid. Stupid. Stupid. The cap. He had to get his baseball cap back — it had his fingerprints all over it — and then he needed to get out of the park.

He raced back to the tree he'd crashed into, dropped to his knees, and began to search in the dark. What's this? His hand curled around a silver cell phone, and his heart leapt with joy. She hadn't called the police. When she'd dropped her folder, she'd also dropped the phone. Yes, yes, it had to be hers.

Relief flooded over him until he remembered he needed to find his cap. Where was it? Frantic now, his mind screamed hurry, hurry. And then he found it and let out a low, anguished sob. Jumping up, he started running to safety, clutching the folder and the cell phone and his cap in his hands, his mind in such a confused state, he could barely concentrate.

He couldn't hear himself think. The roar of the demon blocked out all other sounds.

Chapter Twelve

He came out of nowhere. He was running toward her. She could hear his footsteps on the pavement as she was turning. His face was twisted in rage. He was a big, muscular man. What was he doing? And why was he so angry?

Her mind tried to make sense out of why he was there. He was probably a jogger who just got caught in the rain. Maybe he was trying to get to his car just as she was trying to get to hers, and when she turned toward him, she'd so surprised him that he'd stopped.

No, no. There was something all wrong about him. Without understanding why, she knew the anger was directed at her.

Her instincts were screaming at her to get out of there. Fear, a powerful motivator, overrode the pain in her knee as she struggled to get up off the ground.

Her car key still dangled from the bracelet on her wrist. It was a miracle it hadn't slipped off in the fall. The car was safety. Run, her mind screamed. Run.

The rain was pouring now. Head down,

she stumbled to get to her car.

Was he coming after her? She dared a quick look back. Oh, God, he was running at her, closing the distance.

Wait. He was waving something at her and shouting at her to stop.

No, no, it was wrong. It was all wrong. Faster, she had to run faster. Her brother's warning popped into her head. Spencer had always told her that when in doubt, go with your instincts, and her instincts were screaming at her to get to safety.

She finally made it to the car. The key nearly fell out of her hand when she pulled the coiled bracelet off her wrist, but she grabbed it in time. Her hands were slick from rain, and she was shaking so much it took her two tries to get the key in the lock.

He was almost there. She swung the door open, dove inside, threw her purse out of her way, and pulled the door closed. Twisting around, she hit the lock button down with her fist.

She didn't take time to recover her breath. She shoved the key into the ignition and started the engine, turning the bright lights on as she backed out. Her foot slipped off the pedal.

"Oh, God," she whispered. He was

standing just twenty, perhaps thirty feet away. The light shone on his face, and his expression terrified her. He didn't move. She frantically wiped the rain away from her eyes.

She blinked and he was gone.

She grabbed her purse from the floor and frantically dug through it, searching for her cell phone. Where was it?

A car behind her honked. Cordie and Sophie . . . they were waiting for her to pick them up. And the lunatic was out there.

She gripped the steering wheel and drove like a wild woman to the conference center. Aiden was right, she thought. She did need a new car, one with power locks and an alarm. It had been childish for her to hang on to the old clunker just to spite him.

Her friends were standing on the porch waiting for her. Regan put the car in park and slid across the bench seat to unlock the back door for Sophie. She rolled the window down and called out to Cordie, "You drive."

"What happened to you?" Sophie asked, and after she got in, she scooted to unlock the driver's door for Cordie. "Your face is gray."

"I fell. Actually I —"

Sophie interrupted. "You hurt your knee again, didn't you? Did it just give out on you?"

"Yes, but . . ."

"You really should get that fixed," Cordie said. She was adjusting the mirror.

"Stop interrupting and listen. Something happened. Sophie, give me your phone. I can't find mine, and I need to call the police."

Her voice trembled as she related what had happened. Although it seemed odd to her, retelling was almost as frightening as the experience itself, because she now realized how close she might have come to fending off a madman.

Cordie was so shocked by what she was hearing that she grabbed Regan's hand to comfort her.

"Thank God you got away from him," she whispered.

Sophie wanted more details. "Could you identify him if you saw him?"

"I don't know. Yes . . . maybe. I was so scared. I turned and there he was. He wore thick glasses."

Cordie found her cell phone and handed it to Regan. "Call right now and tell them there's a lunatic roaming around the conference center."

"I'll bet he's long gone by now," Sophie said.

"Are you saying she shouldn't call?" Cordie asked, ready to argue.

"Of course she should call, but after you give the police the description, tell the officer we're on our way to the police station. There's one about two miles from here."

"Let's get out of here," Cordie said. She put the car in drive and headed out while Regan made the call.

"We've got to get some ice on Regan's knee," Sophie said. "And the sooner the better."

Regan motioned for her friends to be quiet when the phone was answered. She worried she would end up talking to another detective like Sweeney, but fortunately, the officer who took the call was efficient and polite. As soon as she explained what had happened, he dispatched policemen to the conference center to search for the man.

"I think he believed me, but I don't know why," Regan said after she had ended the call. "I rambled, didn't I?"

"A little," Cordie said.

"Turn left at the next corner," Sophie directed. "There's a QuikTrip where we can get her an ice pack, and a police station is just about a mile farther down that street."

"How come you know where all the police stations are?" Regan asked.

"Not all of them, just some," she corrected. "I'm going to be an investigative reporter, remember? It's good to know these things."

"I liked Officer Martinez," Sophie said an hour later as the three left the police station.

Regan was replaying what she had said and shaking her head over her descriptions. "I sounded like an idiot. There was a man . . . dressed like a runner," she quoted herself. "He appeared out of nowhere and I fell, and I think he might have been chasing me. But then again . . . maybe he wasn't . . ."

"You were smart to run, Regan," Sophie said. "That's what Officer Martinez said. You went with your instincts."

"He also said there hadn't been any problems at the center in over a year."

"You still did the right thing," Cordie said. "You reported the incident, and if he's some kind of wacko, which, by the way, I think he is, they'll be on the lookout for him."

"Could we not talk about this anymore?"

Regan said. "How about eating in the hotel dining room? I'll get you both settled at a table in the restaurant, run upstairs to change out of these wet clothes, and we'll have a lovely dinner."

"I don't think you're going to be able to run anywhere," Cordie said. "And you need to keep ice on that knee."

"Then come up to my suite, and we'll order room service."

They both agreed, and the rest of the evening was blessedly uneventful. As far as Regan was concerned, the matter was closed.

Chapter Thirteen

He had blown it. After all the worrying and the planning and the practicing, he had let her get away. He'd worked so hard. It wasn't fair. No, it wasn't fair at all. It was his right to take her life, his duty.

She'd tricked him into feeling confused and sympathetic when she'd fallen. She'd blindsided him. Yes, that's exactly what she had done.

He pulled the Jeep over to the curb, put it in park, and began to pound the dashboard with his fists. He knew he was behaving like a child having a full-blown tantrum, but he didn't care. He had failed. He kept beating the console until the shaking subsided. By the time he was able to think clearly again, his knuckles were raw.

Panic didn't set in until he'd reached the safety of his garage. He stayed in the car until the garage door was down and he was safe inside his frigid cocoon. And still he didn't move. He leaned against the seat and closed his eyes while he thought about his situation, his mind jumping from one thought to another. He knew it was only a matter of time before the police found the accident he'd buried. Would they connect him to that crime? If they did, he'd be locked away for the rest of his life, and his Nina, his dear, sweet Nina . . . how could she exist without him?

Stay cool, he told himself. There would be other chances. He wouldn't get caught. The beast wouldn't let that happen. It was going to be okay.

He continued his internal monologue as he crept through the house and opened the bedroom door to check on Nina. She was sound asleep. He quietly closed the door and went into the laundry room just off the kitchen. He stripped out of his clothes, tossed them into the washer, and grabbed the box of Tide.

His mind wouldn't quiet down. He analyzed his poor performance this evening, and he was appalled and disgusted. He had to do better next time. Had to.

He couldn't stop thinking about her. He kept picturing her, his beautiful angel with the broken wing, falling, so gracefully tumbling down. Had he heard her cry out, or had he only imagined she had? His chosen one, his perfect angel, was innocent, as innocent as his beloved Nina.

He closed his eyes and bowed his head. He had seen her weep, and his heart ached for her. He was so confused, torn between worrying about her and raging because she had gotten away.

"Can't have it both ways," he whispered. And he knew, in his heart he knew, that he had to appease the demon.

Stark naked, he went back into the garage. His chest and arms were covered in goose bumps. There was a small mirror propped on a shelf near the door. He paused to admire himself. His body was that of a Greek god, he thought with a great deal of pride. He'd worked hard to get it that way. Flexing his muscles, he smiled at his reflection.

He stood there a full minute before he turned away. He had the sudden urge, no, need, to look at her things, just to make sure they were where he'd hidden them in the small wooden crate with a stack of rags on top. The crate was tucked in the corner. It wasn't a very clever hiding place, and tomorrow he planned to move the box.

The hammer, the girl's driver's license, and her pepper spray were just where he'd put them. He still wasn't sure why he'd taken them, but he couldn't make himself get rid of them just yet. He picked up the license and read her name. Haley Cross. In the photo, she was smiling. The picture he had of her in his mind was a face contorted in terror. He dropped the license on top of the spray and picked up the hammer.

The sound of a phone ringing close by jarred him. He whirled around with the hammer upraised in his hand. It took him a second to realize the noise was coming from his Jeep. Of course. Her phone. Someone was calling her. He waited, frozen, with the hammer in midair, until the ringing stopped. He found the phone and her folder on the backseat.

Shivering from the night chill, he hurried into his kitchen. He placed the phone and the folder on the table, went to the sink to wash his hands and clean the cuts on his knuckles, and then made himself a drink.

He dropped into a chair and opened the folder. He spread the contents across the table and began to read.

Chapter Fourteen

Alec Buchanan was one of the last passengers to leave the plane. A flight attendant had to wake him. He'd fallen asleep about ten seconds after he had clipped on his seat belt and stretched his long legs in a poor attempt to get comfortable.

Alec could sleep anywhere, anytime, much to his brother Nick's consternation. Nick was afraid to fly and went to great lengths to avoid it, which, of course, made him the brunt of many family jokes. Alec didn't mind flying at all, though he thought the flight from Boston to Chicago was too short. Since he'd stayed up most of the night with his five brothers and two sisters catching up on all the news, he would have liked a much longer nap.

He knew he looked like hell. He hadn't shaved since his interview with the FBI Thursday morning. He was pretty sure the job was his if he wanted it. Ward Dayborough, the head of the special crimes division, had been actively recruiting him for over a year and had all but guaranteed that he'd be based out of Boston.

That was just one of the many incentives for taking the job, but even if he didn't make this move, he still needed to find the time to go home more often. He missed his family.

Over the weekend, the entire Buchanan clan had gathered at their parents' sprawling island home on Nathan's Bay to celebrate their father's birthday. Nick and his wife, Laurant, had brought their baby girl to the island for the first time.

While he was there, Nick, along with the oldest brother, Theo, worked on Alec to accept the offer from the FBI. They tried to convince him that it was a family obligation. Theo was an attorney with the Justice Department, and Nick had been an agent for a special branch of the FBI for many years. Alec did love Boston, and Nick, now that he had a family and needed a bigger place, was offering him a great deal on his town house.

It was time for a change, and Alec had a lot to think about. Being back home had been wonderful, even though he'd taken quite a beating playing football with all of his brothers. Ironically, the bruised shoulder that hurt the most had actually been inflicted by one of his younger sisters, Jordan. He smiled when he thought about her. Jordan was brilliant, no argument there, and had made them all a fortune when they invested in her design for a computer chip that revolutionized the industry, but as smart as she was, she had absolutely no common sense. She was also a klutz. She hadn't meant to tackle him; she'd simply tripped over her own feet. Fortunately for her, his shoulder took the brunt of her fall, and he'd caught her before she broke any bones.

It was raining when he drove away from O'Hare. Traffic was a bitch, but it still wasn't as bad as Boston's rush hour. He took shortcuts back to his apartment, unpacked, and put on his favorite pair of worn-out jeans. He was about to check his messages when his old partner, Gil Hutton, called. Gil had recently retired but still kept his fingers in the gossip pie. Alec swore Gil was clairvoyant. He knew things before they happened.

Gil didn't waste words on pleasantries. "I got the lowdown on Lewis."

"Yeah?" Alec laughed as he opened the refrigerator and took out a beer. He popped the tab, and took a long swallow. He could just picture Gil rubbing his head — a habit that used to drive Alec nuts — and gloating. The man loved to gloat when he had hot news.

Alec was feeling a little guilty because he hadn't confided in his friend about leaving the department. He had good reason. Alec knew Gil wouldn't be able to keep quiet about his interview with the FBI.

"Lewis was real pissed you fought him about firing that rookie. Know how he's getting even?"

Alec was suddenly weary. He dropped down on the sofa and closed his eyes. God, how he hated politics. "How?"

"If you try to get a transfer out, he's gonna block it."

"I didn't put in for a transfer."

"Yeah? Why not? I just assumed . . ."

Gil's radar was up. It wouldn't take him long to put two and two together and figure out that Alec was leaving.

"I haven't had time to do the paperwork," he said. That much was true, he thought. He hadn't had time.

"Well, Lewis will block it. I just thought you should know."

Alec didn't ask him where he got his information, but he thought Gil must spend most of his day on the phone, gathering little tidbits.

"You need to get a life."

His ex-partner ignored the comment. "Lewis is a real prick."

"Yes," Alec agreed. "And a game player."

Worse, he thought, the lieutenant didn't back up his men the way he should. He hung anyone in trouble out to dry, like the young policeman who really hadn't done anything wrong except have the bad luck to be in the wrong place at the wrong time.

"He's lost the respect of his detectives," Gil remarked.

"He never earned our respect. So tell me. Did he block the kid's transfer?"

"That kid is only four years younger than you are."

"Yeah, but he doesn't have my experience or cynicism."

"Lewis wasn't able to block that one. Hey, you want to grab a beer down at Finnegan's?"

"Not tonight."

"Maybe tomorrow night then? I want to hear your theories about Detective Sweeney."

"What about Sweeney?"

"You didn't hear?"

Alec was losing patience. "Hear what?"

"Oh, man, I thought you knew, but of course you couldn't have heard since you've been in Boston. Don't you check your messages?"

"I was about to when you called. So tell me. What about him?"

"He was murdered last night."

Chapter Fifteen

Regan had really made a mess of her knee. As much as she wanted to, she knew she couldn't put off the surgery any longer. She called the orthopedic surgeon's office Monday morning, fully expecting that, because of his busy schedule, he wouldn't be able to get to her for at least a month or two. That would give her sufficient time to get ready mentally and physically. As it turned out, he had a last-minute cancellation Tuesday morning. She didn't tell anyone except Henry, her assistant, because she didn't want her brothers or her friends worrying about her.

The doctor was able to do arthroscopic surgery, which meant a much shorter recovery time. She only had to use crutches for two days, and after two additional days of taking it easy, she began rehab.

She had just finished a workout to strengthen her knee when Sophie and Cordie stopped by her suite in the hotel.

"I'm still angry with you, Regan," Sophie said. "We had to find out you had surgery after the fact."

Cordie agreed. "You'd be furious if Sophie or I did that to you."

"You're right. I was wrong," she said. "I just didn't want you to worry, and it was no big deal."

"I don't care if it was a big deal or not. You should have told us," Sophie argued.

"I don't know what irritates me more. That you had surgery without us, or that you bailed on that godawful seminar where we had to listen to that quack doctor do one stupid exercise after another. It was the most miserable weekend of my life."

"It was pretty awful," Sophie agreed. "After the seminar, I talked to Shields's people about refunding your fee, but they refused. I told them you had hurt your knee, but they weren't at all sympathetic. The woman told us Shields has a strict policy. No refunds. How come I'm not surprised?"

"I demanded to talk to the doctor himself," Cordie said. She had spotted a candy dish on the credenza and was sorting through the hard candies looking for peppermints.

"And that's when we found out Shields has gone to his vacation home. Debbie said he needs his alone-time to rejuvenate. I translated that to mean he needs time to come up with more idiotic exercises."

Regan nodded. "I don't think he can top the people-I-want-dead list."

Sophie grinned. "That one was really kind of fun."

"Who did you put on your list?" Regan asked. "Anyone I know?"

Sophie's eyes widened. "Of course not. That would have been . . . barbaric. I made up names. And they all rhymed."

"What about you, Cordie?"

"The Seven Dwarfs," she said.

Regan's face was turning red. Cordie noticed. "You wrote real names, didn't you?"

She didn't have to answer. They both knew she had. She waited until they'd stopped laughing and said, "Okay, it's official. I'm a complete idiot. It just never occurred to me to make up names. I guess I was feeling stressed at the time."

"Which brings me to my proposition," Sophie said. She gave her friend a sly grin and continued. "I think we should take a vacation. I've rented a condo, and it's right on the beach. It would do us all good to get away. You could use a rest, Regan."

"Where is this beach?"

"The Caymans," she answered. "So, what do you say? I've called the airline, and we can leave this evening."

Regan glanced at Cordie, who was looking sheepish, and then turned back to Sophie. She recognized that look in her eye.

"So, what's the real reason, Sophie?" Regan asked. "Something's up. I can tell."

Sophie confessed. "Well . . . I did some digging. And guess where Dr. Shields's vacation home is?"

Regan caught on quickly. "The Caymans," she answered. She turned to Cordie. "And you're in on this?"

Cordie nodded. "I know. I can't believe I'm just dropping everything and running off to the Cayman Islands."

"Daddy says that lots of people use the Cayman banks to hide their money from their spouses or creditors —"

"Or the IRS?" Regan asked.

"Definitely the IRS," Sophie said.

"And you're sure that Shields is in the Caymans now?" Regan asked.

"He's been spotted on the beach behind his house," Sophie answered confidently.

"What do you mean, 'he's been spotted'? How would you know —"

"Daddy gave me the name of a guy to call, and he was happy to check. Shields is there, all right."

"How long are you going to be gone?" Regan asked.

"We've got the condo for two weeks," Sophie said. "It all depends."

"Can you take that much time?"

Cordie answered. "Why not? Sophie's a good two months ahead with her column, and I'm officially through with school until next term. I've got the entire summer off to work on my dissertation, but I'm not going to take any work with me. I plan to sit in the shade and relax. This constant rain is depressing, and when I get depressed, I eat."

"I wish I could go with you, but I can't," Regan said. "The art auction is coming up. I can't miss it, and I've got to get ready for the annual family meeting."

"I don't know why you bother," Sophie said. "Your vote doesn't count for anything. Spencer always votes with Aiden, Walker abstains, and you're always the dissenting vote. You don't have any power —"

Cordie interrupted. "You know that's not true. Aiden can't start another hotel without all four signatures. She has the power to stop any kind of expansion. Without her vote, everything comes to a complete standstill."

"But I won't do that," Regan said. "I

want more money for the art projects Henry and I started last year. You've seen the response. It's been phenomenal." She sighed then. "We're getting off the track. I've got to write a report to justify the increase I want, and that's going to take time. I really wish you'd go somewhere else for a vacation."

"This isn't a vacation," Sophie said.

"It is for me," Cordie countered.

"Shields could be dangerous. If he did send his bodyguards to Mary Coolidge's house —"

Sophie interrupted. "I know, but I'm not going to back away from this. I'm going to nail him, one way or another."

"I don't like the sound of that," Regan said. "Don't do anything illegal. And please be careful."

Sophie shrugged. "He stood me up, you know."

"Excuse me?" Regan said.

"The last day of the seminar, he asked me out . . . to dinner," she said. "And I agreed. We were supposed to meet at the top of the Hyatt, and I waited for over an hour. He never showed."

"You agreed to go out with that creep?" Regan asked.

"I didn't agree to go to bed with him, so

stop looking so horrified. We hadn't been able to get into his computer or find any records at the seminar. I just wanted to get close to him so I could —"

"Get to his records?" Cordie asked. "Sophie, you need to start thinking things through."

"Have you got any better ideas?"

"What will you do when you find him in the Caymans?" Regan asked.

"I don't know yet," Sophie answered, "but I'll think of something."

Chapter Sixteen

It was Regan's first full day back at work and Henry was driving her nuts trying to pamper her. He hovered like a doting grandmother. He wouldn't even let her reach for a pencil. Fortunately, he had a full schedule and several errands to run that morning. As he was leaving, she asked him to stop by the parking garage and get her cell phone from her car. She was sure that's where she had left it.

The second the door closed behind him, Regan turned back to her desk. She was determined to clear her e-mails as quickly as possible. She'd finished thirty without interruption, took a break to answer phone calls and eat lunch, and then went back to her task.

The next e-mail was from Henry. Whenever he received anything he thought Regan would be interested in, he forwarded it to her computer. The subject line was blank, and when she scrolled down, there was just an attachment, but no typed message from Henry. That was a bit peculiar. She assumed he'd been in a hurry.

She clicked on the paper clip icon and waited.

Henry walked into her office just as the picture appeared on the screen.

"Your phone wasn't in your car. I looked under the seats, between them . . . hey, Regan, what's the matter. Are you sick?"

"Oh, my God . . ." She was so repulsed by what she was looking at she couldn't go on.

Henry ran around the desk. He stopped short when he saw the screen. In front of him was a picture of a dead man, hanging by a thick rope from a beam in a basement somewhere, his face grotesquely swollen. His eyes were wide open, and his flabby skin was a chalky gray.

"Gross," Henry whispered. "What kind of pervert would send . . ."

"The e-mail came from you," she said.

"No way would I send anything like this."

She nodded. "Someone must have gotten hold of our private e-mail addresses."

Henry pointed to the screen. "It's not real," he said. "Someone's just playing a sick joke on you. Get rid of it," he added as he reached for the delete key.

She pushed his hand away. "I know this man."

"What?"

"I know him."

"People can do a lot of things with a photo and a computer," he said.

"So he might not really be dead?"

"Maybe not," he said. "I think we ought to call the police and let them figure it out."

She pointed to the screen. "He is the police."

Chapter Seventeen

Alec headed over to the Hamilton Hotel to talk to Regan Madison, the nutcase who had called the office and asked to speak to Detective Benjamin Sweeney. When told by the operator that Sweeney wasn't available, she'd asked if that was a permanent or a temporary situation. And that's when Detective John Wincott and Detective Alec Buchanan got involved.

The operator had told him that either the woman who'd called or her assistant would meet Alec in front of the elevators on the south side of the lobby. He spotted a young man dressed in khaki pants and a navy blue blazer shifting from foot to foot in the elevator alcove and headed toward him. He looked like a bodyguard, maybe even a former linebacker with the Bears, or some other pro football team, but when Alec got closer to him, he saw how very young he was. Hell, he was just a teenager.

"Detective Buchanan?"

"That's right."

The young man stepped forward and thrust out his hand as he introduced himself. "My name's Henry Portman, and I'm Regan's . . . I mean, I'm Regan Madison's assistant."

The kid was nervous. Alec didn't make any attempt to put him at ease. "So where's . . ." he began, and then stopped. He'd almost called Henry's employer a nutcase. Not too diplomatic, he decided. "Where's Mrs. Madison?" he began again.

"Oh, she's Miss Madison," he corrected. "She isn't married. I thought she might get engaged a while back, but it didn't work out, and I was real happy about that." He grinned and added, "I guess that isn't important, is it?"

"Probably not," Alec said. "So tell me. Why were you happy she didn't get engaged?" He thought maybe Henry had a crush on his employer and wondered if he'd admit it.

"The guy was only after her money."

"She has lots of money?"

Henry realized he was speaking out of school. "You'll have to ask her about that. She's waiting for us in her office on the third floor. She's making sure no one touches her computer. If you'll accompany me —"

"She's guarding her computer?"

"Yes, sir."

Henry was wearing a key on a long silver chain. As soon as they'd stepped inside the brass-plated elevator, he inserted the key into a lock and pushed the button for the third floor.

"All the offices are on three," he explained. "And no one can get off on that floor without a key. It's for security purposes. There's a lot of expensive equipment up there."

Alec filed the information away. At six foot three inches, he stood shoulder to shoulder with the kid, but he felt dwarfed by him. Alec had the muscles in his shoulders and upper arms, but Henry had about fifty pounds on him. Still, Alec felt he could take him down if he had to.

Something was making Henry nervous.

"How old are you?" Alec asked.

"Nineteen."

"You still in high school?"

"No, sir. I go to Loyola here in Chicago."

"Loyola doesn't have a football team." He spoke the thought out loud.

Henry smiled. "I get asked what position I play and for what team all the time. A big African-American man with a twenty-inch neck. People make assumptions, like I'm a football player or sometimes even a rapper.

My sheet's clean now, by the way."

Ah, there it was. Alec didn't smile, but he came close. "Yeah?" he said as the elevator doors opened on the third floor.

"You'll probably find out anyway," Henry blurted. He stepped off the elevator and turned to face Alec. "Even though my file is sealed, you'll figure out a way to read it like they do on those cop shows, so I'll save you the trouble and just tell you. I had a couple of problems when I was a kid, and I spent some time in juvie. I was hanging with the wrong people. That's not an excuse. Just fact."

"Okay," he said. "So how come you're so nervous?"

"You," he stammered. "Well, not exactly you. Cops make me nervous. That's not so unusual. They make my friend Kevin nervous too. And he doesn't have a record."

"Your boss called us," he reminded Henry. "So stop sweating it."

Henry smiled. They had stopped and were now standing in the hallway. "Our offices are down that corridor and around the corner."

Alec took his time following. He paused at each office door along the way to look inside. When Henry realized what he was doing, he backtracked.

"That office belongs to Regan's brother Spencer. He's rarely here, though."

"That one?" Alec asked nodding toward the office on the opposite side of the corridor.

"That one belongs to Walker."

Alec made the connection. "Walker Madison, the race car driver?"

"Yes, that's right."

They continued on, turned the corner, and then Alec stopped again in front of another suite.

"That one's Aiden's office. He's the oldest brother. There's four in all. Three boys and one girl."

The hall was as luxurious as the lobby. There were fresh flowers in beautiful vases on each table along the corridor. The carpet was a deep red, the walls a white damask.

"Tell me about your boss."

"What do you want to know?"

"What's she like to work for?"

"Oh, she's great."

"How did you get this job?"

"A teacher in my high school had me fill out some forms for an intern program here at the hotel, working with computers. I thought it was a joke because I didn't know much of anything about computers back then, didn't even know how to do e-mail. We had computers in my high school, but they didn't work half the time. Anyway, Miss Madison chose me and had me working day and night all summer long. I even slept at the hotel while I trained, until she found me a family that had an extra bedroom and didn't mind having an extra kid around. I've worked here ever since."

It sounded to Alec as though the teacher and Regan Madison had worked together to save the kid's ass.

"Are you still living with that family?"

"Yes, sir, I am."

There was a set of double glass doors directly ahead. "That's my office," Henry said, pride radiating in his voice. "Miss Madison's office is behind mine."

"So anyone wanting to see her has to go through you."

"That's right. Except when I'm in class. Then she fends for herself. We do okay."

"What is it you do for her?"

"Oh, just about everything."

"Okay. And what is it she does?"

Henry flashed a smile. "She gives money away." Then he laughed, a deep belly laugh. "I love saying that."

"Yeah?"

"And it's true. She really does give money away. Miss Madison runs the family's charitable foundation."

Alec opened the door and motioned for Henry to go first. The kid rushed ahead to stand behind his desk. "This is my work area, my domain," he said proudly. "It's kind of a mess now. I was reorganizing."

There were papers strewn all over the top of the desk. Henry pushed one stack aside and picked up a clipping from the newspaper.

"Here's a photo of the Madisons," he said. "I cut this out of the newspaper a while back, and I was going to frame it."

He continued to hold onto the clipping as he said, "It was taken at a dedication of Conrad Park. You know where that is?" He didn't wait for a response but continued. "The Madisons donated all the land and paid for a new jogging trail. Well, actually, it was an old trail that they repaved and expanded," he said. "They also paid for a beautiful playground with all sorts of equipment for the little kids to climb on. Like it says in the article, Miss Madison used to go running there all the time, rain or shine, but now that the hotel has a track upstairs, she doesn't have to leave the building." He nodded toward the article and photo and said, "It was a nice profile of the brothers. I'm saving it because it's kind of rare for all of them to be together."

Alec barely glanced at the article. The fact that the Madisons were do-gooders wasn't relevant now.

There was another set of French doors about fifteen feet behind Henry's desk. Alec could see a young woman through the glass. She was on the phone, her back to the door. She ended the call and turned around, then hurriedly walked toward him.

Son of a gun, he thought. He recognized those long, gorgeous legs. She opened the door and stood there, the worry evident in her amazing eyes, her face flushed. Oh, yes. Same beautiful woman, all right.

Henry made the introductions as Regan walked forward and offered her hand. Her handshake was firm, no-nonsense, her smile disarming. He smiled back. Might as well start out charming, he decided. If she was a nutcase, which, after meeting Henry, he sincerely doubted, then being charming might make the difference in her continued cooperation. Noah Clayborne, a family friend also involved in law enforcement, once said that you could catch more crazies with sugar than vinegar. Of course, Noah, a true bull in a china store, had never bothered to test that theory. Like Alec, he much preferred clobbering male suspects who gave him trouble to chatting it up with them.

Apparently Regan didn't remember him. Alec thought about it and decided not to mention the fact that he'd nearly run her down on the street last week. If she had remembered the incident, she surely would have said something. He obviously wasn't memorable; she definitely was.

"You probably don't recall, Detective, but we ran into each other last week just outside the police station."

What do you know? She did remember.

"You know him?" Henry asked Regan.

"Sort of," she answered. "We did run into each other, and if he hadn't caught me, I would have been splattered on the sidewalk."

Alec grinned. "I remember trying to roll over you. You laughed. I remember that too."

"Yes," she said. "You reminded me of . . ."

"Yes?"

She blushed slightly. "The zoo. You reminded me of the zoo."

"The zoo?"

"You smell much better today."

He laughed. "I hope so."

Henry had a speculative glint in his eyes as he watched his boss. Regan turned to him and asked, "Did you explain to Detective Buchanan . . ."

"I thought I'd let you explain. I wasn't sure what to say."

Alec's stare was locked on Regan. "Why don't you tell me what's going on?"

Before she could answer, Henry blurted out, "We don't know anything about that detective. Isn't that right, Miss Madison?"

"What's with the 'Miss Madison'?" she asked.

Henry looked embarrassed. "I didn't think I should call you Regan in front of the police."

"How about you sit at your desk while I talk to your employer?" Alec said.

"But I was hoping . . ."

"Yes?" Alec asked impatiently.

"I was hoping I could stay until you look at the photo and tell us if it's real or computer-generated. I think it's phony, but Regan thinks it might be real."

Alec didn't know what the kid was rambling on about. "Go sit," he repeated. "Now, Miss Madison —"

"Please, call me Regan."

"Yeah, okay. Regan, how about you start explaining?"

"I was checking my e-mails," she said as she walked back to her computer. The screen was dark until she moved the mouse on the pad. "And this came up."

She quickly moved aside so she wouldn't block his view. Alec inwardly winced. The photo wasn't a pretty sight. Regan leaned against the credenza, her back to the computer so she wouldn't have to look at the screen again.

"I wasn't sure how to proceed," she said. "I was afraid to save it or forward it because I was concerned that whoever sent it might have built in some kind of virus that would destroy it, so I just left it alone."

"Good decision."

"What do you think, Detective? Is it real or fake?"

"Real," he said. "Definitely real." There wasn't any hesitation or doubt in his voice.

"You don't seem very surprised or . . . shocked."

"I've worked with the violent crime unit. I've seen a dead body before," he said as he moved closer to the monitor to inspect the picture.

"Yes, of course you have, but . . ." She pointed to the screen. His casual attitude had rattled her, and she was trying to recover. "But he was also a detective, one of your own, a . . ." Her voice trailed off.

"Yes, he was."

From what Alec had heard about Sweeney, he was also a nasty son of a bitch who walked around most days in an alcoholic daze. Everyone knew he was on the take and that it was only a matter of time before he got caught.

"Did you know him well?" she asked.

"No."

She hoped that explained why he seemed so casual about Detective Sweeney's demise. If not, then Detective Buchanan had about as much compassion as a fish. She suddenly felt nervous standing so close to him. She was trapped between the desk and the credenza, and unless she wanted to hike up her skirt and vault over the top, she was going to have to wait until he moved. He did smell a lot better today. In fact he smelled great, like the clean outdoors.

He stepped back from the computer, "Why do you think it was sent to you?"

"I don't know," she said wearily. She rubbed her arms as she thought about it. "If you scroll back up, it shows it came from Henry's computer, but of course it didn't. Someone has both our e-mail addresses. I've been racking my brain trying to make sense out of this. So far, no luck. What is the procedure now?"

"We need a tech," he said. He pulled out his cell phone and made the call, walking away from her as he spoke softly into the phone. When he was finished, he motioned for her to join him across the room. Two easy chairs faced a sofa in front of the windows overlooking Michigan Avenue. Regan often curled up on the sofa to do paperwork.

"While we're waiting for the tech, you could tell me about your relationship with Detective Sweeney."

"That will take all of five seconds. I didn't have a relationship with him."

The mere thought was appalling. Though it was wrong to speak ill of the dead, Sweeney was one of the most obnoxious men she'd ever met. Still, no matter how repulsive, no one should have to die in such a way.

"Okay," he said. He leaned against the window ledge, folded his arms across his chest, and asked, "So tell me how you know him."

His eyes weren't missing a thing. The way he was watching her made her even more nervous, but she was determined not to let him know it. She hadn't done anything wrong, and he wasn't going to make her feel as though she had.

She went to the sofa and sat down. "I don't actually know the man. I only met him once, when I went to the police station . . . the day I bumped into you."

She tried to get comfortable so she would look calm. One of the pillows was poking her in her back. She leaned forward, pulled the pillow out, and dropped it on the cushion beside her. "I went to the station as a favor for a friend to find out how Detective Sweeney was progressing on an investigation he was supposed to be handling."

He homed in on the key word. "*Supposed* to be handling?"

"I wasn't certain if he was looking into the matter or not," she said. "But I got the distinct impression he didn't much care about the case or anything else, for that matter."

"Tell me about the investigation," he said.

Straightening her skirt, she crossed one leg over the other and leaned back against the cushions.

"Have you ever heard of Dr. Lawrence Shields?"

"No," he answered. "What kind of doctor is he?"

"A quack," she blurted. "At least I think he is." She shook her head and then said, "He runs those self-help, turn-your-life-around seminars twice a year in Chicago. You've never seen his commercials?"

He shook his head. "What about him?"

She explained in great detail who Shields was and what he had done to Mary Coolidge. She told him Mary's daughter had gone to the police and filed a complaint against Shields and that Detective Sweeney had been given the file. "Mary's daughter didn't get anywhere with the detective. She went back home, but my friend Sophie read copies of Mary's diary and decided to get involved. Sophie sent another friend, Cordie, to talk to Sweeney about the investigation, and she couldn't get any answers either."

"And then it was your turn to talk to Sweeney?"

"Yes. Wait a minute . . . don't you see, that has to be it." She was suddenly too excited to sit still. She stood and began to pace while she worked the hypothesis out in her mind. "It all makes sense," she said. "There's your connection."

"Want to tell me about it?"

"Shields and Sweeney. Maybe Shields found out that my friends and I were investigating him. What if he knew that we were pressuring Detective Sweeney to do his job. Maybe Shields decided to have Sweeney killed to warn us off, and he sent me that photo to scare me."

She stopped pacing and stood in front of Alec, her hands on her hips as she eagerly waited to know what he thought of her supposition. He didn't respond quickly enough.

"What do you think? It is possible, isn't it? Shields manipulated Mary into handing over more than two million dollars. Maybe Shields thought that was worth killing for. And Mary's daughter believes that Shields drove Mary to suicide, or maybe he had her killed, because she threatened to go to the police. And if he killed once, why would he hesitate to kill again? Maybe Shields thought my friends and I were getting too close." She put her hands out, palms up. "Maybe that's our connection."

He didn't say anything.

"Doesn't that make sense?"

He couldn't resist. "Maybe."

She didn't realize he was teasing her. She looked inordinately pleased with herself. "Okay, then," she said. "Good," she added with a firm nod. "Now what?"

He pulled a ragged little notepad out of his suit pocket. "Now we start over."

"Oh, my God, Cordie and Sophie . . . could I make a phone call first?" she asked. "My friends are in the Caymans with Shields. I've got to warn them." She hurried to her desk.

"Before you leap to conclusions, let's get a few facts," he cautioned.

She was already dialing Cordie's cell phone. She was routed to voice mail, which told her that Cordie was either using the phone or had it turned off.

"Cordie, call me as soon as you get this," she said. "It's urgent, and you and Sophie stay away from Shields. Call, no matter what time it is."

She hung up the phone and walked back to Detective Buchanan. He didn't ask her what her phone call was about, and she didn't offer to explain.

"You said we needed to start over?"

"That's right." He motioned for her to sit down. "Let's start with Mary Coolidge."

Then the questions began, one after another and another. She was beginning to tell him about the reception for Shields that she and her friends had attended when a man and a woman walked into the office with Henry. The woman carried what looked like a tool kit.

Alec grinned when he saw who the tech was. Melissa What-A-Bitch Hill. And that was only one of the many colorful names bestowed upon her by various detectives. Hill was a short, angry woman with a buzz cut and premature wrinkles, no doubt caused by her perpetual frown. She was nearly impossible to work with, but also one of the best computer nerds in the business.

The detective following in her wake was Matt Connelly. He was glaring at Hill's back, which probably meant he'd had to ride over to the hotel with her. He nodded to Alec in greeting. His gaze moved to Regan and stayed there. "So what's going on?"

"See for yourself," Alec answered. "Look at the computer screen. Hey, Melissa," he added.

Her grunt was her response. She wasn't one for chitchat or pleasantries. "Is that the piece of crap computer you want me to take apart?"

Connelly answered her. "It's the only piece of crap computer in the office. What do you think?"

"Up yours, Connelly," she replied.

Alec quickly made the introductions. Connelly nodded in response, but Hill ignored Regan.

They both went to the computer and looked at the screen. Hill didn't show any reaction, but Connelly visibly blanched. "Jeez. Sweeney naked. Man, that's harsh. I'm gonna have nightmares."

Regan joined them. "Did you say you were going to take my computer apart? Is that necessary?" she asked.

The woman plopped down in Regan's chair. A second later her fingers were flying over the keyboard. "If I think it's necessary, I'll tear it apart. Now go sit somewhere and let me do my job."

Regan was shocked by the woman's rudeness. She wanted to grab her computer and protect it from her. "My files are all in there and my —" she began.

Alec moved in front of her to block her. "It's okay," he assured her. "Melissa won't destroy your computer. She realizes she doesn't have the right to touch it without your permission, and she certainly understands the legal ramifications if she were to deliberately break anything. Isn't that right, Melissa?"

"Up . . ." She was about to use her standard reply when she glanced up and saw the look in Buchanan's eyes. She'd heard he'd been a hard-ass while working vice, and she figured he hadn't lost that mean edge yet. "Yeah, all right," she muttered in a voice that resembled a pit bull's growl. "Now, if you'll leave me alone, I'll try to get past these walls."

"Let's give her some breathing room," Alec suggested.

Regan ignored him and thrust her hand out to the tech. She introduced herself once again. Melissa didn't want to be bothered, but the hand was hard to ignore, since it was just inches from her face. She finally stopped typing and shook Regan's hand.

"We were already introduced," she muttered.

Melissa was a nervous woman. Her fingernails were bitten down to the quick. She gripped Regan's hand tightly and then impatiently jerked her hand back.

"Now can I get on with my job?"

Regan pretended she hadn't heard the question. "What did you mean when you said you had to get past the 'walls'?"

Melissa looked resigned. "Whoever sent you the e-mail of Sweeney was a clever one, all right. He knows his way around computers. He's set up barriers so no one can track it. But don't worry. There isn't a barrier I can't get around."

"Even with a piece of junk computer like mine?" Regan asked, smiling.

Melissa chuckled. "Actually, I called it a piece of crap computer, but I was exaggerating. It's a little outdated. You ought to upgrade."

Alec was impressed. He'd never seen Melissa smile before, and to listen to her chat it up with Regan was astonishing. With very little effort, Regan had cut through all of Hill's barriers. Definitely impressive.

The photo of Sweeney appeared on the screen again. Melissa pointed to it and said, "That's just how they found him."

"I'm sorry?" Regan replied.

"I heard that's how they found him, in his basement, hanging like that. Someone called it in, said Sweeney would be there, and he sure was. Pretty awful crime scene, I was told. Sweeney had a lot of enemies," she thought to add. "There was a rumor he was blackmailing some dealers. Do you know why the photo was sent to you?"

"No, I don't," Regan answered. "It's grotesque."

"I've seen worse," Melissa boasted.

"Like your old boyfriend?" Connelly asked.

"Up yours."

Regan backed away from the desk and turned toward the windows so she wouldn't have to look at the photo again. "Did anyone else get this?" she asked. "Or was I the only one —"

Melissa interrupted in a near shout. "I'm in."

"In where?" Connelly asked. He was squatting down and peering at the blank screen when his cell phone rang. He impatiently answered it as he walked into the outer office.

"The photo was sent from a cell phone," Melissa said. She rattled off the number as Alec pulled out his notepad again.

Color flooded Regan's face. "Oh, my," she whispered.

Alec heard her. "What? Oh, my, what?"

"The phone number . . . it's mine."

Chapter Eighteen

Her theory was springing leaks. If Shields was indeed behind the murder of Sweeney, how did he get hold of her phone? Maybe her theory wasn't right, after all. She was thinking about that while Detective Buchanan patiently waited for her to tell him how the photo of Sweeney had been taken with her cell phone. She wanted the answer to that question too.

"It is your phone number."

"Yes," she said. "But I certainly didn't take that picture."

Detective Connelly interrupted. "Plea bargain fell apart," he called out as he shoved his cell phone into his pocket and headed for the door. "I've got ten minutes to get to the courthouse. You want me to get someone over here to help you?"

"No, I'm good," Alec answered.

"The lieutenant wants to see you in his office as soon as you finish up here," he added.

That news put Alec in a foul mood. The second the door closed behind Connelly, he gave Regan his full attention. "Okay, tell me about your phone."

She assumed he wanted to know the model or the style. She didn't remember either of those things, and so she told him about the capabilities. "It has a built-in camera," she began. "And an extensive phone book with personal and business e-mail addresses. It's Internet friendly," she added with a brief smile.

"And you don't remember where you lost it?"

She shook her head. "I thought I had left it in the car, but Henry looked, and it wasn't there. I don't know what happened to it."

Henry heard what she said and rushed over to join the conversation. "That's right. You can check with the guys in the garage. They all saw me, and I told them what I was looking for. They weren't surprised. I mean, no offense, Regan, but you're always leaving your phone somewhere. It's small," he told Alec. "And it sometimes falls out of her purse. One time I found it wedged between the seat and the console. I couldn't find it today, though. I searched everywhere inside that car, and it wasn't there."

He took a protective step closer to Regan and said, "She isn't in trouble, is she, just because someone else used her phone? You aren't going to blame her, are you?"

The kid's loyalty to his boss was admirable, but at the moment he was also a nuisance. "Last time I checked, losing a cell phone wasn't a criminal offense. Don't you have some work to do at your desk?" Alec asked.

Regan waited until Henry was out of earshot and then whispered, "He's a worrier. He used to be much worse when he first started here. He's getting better, but he still worries too much."

Melissa's loud grunt turned their attention. The woman was certainly in her element. Her fingers continued to whiz across the keyboard in a blur, and every minute or two she would let out a sigh or another crude grunt.

"Should I call and cancel the phone or report it stolen?" Henry asked from the doorway.

"No, don't do that," Alec said. "If we're lucky, maybe he'll try to contact her again."

"He's not going to use her phone again," Melissa said. "He knows his way around computers, and he surely knows her phone can be tracked. The e-mail was sent five days ago, and he hasn't sent anything else."

Her fingers suddenly stilled on the keys. "Okay, I've sent everything on to my computer, and I'm also printing out the picture of Sweeney to take with me. Until further notice, any e-mails she receives will automatically come to me too. That's okay, isn't it? I'm going to assume that's okay."

Regan wasn't paying much attention. She was standing in front of the window looking down at the traffic on Michigan Avenue, her mind racing as she tried to remember the last time she used her cell phone. She knew Detective Buchanan would check with Sprint for the log of calls coming in and going out, but if she could remember now, it would save him valuable time. Since her surgery, however, the days all blended together, and she hadn't kept track of her appointments in her PDA the way she usually did. The godawful photo of Sweeney was also disrupting concentration. She hadn't realized a face could become so bloated, so grotesque. That image kept popping into her mind.

She didn't hear Henry come up behind her. She jumped when he touched her shoulder.

"Sorry," he whispered. "I didn't mean to startle you." He glanced over at Detective Buchanan to make sure he was still busy talking with the technician and then said, "I just wanted you to know I checked my computer again."

"What were you checking?"

"I wanted to see if the photo of that dead man was sent to me," he whispered. "But it wasn't. I wish it had been. I wish it had been sent to all the e-mail addresses you had programmed into your phone. It's not good that it was sent just to you."

She nodded. "I know."

"It was clever, the way he sent it," he said, "making it look like it came from my computer."

"I never would have opened the attachment if I hadn't recognized the sender. I guess he didn't want to take the chance that I'd delete it."

"I think he's targeted you for some reason," Henry said. "But why?"

Alec heard the comment. "That's what we're going to find out."

Alec was digging through his pocket looking for a card to give Regan when his cell phone rang. It was the third call in the past fifteen minutes from the office. Lewis's assistant kept calling to demand that he get back to the station as soon as possible. The lieutenant was waiting to talk to him. Alec knew why. Lewis had obviously just found out that Alec had gone over his head to the commander to save the job of the young cop who had interrupted the sting operation.

"Aren't you going to answer that?" Regan asked.

"I guess I should." He flipped the phone open, listened for a minute, and then said, "I'll get there when I'm finished here."

Before the assistant could argue with him, he disconnected the call and turned back to Regan. He found one of his cards and handed it to her. She gave him a grateful smile. Gorgeous woman, he thought. And damn, was she sexy. Another time, another place, and he definitely would have asked her out, but he couldn't now. Not with an investigation pending. Besides, even if he didn't get the job with the FBI, he was still going to give notice and leave Chicago within the next month or two, so getting involved with any woman was out of the question. Unless the woman was into casual sex. Regan Madison wasn't. He knew that much about her just by being with her for a half hour.

He mentally shook himself. He had no business thinking such thoughts now. Funny how the mind worked. Guess his brother Dylan was right. He was perverted.

"Detective Wincott is running the investigation into Sweeney's murder," he said. "I'm helping him out, but he's senior man, and he'll be over to talk to you soon. You'll want to stay in the hotel."

"Yes, of course."

"But in the meantime, if you think of anything else," he said with a nod toward the card she held in her hand, "there's my number."

"I have physical therapy for my knee in an hour, but I can cancel."

"I thought that scar looked new. It wasn't there when I ran into you on the street. What happened?"

She was surprised he'd noticed. The incision wasn't large, but the scar was raw, the skin puckered.

She said what she was thinking. "You noticed it wasn't there the first time we met? That's impressive, Detective."

Not really, he thought. He'd have to be a eunuch not to notice those sexy legs of hers.

"Baseball," she continued. "I twisted it sliding into third base. It happened last summer."

"Baseball, huh?" He smiled. He was having trouble picturing her in a uniform with a ball and bat. She seemed too soft for that sport.

"Yes, baseball," she said. "It was a charity game. Why is that funny?"

He didn't answer. "You wrenched it last year, and you only just now had the surgery?"

"I was procrastinating, but then I hurt it again . . ." She suddenly stopped and then blurted, "What an idiot."

"Excuse me?"

"No, not you," she said. "Me. I'm the idiot." In her hurry to explain, her words tripped over one another. "I know who has my phone. At least, I think I know, and I can't believe it took me so long to remember. You see, I dropped my purse, and that's when I lost it. I'm sorry. I'm not usually so rattled. There was this man. He chased me to my car, and he —"

That statement gained his full attention. He put his hand up. "Whoa," he said. "Slow down and start at the beginning."

"Yes, okay," she said. "It was a week ago Friday night. That's the last time I used my cell phone. I'm sure of it."

He pulled out his ragged notepad again and began to search his pockets for his pen. "And where were you?"

"At the reception."

"You sound like I'm supposed to know about a reception."

"Oh, I'm so sorry. I thought I had told you about that when I was explaining the connection between Sweeney and Shields."

He didn't look happy with her. "Why don't you tell me about it now?"

She couldn't believe she'd forgotten about the man in the parking lot, but then, in her defense, she had been bombarded first by the e-mail and then Detective Buchanan, the technician, and Detective Connelly. And all in the past hour.

She explained as quickly as possible all about the reception she and her friends had attended at Liam House. "Sophie had signed us up for Shields's weekend seminar, and I know I told you that Shields runs two seminars a year in Chicago."

"What were you hoping to accomplish?"

"It was apparent to all of us that Detective Sweeney wasn't going to do anything about Shields, and so we decided . . ."

"Yes?"

She shrugged. "To do his job for him."

His frown indicated he didn't like hearing that. "And how were you going to do his job?"

"We decided we would investigate Shields and hopefully we would get enough evidence to give to the prosecutor. Sophie was doing the investigative work, and

Cordie and I went along to be supportive. Actually, we were going to try to find a way to break into his computer so we could get the names of the other women who'd attended past seminars. We thought we could match his deposits with —"

He stopped writing. "You do know that isn't legal, right?"

"Of course, I know that," she said. "We didn't break into his computer. We just wanted to. That was the plan anyway."

The woman was honest to a fault. "It sounds like a half-baked plan."

She agreed. "Yes, well, Sophie did come up with it, and she does tend to rush in without thinking things through. She believes things will work out, and the fact is, they usually do."

Regan folded her arms and began to pace in front of the windows while she thought about that awful night. "I remember I had my cell phone with me. We were late," she said. "But then whenever Cordie and I go anywhere with Sophie, we're always late. Anyway, the reception was in full swing by the time we arrived, and Shields was there speaking to the group. He's such a fraud and very full of himself. I wasn't impressed, but judging from the reactions of the people around me, they were dazzled by him. There was this exercise he had us do that was absolutely insane."

"What about your cell phone?" he said, trying to keep her on track.

"I should have remembered to turn it off, because it rang right in the middle of Shields's talk. I hurried out to the hallway to answer it before one of his bodyguards tried to take it away from me."

"Bodyguards?"

"Two of them. He calls them his assistants, but they're his bodyguards. Real musclemen."

"Okay," he said. "So you think you left your phone in the conference center?"

"No," she said. "I'm sure I put it back in my purse. I think it dropped out when I fell."

Alec was trying to remain patient. "And when did that happen?"

"When I went to get the car," she said. "It was raining, and so I told Cordie to find Sophie and wait by the front door and I would drive up to get them. I was running along the path to my car, and I thought I heard someone calling my name. The wind was up, though, and it was raining hard, so I wasn't sure. I turned to look behind me, and there was this man . . ." It all seemed such a long time ago. "Everything happened so fast. When I turned, I wrenched my knee."

"And you're just now mentioning this?" He was irritated and making sure she knew it.

"I just didn't think . . . I didn't connect. I was lucky I got away from him."

"He chased you?"

"Yes. You don't think . . ."

"Think what?" he asked when she hesitated.

"Maybe Shields hired him. Maybe he was waiting outside the conference center because he knew I was inside, and maybe he was there to scare me, which he certainly did."

"You're really hooked on your idea that Shields is behind it all, aren't you?"

"It makes sense, doesn't it?"

"I'm not going to guess yet because I don't have enough information to form an opinion, but when I do, I'll let you know. Now, I want to know exactly what happened from the minute you stepped outside Liam House."

"I just did tell you everything that happened."

"Tell me again."

She went through it again just as he'd instructed. "When I fell, everything spilled out of my purse, but at the time, I thought I'd shoved it all back in. I must have left the phone on the ground. I was desperate to get into my car and lock the doors," she said. "He was holding up something and yelling at me to stop, but I didn't. There was something all wrong about him."

"Like what?"

"His face," she said. She rubbed her arms to ward off a sudden chill. "It gives me the shivers to think about it. I called the police," she added. "And I went to the police station nearby to make a report."

"That was good. Now tell me. What about his face?"

"Rage," she said. "I've never seen rage like that in anyone's eyes. And then the oddest thing happened."

"Yes?"

"It might be my imagination. I was in pain because of my knee and soaked from the rain, but when I was inside the car, I looked, and he was standing under the streetlight, still staring at me. I was crying," she admitted. "And I think he could see me crying. His expression changed."

He cocked his head. "Changed to what?"

"Sympathy," she said. "I think he felt sorry for me."

Chapter Nineteen

The timing couldn't have been better. Alec was on his way back to the station for round two with Lieutenant Lewis when the call came in on his cell phone. Ward Dayborough, the FBI agent who had been relentlessly recruiting him, was on the line welcoming him into the Bureau.

Ward was all but gloating. "I knew I'd get you," he boasted. "Tenacity," he said then, drawing the word out in his deep southern accent. "I have a butt-load of tenacity. How many years did it take me to get you interested?"

The question obviously didn't require an answer because Ward, still high on his conquest, continued on. "Training's going to be tough, but I'm not worried about you. You'll do just fine. Your scores on that test were phenomenal. You've got seventeen weeks ahead of you at the academy," he added. "No matter how much law enforcement experience you've had, you've still got to do the full seventeen weeks."

"Are you trying to get me to change my mind?"

"No, no, of course not."

"When do you want me to start?"

"New sessions start every two weeks, but I went ahead and slotted you to start two months from now. That's eight weeks from today. I figured you would need time to pack up everything and tie up loose ends there in Chicago and get a little time off."

"Yes, that's good," Alec said. "Eight weeks will give me time to get organized."

Like that's ever gonna happen, he thought to himself as he hung up. Though he was extremely organized in his professional life, he was extremely disorganized at home. He was considered the slob of the family. When he was a boy, his room always looked like a cyclone had hit. He'd gotten better about all that, though. He'd hired a cleaning crew to blitz his apartment every other week. One of the women even did his grocery shopping and made sure his refrigerator was stocked with all his favorite foods. She was an expensive luxury, but one he'd hate to do without.

She couldn't go with him to the academy, however, and for those seventeen weeks, he was going to have to shape up. That seemed tougher to him than any obstacle course.

Alec felt good about his decision. He

knew he was going to miss Chicago, and he had absolutely no guarantee that when he graduated from the academy, he'd be assigned to the Boston office. Ward had told him it was as good as guaranteed, but Alec wasn't banking on it.

He decided to stop by Human Resources and give his notice before seeing Lewis. The woman behind the desk was a real sweetheart who had been with the department for close to twenty years. She wore such thick bifocals her eyes looked milky and twice their size.

She smiled and shook her head the minute she spotted him. "Oh, no."

"Oh, no, what?"

"You can't put in for a transfer. I mean, you could, but it's not going to go anywhere. Lewis has made it abundantly clear that he needs you in his department." Her voice softened as she added, "Which means he wants you under his thumb. I'm sorry, Alec. I think just about everyone knows what a worm he is, but he's got seniority and his wife has connections, if you get my drift. We're not going to be able to get rid of him unless he really screws up."

"I understand. You *are* going to get rid of me, though. I'm giving my notice today. What papers do I need to fill out?"

She became teary-eyed. "I hate to see you go. You're one of the good ones." She pulled a tissue out of the box she kept on her desk and dabbed her eyes. "It's like the old song Billy Joel sings. You know, only the good die young."

He rolled his eyes. "Hell with that. I'm not planning to die young."

"But you're leaving." She sniffed as she opened a file drawer and pulled out the necessary papers.

Resigning turned out to be more complicated than Alec had anticipated. There were all sorts of forms to fill out and a long conference with the commander, who was determined to talk him into staying. What Alec had naively estimated would only take a couple of minutes dragged on for over an hour.

By the time he got back to the office, Lewis had worked himself into a fury. He was on the phone, but the second he spotted Alec making his way across the room, he jumped up and angrily motioned for him to come in.

Alec was halfway there when his cell phone rang. He knew it couldn't be Lewis's assistant calling him yet again because he'd just passed the man on the steps.

Gil was calling. The second he heard Alec's voice he exclaimed, "Say it isn't so."

Alec was impressed. "How did you find out so soon?"

"You know me. I've got my sources. It's true then? You're really leaving the department?"

"Yes," he said. "I'm about to go in and tell Lewis. I'll call you later."

He ended the call and walked into Lewis's office. The lieutenant had a white-knuckle grip on the receiver. Alec shoved his hands in his pants pockets and patiently waited until he ended the conversation.

"Yes, sir," Lewis said, his voice a tight whisper.

The call finally ended. As Lewis slammed the phone down, Alec casually asked, "You wanted to see me?"

"You know damn well I want to see you," Lewis shouted. "I've been waiting for over an hour. My reasons have changed, however."

He stood there glaring at Alec for what seemed like a full minute. Alec wasn't fazed. He simply stared back.

"You resigned."

"Yes."

The vein running down Lewis's forehead began to pulsate.

"And you didn't think you owed it to me to give me your notice first? I had to find out about it over the phone from *my* superior?"

By the time he finished his question he was bellowing. The vein in his forehead was going wild. Alec couldn't stop staring at it. If Lewis had a heart attack and suddenly stopped breathing, would Alec give him CPR? Hmm . . . definitely a tight call, Alec thought.

He continued to contemplate the philosophical dilemma while Lewis ranted and raved.

"Do you know what that made me look like? Emmett is furious with me," he said, referring to the area commander.

Alec shrugged. "I don't know what to tell you," he drawled. He'd be damned before he'd apologize for making the jerk look bad.

Three more weeks with Lewis calling the shots suddenly seemed like an eternity, and Alec wondered if he could make it. He could barely stomach looking at the man. Lewis looked and acted like a freak. Vain to a fault, he always had a deep tan, no doubt from the tanning bed it was rumored he slept in at night. His exceedingly bright white capped teeth made his scowl all the more garish.

"I gave three weeks' notice," Alec said. "But if you'd like me to leave now, that'd be fine with me."

"You've put me in a hell of a spot."

"How's that?"

"Emmett told me I had to talk you into staying. He seems to think you're an asset. Needless to say, I don't share that opinion."

Alec shook his head. "My mind's made up."

Lewis slapped his palms down on his desk and leaned forward. "You know what your problem is, Buchanan? You're not a team player."

If the goal of the team was to make Lewis look good, then no, Alec decided, he wasn't a team player.

"Do you want me to stay for three more weeks, or do you want me to leave now? It doesn't matter to me."

"You stay," Lewis snapped. He sat down heavily behind his desk and began to push folders around, obviously trying to give the impression he was a busy man. He opened one and closed it. Reaching for another, he said, "You can clean out your files. Give whatever you've got pending to me, and I'll distribute them to my loyal detectives."

Alec wanted to ask who those men might be, but he didn't think it was a good idea to antagonize Lewis, who could and would make his life miserable.

Without looking up, the lieutenant said, "For the next three weeks, you sit at your desk. You can do the phone work for Wincott."

"Phone work for Wincott? What exactly does that mean?"

"It means you can answer the damn phone, and if Wincott needs any help, you'll help," he said. "From your desk."

The urge to punch him was getting stronger. Alec was leaving when Lewis asked, "Do you have another job lined up?"

"Yes."

"In Chicago?"

"No."

He didn't offer any more information, and Lewis didn't press. Alec went to his desk and began to sort through his files. John Wincott came rushing across the room. He and Alec went way back. They had gone through the police academy together and had become good friends, but they hadn't worked together until recently. Wincott used to be able to drink him under the table. Alec thought maybe he still could.

"Man, do you look bad."

Alec wasn't exaggerating. Wincott looked as if he hadn't had any sleep in a decade. There were fat bags under his eyes and deep creases running down the length of his cheeks. He was only a couple of years older than Alec, but at the moment he looked ancient.

Wincott ignored the comment about his appearance.

"Did you get my message about the e-mail Regan Madison received?" Alec asked.

"Yes," Wincott answered. "And I'll be happy to talk about it in a minute. First, I want to ask you something. Is it true? You're leaving the department?"

Alec nodded. "Yes." His chair squeaked when he leaned back. "I was going to call you and tell you, but I guess Gil beat me to it."

Wincott sat on the edge of Alec's desk. He glanced beyond Alec's shoulder to the lieutenant's office. "I can't blame you. I'd get out if I could."

"I was ready for a change." That response was becoming the pat answer. Alec decided he'd stick with it and wondered how many times he'd say it in the next twenty-one days.

"A change, huh? A change where?"

"I'm hoping Boston. I'm kind of home-sick."

Wincott lowered his voice and leaned toward Alec. "There's a nasty rumor going around that you're heading to the FBI."

Alec smiled but didn't confirm or deny it.

Wincott went on, "You have to come over for dinner before you leave Chicago. It's gonna upset Suzie when she hears. My wife's had the hots for you for years."

"Is she still screaming my name when you're having sex?"

Wincott laughed. "How the hell would I know? I can't remember the last time I had any. There's always at least one kid in bed between us, and now with the baby getting up every couple of hours, the only thing I want to have is sleep."

"Spoken like a true married man," Alec said.

Wincott grimaced. "Back to Sweeney," he said. "We're discovering that a lot of people wanted him dead, so I won't be running out of suspects. We've been going through his stuff. No one can find his wallet. Hey, guess what? Sweeney kept a diary."

Alec raised an eyebrow. "That's a girly

thing to do. I didn't think Sweeney was the dear-diary type."

Wincott laughed. When he smiled, he looked ten years younger. "It wasn't that kind of a diary," he said. "The idiot kept notes on all the people he was going to blackmail. I'm not speculating about that. He wrote it all down. Guess who was in the notebook with the drug dealers and the pimps?"

"Who?"

Wincott leaned in again. "Lewis."

Alec perked up. "No kidding."

"That's right. Sweeney was going to take pictures and send them to his wife."

"What kind of pictures?"

"Lewis with his mistress."

Alec shook his head. "Now, that's shocking."

"I don't think it's so shocking," Wincott argued. "I don't know anyone who wouldn't like to see Lewis take a fall."

"I think it's shocking that he could get two women to have sex with him."

"One woman's built like an ironing board but has some money, which is why he married her, and the other one doesn't have any money but from what I hear, she's loaded in other areas, if you know what I mean."

"Who else was in there?"

Wincott told him about some of the other deviants Sweeney was already blackmailing. "He even had a ledger of the cash he was going to be taking in and the amounts he was going to charge, kind of like a bank account. Who would write all that down?"

"He must have thought he'd never get caught."

"Like I said, we've got a lot of suspects, but we're narrowing it down. It looks like one of three drug dealers didn't want to pay Sweeney's bills. Maybe he was already shaking them down."

"What about Regan Madison? How does she figure in this?"

"Don't know," Wincott said. "I haven't had a chance to talk to her yet. I had to go back to the crime scene and I got stuck there. We did find her cell phone."

Alec straightened. "Yeah? Where'd you find it?"

"In the bushes behind the dump Sweeney called home. We're running what's left of it for prints, but I don't figure we'll find any. The basement was wiped clean. Only prints around were Sweeney's. The killer had to know what he was doing, and he was strong, real strong. Had to be," he added, "to lift Sweeney's body up like that with the rope. Oh, and by the way, we got the autopsy report. He was dead before he was stripped and hung."

"How was he killed?"

"Asphyxiation," he said. "So now I've got to wonder why the killer went to all that trouble to strip him and hang him. Bradshaw thinks it was for drama," he said, referring to his partner.

"What do you think?"

"I think he was showing off for his fantasy girlfriend . . . you know, trying to impress her."

"The girlfriend being Regan Madison?"

Wincott raised his eyebrows. "I hear she's a real looker."

Alec didn't comment. Wincott didn't seem to notice.

"You know how those sickos are. Bradshaw thinks maybe he saw her someplace and got fixated on her. He's going to talk to Matlin about it," he added, referring to the psychiatrist on staff.

"Good idea," Alec said. He then filled Wincott in on his interview with Regan and told him about the man who had chased her to her car. He also mentioned her theory about Sweeney and Dr. Shields. "She's sure she lost her phone when she fell."

Wincott was trying to work it out in his mind. "Okay, so he found the phone, saw it had a camera built in, and decided to have a little fun with it. Her e-mail address was there. All he had to do was take the picture and then push a button."

"Still doesn't explain the connection to Sweeney."

Wincott agreed. "And I don't see a drug dealer having that kind of fun. I can see one of them killing Sweeney, but . . ." He stopped, shrugged, and then said, "Not making any sense yet."

"What did you mean when you said you were running prints on what was left of the phone?"

"He'd smashed the phone to pieces while he was still in the basement. Crime team found a couple of tiny pieces on the workbench."

"And of course no prints on the hammer."

"Nope," he confirmed. "Not a one. Listen, I appreciate you working this with us. There's going to be a lot of legwork. Since that e-mail was sent to Regan Madison, we're going to have to check out anyone who's connected to her. Maybe there's a vendetta from a jilted lover or an unhappy employee. I can use all the help I can get. Be kind of nice finally working to-gether and me getting to tell you what to do. I'm gonna like that."

"Yeah, well, before you get all worked up about adding me to your team, there's something you need to know."

"What's that?" Wincott happened to look up, and then muttered, "Ah, hell. Lewis is motioning to me."

"He's gonna tell you he wants me out of the loop. I can make phone calls for you, but that's about it."

"Wincott," Lewis shouted from his doorway. "I want to talk to you."

"Prick," he mumbled.

"Keep me posted," Alec said.

Wincott nodded. Alec could hear him sigh as he threaded his way around the desks to get to Lewis.

Chapter Twenty

"You're back in."

Lewis made the announcement from the doorway of his office. "Buchanan, did you hear what I just said? You're back in."

Alec didn't bother to stand. He simply turned in his swivel chair and asked, "Back in what?"

Lewis strode forward. "I just got off the phone with the superintendent of police. That's right," he said. "The superintendent." His chest actually swelled like a blowfish when he repeated the news.

"And?" Alec prodded.

"Did you have any idea who Regan Madison was when you interviewed her?"

Alec wasn't in the mood to play guessing games. He'd been in the middle of doodling on his blotter while he watched the second hand circle the clock on the wall. It had been only a couple of hours since Lewis had taken his cases away from him, but he was bored out of his mind. He wasn't sure how much longer he could stomach sitting there and knew that Lewis expected him to show up at eight every morning and do nothing for nine frickin' hours. If Lewis had wanted to drive him nuts, he couldn't have picked a better punishment. Three weeks of sheer boredom. Like it or not, he was going to have to deal with it.

"Well, did you?"

"Okay, I'll bite. Who is she?"

"A Hamilton," he said. He all but smacked his lips as he said the name.

Lewis stood in front of Alec's desk and planted his sweaty palms on Alec's blotter. "She's Regan Hamilton Madison."

"And?"

"Her family owns all those hotels." He was frowning now, obviously irritated that Alec hadn't been suitably impressed. "The Hamilton in Chicago is just one of several. They're all top-of-the-line. The woman comes from money, old money."

"So?"

"That wasn't in your report. I checked. You should have said something. Why didn't you?"

Alec didn't know how to respond to the absurd question. "So what about her? And what did you mean when you said I was back in?"

"She has brothers."

"Yes, I know."

"Three of them," he continued, acting as though Alec hadn't acknowledged the fact. "The oldest one just called the superintendent. Seems he knows the Madisons quite well. They belong to the same country club," he added. "The Clairmont Country Club, to be exact. My wife and I have been trying to get in there for over five years."

"And?" Alec asked, trying to force him to get to the point.

"Aiden's the oldest Madison," he said. "He's a very powerful man."

He sounded like a fan now. Alec was disgusted. "So?"

"So he's concerned about his sister's safety."

Alec leaned back. "Why are you talking to me? Wincott's in charge of the investigation. Refer the brothers to him."

"Wincott has enough to do," he said. "And Regan Madison isn't a suspect . . ."

"Did Wincott tell you she wasn't?"

"I'm telling you," he snapped.

He wasn't going to argue. Come on, he thought. Spell it out. Lewis was taking forever to tell him what he wanted. And Alec had so many other things to do. Like doodling. He almost laughed out loud then. Lewis had made sure he'd be excluded from any and all investigations, wanting him to sit at his desk and stare into space. Fortunately, he had a lot of doodles to finish, and right now Lewis's palms were sweating all over one of his more creative ones.

"I want you to look after her until Wincott brings in Sweeney's killer."

Alec dropped his pen. "You want me to be her bodyguard?" He got angry just thinking about it. "I'm not a damned bodyguard," he muttered before Lewis could speak.

"You are now. Know why I decided on you?"

"Because you knew I'd hate it?"

"That too," Lewis said, grinning. "You have a bad attitude, Buchanan. That's why you were so good working vice. You fit right in with all those perverts and psychos."

His insults didn't faze Alec. "Nice of you to notice."

"You're going to stick with the Madison woman night and day, day and night. You got that?"

Was he more concerned about the wealthy woman being upset or Sweeney's murder? It was hard to tell.

"If her family has so much money, why can't they hire bodyguards?"

"They could. Of course they could," he said. "And they might."

Every time he opened his mouth, he spit all over Alec's desk. Man oh man, three weeks suddenly felt like a life sentence.

"But I want someone from this office with her at all times, and I want Aiden Madison to be beholden. Got that?" He didn't expect a reply. He straightened and headed back to his office. He was shutting the door when he paused and shouted, "Buchanan?"

Alec didn't answer.

"This is my ticket into Clairmont. Don't screw it up."

"Yeah, right."

"Keep her alive."

Chapter Twenty-one

Due to the incessant rain, the maintenance crew didn't get around to clearing the five-foot-high pile of dead shrubs and branches for days. The men wore black rubber boots and yellow slickers over their work clothes and were soon covered in mud as they hauled the refuse away. Vernon, the most energetic of the three-man crew, had tossed the last gnarled branch into a nearby wheelbarrow and was heading back to the shed to take a break and smoke at least two unfiltered Camels when one of his coworkers, a whiner named Sammy, started screaming like a girl, pointing and backing away. Sammy's hazel eyes looked as if they were going to pop right out of his head.

Harry, the new man, wore large bifocals, which were splattered with mud and drizzle. When he walked closer to see what Sammy was carrying on about, he too started screaming. He didn't sound like a girl, though; he sounded like a squawking bird.

"What's the matter with you two?" Vernon returned to the men as he asked the question. Then he saw what they were looking at. A toe was sticking up out of the mud.

He squatted down, saw the chipped red polish on the toenail, and fell back on his ample butt. "Don't touch nothing," he choked out as he scrambled to his feet. "The police won't want us touching nothing because this here is now a crime scene."

Harry was staring hard at the toe, half expecting it to wiggle. "How do you know, Vernon?"

" 'Cause this is where the crime was perpetrated, you twit, or at least where the body was buried." He paused to point dramatically at the toe before continuing. "And that makes it a crime scene. That's what they call it on television when they wrap yellow official tape all around the perimeter. Sammy, for the love of God, stop your yelling."

Sammy pulled a soggy handkerchief out of his pocket and wiped his eyes. "We should do something for her . . . shouldn't we try to do something for her?"

Given the circumstances, Vernon was surprisingly calm. "No one can do anything for her now."

"It is a real toe, isn't it, Vernon?" Harry asked.

"What do you mean, 'real'?"

"I'm thinking it could be a rubber one or a plastic one. One of those smart-ass college kids might be trying to prank us."

It was a viable possibility. Vernon leaned in. "It's real, all right. Rubber don't decompose so fast, and I can see it isn't plastic 'cause there isn't any shine to it."

Sammy gagged. Harry gave him a sharp look and waved him back. "The police won't appreciate it if you puke on their crime scene. Take a couple of deep breaths," he suggested.

"Are you sure the toe's attached to a body?" Harry asked Vernon.

"You come up with the stupidest questions. I'm not touching it or tugging on it to see if it's attached or not. That's for the police to figure out. Why don't you run over to the lecture hall and use their phone to call the police? Sammy and I will wait here."

"Wouldn't it be quicker if I just use my cell phone?"

"For crying out loud, does everyone in the U.S. of A. have a cell phone?"

"I don't know about everyone else in the U.S. of A.," Harry said. "But I sure do. Had it for over a year."

He unfastened his slicker, pulled out a bright red phone, and dialed 911.

Chapter Twenty-two

The last thing Regan wanted or needed was someone shadowing her every second of the day. Detective Buchanan didn't particularly care how she felt, though. He strolled into her office, looking as scruffy and as sexy as she remembered, leaned against the side of her desk, and calmly announced that he was going to be her bodyguard for the next three weeks, or until the man who had e-mailed her the photo of Detective Sweeney was apprehended.

"Shouldn't you be out there looking for the murderer instead of following me around?"

"I've been assigned to you," he said. "Detective Wincott is out there looking," he added.

She was frustrated and weary. She was also scared but wasn't going to admit it. Cordie still hadn't called her back, and Regan was worried sick about her and Sophie.

"Yes, you already told me that Detective Wincott was in charge. I haven't met him yet. I have been cooperating, haven't I?"

she said. "And it seems you only just left. There's been such commotion here since then. I need some time to just sit down and think. My head's reeling. I have some work to finish, and then I want to . . ."

He tried not to smile. "Think?"

"Yes, think."

"No problem," he said.

He removed his tie and stuffed it in the pocket of his jacket before taking it off and draping it over a chair.

She watched him get comfortable on the sofa. "What happens in three weeks?"

"Sorry?" He was rolling his sleeves up as he turned to her.

"You said you were going to be my bodyguard for three weeks. What happens then?"

He undid the top button of his shirt before he answered. "I'm finished with the job and leaving Chicago, but don't worry, if he's still out there, then someone else will be assigned to guard you. Until then, you're stuck with me."

"Who made that decision?"

"Does it matter?"

"Yes, it does," she said.

"Okay."

"Okay, who?" She wasn't going to let it go.

"Lieutenant Lewis."

"Do I have anything to say about this?"

He flashed a smile and picked up the latest *Forbes* magazine from the coffee table. "Not really," he said. "Like it or not, I'm here to stay."

She didn't like it, not one little bit. Detective Buchanan was a clear distraction, but she had to put the discussion on hold when his cell phone rang. Her office phone rang at the very same time.

Peter Morris, the man she had turned down for a second grant, was on the line. He was absolutely thrilled he'd gotten through to her.

"This is wonderful," he stammered. "Your assistant kept putting me off, and I can't believe I'm finally talking to you. I know you didn't have anything to do with turning me down for the grant renewal, so I'm not blaming you. It was just a huge misunderstanding, wasn't it?"

Before she had time to answer and set him straight, he rushed on. "My work is important. I need that money, and I was guaranteed that, once I qualified — and I did qualify last year — that it would be an automatic renewal. How about I come by tonight and you could have the check ready?"

"That's not going to happen, Mr. Morris. I am the one who turned you down for the grant, and the information each applicant received was quite specific. There is no such thing as an automatic renewal."

He refused to believe her. His voice had lost a little of its cheer as he said, "No, that's not true. You couldn't have turned me down. You understand how important my work is."

"Mr. Morris —"

He interrupted her again. "I know what you're going to say. Your assistant already told me that I could reapply next year, but the community center desperately needs the money now. Pulling the rug out at the last minute . . . it just isn't right. Now, about the check —"

Determined to end the conversation as quickly as possible, she interrupted, "You are not going to receive any grant money. Your application was denied, and I think it would be a waste of your time, and mine, for you to reapply next year."

His gasp was loud and clear as she hung up. She noticed Detective Buchanan was off the phone and said, "Henry was right. Peter Morris can't take no for an answer."

She repeated almost word for word the

conversation she'd had with the man. When she was finished, Alec said, "I'll mention him to Wincott again and make sure he's looking at him." He stood, rolled his shoulders, and then picked up his suit jacket and put it on.

"Are you leaving?" she asked.

He smiled. "Yes, and so are you. The sketch artist is back and is waiting for us. We need to go. Hopefully, the two of you will be able to come up with a good likeness of the man who chased you."

Her response was immediate. "Yes, okay."

"No argument?"

She shook her head. "No, this is too important."

"Yes, it is."

She grabbed her purse from her drawer and was heading toward the door, where he stood waiting, when her fax machine began to buzz.

"Do you need to see what that is, or can it wait until we get back?" he asked.

"It's probably just an advertisement," she said, but she had already turned around and was circling the desk to get to the fax machine. "It is so rare to get a fax these days. Everything's sent through e-mail."

She glanced over her shoulder to see if he was irritated that she was making him wait. He was busy buttoning the collar of his shirt and didn't appear out of sorts over the delay.

"Do you mind? It will only take a minute. The cover sheet's coming through."

"No problem." He was looking for his tie now.

"It's on the floor by the sofa."

"What is?" he asked.

"The tie you're looking for. It fell out of your suit pocket."

"Thanks."

He headed back to the sofa. She turned to the machine. The cover sheet had dropped into the tray below. The sender line was blank, but there was something written on the subject line. She couldn't quite make it out. She picked the sheet up and turned toward the light. A cold chill raced down her spine as she read the three words scrawled across the line: *Your Murder List.*

"Murder List? Oh, God . . ."

It suddenly all clicked. She inhaled sharply and took a step back as though that simple action would separate her from the truth.

She shook her head. "No . . . it couldn't

be . . . it's just not possible . . ."

Alec heard the panic in her voice. He gently pried the cover sheet out of her hand just as the fax machine began to hum again. Page two was slowly coming through.

Regan had been so stunned by the heading on the top of the page that she missed the message, written in what looked like chicken scratches, on the bottom. Alec read it out loud: "Sorry, I can't take credit for this one. I was too late. She was already in the mortuary. Had herself a fatal heart attack, but I went ahead and marked her off your list anyway."

Alec was on the phone to Wincott by the time Regan held up the second page. He rattled off the fax number. "Everything else is blocked out."

"We're on it," Wincott said. "I'll see you back at the station." He was shouting to his partner as he hung up.

Alec turned to Regan. "Murder List? What the hell is a murder list?"

She didn't immediately answer. She was anxiously gripping her hands together as she continued to wait for the machine to spit the page out. It seemed to be taking forever.

And there it was.

Oh, God, another picture, this one of a woman lying on what looked like a metal slab. Her ashen face was peaceful in death.

It took Regan several seconds to remember where she'd seen the woman before.

"This can't be happening."

"Tell me," he demanded.

"I know this woman," she said. "She works at Dickerson's Bath Shop on Michigan Avenue. I stopped in there a couple of weeks ago to buy a bottle of body lotion. She's a saleswoman."

Her knees felt as though they were going to buckle on her. She fell back against the desk and took a deep breath. Her mind was reeling.

"She was wearing a name tag . . . Ms. Patsy."

"You remembered her name?"

She nodded. "She was rude, terribly rude. She was probably just having a bad day, and it was wrong of me to judge her so harshly. And now she's dead."

That much was pretty obvious. "Are you going to get sick?" Alec was already looking around for a trash can.

"No, no. This is all my fault."

"How could this be your fault? If what

this maniac says is true, she died of a heart attack."

She was barely listening to him. Oh, God, what had she done? What had she done?

"Regan?"

She took another deep breath. "You read the note. He said he was too late, that she was already dead. It's obvious to me he went after her to kill her."

"You didn't kill her."

Her face was turning gray. Alec was becoming concerned she might pass out on him now. He stepped closer just in case so he could catch her if she collapsed.

"No, but I put her on the list."

His head snapped back. "You what?"

"The murder list . . . it's mine."

Chapter Twenty-three

Regan was a little surprised he didn't put handcuffs on her and read her her rights. Actually, Detective Buchanan took the news well, considering that she surely now was his number one suspect.

He was quite good at hiding his reactions. Had she not been looking into his eyes, she wouldn't have noticed his attitude had hardened toward her.

She was too shaken to care what the detective thought about her. She was scared and worried and didn't like feeling that way at all. She checked the time, calculated that Henry would be back at his desk in about fifteen minutes, and left him a note explaining where she was going. She also instructed him to call Sam Baldwin, the in-house attorney who, with an overworked staff of three other full-time attorneys, handled all the legal problems involving the Hamilton Hotels and/or any of the Madisons. Spencer jokingly referred to the attorneys as Walker's personal team, since he was the family member who most often needed their expertise. Sam would be shocked to hear it was Regan who now needed him.

She rode in the detective's car to the police station, and on the way she tried to explain all about the spontaneous exercise Dr. Shields had had the registrants do during the reception.

He was weaving in and out of traffic, narrowly missing one car after another. The man drove like a maniac, and she felt it was her duty as a concerned citizen to tell him so.

"Are you kidding me?" he said. "You're Walker Madison's sister, aren't you? If anyone drives like a maniac, it's your brother." He paused to think about what she had been telling him and then asked, "What did you mean when you said the bodyguard was still watching you? Had something happened earlier that got his attention?"

"No," she answered. "But from the minute I walked into the room, he locked in on me. It was really strange. I hadn't done anything to draw his attention, but he wouldn't stop staring at me."

Alec didn't think it was strange at all. Rude, maybe, but not strange. Hell, he himself was having trouble not staring. The bodyguard was a man, and Regan

Madison was a very beautiful woman.

"I can prove all of this happened," she said.

He glanced at her. "Prove what?"

"That I'm not making this up . . . the exercise, I mean. Sophie taped it. She had a recorder in her purse, and she sat close to Shields. You can listen to it."

"Yes, I will."

"And just so you understand, I didn't have any intention of doing the exercise, but then Shields said that, when time was up, we all had to hold up our lists, and he was going to walk around the room to see if we'd all written names. I decided then I'd let him know what I thought of him. He posed the question, after all, and he told us that if the world would be a better place without certain people in it, then put their names down."

"His name was on your list?"

"Yes."

"How many names did you write on your notepad?"

"Six . . . no, five."

"You're sure?"

"Yes, there were five names." She prayed to God she was right.

"Okay, so Shields was one, and the Patsy woman, and Detective Sweeney," he said.

"Who are the other two?"

"The bodyguards."

"Ah."

"I'm not normally so bloodthirsty."

He flashed a grin. "I didn't think you were."

"The reception seems such a long time ago. I had surgery shortly after that and the days all blended together. As far as the list goes . . ."

"Yes?"

"I thought I was going to tear it up and throw it in the fire like all the other people were doing, but I had to step into the hall to take a phone call, and when I went back inside, Shields had moved on to what Cordie called his inspirational, aren't-I-wonderful segment."

"What was that like?"

"I don't know. I didn't listen. I went to get the car. That's when the man came after me, and I fell. I dropped everything. I didn't realize I'd left my phone and the folder there."

"So, tell me exactly what was in the folder."

She looked off into space trying to remember. The image of the blue folder filled with the glossy pages vaguely emerged. "There was the notebook I wrote the list on . . . and there were testimonials about Shields . . . and photos . . . I took one of them and began a reminder list . . . notes, work stuff . . . things I needed to get done . . . just stuff."

"You're going to have to remember what all the 'stuff' was and, when we get to the station, you can write it down for Detective Wincott."

"Why?"

"Those notes were left in the folder. He's going to want to know about them."

Regan didn't know if she could remember what she'd written. She thought about it and didn't say another word the rest of the way to the station.

Alec parked the car in the adjacent parking lot, opened her door for her, and took hold of her arm when they crossed the street.

"It's going to be a long afternoon," he said. "Everything you've gone over with me, you'll have to go over with Wincott." Again and again and again, he silently added. Wincott was big on repetition.

"And what will you be doing?"

"I've got some calls to return and some paperwork to finish up. Wincott will let me know when you're finished."

"I don't need a bodyguard."

"I think maybe you do."

"Then I'll hire —"

He interrupted. "Look, you're stuck with me no matter how many others you hire. The choice isn't yours."

She decided that arguing with him would be pointless. She must have looked forlorn, though, because he said, "Cheer up. It could be worse."

"How?"

"You could have written ten names on that list, or twenty, or thirty . . ."

They started up the flight of stairs. "How many names did your friend Cordie write?"

"Seven," she said.

They reached the landing, and he led her down a narrow hallway. "There you go," he said. "Your friend's more bloodthirsty than you are. That ought to make you feel better."

"Not really. She wrote the names of the Seven Dwarfs."

He laughed. "You're kidding."

She shook her head.

"What's she got against the Seven Dwarfs?" he asked.

She gave him a weak smile. "Nothing."

"It's impressive," he added. He opened the door and stepped back so that she could go inside first.

"What's impressive?" she asked as she walked past him. "That Sophie and Cordie were smart enough not to write names of real people?"

"No, it's impressive Cordie could name all Seven Dwarfs. I can only get to four. Let's see. There's Doc and Sleepy and Dopey and Slurpy —"

She interrupted. "Slurpy isn't one of the Seven Dwarfs. It's a beverage."

"Huh. What about Loopy?"

"Sorry, no," she said. And then she laughed. "Are you trying to make me feel better?"

"Maybe a little."

"Why?"

"Because you look like you're on your way to a firing squad. And we stopped doing that over a month ago. And like I said, it's going to be a long afternoon for you."

The police station seemed to be a maze of corridors. Alec reached around her to open yet another door. She was going to need bread crumbs to find her way out of here.

"Where are we going now?"

"The coffee room. I told Wincott we'd wait there for him to get back."

"What about the sketch artist?"

"He's next."

He pulled a chair out for her and got a whiff of her perfume. Damn, she smelled good.

"Do you want something to drink?" he asked.

"Water, please."

Regan looked around with interest. The coffee room was nothing like the ones she had seen on television with peeling paint and dirty barred windows. This one was spacious and clean and had obviously just been remodeled. The faint smell of paint still lingered in the air. The walls were bright — almost too bright — and the color was a rather putrid shade of turquoise. There were two square tables with chairs that looked new.

Alec noticed her staring at the walls. "Makes you want to put on sunglasses, doesn't it?"

"Who picked out this color?"

"No one will own up to it."

The refrigerator was also new and was stocked with water and soft drinks. Alec handed her a bottle of water and then pulled out a chair across from her and sat down.

There was a steno pad and a ballpoint

pen in the center of the table. Alec pushed both toward her. "You might as well get a head start and write the names you put on your murder list."

Murder list. Oh, God, what a mess this was. She picked up the pen and quickly wrote the five names. She labeled the bodyguards *A* and *B* since she didn't know their real names. When she was finished, she pushed the pad toward him.

He leaned across, glanced at the list, and then pushed the pad toward her again.

"Okay, now write down all the notes you were making while Shields was talking."

That was easier said than done. She tapped the toe of her shoe on the linoleum floor while she tried to concentrate. Emily Milan came to mind. Regan remembered she'd made a note to have it out with Aiden's assistant. Oh, and Peter Morris. How could she have forgotten him? She'd made a note to talk to security about him. But who else? Was there anyone else?

The tapping increased. "There's no need to be nervous," he said.

"I'm not nervous." It was a lie, and he knew it.

Then she realized she was jiggling the table with her knee, making a racket with her foot. She forced herself to stop.

"Maybe I'm a little nervous."

She put the pen down and once again pushed the notepad toward him. He looked at her notes but didn't comment.

She stared at the tabletop while she tried to recall what else she'd written on those papers. Had she left anyone off her doom list? She remembered wanting to add Emily's name at the last minute, but she never got the chance.

She looked up at Alec, and for a second she actually lost her concentration. That had never happened before. But then, Detective Buchanan was a very interesting man — and a definite contradiction. He was a bit disheveled with his tie still askew, his wrinkled suit jacket, and his desperate need for a shave, but he had impeccable manners, was obviously well-educated, and had a sense of humor — a trait she thought would have been the first to vanish in his line of work. When he was giving her his full attention, she could almost feel a magnetic pull.

Okay, I'm losing it, she thought. She cleared her throat and said, "I saw you in Lieutenant Lewis's office when I was there before, talking to Detective Sweeney."

"I saw you too."

Momentarily sidetracked by his admission, she said, "You did?"

"Uh-huh."

"Yes, well, the thing is . . . the lieutenant was shouting at a police officer," she said. "Actually, as I remember, he was screaming. I had never seen anyone behave like that. No one in such a position of authority, anyway. I thought his conduct was appalling."

"He wanted to get rid of the officer."

"You defended him."

He smiled. "You saw that too?"

"Yes," she said. "I saw you arguing with the lieutenant, but I couldn't hear what you were saying to him. Unlike your superior, you didn't raise your voice. I remember thinking that he . . . Lewis . . . was humiliating that officer."

Alec disagreed. "No," he said. "He tried to humiliate him, but he didn't succeed. The officer knew he hadn't done anything wrong. How come we're talking about this now?"

She couldn't hold his stare but looked over his shoulder. "I was going to put the lieutenant's name on the list."

He was trying hard not to smile. "But you didn't?"

"No, I didn't. I would have, though, if I hadn't been interrupted. My cell phone rang, and I had to hurry out into the hall to answer it. I would have added his name if I'd continued. I just thought you should know."

"I wouldn't tell Detective Wincott if I were you."

"Why not?"

He shrugged. "It'd be cruel, getting his hopes up and then disappointing him."

"But I didn't put Lewis's name on the list."

"There you go."

Chapter Twenty-four

Regan finally asked the questions that had been nagging at her.

"Why are you leaving Chicago?"

"It's a long story." He didn't go on.

"Where will you go?"

"Back to Boston. That's where I'm from."

"We have a hotel in Boston."

"I know," he said.

He didn't offer any information, and she didn't press him to explain. They both turned when the door opened. Detective John Wincott took a step inside, then bent down to pick up some papers he'd dropped. The perfectly round bald spot on the crown of his head was visible and shiny. Wincott's partner told everyone in the precinct that Wincott was sensitive about his hair loss, so of course at every opportunity he was teased and tormented. One of Wincott's least favorite nicknames was Friar Tuck, but fortunately, he had a good sense of humor.

He reminded Regan of a harried accountant, probably because he was carrying what looked like a ledger with papers sticking out every which way. Then she noticed the gun holstered to his side, and the possibility that he was an accountant went out the window.

"Sorry to keep you waiting."

"You still look half dead," Alec told him after introducing him to Regan.

Regan thought the man was actually rather nice looking, but with the dark circles under his eyes and the gray complexion, he did look worn-out.

"Yeah, well, I missed my day at the spa this week," Wincott said.

Alec laughed. "I forgot to ask. How's the baby?"

Wincott turned to Regan to explain, "Our baby's cutting teeth," he said. "And she's not happy about it, which means my wife and I aren't happy either. Neither one of us is getting any sleep."

"I hear whiskey helps," Alec said.

"I tried that, but it only gave me a bad hangover the next morning."

"You're supposed to rub some on the baby's gums. It numbs them."

"I've never heard of such a thing. Besides, what if she likes it? What if she develops a real taste for it? Before you know it, I'm driving my two-year-old over to AA.

Too risky," he said with a straight face.

Alec stood. "I told Regan you're an adequate detective. Don't make a liar out of me."

"Don't you want to sit in on this?"

He shook his head. "I've got some phone calls to make. I'll be at my desk if you need anything," he told Regan. "Okay?"

He was being very sweet, she thought. And looking worried about her. "Yes, okay," she said.

Alec pulled the door closed behind him. He turned and bumped into Lyle Bradshaw. Wincott's partner looked impeccable as usual. His striped tie had a perfect knot in it, his dark suit was wrinkle free, his shirt was immaculate, and his shoes, like always, looked brand-new. Standing next to him, Alec looked as though he'd just recently been mugged.

"Is she in the coffee room?" Bradshaw asked in lieu of a greeting.

"Yes," Alec said. "Wincott's with her."

"Is he drooling?"

"Excuse me?"

"I hear she's a stunner."

"Yeah? Where did you hear that?"

"The pool," he said, referring to the open area where all the detectives worked. "She's been the topic of conversation since you brought her in. I hear she's got a gorgeous face and a body that just won't quit."

Alec was surprised by the spark of anger he felt. It came out of nowhere.

"She's definitely out of your league, Lyle."

Newly divorced, Bradshaw considered himself a ladies' man. Women found him attractive and attentive, and he never lacked for female companionship, but Alec thought he was a little too arrogant for his own good, and on occasion he could be downright obnoxious. His only saving grace was his skill as a detective.

Bradshaw was opening the door to the coffee room when Alec called out, "Hey, Bradshaw."

"Yes?"

Alec was going to tell him not to hit on Regan but stopped himself in time. "Go easy on her," he said instead. "She's scared."

Alec picked up his messages and went back to his desk. Lewis had doled out his cases to several other already overworked detectives, and in a childish attempt to punish him, Lewis had had his computer removed. The top of Alec's desk was now completely bare.

If the other detectives hadn't gotten stuck with his work, he would have thought Lewis's behavior was funny. Alec sat down at his desk and used his cell phone to call his brother Nick.

"So I guess I'm in," he said.

Nick laughed. "Hi, Alec. By *in,* I assume you mean the FBI?"

"You already knew, didn't you?"

"Yeah, I did. Ward called to tell me about five minutes after you were accepted into the academy. Your test scores were impressive."

"Better than yours?"

"If they were, do you think I'd admit it?"

"Probably not. Tell Theo, will you?" Alec asked. He didn't know if he'd have time to track down his oldest brother.

"He already knows. Ward called him too. Have you made up your mind about buying my town house? Laurant's been out looking every Sunday with a realtor. The town house is great for a bachelor, but with the baby, it's too crowded, and Laurant wants to get pregnant again."

Alec smiled. Nick had hit the jackpot when he'd married Laurant. She was such a sweetheart, and perfect for his brother. She was so laid-back and easygoing, which was exactly what Nick needed when he came home from work. Theo often described Nick's job as a real pressure cooker. He and his partner, Noah Clayborne, worked for a special branch of the FBI. They were called in when the search for a missing child had gone cold. It was a hard, tear-you-up-inside kind of job.

"I am going to buy your town house," Alec said. "Even if I don't get assigned to the Boston area . . ."

"Ward says you will."

"He'd say anything to get me to sign up," he said. "Ward doesn't make the decision, but even if I don't end up in Boston, I'll still keep the property. It's a good investment."

"Hold on," Nick said. "I can barely hear you. I've got two conversations going at the same time."

"Who's talking to you?"

"Noah."

"Where are you?"

"In Dallas," he said. "We just finished up a case. This one went well."

"That's good."

Noah was suddenly on the line congratulating him. "They're gonna work your butt off at the academy, but you'll do fine. When are you leaving Chicago?"

"Not for at least three weeks, maybe

four," he said. "If you still want to see a Cubs game, you better get here soon. I'll need a little notice to get tickets from Gil."

A second later Nick was back on the cell phone reminding him that their sister Jordan was still planning a trip to Chicago.

"I know, but she won't commit to a date. I won't be able to start packing until my job ends here. I've got a new assignment that's going to take up most of my time for the next three weeks, but then I'm done. If Jordan waits too long, she'll get stuck helping me pack."

"What's the new assignment?"

"I don't want to talk about it."

Nick laughed. "That bad, huh?"

A young cop dropped a fat file on Alec's desk and turned to leave. Alec motioned him to stay. "I've got to go, Nick." He flipped the cell phone closed and put it back in his pocket. "What's all this?" he asked.

"Forms you need to fill out. H.R. sent them over."

"You're kidding."

"No, sir. I never kid."

"I've already filled out papers." He silently added, *damn it.*

"No, sir. You filled out some of the forms, but not all of them. They said they'd need these back by the end of the day."

"It's harder to get out of this place than it is to get in."

"That's what a lot of criminals tell us," the cop responded dryly.

Alec decided he might as well get it over with, opened the folder, and started filling in the first form. It took him close to an hour to finish up, but only because he kept getting interrupted. A detective had gotten a photocopy of Sweeney's blackmail book and was reading out loud from it.

Alec had just signed the last form when he looked up and saw Bradshaw motioning to him. He picked up the folder to take with him, intending to drop it off on his way downstairs. Bradshaw was waiting by the steps.

"Are you finished with Regan?" Alec asked.

"For now," he answered. "Wincott took her upstairs to his favorite sketch artist."

"That shouldn't take too long."

Bradshaw snorted. "You don't know Tony, do you? He'll keep her for the rest of the day if he has to, until she tells him it's a perfect likeness. You'll need to stay with her. I just got a call from Lewis's kiss-ass assistant. He told me that Regan's brother and her attorney are headed over here."

"She's not a suspect. Did you explain that to her?"

"Of course I did," he said. "I came close to asking her out too, but I controlled myself."

"Jeez, Bradshaw. Try to stay focused."

Bradshaw grinned. "That's hard to do around her."

"Who called the brother and the attorney? Do you know?"

"No," he said. "They're going to have a conference with Lewis."

They simultaneously turned to look at the lieutenant. They could see him through the glass clearing the clutter from his desk.

"He's getting ready for company," Alec said.

"Important company," Bradshaw added. "The Madisons have money."

Money. That was what it was all about with Lewis, Alec thought, as he headed to the front desk to drop off the papers. On his way back, he ran into Melissa and said hello to her. She grunted her reply. When she was past him, she stopped and called out, "Hey, Buchanan."

"Yes?"

"Tell Regan that when I was working on

her piece of crap computer, I removed her from the loop and I forgot to put her back."

"What are you talking about?"

"She's got a couple of stations hooked on in network."

"Melissa, I still don't know what you're talking about."

She looked vexed. "Do you know anything about computers?"

"Apparently not as much as you'd like me to know, so just explain in layman terms."

"There are a couple of other people reading her e-mails."

"Now, how hard was that to say?"

She ignored his sarcasm. "There are a bunch of computers over there at the hotel, and they're all on the same network. Think of her e-mail like a ball. Yeah, like a ball. When she gets a message, the ball bounces to other stations. Her assistant gets her messages the same time she does. It was set up that way to save time," she explained. She squinted at him and asked, "Are you getting any of this?"

He wasn't going to let her irritate him. "You said that there were a couple of people reading her e-mails. Her assistant is one. Who's the other ball breaker?" he asked with a straight face.

"The ball bounces, Buchanan. It doesn't break. And it's someone else in-house."

"Can you track it to a specific computer?"

"I already did. I don't remember the computer ID, but it's in one of her brothers' offices. I can't remember which one. It's all in my notes, which I sent to Wincott. Ask him."

"Send me a copy of your report." She was walking away when he stopped her again. "Regan might not know someone else is reading her mail? Is that possible?"

She shrugged. "She might not know."

Alec turned the corner and spotted Regan through the glass in the door. She was sitting at a computer with the sketch artist at her side. She must have sensed that he was watching her because she suddenly turned and looked at him. And then she smiled. And he smiled back.

Tony tapped her on her arm to get her attention again. Regan reluctantly turned to the screen. Tony was a hard taskmaster. He was an older man who looked like a comedian she'd seen perform at a comedy club a couple of months ago. For the first five minutes or so, she kept expecting him to tell her a joke. Tony didn't have much of a sense of humor, though. After he shook her hand, he announced that he was a per-fectionist and told her that they would work together for as long as necessary to achieve a perfect likeness of the man who had chased her in the park.

It was a surprisingly difficult under-taking. Until she sat down with Tony, she thought she had a good picture of the man in her mind, but that wasn't the case. Several times she had to close her eyes and try to visualize him again. Being exact about the shape of his nose, his eyes, and his chin was extremely challenging.

When they were finished, she believed the sketch was a good likeness, but it wasn't perfect by any means. And when Tony removed the glasses and the beard, the man's appearance completely changed. She didn't have a clue if that was accurate or not.

Alec was waiting for her outside the sketch artist's workroom. She handed him the printout and said, "Tony thinks the hair and the glasses and the beard could all be props." She handed him the second printout of Tony's drawing. "This is what he might really look like."

"Does he look familiar?"

She shook her head. "He's very . . . ordi-nary, isn't he?"

He nodded. "So this might be the . . ." He started to say *bastard* and then substituted, ". . . crazy we're looking for. He's nondescript and will blend in with a crowd."

"Maybe not," she said. "He was big, as big as you, and just as muscular. His size alone might make him stand out. I don't know." She took a breath and then said, "If he's the man who stole my phone, and if he's the man who killed Detective Sweeney, and . . ." She was too disheartened to go on. "I think Detectives Wincott and Bradshaw are finished questioning me, so I'll head back to my office. If you or the other detectives need to speak to me, just call or stop by."

Alec stepped in front of her. "Now, I know you're smarter than that, and we have been over this, but I'm gonna pretend you still don't understand. I've been assigned to you, and that means that everywhere you go, I go."

She folded her arms and frowned. The day was proving to be long and arduous. "And as I explained, if I feel I need a bodyguard, I'll hire one."

His smile was distracting, and when he stepped closer to her, forcing her to tilt her head back to look into his eyes, she actually felt a rush of goose bumps.

"Are we going to get into an argument?" he asked.

"I believe we are."

"You can't win."

"Why? Because you've got a gun?"

He didn't say a word. He just nodded.

"Because you're bigger?"

He nodded again.

"Stronger?"

He smiled.

She rolled her eyes. "You'll notice I didn't say smarter." He did laugh then. "Detective —"

It was as far as he would let her get. "Neither one of us can leave just yet."

"Why not?" she asked, temporarily side-tracked from the bodyguard issue.

"Your brother and your attorney are downstairs in Lewis's office with Wincott and Bradshaw. I came up here to get you. They're all waiting to talk to you."

"Which brother?" she asked, trying not to let him see how irritated she was.

"I don't know. Does it matter?"

"Yes. I hope it's not Aiden," she said. She didn't tell Alec what she was thinking, but she did hope that Spencer was back in town and was waiting downstairs. He was much easier to deal with.

She shook her head as she attempted to go around him. "I guess we should go downstairs then."

He maneuvered in front of her again and leaned against the wall. "What's going on with you?"

He acted as though they were old friends and he knew her so well he could tell when she was out of sync.

She shifted from one foot to the other as she said, "If I hadn't made that stupid list . . ."

"You didn't kill anyone, did you?"

"No, but . . ."

"You simply took part in an exercise."

"I made a murder list, for heaven's sake."

"Along with a whole lot of other people," he pointed out. "You just didn't get the opportunity to toss your list into the fire." He stepped aside to let her go ahead of him. "I can't wait to meet this Dr. Shields. He sounds like a snake charmer."

"Not so charming. Just a snake. I wish I had never heard of him," she answered over her shoulder.

"So what's wrong with Aiden?"

The questions jarred her. "Nothing's wrong with him. He's a wonderful brother."

Alec wasn't buying it. "Yeah?"

"He's just a little . . . uptight. That's all."

Alec didn't have to ask which of the two strangers in Lewis's office was Regan's brother. The family resemblance was obvious. Though Regan was only five five or five six and her brother was over six feet, they shared the same coloring and patrician features. Aiden was impeccably dressed in a well-cut, dark suit, which Alec assumed had a fancy designer label inside. His own brother Theo had a suit just like it. Calvin Klein, Alec thought. Or maybe Armani.

The well-fed man sitting in a chair facing Lewis's desk was also wearing an expensive suit. The man was short, round as an egg, and his face was as wrinkled as an unironed cotton shirt. Alec assumed he was the attorney.

Detectives Wincott and Bradshaw stood by the windows, watching. They both looked bored senseless.

Regan's brother happened to glance up, spotted her coming toward him, and for a fleeting second, Alec saw relief in his eyes. No matter how many flaws the man might have, it was apparent he loved his sister.

Chapter Twenty-five

Sam Baldwin, the Madisons' attorney, closed his notebook and stood when Regan walked in.

"You're not a suspect," he told her immediately.

"No, no, of course she isn't," Lewis agreed. He stood and leaned across the desk with his hand outstretched. He introduced himself, shook her hand, and wouldn't let go as he said, "I know this must be a terrible ordeal for you."

Before she could respond, Sam said, "I'll get back to you within the hour, Aiden." He nodded to Regan, who was trying to pull her hand away from Lewis's grasp and then left the office.

"Regan?" Aiden said.

"I'm fine," she replied.

The second Lewis let go of her, she crossed the room to stand next to her brother. Since the lieutenant hadn't bothered to introduce Alec to him, she did.

The two men were the same height. Aiden was thinner, but both men were quite handsome and fit. Her brother looked tired, though. Tired and worried.

"The lieutenant tells me you've been assigned to protect my sister until the man who sent those photos is apprehended."

"That's right," Lewis said before Alec could answer.

Wincott drew Lewis's attention when he asked, "Who else are you going to put on this, or is it just Buchanan and Bradshaw and me working the case? Connelly's already been reassigned, hasn't he?"

"Yes, he has," Lewis said. "You'll have help, but it won't be Buchanan." He sat down in his chair and scowled at Wincott. "You understand what I'm saying? Buchanan's got bodyguard duty and that's all."

"Did Sam call you?" Regan asked her brother. She whispered so that the lieutenant wouldn't hear her. "Is that why you're here?"

Wincott and Bradshaw were occupied arguing with Lewis about manpower, ignoring Regan for the moment, but Alec was paying attention.

"No," Aiden said in response to Regan's question. "Henry called Sam and told him you were on your way here. He also told him about the e-mail and the fax you received. I saw the photos."

"You did?"

"There were copies on my desk when I arrived. As soon as I saw them, I called Sam. Neither one of us found out you had made a murder list until we got here. Regan, what in God's name were you thinking?"

"Excuse me?" Anger radiated in her voice.

"You heard me. I cannot imagine why you would do such a thing."

She didn't bother to explain because she knew that no matter what she said, she would still be put on the defensive. And be found guilty.

She took a breath and whispered. "How did you get those photos? Henry wouldn't have placed anything on your desk without checking with me first."

"Someone put them there. I just assumed they came from your assistant. That really isn't important, is it?"

Yes, she thought, it was very important, but she knew that now wasn't the time to argue about it. "I would appreciate it if you didn't bother Spencer and Walker about any of this. I don't want them to worry," she said.

"Too late. Someone e-mailed them the photos."

"The photos of Detective Sweeney and

the saleswoman? They've seen those photos?" she asked, trying to understand.

"Were there others?"

"No, no there weren't."

"Then the answer is yes. They've seen the photos of the detective and the saleswoman."

"I wish they hadn't seen them. They're going to worry, and —" Her anger and frustration were building.

Aiden, on the other hand, was his usual stone-faced self. "Worry? They're frantic. Spencer wants you under lock and key until he gets here, and then he hopes you'll fly back to Melbourne and stay with him until the police catch this maniac."

"I'm not going to do that."

"He thinks he can talk you into it. Walker also wants you to stay with him."

"Where is he this week?"

"Paris until the day after tomorrow. He wants you to travel with him, and that, of course, is out of the question."

"Aiden, I can make my own decisions."

"You won't even get in a car with Walker. Why would you consider traveling with him?"

"I'm not going to travel with him, and I'm not going to Melbourne."

Aiden nodded and turned to Alec. "As I

was explaining to Detective Wincott, we have an excellent security force at the hotel. I'll go ahead and hire additional men."

Was he dismissing him? Alec thought maybe he was and was vastly amused. Did Aiden think Alec worked for him? Even though he found the job of bodyguard a little demeaning, he would keep Regan safe until Lewis replaced him.

Detective Wincott joined them. Aiden assured him that he and his brothers, and Regan, of course, would do anything they could to help with the investigation.

"She's living at the hotel now, and her office is on the third floor, so she never has to go outside, and that should make your job a little easier," he told Alec.

Regan was shaking her head. "I can't just cancel my schedule. I've given my word that I would help with some important events coming up. I won't miss the hospital fund-raiser."

"You're going to have to cancel everything for now," Aiden said. "If you insist on staying in Chicago, then you're stuck in the hotel. I'm postponing my business trips until this matter is settled."

"But, Aiden —" she began. Her brother had already turned to Wincott and was now discussing the plan for her protection.

Neither one of them asked her opinion. Aiden still firmly believed she should be put on their private jet and sent into seclusion.

In the midst of their conversation, Regan walked out of the office. Alec was right behind her.

"Would you mind driving me back to the hotel?" she asked. "If it isn't convenient, I could walk or grab a cab."

"What is it with you people? First you and then your brother. I'm not going to go away, so stop trying to dismiss me. Got that?"

She didn't turn around. "Yes, all right."

"Wait a minute. What about your brother?"

She kept right on going. "What about him?"

A slow smile crossed his face. He followed her down the stairs, half expecting her brother to come chasing after her.

"How come you didn't defend yourself back there?"

"When?"

"When your brother asked about the murder list. He gave me the impression that he thinks you're responsible."

"In a way I am, aren't I?"

"No."

He grabbed her arm and pulled her back so she wouldn't go outside ahead of him. They crossed the street and went into the parking lot. Alec opened the passenger door for her, but his gaze, she noticed, was never still. It was as though he expected a sniper to pop up somewhere. He scanned the roofs and the street beyond.

Once he was behind the wheel, he pushed a button that locked the doors. The sound turned her thoughts. "I'm going to buy a new car today."

"You are? What's wrong with the car you have? You do own a car, don't you?"

"Yes, I do." She wondered if he thought she was driven around in a limo whenever she wanted to go out.

"So what's wrong with it?" He pictured her driving a Mercedes or maybe even a Porsche, definitely something expensive and trendy.

"It's old."

"How old? A year? Two?"

"You think I'm spoiled, don't you?"

"Does it matter what I think of you?"

"No." She told the lie well and was certain he believed her. It did matter, though, a little anyway.

The traffic was heavy. When Alec veered to the left to avoid a car that pulled in front of them, Regan flinched, and when he sped up to work his way onto the highway, she reacted again. "Listen," he said. "You're making me nuts grabbing the dashboard every time I turn a corner. Try to relax, or is that possible?"

"Of course it's possible. Slow down and I'll prove it."

"I know what I'm doing." There was a bite in his voice now.

His tone didn't faze her. "So does Walker, and he's had God only knows how many accidents."

"I'm not your brother," he said. "And the name is Alec."

She noticed he'd slowed the car down. "What did you say?"

"You might as well call me Alec. You and I are going to be real tight for a while."

"If Lieutenant Lewis knew I was going to put him on that murder list, he'd reassign you and hang me out to dry. That's what I'd do."

He laughed. "No, you wouldn't. You're too softhearted to do anything like that."

"You can't know if I'm softhearted or not."

"Sure I can. I'm a detective."

"Meaning?"

"I detect," he said with a grin.

"Are you married?" Now, why had she asked him that? It really was none of her business.

"No."

"I'm not either," she said.

"Yeah, I know."

Regan was trying to come up with a suitable reason she'd asked such a personal question. "I was just curious," she said. How lame was that?

They reached the hotel a minute later. Wincott called Alec's cell phone just as the doorman opened the car door for Regan.

"I wanted to talk to you about the schedule," Wincott said as Alec followed her into the lobby.

"What about it?"

"You can't be with the woman twenty-four hours a day, despite what Lewis thinks. You're gonna have to sleep sometime. You could sleep with her, I guess. That would be one way to keep an eye on her during the night."

"There's a plan," Alec said dryly.

"Of course, there's a chance she might not cooperate."

"So what do you suggest? You're running the show."

Regan had stopped at the front desk and was going through some papers one of the staff had handed her. Alec stood about ten feet away, his back to her, watching the people in the lobby.

"Her brother wants her under lock and key," he said. "That would make our job easier; however, we both know there will be times when she absolutely has to leave the hotel, so how about this? You're with her all day, in and outside the hotel. Wherever she goes, you go, but when she's in for the night, we let the hotel security staff babysit her."

"I don't like it."

"I don't like it, either."

Alec laughed. "Then why did you suggest it?"

"Bradshaw wanted me to."

"Since when do you listen to your partner?"

"Pretty much never, but he came up with the idea, and I promised I'd run it by you," he said. "Her brother's hiring additional security."

"Yeah, I know, but I still don't like it. I don't trust any outsider to do our job."

Wincott agreed. "This bastard . . . he's playing a sick game with her, isn't he?"

"That's my guess."

"I've got a feeling he's going to want some feedback from her."

"I think so too. You do something nice for someone, you want to hear *thank you*."

"Matlin agrees with you," he said, referring to the staff psychiatrist. "He thinks he'll want to contact her again, but he'll do something a little more personal than a fax or an e-mail."

"What else did he say?"

"Bradshaw only just gave him the file, so Matlin's going to need a little time, but he did notice the 'your' was underlined a couple of times. You know what I'm talking about, don't you? On the subject line of the fax. He wrote, 'Your Murder List.'"

"Yes, I know."

"Matlin thinks underlining the 'your' is significant."

"Did he say why?"

"No."

"That's a big help."

"I'll talk to him in a couple of hours. He should have had enough time to go over our notes."

"Let me know what he says."

"Okay. I'm going to get someone over there tonight to relieve you. Tomorrow we'll figure out a schedule that works for everyone."

"Have whoever you assign call me before he comes over."

Alec ended the call and turned to Regan. She handed some papers back to the clerk and said something to the woman that made her smile.

"Are you ready?" she asked Alec.

"Ready for anything," he said. "What did you have in mind?"

"I'd like to test drive a couple of cars this afternoon."

He shook his head. "You're going to have to put that on hold."

"I'm stuck here, aren't I?"

"Yes. Do you have a lot of work to do?"

They crossed the lobby to the bank of elevators.

"Actually, once I get caught up, I won't have much to do for a while. This is our slow time, or wind-down time."

"How come?"

"All the grant letters have gone out. The money's been allotted for this next year, but the process starts all over again in August, when Henry and I begin sorting through all the new applicants."

Regan was digging through her purse, looking for her elevator key. She handed Alec her billfold, a pen, lipstick, a packet of tissues, an inhaler, and a notepad before she found it.

She smiled. "It's always on the bottom,"

she said. She put the key in the slot and pushed the button for the third floor before she opened her purse wide enough for Alec to dump everything back in.

"I understand no one can get up to the offices without a key," he said as the doors opened.

"That's right."

"Bet it would be easy to steal a key."

She thought about it. "Yes, it would be easy. So many of the staff have keys, and they get misplaced."

"Not good." The elevator stopped on the third floor as he said, "You need to talk to the head of security."

"Yes, of course. I'll make a note to talk to her tomorrow."

"Her?" He sounded surprised.

"Do you have a problem with a woman in charge of our security?"

"Not if she's good."

Henry must have heard them talking, because he came rushing toward them when they turned the corner.

"Man, have I got news," he said. He was so excited he sounded out of breath. "Aiden called and left a message. He's posting a guard in front of the elevators and the stairwell downstairs, and another one on this floor. No one gets past without proper identification, and it's got to be a photo ID. He's also putting a guard outside your door upstairs, your bedroom door."

"When is this supposed to happen?" Regan asked.

"Now," he answered. "They're all on their way, I guess. Anyway, there's more . . ."

He was walking backward as Regan and Alec headed for her offices. "More guards?" she asked.

Henry shook his head. "No, more news. You're not gonna believe this."

"What is it?"

"Nothing's wrong," he said in case she was worried about that. "It's just . . . well, you're not going to believe . . ."

"Try me."

"You might get mad."

"For heaven's sake, just tell me," she said, her exasperation obvious in her tone.

They had reached her offices. Alec stepped around Henry to hold the door for both of them.

"Before Aiden went with the attorney to the police station, he stopped in here."

"For what purpose?"

"He told me to tell you that he had your car towed away, and he left this for you," he said. He turned and picked up a padded envelope from his desk.

Regan looked astonished. "He had my car . . ."

"Towed away," Henry said.

"Did he tell you where he had it towed?"

Henry looked miserable when he said, "To a junkyard, but he wouldn't tell me which one."

She took a step back. She could feel her face heating up. She tried to remain calm in front of Alec and Henry, but inside she was doing a slow burn. She took a deep breath. It didn't help. The burn was getting hotter.

"Aren't you going to open the envelope?" Henry asked.

"Yes," she said. She tore the seal off and pulled out a set of keys.

"Did Aiden explain this?" she asked, holding the key chain up.

Once again, Henry was looking excited. "He bought you a car."

Alec noticed that Regan's left eyelid twitched ever so slightly. It was apparent she was struggling to keep her temper under control. She was doing a fair job of it too.

"Your brother bought you a new car," Alec commented cheerfully. "Wasn't that nice of him?" He added the question just to see how she would respond.

Her eyelid twitched again. "Yes," she said, all but choking on the word.

"It's a Beemer," Henry announced. He was looking at the emblem on the key ring.

When Regan didn't immediately show any reaction to that news, Henry thought she didn't understand. "You know what I'm talking about, right? A Beemer's a BMW."

She didn't trust herself to speak, and so she simply nodded. She was at a loss for words and so furious with her brother she wanted to scream. His audacity was stunning. Why was he so hell-bent on running her life?

"Regan, are you okay? You've got a real funny look in your eyes," Henry said.

"I think she's still reeling from the surprise," Alec said. He was trying to be diplomatic. In reality, she looked as if she wanted to kill someone.

Henry couldn't quite contain his eagerness. "Yes, I guess I would be reeling too. A Beemer costs a small fortune." He turned to Regan again and said, "Aiden didn't mention what color the car was, and I didn't think to ask him until after he left."

She took another deep breath. "The color isn't important."

"Would you like me to test drive it for you?" Henry asked. "I mean, you know, just to see if the car measures up. Aiden told me it's already insured, and I've got the time. My desk is clear, and I'm all caught up."

The kid was dying to drive the car, and judging from the look in Regan's eyes, she was dying to get her hands on her brother's neck.

Alec couldn't help but be impressed with her restraint. Keeping all that anger bottled up inside couldn't be good for her, though. And what was her brother's problem? Alec thought it was damned gutsy for him to have her car towed away, no matter how old or junky it was.

Not my worry, he told himself. He was out of here in less than a month, and he wasn't going to get involved with anyone before he left. Every family had problems, of course, but Regan's brother put a whole new spin on the word "dysfunctional." Alec couldn't imagine one of his brothers or sisters having his car towed away. If they did, he'd have to kick some serious butt. Aiden didn't seem to have any problem interfering in Regan's life, however. Were her other brothers like him? Three men trying to run her life. Good Lord. If that were true he couldn't help but feel sorry for her . . . and for any man who tried to get close to her.

But not his concern, he reminded himself. No, sir. No problem, no worries. Yeah, that was going to be his motto for the remainder of his time in Chicago. He'd do his job to the best of his ability and then get out. Sounded simple enough.

"So what do you think, Regan?" Henry asked.

She mentally shook herself. "I'm sorry. What do I think about what?"

"Do you want me to test drive the new car for you?"

She forced a smile. It wasn't Henry's fault she had a jerk for a brother. "Yes, I do."

She dropped the keys into his hand, told him to be careful, and then slowly walked into her office and closed the door.

Henry was putting his blazer on as he headed for the door. "I won't be gone long," he told Alec.

"Wait a minute," Alec said.

Henry paused with his hand on the doorknob. "Yes?"

Alec tilted his head toward Regan's office. "Is she going to start throwing things, or is it safe for me to go in there?"

Henry laughed. "Regan throwing things? Like in a temper tantrum? She'd never do that. She never loses her cool, and she would never ever throw things. That's just not her style. She is angry, though, but I guess you could tell that."

"Yes, I could."

"Don't worry," he said. "She won't take it out on you."

That thought hadn't entered his mind. Alec considered himself a good judge of character, and it had taken him about five minutes to figure out that Regan didn't have a mean bone in her body. She could never deliberately hurt anyone. The way that her staff responded to her indicated she was kind and good-hearted. The problem, as he saw it, was that she was too sweet for her own good. She ought to find Aiden and give him hell for poking his nose into her affairs. Yeah, that's what she ought to do, but he doubted she would. She was too nice to ever blow up.

No, not his problem, he reminded himself. It wasn't his job to teach her how to stand up for herself. He did think it was odd, however, that growing up with three older brothers hadn't toughened her up.

He knocked on her office door but didn't wait for her to give him permission to enter. The sofa was calling his name. He remembered how comfortable it was, and while she worked, he was going to take a nap. Alec was a light sleeper. He wasn't concerned she would leave, because he'd be wide awake before she reached the door.

Regan was on the phone. Her face was flushed, and she was obviously agitated. She was pacing back and forth behind her desk. He heard her say, "Have him call me the second he returns," before she hung up the phone.

"Is everything okay?" he asked, knowing full well it wasn't.

"Yes," she said. "Everything's fine."

He leaned to the side to look behind her.

"What are you looking for?" she asked.

"I just wanted to see if your pants were on fire. You know," he drawled. " 'Liar, liar . . .' "

She smiled. "Everything isn't okay," she admitted. "I'd like to get my brother alone and . . ."

He was removing his jacket, but his eyes were locked on hers. "And what?"

She didn't answer.

"How do you get rid of it?" he asked then.

She pulled her chair out from behind her desk and sat down. "Get rid of what?"

"The tension, the frustration," he said. "Or do you keep it all bottled up inside? If that's the case, you'd better find a way to get rid of it, or you're going to die young. Stress will kill you."

"I take a yoga class."

He laughed. "Yeah, well, you need a little more than yoga with those brothers of yours. Do they all interfere, or is it just the oldest, Aiden?"

She didn't pretend not to know what he was talking about. "All of them," she said. "And it's getting tiresome."

"I would think so."

"What do you suggest I do?"

He draped his jacket over the back of a chair and started working on his tie.

"About your brothers?"

"No, about stress . . . tension."

He suddenly realized he was breaking his own rule of not getting involved, but he couldn't stop himself. "Stop being so nice."

She looked surprised and also pleased. "You think I'm nice?"

"Being nice isn't always a good thing."

She leaned back in her chair and folded her arms. "What about you? You're in a high-stress job. How do you get rid of all the tension?"

"I shoot bad guys, and I get to break a lot of heads . . . and noses and arms."

She laughed and shook her head. "You do not. I've got news for you, Detective. You're not such a tough man. You're actually kind of sweet."

Now it was his turn to laugh. "Sweet? That's a new one. I'm definitely not sweet. I've been told I can be a real mean mother . . ."

"Yes?"

"Trust me on this. I can be mean, real mean."

She didn't believe him, but she wasn't going to argue. She realized he had to be tough because of his job, but she also sensed that there was an ingrained goodness and decency about him.

Alec stretched his shoulders and rolled his head, trying to work out the knot in the back of his neck. Regan was distracted by his broad shoulders. The man was way too sexy for his own good.

Get control of your thoughts, girl, she told herself. She cleared her throat, straightened in her chair, and folded her hands on the desk. "You don't need to stay, Detective."

"Alec," he reminded her.

"Okay," she said. "You don't need to stay, Alec. I'll be fine here. I'm sure you have better things to do than babysit me."

"You're still not catching on, are you? You're not getting rid of me. The only place I'm going is to your sofa." He added, "And just so you understand, I'm with you until you're bedded down for the night."

"Are you going to tuck me in?"

She was actually being a bit sarcastic, but he didn't take it that way. "That depends on you," he said.

His eyes sparkled with devilment. She swallowed. "Oh?"

She inwardly groaned. Was that the best she could come up with? *Oh?* Sophie would know what to say, and she'd say it in a teasing, come-get-me voice.

Alec leaned against the side of her desk. "How long have you been living here?"

"A while." She didn't want to explain why. She picked up a stack of what looked like messages and began to go through them.

"So how come?"

Ignoring him hadn't worked. He was still half sitting on the side of her desk while he waited for her to explain. She watched him pull his tie loose and drop it on the corner of her desk. She wouldn't be surprised if he kicked off his shoes next.

"Could you get any more comfortable?"

"Yes, I could. So how come?"

He definitely wasn't going to give up. "I had an apartment . . ."

"Yes?"

She sighed. "But I moved back home when my mother became ill."

He frowned. "Was she alone?"

"No. She had nurses and a full staff to see to her every need, and my stepfather, Emerson, was still living there, but she wanted me close to her . . . until it was over."

"And when was it over?"

"Eleven months ago."

"And your stepfather?"

She stiffened. "What about him?"

Alec knew he'd poked a sore spot. Her body language intrigued him. She looked as tightly wound as a clock spring. "I just wondered what happened to him."

"Nothing happened to him. He's still living in the house."

"With the staff?"

"Yes," she said.

"That must be lonely for him."

She scoffed. "He isn't lonely."

"How come?" he prodded.

"He lives there with his new wife."

"Ah." Now he understood the reason for her prickly, uptight attitude.

He said the obvious. "He didn't mourn long, did he?"

He'd hit a nerve. Regan decided not to mince words. "No, he didn't mourn long. In fact, he didn't mourn at all. He was never faithful to my mother for the very short time they were married, and he was already sleeping with Cindy before my mother became ill."

"And he married Cindy."

"Yes."

"When?"

She was as stiff as a surfboard again. "Three days after the funeral."

Man, that was cold, he thought. "I guess it bothers you to talk about this, doesn't it."

"It's a little late for that question, isn't it? How come you're so curious about my family?"

"I'm not curious about your family."

"Oh? Then why all the questions —"

He cut her off. "I'm curious about you."

It wasn't what he said so much as how he said it, with a warm glint in his eyes she couldn't quite decipher. Was he flirting with her? No, of course he wasn't. Why would he be interested in her when he could have any woman he ever wanted? And probably had. She was such a straitlaced . . . nerd. Yes, a nerd, she thought, especially when compared to her friends. Regan believed that everything about her was ordinary, boringly ordinary.

She did have money, however, as Spencer and Walker pointed out every chance they got, and Regan was sure money was why most men paid attention to her. At various functions they swarmed around her like hungry bees. Spencer called them parasites. Alec wasn't a parasite, though, and he didn't seem to be the least impressed with her money. The man was simply being a good detective, and that was why he asked so many personal questions.

"You've been assigned to protect me," she said. "And that's why you're so curious about me."

He didn't miss a beat. "That too," he said as he turned and walked across the office.

She swiveled in her chair to face the computer and pretended to be busy. Out of the corner of her eye she watched him. He plumped a couple of pillows and sat down on the sofa with a loud sigh.

"Damn, this is comfortable," he said. "So tell me, Regan. How long was your stepfather married to your mother?"

She didn't look at him when she answered. "Long enough to think he should get half of everything she owned."

"Is there a legal battle brewing?"

"I know he's consulted a couple of attorneys in hopes that one of them will find a way to break the prenup. By now he must know that my mother didn't own much of anything, not even the house she lived in."

"The house Emerson's living in with Cindy?"

"Yes."

"Huh. So who owns it?" Before she could answer, he said, "Aiden? Or do you and all your brothers own it jointly?"

"All of us."

He leaned forward. "And yet you're the one who moved out?"

"Yes, that's right."

She turned back to the computer screen, hoping that he would let the subject drop.

No such luck. "So how come?"

She began to laugh. "You just don't give up, do you? No wonder you're a good detective."

"How do you know I'm good?"

"I just do."

"Not good," he said, and in a burst of ego, he added, "Great."

She laughed again. "I wish I had your confidence."

"You still haven't answered my question," he reminded her.

He took his loafers off, swung his feet up on an ottoman, and stacked his hands on his chest.

"How come I moved out of the house? I promised my mother that I would let Emerson stay on in the house for a year. She hoped that he would be able to get it together in that time."

"You mean get a job?"

"Yes," she said. "She never knew he cheated on her, at least I don't think she did, and she certainly didn't think he would remarry so quickly."

"Aiden agreed to this year plan?"

"Of course. It's what our mother wanted. Why wouldn't he agree?"

"He seems to be the one who calls all the shots and runs things around here."

"He's the most ambitious one in the family and certainly the most driven," she said. Frowning, she added, "But you're right. He does like to run things around here. I just wish . . ."

"What?"

"I just wish I understood why he thinks he can run my life."

"That one's easy."

"Oh? Why then?"

"You let him."

Chapter Twenty-six

Regan had cleared her desk. Every piece of paperwork had been signed, mailed, or filed; every e-mail had been read, deleted, or answered, and every phone call had been returned.

She had miscalculated and had thought it would take her several more days to get everything done, and she wasn't happy about being caught up. She wanted to bury herself in work to keep busy. An idle mind . . . worries. At least hers did. She drummed her fingertips on the desk.

She still hadn't openly acknowledged that she was in danger and that she needed a bodyguard, because to do so would put it all right there in front of her face, and she would have to deal with it. She knew she was being foolish, maybe even a little cowardly, but at the moment she didn't particularly care. She was scared and feeling powerless, and that was just plain awful.

Alec closed the magazine he was reading and then picked up a remote and turned to her. He saw her expression and asked,

"What's the matter?"

"Nothing."

He knew she had to be feeling caged. Every move she made was being watched. He decided he wouldn't press. "Okay," he said. He held up the remote and asked, "Where's the television hidden?"

"Push the top button," she said.

He was intrigued. As soon as he pushed the button, a seam in the wall adjacent to the window slowly slid back to reveal his dream come true. An entertainment center filled with all the latest technology. He whistled over the size of the flat-screen plasma TV.

He settled back to watch the news but glanced at her again and noticed the frown hadn't gone away. "Come on. Tell me. What's the matter?"

"Nothing. I was just thinking."

"About what?"

She wasn't going to tell him the truth — that she worried she wouldn't have enough courage when she needed it — or admit that she was afraid of being afraid, because she knew he wouldn't understand. How could he? He probably put himself in harm's way all the time. He was used to danger, and he was used to standing up when it mattered.

Was he ever afraid? Probably, but she doubted that fear would ever stop him from doing what was needed, and wasn't that what courage was all about — not letting the fear stop you from doing the right thing?

"Regan?"

She realized she hadn't answered him. "I was thinking about that expression, an idle mind . . ."

"Gathers no moss?"

She smiled. "I don't think that's how it goes."

She lost him then. The sports portion of the news came on, luring him like a siren with the promise of scores and clips from all the games. As though in a trance, he immediately turned back to the television screen. She was exasperated. What is it with men? At least the men in her life. Alec's behavior was like Aiden's and Spencer's. No matter how busy her brothers were, they stopped everything at the sight of a baseball, football, or soccer ball. Any kind of sports game grabbed them. They were addicted to the Sports Channel and couldn't go to sleep without knowing the latest scores. She had a feeling her bodyguard had the same affliction.

Regan dusted her desk blotter and then

began to turn one of the pages of her *Far Side* calendar back and forth while she surreptitiously studied Alec. He had a beautiful profile, she decided. A nice, straight nose, a great mouth. His hair was dark and thick and kept drooping down on his forehead. He needed a haircut. His hair was given to curl, and she had the insane urge to touch it. Were other women drawn to him the way she was? No doubt, she thought. With his good looks and his sexy aura, he probably had women falling all over him. Oh, she knew his type. He had that bad-boy, love-them-and-leave-them thing down pat. How many tears had been shed over him? How many hearts had he broken?

"You about finished?" His gaze never left the television when he asked the question.

How long had she been staring at him? "Just about," she answered as she quickly looked at her desk and began to shuffle papers around.

She was saved from having any other discussion about her behavior when her phone rang. She almost fell out of her chair when she lunged for the receiver.

Cordie was on the line. Just hearing her voice made Regan feel better.

"Are you all right?" she asked. "Is Sophie?"

"Yes, we're both fine."

"You took your time calling me back. I've been worried."

"Worried about what? Everything's fine, and I only just now checked my messages. Sophie and I have been real busy, and I've got loads to tell you, but first things first. I've got to make you feel bad because you didn't come with us."

Regan smiled. She was so relieved to know her friends were okay. Now that she had Cordie on the phone, Regan could take her time telling her everything that had happened.

"And how are you going to make me feel bad?"

"The weather. It's beautiful here, and do you know why?"

"I'll bite. Why?"

"It isn't raining. How is it there?"

"Eighty degrees, not a cloud in the sky, absolutely no humidity, and there's a soft breeze —"

"Tell the truth," Cordie interrupted.

Regan laughed. "We're supposed to get more rain tonight, and it's chilly here. And now I do feel bad because I didn't go with you. Satisfied?"

"Yes," she said. "And since it's still so awful in Chicago, I'm staying here, until I run out of sunscreen, anyway."

"If you're about finished talking about the weather, I've got some news."

"Oh? How much do you want to bet my news is bigger?"

"I doubt that, but you go first."

"We're already piling up evidence against Shields."

Regan straightened in her chair. "Really? So soon?"

"Yes," she answered, her voice brimming with enthusiasm. "It was easy, too, because Shields always has the women he brings down here stay at the same hotel. It's called The Murdock, and it's a small, family-owned place with lots of charm. Most of the staff have been working there for years. They're very loyal."

"And that's important because . . . ?"

"They remember past guests."

"Okay. Go on."

"We've gotten the names of two women Shields had down here last year, and guess what? They were both widowed, and they were both very rich. Oh, and we also got copies of Shields's bank accounts."

"You what?"

Cordie repeated what she'd just said. Then Regan blurted, "That's illegal."

Alec was watching her. She was pretty

sure he'd heard what she'd said. She smiled at him, then turned her chair to face the wall and lowered her voice. "How in heaven's name did you get his bank records? If you aren't careful, you'll both end up in jail."

"We are being careful," Cordie assured her. "We didn't break into the bank to get the records. Someone got them for us."

"Who?"

"A friend of a friend of Sophie's father," she said. "And so far we know for a fact that Shields has taken huge amounts of money from these two women."

"How do you know that?"

"With copies of the checks the women wrote. The bank keeps records, for heaven's sake, especially when the deposits are so large."

"But how did you get copies of the checks? No, don't tell me. I don't want to know."

"Sophie's dad has a lot of friends down here."

"That's not good."

"I know, but I'm watching out for Sophie. It's okay."

"And who's looking out for you?"

"Regan, stop worrying."

"Where's Sophie now?"

"She went back to The Murdock. We already have the names and addresses of the two women we can prove gave Shields money, but Sophie wanted to make sure there weren't any others. So what do you think? We've made a good start, haven't we?"

"I'd say so," she replied, "but . . ."

"We haven't seen Shields yet, but we know he's inside his beach house because we've seen his bodyguards, Huey and Louie, on the beach. They're wearing their uniform black suits and dark ties and sunglasses while they walk on the sand. They look like Feds."

" 'Huey and Louie'?"

"I've got to call them something, don't I?"

"I guess so. Do they stay out on the beach all day?" She could picture them melting in the hot sun.

"No, they have a schedule. During the day they come out every hour on the hour, and they stay outside ten minutes tops. Shields obviously isn't feeling very safe if he has to have his bodyguards with him all the time. Sophie thinks he's becoming paranoid because of all the horrible things he's done."

"But you haven't seen him?"

"No."

"Thank God," she whispered.

Cordie didn't hear her. "Here's the odd thing. Shields's neighbor to the south is keeping tabs on the bodyguards —"

"How did Sophie get the neighbor to do that?"

"She asked. They're very friendly down here."

"Is the neighbor a man?"

Cordie laughed. "Yes," she said. "Anyway, Huey and Louie have stopped patrolling. Something is definitely going on, but we can't figure out what yet."

"Are you finished with your news? Is it my turn?"

"Just one more thing. A woman has visited Shields twice now. Sophie swears she saw her at the seminar. I don't remember her," she said. "But Sophie is much better with faces than I am. Anyway, the woman is staying at The Murdock and we're pretty sure she's Shields's next target."

"He doesn't waste any time, does he?" Regan kicked off her heels, crossed one leg over the other, and began to swing one foot nervously back and forth.

"No, he doesn't. Sophie's becoming obsessed about spotting him. She's jogged on the beach behind his house a couple of times, but she hasn't had any luck. We're going to take one of the boats out to-morrow with our binoculars and see if we can spot him inside. The back of his house faces the ocean, and it's all glass. If he's in there, we'll see him. Knowing Sophie, if she doesn't spot him soon, she'll jog right up to his front door and start pounding."

Regan almost dropped the phone as she jerked upright in her chair. "Oh, no, she mustn't do that."

"All right, I'm finished. Now it's your turn. Try to beat my news."

"Okay. Remember that little exercise we did during Shields's reception?"

"The make-a-list-of-the-people-you-want-dead exercise?"

"That's the one."

"What about it?"

"A madman got hold of my murder list and is now killing everyone on it."

A long silence followed her announcement, and then Cordie said, "Okay, you win."

"I thought I might."

"Wait a minute. You are joking, aren't you?"

Regan's voice dropped to a whisper. "I wish to God I were. It's true, though."

"Tell me."

Her friend didn't say another word

during Regan's lengthy explanation of what had happened, but she did gasp, several times as a matter of fact, and when Regan was finished, she whispered back, "Who else did you have on your list?"

Regan told her and then said, "I was so certain there was a connection between Sweeney's murder and Shields."

"But now you're not so sure?"

"I'm not sure of anything. Until we know, you and Sophie have got to stay as far away from him as possible."

"No wonder we can't find Shields, and no wonder his bodyguards aren't patrolling the beach. I'll bet the police have warned them, and they've all gone into hiding."

A minute later, just as Regan was about to hang up, Sophie got back to the condo. Cordie shouted at her that Regan was on the phone. Sophie picked up the extension in the kitchen.

"Hey, guess what?" She didn't give Regan time to answer. "Shields and his bodyguards have left the island, and no one, not even the police, know where they went."

"How'd you find that out?" Cordie asked.

"A friend of a friend."

"Are you going to tell her or should I?"

Cordie asked Regan.

"I'll hang up and, you can —"

"Tell me what?"

While Regan waited, Cordie repeated what Regan had told her. Sophie was shocked into silence.

"What are the police there saying?" she finally asked.

"Detective Buchanan is hoping that whoever sent the e-mail and the fax will try to contact me again. Detective Wincott agrees."

"Okay, who's Detective Wincott?"

"He's in charge of the investigation."

"And Detective Buchanan? Is he his partner or something?" Cordie asked.

"No, he's my temporary bodyguard."

"Dear God . . ."

"It's okay, Cordie."

"We're coming home on the next flight."

"No, Sophie, don't do that. Since Shields has already left the island, you're probably as safe there as any place."

Cordie added, "She thinks Shields is somehow involved in what's been happening because Sweeney was investigating him."

"I admit, it's not a firm connection," Regan said.

"Sweeney hadn't done anything yet, so

how could Shields have known about him?" Sophie asked.

"I still think we should pack it up and head back to Chicago. We should be there with you, Regan."

"No," she replied. "Stay there and finish what you started. What you're doing is important, and it sounds like you're making great progress."

"We are," Sophie agreed. "But we'll need to stay here another week, maybe even two. There's so much cross-checking to do with names and dates, and now that I've got the hotel's registration records that go way back —"

"Did a friend of a friend get those for you too?"

"No," Sophie said. "I just asked, and they handed them over."

"We are making progress," Cordie said. "And, Sophie, you did want to talk to that woman who's staying at The Murdock, and you better do that soon before she finds out Shields has left. This is the perfect opportunity, and we both want to know what Shields promised her."

"Wouldn't it be something if she would help us?"

"We could nail him."

"Call me with updates, okay?"

"Wait, Regan. Are you going to be okay?" Cordie asked.

"I'll be fine." She looked at her empty desk and decided to lie to ease Cordie's anxiety. "I've got so much work to do. I won't have time to worry, and I'm perfectly safe in my office."

"Okay," Cordie said. "No matter what, we'll be home in time for the country club charity thing, but that's two full weeks away."

"By then, the police will probably have the madman behind bars," Sophie said.

Regan hoped she was right. By the time she finally hung up the phone, Alec had stopped watching the television. She stood, stretched, and then told him about some of her conversation with her friends.

"The police down there verified that Shields and his bodyguards have left the island. Do you think Cordie and Sophie will be safe?"

"Yeah, I think they will be, as long as . . ."

"As long as what?"

He decided to be blunt. "As long as they stay away from you."

Chapter Twenty-seven

Regan was reaching her breaking point. Two full weeks had passed since she had received the photo of Sweeney, and her nerves were becoming more and more frayed. One day dragged into another and another. She thought she was going to go stir-crazy being cooped up inside the hotel. Detective Wincott would check in periodically and let her know how the investigation was going. The police had ruled out any connection between Shields and Sweeney, which meant that the killer was still out there, and still unknown. Waiting for something to happen was making her anxious and irritable.

Keeping busy helped, and since she was caught up with work, she decided to tear her office apart and reorganize. Behind one long wall were file cabinets crammed with papers, and all of them needed to be cleaned out.

Regan really got into the task. Some of the files had already been transferred to discs, and those files could be shredded. Other files needed to be consolidated, and she was determined to see that was done too. There was a system to her reorganization, but she was the only one who knew what it was. There were stacks of file folders and papers all over her office floor. It had become an obstacle course from Henry's office to her desk, but she felt she was making headway.

She wasn't making any headway with her brothers, however, and she was developing a real love/hate relationship with them. Spence had been delayed in Melbourne, but he called her at least three times a day just to check in and make certain she was doing okay. Walker was also calling. His messages always had the same theme. He wouldn't give up on the idea of her traveling with him until this situation was resolved.

After two weeks of the constant phone calls, Regan decided she was through placating them. She asked Henry to screen her calls and not put Spencer or Walker through.

Aiden was also making her nuts. She wanted to have a long talk with him. She had had it with his constant interference, and she was determined to make him listen to what she had to say. Then she would go to work on the other two. She didn't care if it was bad timing or not. She was sick and tired of all three of her brothers trying to run her business and her personal life, and if she wanted anything to change, she would have to start with the most aggressive brother, Aiden. If she could just get him to stop interfering, then the other two, like dominos, would follow his lead.

That was the plan, anyway . . . if Aiden would stand still long enough to listen. He had canceled a business trip to stay in Chicago and was looking in on her a hundred times a day, and yet he just couldn't find the time to sit down and have a conversation. He knew where she was every second, and when he couldn't personally look in on her, the security guards he'd hired kept tabs for him. She knew he was worried, and in this instance, she understood why he was being so overly protective. What she found amazing, however, was the way he could vanish whenever she asked for a few minutes of his time.

Emily sent a message through Henry that Aiden simply didn't have time to listen to Regan's petty complaints. Henry had been furious when he conveyed it.

"I've finally figured out her plan," Henry said. "She wants you out of here, and she's going to do anything and everything to make that happen."

"She does know I'm Aiden's sister, doesn't she?" She was teasing to let Henry know she wasn't upset.

"Of course she knows, but when she started, she didn't know who you were. She was rude and obnoxious. Since she can't fix the past and she knows you don't like her, she's got to make you look incompetent. That way, Aiden won't listen to you about anything, including your opinion of her."

Before Regan could say a word, Henry continued. "She's after your brother. She wants to marry him, and you, Regan, are messing with her plans."

"Aiden will figure out what she's doing, and he would never have said 'petty complaints.' "

Aiden was deliberately avoiding Regan, though, giving her time to cool down. He had to have known how furious she was about her car — she still couldn't believe he'd had the audacity to have it towed away — but he also knew that if he waited long enough, she would eventually get over it and let it wash over her the way she let everything else these days.

She knew what the problem was. She loved her brothers and would do anything for them. She went to great lengths to keep them happy, even to the point of trying to change who she was.

When she was growing up, Aiden had always been the one she went to with her problems, probably because he was the oldest and more of a father figure. He was also the most rigid. He couldn't stand to see her cry — which she seemed to be able to do at the drop of a hat back then — but over the years she'd tried really hard to learn to hold her feelings in. Sometimes, though, they bubbled to the surface.

Regan took after the Hamilton side of the family. They were all emotional twits, at least that was what Spencer had told her. The Madisons, on the other hand, were stoic and very disciplined. They were also workaholics like Aiden and Spencer. No one knew what side of the family Walker took after, but it was theorized that he was a throwback to a great-great-uncle who began to sow his wild oats when he hit puberty and didn't stop until he was on his deathbed. It was rumored that he was propositioning a young, pretty nurse when he took his last breath.

At the moment, Regan didn't want to be related to anyone. The conditions of the will had put her in a no-win position with her brothers, and just as Alec had said, the stress would do her in if she didn't find an outlet.

Her brothers weren't the only ones giving her trouble. She was also developing a love/hate relationship with Alec. The truth was, she loved being with him — he was smart and funny and sweet and kind — but she hated the reason why he was always there at her side.

For two weeks now, she and Alec had been inseparable. He refused to take any days off and only left her after a policeman had been posted on her floor, between the elevator doors and the stairs, which were the only ways to get to her suite. Alec was the last person she saw every night before she locked her door, and the first person she saw in the morning when she stepped out into the hall.

He was definitely growing on her, but she kept wondering — would he even have given her the time of day if it hadn't been his job to protect her? If he had met her under different circumstances, would he have been interested? Would he have wanted to ask her out?

Henry also liked having him around. The two seemed to talk for hours about sports trivia and rock bands, and when Henry was struggling over a paper he was writing for a summer political science course, Alec offered to help him. Before long, Henry was asking his advice about girlfriends and his own future.

In the evenings, Regan and Henry and Alec changed into running clothes and worked out together in the gym. Alec beat the socks off her and Henry on the track. He was in much better shape than she was and gleefully pointed that out, several times, as a matter of fact. She used her recent surgery as an excuse for having to hold back, but each day she went a little faster and a little farther. There was an annual charity race coming up, she told him, and she wanted to walk as much of the course as she could.

Regan knew she couldn't follow her normal routine, and she cooperated as much as she could, but there were a couple of events she refused to cancel or postpone because she felt they were too important. One of them took place at the hotel, and that made things easier for Alec.

It was toward the end of the second week, and Regan was getting ready for the reception she was hosting that evening. She wanted everything to go smoothly. Alec helped her measure the spacing between hooks on the walls in the corridor leading from the lobby to the gift shop, and when they were finished there, he followed her to the atrium and she checked the measurements there. She had already had the electricians work on the gallery lighting, and Frank from maintenance was happy to lend a hand.

"Are you going to tell me what we're doing and why?" Alec asked as he handed her the measuring tape again.

"We're measuring the distance between the paintings one last time just to make sure the spacing is right. I don't want them to look crammed together."

"Where are these paintings?"

She smiled. "You'll see."

He could feel her excitement, and his curiosity was aroused. He didn't even mind that he had to wear his suit a little longer.

Regan changed into a simple black dress with a jewel neckline. Because she was running late, she didn't have time to put her hair up. She brushed it, sprayed it, and then put on lip gloss and blush and was on her way out the door with five minutes to spare.

The reception began at seven o'clock. Alec wasn't happy about the crowd gathered in the atrium. She was ecstatic. When she tried to walk away from him, he grabbed her hand and forced her in to his side.

He leaned down and whispered, "Stay with me."

She nodded to let him know she had heard what he said.

They were both getting speculative looks from men and women. Regan introduced Alec as her friend, but Henry was being plied with questions. Was Regan serious about this man? Who exactly was he, and what did he do for a living?

Henry's friend Kevin had also been invited, and he helped Henry with last-minute details.

After Regan had welcomed her guests, she took Alec's hand and led him to the first of twelve beautifully framed paintings. The cream-colored walls came to life next to the vibrant and joyful colors. Yes, joyful, Alec thought as he studied one bold abstract. The names of the artists were printed in black block letters on a white square plate underneath each painting.

"I've never heard of any of these artists," he said.

"You'll get to meet them before they become famous. Do you have a favorite painting?"

He shook his head. "I like all of them."

Henry and Kevin stood together while they waited for a quiet moment to talk to Alec. Kevin's hands were jammed into his pockets, and he was shifting from foot to foot.

"Don't lose your nerve," Henry whispered. "Alec will help you. I know he will."

"I won't lose my nerve. I'm gonna do it. So when do you think —"

"After the presentation but before he takes Regan upstairs." Henry's gaze was on Regan and Alec. "They look good together, don't they?"

They were laughing and talking, and Henry noticed Regan taking Alec's arm as she guided him from picture to picture. They seemed so comfortable with each other. As they headed back to the atrium, Henry and Kevin intercepted them. Alec shook Kevin's hand when Henry introduced him. He could feel the kid trembling, but he already knew from the look in his eyes that he was scared.

"You look familiar," he said, thinking he might have busted him at one time.

"I work at The Palms," Kevin said. "Maybe you saw me there."

"Maybe."

Regan didn't seem to notice there was

anything wrong. She spotted a woman who nodded to her. "They're here," she told Henry.

"Maybe later we could . . . uh, you know, maybe talk," Kevin said to Alec.

"Yeah, okay. Later."

"Are you ready, Henry?" Regan asked.

"Let's do it."

Alec stayed by Regan's side as they made their way through the crowd to the podium. The guests had all been plied with food and drink, and the mood was quite jovial.

The uninvited guest stood in the crowd watching her, waiting for his opportunity. Slowly he maneuvered his way toward her, closer and closer. For a few minutes he stood just feet away pretending to admire a painting while he eavesdropped on her conversation with a man she called Alec. If he could just get close enough to touch her, maybe he could separate her from the throng of people, get her alone, but each time he made his move, the man she was with got in the way and wouldn't let her out of his sight. She was the center of attention, the star. Wherever she turned, there was another guest eager for a moment of her time. It took him twenty minutes to weave his way close again, but just as he was extending his hand to take hers and request a moment of privacy, Alec ushered her in the opposite direction. His frustration grew. He couldn't get to her. Tonight would not be the night. He would have to wait for another opportunity, but eventually the right moment would come, and he would be ready. Unnoticed, he slipped out the side door.

Henry motioned to the string quartet to take a break. He stood next to Regan as she once again welcomed everyone, and then she introduced Henry and moved back so that he could speak into the microphone.

As he was talking about the importance of art and music in the public schools, the twelve artists filed in and stood in front of the podium. With a great deal of pride in his voice, Henry presented each one.

Alec was impressed and a little stunned. Not one of the artists was more than fourteen or fifteen years old. Now he understood what Regan had meant when she said he would meet them before they became famous, for their amazing talent was just beginning to blossom. The paintings were for sale, the price of each steep, but

every dollar would go to the art depart-
ments in the schools the artists repre-
sented. Henry also introduced the teachers
involved in the new program and explained that the artists would receive
scholarships and art supplies.

Every painting had been sold by nine
o'clock. Regan was thrilled and so proud
of Henry, she hugged him. She kept giving
him all the credit, but Henry told Alec that
Regan had come up with the idea. He'd
merely implemented it.

The party was over by ten, and though it
wasn't all that late, Regan was tired and
wanted to go up to her suite, take a hot
shower, and fall into bed.

They were crossing the lobby together
with Henry and Kevin trailing behind. She
was telling Alec the reason behind the art
project.

"Whenever schools run into financial
trouble, they take away money for art and
music. The administrators . . . they
forget."

"Forget what?" he asked.

Henry answered. "It's like Regan says.
Education isn't just about feeding the
brain. Art and music feed the heart and
the soul."

Alec agreed. Then Henry said, "There

will always be paintings hanging on those walls, and when one sells, we'll put another one up. It will be an ongoing thing. It's a cool idea, isn't it? The goal is to do this in all the Hamilton hotels."

Kevin nudged Henry and whispered, "I want to get this over with."

Henry spoke up. "Hey, Regan, how about stopping for a drink?"

The bar was just off the lobby, and there were only a couple of people inside. Alec suggested they get a table and order a drink, a nonalcoholic drink he stressed.

Alec squeezed Regan's hand. "If you want me to take you upstairs, I'm sure the policeman is already stationed outside your door. I'll check your suite, lock you in, and come back down here. The guys won't mind waiting."

"That's okay," she said. "I'll get a drink with you."

The bar was dark and cozy, the walls a rich walnut paneling. Candlelight flickered softly from votives on all the tables. Henry rushed ahead and found a table tucked in the corner that faced the side exit. He pulled out a chair for Regan, but Alec didn't approve. He wanted her to sit with her back against the wall. Once Regan was settled, she expected the three men to join her, but none of them sat down. Henry and Kevin had their heads down and were looking very ill at ease.

"What's going on?" she asked.

Henry darted a quick look at Alec before answering. "What it is . . ." he began, and then nudged Kevin.

"Yes?" she asked.

She marveled at the change in Henry. When he had stood at the podium and had spoken to the guests tonight, he had been polished and eloquent. Now he was acting like an insecure teenager. Henry only reverted to that behavior when something was very wrong or had him riled up.

"I just thought that maybe Kevin would want to talk to Detective Buchanan for a couple of minutes, and he said okay, about talking . . . you know, so Kevin can run something by him."

Henry seemed to need her approval, and so she said, "That's fine."

Alec put his hand on Henry's shoulder. "Henry, sit with Regan while Kevin and I talk." He turned to Regan. "Don't you move," he said.

She rolled her eyes. Ordering her to stay put hadn't really been necessary, since he never let her out of his sight. He and Kevin went down the three steps to the corridor and stood off to the side. Alec towered over Kevin, so he leaned down to hear what he was saying.

Regan couldn't read anything in Alec's expression, but poor Kevin was clearly falling apart. His complexion went from ashen white to flushed red, and he was talking fast and gesturing with his hands. A tear slipped down his cheek, and he angrily wiped it away. Then he glanced at Regan. She quickly turned to Henry, so Kevin wouldn't know she had been watching him.

"Is Kevin in trouble?"

"Not Kevin . . . someone else. It's kind of private stuff, but he said I could tell you."

The waiter appeared with a small silver bowl filled with cashews. Henry ordered soft drinks for all of them and then sat back. He continued. "He's scared. His mother . . . you know, she left a couple of years ago. She just walked out."

"Yes, I know," Regan replied.

"His dad got a divorce, and that was a good move, and he got sole custody of the kids too. Anyway, Kevin's mother suddenly showed up again and she wasn't alone . . . and they're bringing the junk back into the house . . . you know, drugs."

"Why didn't Kevin's father — ?"

"Kick them out? He tried, but they aren't going anywhere. His dad farmed the kids out to friends, and Kevin thought maybe Alec could help him."

"Poor Kevin," she whispered. "I can't imagine how he must be feeling."

"He thinks he's playing it cool, but he isn't." Henry watched his friend for a minute and then turned back to Regan. "How do you do it?"

"Do what?"

"Stay cool. I mean, come on, you've got a nut out there doing crazy stuff. You've got a bodyguard and security —"

"I'm not cool about it," she said. "But I try not to dwell on it."

"Waiting for something to happen . . . that's what's scary. I get freaked out thinking about it. If anything happened to you, I don't know what I'd do. I mean . . ."

She put her hand on top of his. "It's going to be okay. You'll see."

She sounded as though she knew what she was talking about, but like Henry, she got scared thinking about it. Then she looked at Alec and she relaxed. As long as she was with him, she was safe.

The waiter placed the drinks on the table. She thanked him, picked up her glass, and took a sip. Her gaze kept going back to Alec. Henry noticed.

"What are you going to do when he leaves?"

"I guess someone else will be assigned to follow me around."

"That's not what I mean. Come on, Regan. You're talking to me. You don't have to pretend. I've been watching you two. You've got this connection. You know what I'm talking about?"

Oh, boy, did she. "I like him," she admitted. "He kind of grows on you, but he isn't at all my type."

"You mean the sterile type?"

She smiled. "What's that?"

"Every button buttoned, always in a suit and tie, and looking immaculate all the time. I used to think Aiden was the sterile type, but then I played rugby with him in that charity game, and man, did I change my mind. He was muddy and brutal. Definitely not the sterile type. And neither is Detective Buchanan — I mean Alec. He told me to call him Alec — I'll bet he'd be brutal on the field too."

"I'm sure he'd play to win," she agreed. "He is kind of . . . sloppy," she added, and almost made it sound like a compliment.

Henry finished his drink, then picked up

the one he'd ordered for Kevin and gulped it down in two swallows. He couldn't seem to figure out what to do with his hands. He lifted his empty glass, swirled the ice around a couple of times, and then put the glass back down. Regan handed him her drink, and he gulped that down too.

"I'm thirsty," he said.

"You're nervous."

"That too," he agreed.

Regan's heart went out to Kevin. He had backed away from Alec, but Alec grabbed his arm and shook his head. He put his finger in front of the teenager's face and started talking. Regan couldn't hear what he was saying, but Kevin appeared to be hanging on his every word. He didn't look as anxious or fearful.

Alec Buchanan was a good man. She felt a tightness in her throat as she watched him, and she suddenly realized that the attraction she'd felt for him had grown into something much more complicated.

"Here they come," Henry whispered.

Kevin came back into the bar first. His eyes were red. "We should probably go," he said to Henry.

"So should we," Alec said. "It's getting late."

Regan immediately stood. She said good

night to the boys. A few minutes later, Alec was seeing her to her suite.

"Listen, I'll be a little late in the morning. I've got some things to do . . . packing and stuff. I'll make sure the policeman on duty stays until I get here."

She had a feeling that the "stuff" had something to do with Kevin, but she wasn't going to ask.

"That's fine," she said.

"Good night, then."

He was pulling the door closed. "Wait," she said.

He stopped. "Yes?"

"Tomorrow . . . be careful . . . packing. Okay?"

"Yeah, okay."

She bolted the door and leaned against it. She knew she would be dreaming about him tonight, but she vowed that tomorrow she would take that step back and start being practical again. There was only one little problem with her decision. She didn't know how.

Chapter Twenty-eight

Henry told her what had happened. He rushed into her office, closed the doors behind him, and said, "I know you were worried about Kevin, so I just wanted you to know it all worked out."

She'd been searching through her desk drawers looking for her stash of M&M's. She immediately gave Henry her full attention. She looked up and saw how relieved Henry was. "That's good to know."

Henry wanted to talk. "Kevin is on his way up. That's okay, isn't it?"

"Of course it is."

"He said it was real bad for a while."

"It was?"

"Alec had it all set up. He told Kevin's dad to keep the kids out of there, and he did. Anyway, Kevin didn't want to leave, so he saw it go down."

"Was Kevin in the house while this was happening?"

"No," he said. "He was across the street, staying out of the way. I think maybe he was hiding so Alec wouldn't make him leave. He said that for a minute there he was afraid of Alec. I guess a couple of his mother's friends resisted, and Alec and the others with him had to get . . . uh, physical so they could get the cuffs on them. I sure wish I'd been there. Kevin said the look on Alec's face when he was . . . you know, having to get physical, was scary."

"I'm glad you weren't there," she said.

He pushed some papers out of his way and sat on the edge of her desk. "I'll bet they knew Kevin was there. Alec told Kevin's mother she'd get the opportunity to go into rehab, but she turned it down."

"How's Kevin doing?"

"He's okay. He's kind of come to terms with the way things have to be."

"You're a good friend, Henry."

"Yeah, well, he's helped me get through some tough times." He spotted Kevin in the outer office and said, "Kevin was okay with me telling you what happened, but . . ."

"I still won't mention anything," she assured him.

Regan bent down to check her bottom drawer for the M&M's, and when she looked up, she saw Alec standing next to Henry's desk talking to him. Kevin was there too, standing beside his friend.

Alec evidently hadn't gone home to

change clothes after the action at Kevin's house. He walked into her office, asked her if anything was going on, and then told her he'd dismissed the policeman and was taking over the bodyguard duty.

"Everything okay?" she asked.

"Yes," he said.

He looked comfortable in his jeans and T-shirt, but the gun and holster were very noticeable. He caught her staring at it. "It's part of the job, Regan."

"I know."

"Good, because you need to be okay with it."

Why was he getting all worked up? "What's the matter with you?"

He glanced into the outer office, saw Kevin, and shook his head. "Nothing's the matter. Some people just don't get the breaks they should. It was a bad way to start a morning, that's all."

"But it turned out all right?"

He shrugged, and that was the end of the conversation.

Alec could close up quicker than a clam. If he hadn't been so aggravating, she would have been impressed.

By midafternoon they had fallen back into their routine. Alec took a nap on her sofa while she cleaned out files.

That evening they went back to her suite, ordered pizza, popcorn, pop, and beer, and watched a movie. It was an old classic, a love story that made her cry and made him laugh. She accused him of not having a sentimental bone in his body, and he took that as a compliment.

The next night he chose the movie, and they watched another old classic. It wasn't a love story, though, it was a rip-'em-up, shoot-'em-up, skin-'em-alive movie with lots of special effects and aliens. He loved it.

Both of them had their feet propped up on the ottoman. She was barefoot; he was wearing socks. One had a big hole in it.

The credits were rolling when he asked, "Want to watch it again?"

She didn't think he was kidding. "No, thank you. It was too violent for me."

"You thought it was violent?" He acted surprised by her reaction.

"Alec, I counted thirty-two dead bodies."

"That's not so bad," he said with a straight face.

"Thirty-two in the first half hour. I stopped counting after that."

"Hey, they were aliens, and humans were their food source. What did you expect?"

"A little less face eating would have been nice."

"Yeah, but not as scary. Man, I loved those kinds of movies when I was a kid."

"You liked being scared?"

"Sure."

"What about nightmares?"

"I shared a room with my brother Dylan, and I figured if any monsters got in, the two of us could take them." He grinned as he added, "I was kind of cocky back then."

"Back then? I've got news for you, hotshot. You still are."

He laughed. "Hotshot? I come from a family of eight, and we were all hotshots at one time or another."

"Where do you fit in?"

"I'm third down from the top. There's Theo, the oldest, then Nick, then me, then Dylan, Mike, two sisters, Jordan and Sydney, and then baby Zack. He's still a wild man."

She nudged his shoulder. "I'll bet you gave your parents gray hair when you were a child. It's lucky you grew up. But I guess I did some pretty foolish things too."

"Is that a boast?"

When she didn't answer, he nudged her shoulder.

"I'm sure I was just as reckless as you

were," she finally said.

They then spent the next hour trying to one-up each other with the dumb stunts they'd pulled as children. Alec won hands down.

"How come all of your stories about your childhood involve power tools?" she asked.

He laughed. "Not all, just some. How come you never mention your parents in any of your stories?"

"I know I told you my father died when I was little, and my mother was never at home. I remember saying good night to her over the phone."

"Now, that's just sad."

She laughed. "No it isn't. It's just the way things were."

"That's no way for a little girl to grow up. How come you turned out so normal?"

"Who says I'm normal?"

"I do. I'll bet that I know just about everything there is to know about you." He was teasing her and being very arrogant. "I know what you like and what you don't like."

"I doubt that," she said.

"You hate salmon; you're allergic to strawberries, and you sneeze whenever you're around roses."

She retaliated. "You're a ketchup freak. You put it on everything, even peanut butter sandwiches. You hate thin-crust pizza, and you aren't allergic to anything."

"My turn again? Okay. You're very competitive; you're a full-blown liberal trapped in a family of conservatives, and honest to God, I don't know how that happened; you think you're good at hiding your emotions, but you're not, and you don't trust men or marriage."

He had touched a nerve, and she sounded a bit defensive when she responded. "You're far more competitive than I am; you think you're a liberal, but you're really very conservative; you have strong, unbendable values, and, Alec, I do trust some men."

"And marriage?"

"My mother was married twice, and both of her husbands were unfaithful. I don't want to make her mistakes, and I've learned there's no such thing as now and forever."

"Unless you marry the right man."

"That's the trick, isn't it? Knowing who's right and who's wrong. I think it's all a guessing game."

"No, it isn't," he argued. "And it's not a science either."

"Oh? Then how will you know who's right for you?"

"Are you asking me to describe my perfect woman?"

"There's no such thing as a perfect woman."

"Sure there is," he said.

"Oh? What does she look like?"

Their arms were touching, and neither one of them moved away. "She has dark hair."

"Yes?"

"And blue eyes. The color of violets. Incredible blue eyes."

He was leaning down toward her now, and she thought he might kiss her. She hoped he would.

"She's got a great body."

"Of course she does."

"Are you mocking my fantasy woman?"

"No," she said, smiling. "Go on. What else? Does she have magic powers?"

He leaned a little closer. "It's gonna be magic when we're together."

Oh, God, he was going to kiss her. She held her breath.

"And long legs," he said, his voice whisper-soft now.

His knuckles gently trailed down the side of her face. She had to force herself to stay still and not lean into the caress. Why wouldn't he kiss her? What was taking him so long?

"Does this perfect woman have a brain, or is not having a brain what makes her perfect."

"Of course she has a brain. She's very intelligent, has a quick wit, and she makes me laugh. She's got this wonderful combination of vulnerability and stubbornness. And that, Regan, is my perfect woman."

His mouth was just inches from hers. She closed her eyes and waited.

He tweaked her nose. "Got to go."

She blinked. "You . . . what?"

"Got to go."

He had his tennis shoes on, his laces tied, and was halfway to the door before she had her wits about her.

She stood, grabbed the bowl of popcorn she'd forgotten was in her lap, and put it on the coffee table.

"You have fun teasing me, don't you?"

He was tucking his T-shirt into his jeans. "You make it easy." He opened the door and stepped out into the hall. "Come here, Regan."

The way he was looking at her made her stomach flutter. She walked over to the door. "Yes?"

"Let me hear you flip the dead bolt."

"Oh. Yes, okay."

He pulled the door closed. "Night."

She could have sworn she heard him laughing as he walked away.

Chapter Twenty-nine

Regan awakened Saturday morning to another foul-weather day. There'd been so much rain in the past three weeks, she thought she might start sprouting mold. Her allergies were driving her nuts too. She sneezed at least five times before she'd even gotten out of bed, and when she looked at herself in the bathroom mirror, she grimaced. Her eyes were so bloodshot she looked as if she'd tied one on the night before. Tonight there was a large, formal charity event, and she hoped she could get her allergies under control, otherwise everyone would think she'd been crying.

A hot shower helped, but not much. She still had to use eyedrops, nasal spray, and her inhaler after she got dressed. She hated being dependent on medicines to control her allergies, but at least it wasn't an all-year thing. Spring was the worst, then fall, but she managed to function without any medication in the winter and summer.

She put her hair up in a ponytail and was ready to go.

Detective Wincott had insisted that Alec

take the day off, and when she left her suite to go downstairs to her office to tear through more files, she was accompanied by one of the new security guards Aiden had hired, an ex-policeman named Justin Shephard. Wincott approved because Justin used to be a cop and knew the job. She spotted Detective Wincott sprawled in a chair that faced the elevators. He stood and adjusted his tie as they walked closer. From his ragged appearance, Regan assumed his baby girl had kept him up yet another night.

"It's Saturday," she said. "You should be home with your family."

"I just put the family on a plane to go see my wife's mother, but if she were home, she'd have me fixing things, and I'm no good at that kind of stuff."

He stepped back as the elevator doors silently opened. "I'm filling in for an hour," he explained. "The officer who was supposed to hang with you today couldn't do it. His wife went into labor. I've got another man coming in."

Regan was dressed in jogging clothes, and Wincott frowned as he gave her the once-over.

"I thought we had an understanding," he said. "We're letting you go to that country club for the hospital thing, but running outside . . . that just can't happen."

The poor man looked as if he was bracing himself for an argument. She realized that if she insisted on running outside, the detective would have to run with her. From the shape he was in and the loafers he wore, she guessed he would have lasted about ten minutes tops.

"I don't plan to go outside at all today. We have a gym upstairs with a brand-new track, so when I do work out, I go up there."

He looked relieved. "Where are we headed now?"

"My office."

"Do you work every weekend?"

"I really don't have much to do, but since I'm stuck in the hotel, I'm reorganizing the office. This is our slow period. The charity projects and the work on the grants start all over in August."

"Bet that's a lot of hard work."

"Not really. Henry could do the grants blindfolded. As soon as he graduates from Loyola, he'll be taking over my job and working on his MBA. He'll hire someone to help, of course."

"And what will you do?"

She smiled. "I'm going global. I want to

set up our programs at all the hotels."

They reached the first floor and crossed the lobby to another bank of elevators. There was a security guard stationed in the alcove. Regan nodded to him as she walked past. She stepped into the elevator, inserted her key and pushed the button for the third floor.

"Do you think all of these extra guards are necessary, Detective Wincott?"

"Hey, if you're calling Buchanan, Alec, you can call me John, and I've got mixed feelings about the guards. If they don't get in our way, I guess they're okay."

The hallway was quiet, the doors to the other offices locked. Regan led the way into her office. Like Alec, Wincott immediately went to the sofa and made himself comfortable.

She grabbed another stack of files, dropped them on her desk, and sat down. Wincott had spotted the remote on a tray on the table and picked it up. She watched him look around.

"Hey, Regan . . ."

"Top button," she said as she opened the first folder.

He didn't understand her instructions. "Push the top button on the remote."

The second the panels began to move,

Wincott whistled. "Holy heaven. Did Alec know about this?"

She laughed. "Yes."

"No wonder he didn't want to share this detail. With this television and . . ."

"And what?"

Wincott shook his head. And "you," he was going to say. "The sofa. It's nice and soft. And this TV. It's bigger than my house."

"My brother Spencer had it installed a couple of months ago. He can't be in a room without a television blaring."

"I bet I'd like your brother."

"I'm sure you would. Spencer's the easy-going one," she explained.

"And he hangs out here when he's in town?"

She nodded. "Pretty much."

"Will the noise bother you while you're working?"

"Not at all."

Her computer screen was on and she immediately noticed a little square light blinking in the corner. Had she forgotten to turn it off? Or had someone else turned it on this morning?

She drummed her fingers on the mouse pad while she thought about it. Melissa, the computer tech from the police department, had told Alec that she had removed Regan from the loop.

Melissa had given Regan her card. She found it in her desk drawer and called the station. She didn't expect Melissa to be at her desk, but she wanted to leave a message asking her to call her Monday.

The woman answered on the second ring.

Regan told her who she was and said, "I didn't think you would be working on a Saturday."

"Then why did you call?"

Melissa's antagonistic tone didn't deter Regan. "I thought I would leave you a message, and you'd call me back on Monday. Since I have you on the phone, I wonder if you have a minute to answer a couple of questions for me. I could call back if it isn't convenient now."

"What kind of questions?"

"Computer questions."

"Yes, sure," she said. She sounded almost perky now. "I know everything there is to know about computers."

"That's what I understand," she said. "Detective Buchanan told me that you had discovered my e-mails were going to other terminals in the hotel."

"That's right," she said. "They went to

your assistant's terminal and to one in your brother's office. Did you want me to pinpoint the exact location?"

"No, that isn't necessary. I'm almost positive my e-mails were going to my brother Aiden's assistant."

"Okay, so what do you want?"

"This morning, when I came into my office, I noticed my computer was on."

"And you think maybe he or she hooked up again?"

"Yes."

"It's easy to find out. I mean, easy for me to find out," she qualified. "Are you sitting at your keyboard now?"

"Yes, I am."

"Then let's get started," she said impatiently.

For the next five minutes Melissa barked one order after another. Regan had to ask her to slow down a couple of times, but eventually she found the link that indicated someone else had locked onto her private and her business e-mails.

A couple of commands later, Regan knew exactly where her e-mails were going, and the link was broken. "Snoop's gone," Melissa said. "Now I'm going to talk you through this, and we're going to make it impossible for anyone else to get in there."

Melissa once again rattled off one command after another. Regan came up with a new password and typed it in.

"Okay, we're done. If you do forget the password, just get hold of me and I'll tell you what it is. You tell Henry what it is and to memorize it too."

Regan thanked her for her help and said, "If you ever want to change jobs, please let me know. We could certainly use you at the Hamilton."

"Honest? Or are you just saying that to be nice?"

"Yes, I do mean it."

"Would I get to travel to the other hotels, like the one in London and the one going up in Melbourne?"

"Yes, you would."

"Are there good benefits?"

"Oh, yes."

"We'll see," she said, and then abruptly hung up the phone.

Melissa's rude dismissal was both startling and somewhat humorous. Regan wasn't sure what "We'll see" meant, but she hoped the tech would seriously consider a move. She would be an asset. Regan was sure of that, and she also liked her. There didn't seem to be an artificial bone in her body, and it was refreshing to talk to someone who didn't have a hidden agenda.

While Regan had been working on her computer, her back was to the door, but when she swung around in her chair, Alec was standing there, not five feet away from her desk. He hadn't made a sound when he'd entered her office, and she didn't have any idea how long he'd been watching her.

She felt a surge of joy and hoped to heaven her reaction didn't show in her face.

He looked as if he was about to change the oil in his car or maybe make his third trip to the hardware store. His gray sweatshirt had seen better days.

He looked amazing . . . and just about perfect. Surely she could find something wrong with him. Okay, she thought, he looked like a slob, and that wasn't good, was it? Focus on the flaw, she told herself. Had he bothered to comb his hair? She didn't think so. There you go, she thought. Another flaw to think about. God, who was she kidding? The slob was sexy and gorgeous and —

"What are you doing here?" Wincott called out.

Alec kept his gaze locked on Regan as he answered, "Just checking. I thought you were asleep when I walked in here."

"Hey, I'm on duty. I heard you and I saw you."

"Yeah, right."

"I did. What did you mean when you said you were just checking? Checking what?"

Regan was the first to break eye contact. She leaned back in her chair and glanced over at Wincott, who admittedly did look half asleep. He had that glazed, I'm-watching-the-Sports-Channel look about him.

"Why *are* you here, Alec?" she asked.

"I was in the neighborhood."

"You live in the neighborhood, Buchanan," Wincott said without turning away from the TV.

"Yeah, well, I just wondered if anything was happening."

She shook her head. "I've just been finishing up some things."

"I thought you were going to pack today," Wincott said. He hit the mute button on the remote and stood. "I don't know why you think this is punishment. I feel like I've died and gone to heaven. Just being able to order room service and watching television without kids climbing all over me . . . yeah, this is heaven."

"Being with me is punishment?" she asked. She didn't sound wounded, just curious.

Alec shook his head. "Lewis gave me the assignment as punishment. He thought I'd hate it."

"And do you?"

He grinned. "What do you think?"

He didn't wait for her to come up with a clever reply but turned to Wincott and said, "You want to explain why the head of the investigation is doing bodyguard duty?"

"I'm filling in until a replacement gets here."

"Who's on for tonight?"

"Lyle's going to escort her to that formal thing she has to attend. He's probably out renting a tux now."

Alec shook his head. "Get him on the phone and tell him he's off the hook. I'll take her."

"Off the hook?" Regan repeated. She didn't know if she should be insulted or amused.

Alec ignored her and continued to frown at Wincott because he hadn't pulled out his cell phone and dialed Bradshaw yet. "Call him," he insisted.

"How come?"

"What do you mean, 'how come?' I just told you how come. I'm going to take her."

"And I'm still asking how come you're going to take her."

Alec was glaring now. He knew Wincott was deliberately baiting him, and from the stupid grin on his face, he was having a fine time doing it too. Alec had the sudden urge to punch him.

"Because I said I would take her, that's how come, and I've got a tux hanging in my closet."

"But Lyle's looking forward to tonight."

"I'll just bet he is," he snapped. "We both know Bradshaw's a . . ." He suddenly stopped.

"A what?" Wincott stretched as Alec crossed the room.

"Listen up," Alec said, his voice low so Regan wouldn't overhear. "Stop messing with me. Got that?"

"Last I checked, I was still in charge of this investigation, Alec."

"That's right, you are, John," he replied, stressing the detective's first name. "So go somewhere and investigate. I'm in charge of her protection, and you know what that means?"

Wincott grinned. "Yeah, yeah, I get it.

You're going to protect her."

"Make the call."

Alec turned to Regan and knew from her puzzled expression that she had heard every word of the exchange and most likely didn't understand. She probably thought he was out of his mind, and maybe he was. At the moment he didn't care. He wasn't going to let anyone get near her, especially Lyle Screw-Anything-That-Walks-By Bradshaw.

"What time do you want to leave?" he asked Regan. He sounded downright surly.

"I'd like to be there a little early."

"Okay. What time do you want me at your door?"

"Seven-thirty."

Wincott walked with Alec into the front office.

"Have you got any leads yet?" Alec asked.

"We've checked out almost everyone connected with Regan, and we looked hard at Shields and his sidekicks. I didn't see anything there. The three of them are in protective custody, and I'm told that Shields is scared sick."

"No one else looks good?"

"Not yet. We're checking out Peter Morris. You know, the guy Regan turned down for a grant. We don't have much on him yet."

"What about former employees? Maybe someone who got fired is trying to get even."

"Alec, I know how frustrated you must be because you can't work on this case, and I'll call you the second I do have something."

"Are you looking at the employees?"

"Yes. Her brother Aiden is getting a list together."

The two detectives continued to talk for another ten minutes. Regan was on the phone, but she'd been placed on hold, and while she waited, she tried to overhear what the men were saying. Alec caught her watching. He didn't smile or frown, but he did wink before he turned and walked out of the office, and despite all her attempts to remain unaffected, every one of her senses reacted.

She would never ever admit any of this foolishness to her friends. Sophie would start nagging Regan to make a move on him, and that was something Regan wasn't prepared to do.

Cordie would probably tell her that Alec was safe because he was untouchable, which made him great for a fantasy man.

He was someone who had a job to do and would do it well, but when he was finished, he would walk away without a backward glance.

But still, Regan was relieved to find voice mails from each of her friends saying they'd returned to Chicago in time for the dinner dance. Sophie's message said that she was bringing a date and that she had loads to tell Regan about their investigation.

Cordie had left two messages. The first was to inform Regan that she was going to the country club alone — she'd probably get a cab and catch a ride home with Sophie — and that she would wait for Regan in the reception area just outside the ballroom door. The second message was all about clothes. She described in great detail the sapphire blue gown she was wearing and ended her call with the suggestion that Regan stop being such a wimp and wear the "S" dress.

In the matter of the dress, Regan had no one to blame but herself, she supposed. She never should have let Cordie and Sophie talk her into buying the dress Cordie was referring to in the first place because they weren't going to let up until she wore the thing. She had to admit, though, it really was a stunning dress, and the silky fabric was a rich, deep burgundy color that even Regan knew looked beautiful against her skin.

It was a simple slip dress, and while the plunge between her breasts wasn't all that low, it was certainly lower cut than Regan was comfortable with. She usually went to great lengths to downplay what her friends called her assets, and wearing the dress would make her feel so self-conscious she would be tugging and pulling all night.

Regan decided to make up her mind about what she would wear when it was time to get ready. Until then, she had other more important things to do. She turned her computer off. Wincott had been replaced by a uniformed policeman who followed as she headed upstairs to the gym. It took her an hour and a half to get through the regimen of exercises the physical therapist had given her to strengthen the muscles around her knees, and then, because she still had nervous energy to burn, she put on her protective brace and walked the track. She was usually able to block out all her worries and concentrate only on the sound of her breathing and the pounding of her feet against the cushioned floor, but that wasn't working today.

For the last couple of weeks, her life had been turned upside down. It seemed that everywhere she looked, she saw security guards, and of course Alec or a policeman was always with her. Everyone was waiting for something to happen. Wincott was as convinced as Alec that the *crazy* — Alec's name for the suspect — would try to contact her again, but thus far, that hadn't happened.

Regan was pretty certain she had fooled everyone, even Henry, into believing she was taking it all in stride, but inside she was a nervous wreck. The only time she felt safe was when she was with Alec.

The wait was taking its toll. Her appetite was gone; she couldn't sleep, and lately she was having trouble concentrating. She couldn't stop worrying that the killer had already taken off for parts unknown — or what if he had simply gone to ground, waiting for them to drop their guard? How long would the detectives continue to shadow her before Lieutenant Lewis decided he was wasting valuable manpower? What would happen then?

Maybe Alec would have some answers, and if there was a quiet moment tonight, she would ask him what the next step was.

Wincott stopped by again that evening.

He had returned to pick up a couple of employment files from Aiden and decided to sit with Regan until Alec got there. Wincott's family was out of town, and he didn't want to go home to an empty house, so he relieved the policeman on duty.

He was lounging on the sofa in her parlor while she took a long hot shower. At her insistence, he'd ordered dinner and was now watching a baseball game while he ate. She had grown accustomed to having someone sitting in the outer room. She hadn't bothered to lock the French doors separating the bedroom from the parlor, but she was mindful not to walk in front of the windowpanes. There were sheers covering the glass, and he could probably see only her outline, but she still kept her robe on until she was inside the walk-in closet.

She took the "S" dress off the hanger and held it up. It really was lovely. The fabric was as light as air, and when she put it on and zipped up the back, the fabric clung in all the right places and felt wonderful against her skin.

Definitely too racy for tonight, she told herself.

She reluctantly removed the dress, put it back on the hanger, and sorted through her closet several times before settling on what Cordie called her old lady's mourning dress. The thing was shaped like a sack. Even Regan, who usually didn't focus very hard on her appearance, was so appalled when she looked at herself in the full-length mirror, she actually took a step back.

Her brothers would definitely approve of this one. "It's fine," she said out loud, trying to convince herself that the safe black sheath was better than the I-want-to-sin-tonight dress, which made her feel so sensual and feminine.

"Yes, this is fine," she repeated. Then she sighed. "If I were eighty."

Sick and tired of acting like a prude, she put on the sinner dress again. Then she searched through her drawers until she found the black, fringed silk wrap she'd purchased in Italy a couple of years ago. When she draped it around her shoulders just right, her back and chest were nicely covered.

Her only jewelry was a diamond pendant that hung on a platinum chain and a pair of diamond stud earrings.

She folded the wrap on the back of a chair, took a deep breath, and then opened the doors and walked into the parlor.

Wincott had picked up a french fry and had it halfway to his mouth when he saw her. He froze, the forgotten french fry dangling in the air from the tips of his fingers.

He gaped at her. She waited for him to say something, and when he didn't, she asked, "Do you think this dress is okay? It's . . . decent enough, isn't it?"

She'd put him on the spot asking him such a foolish question, and she was sorry she'd said anything. Not that it mattered. And still he gaped. Oh, dear, she thought. He had given her the once-over and was staring at her strappy, high-heeled sandals.

"I'll go change."

"No, no, it's okay. Honest. You just took me by surprise. Your legs . . ." He realized what he was about to say and stopped in time.

"Yes?" she asked, looking down. Her dress had a ragged hemline, and in places the fabric floated well above her knees. "What about my legs?"

"Long," he said, nodding. "Yeah, they're long . . . I mean tanned. Have you been in the sun?" He cleared his throat, dropped the french fry on his plate, and stammered, "Your dress is pretty."

"Thank you."

He wanted to say, *Wait until Alec gets a*

look at you, but he didn't. She was already feeling self-conscious, and for the life of him, he couldn't understand why. The woman was a knockout. How could she not know it?

The knock on the door pulled him from his thoughts. Regan went into the bedroom to collect her wrap and her evening bag while Wincott let Alec in.

She could hear the two men talking as she turned the lights off and walked back into the parlor. Wincott was watching Alec as he spotted Regan in the doorway. He gave her a quick glance and said, "You'll need a raincoat."

"Yes. All right."

She disappeared into the bedroom again. Wincott stood in front of the sofa staring at Alec, willing him to say something. Wincott couldn't stop grinning. Alec was good, all right. He hadn't shown any outward reaction to the vision standing before him. He hadn't even blinked. Come to think of it, he hadn't taken a breath either.

He kept staring into the bedroom, though, even when he said to Wincott, "What are you looking at?"

"You."

"And?"

"And I'm wondering how come you're

not drooling. Must have a lot of discipline," he said.

Alec looked at him. "We're here to do a job, and that's all."

"You're saying you're not going to try to get her to —"

Alec cut him off. He knew where he was going. "Not another frickin' word, or I swear I'll shoot you."

"Hey, I wasn't going to say anything offensive. Well, maybe I was gonna say something like, 'You kids have a nice time tonight, but you keep your hands to yourself.' You know, I might have said something like that."

Chapter Thirty

Alec was wearing a black raincoat over his tux and looked devastatingly handsome. He opened the door for her, stepped back, and said to Wincott, "Replacement's here."

Wincott's phone was ringing. "I'll go over a couple of things with him. You two go on."

The door closed as he was answering the phone.

They didn't speak until they were in the car and on their way north. Regan gave Alec directions to the country club — she'd written them down on a three-by-five index card — but he already knew where it was located.

"Are you always so organized?" he asked.

"I try to be," she said. She pulled out a handful of cards, shuffled through them, and put them back in her purse.

"What are all those?"

"Notes for tonight," she said.

"Do you have to give a speech?" he asked.

"Just a couple of words."

She didn't expound, and he figured he'd find out what it was all about when he got there. He was having a difficult time paying attention to the road. Her perfume was playing havoc with his concentration, and all he wanted to think about was how sexy she had looked when she walked into the parlor.

Yeah, right. Who was he kidding? He was trying to picture her naked, and that was what was playing havoc with his concentration.

They'd driven a couple of miles without speaking again, and the silence was awkward. Regan wished he would say something, even if it was a mundane remark about the weather. He had a ferocious frown on his face. What in heaven's name was he thinking about?

"Is everything all right?" she asked.

"What? Oh, sure. Everything's fine."

"You were frowning."

He glanced over at her. "I was?"

"What were you thinking about?"

You. Naked. Stalling while he tried to come up with a suitable lie, he said. "Just now?"

He eased the car down the ramp onto the interstate and swung in behind a pickup. Traffic was unusually heavy, even for Saturday night, but he still didn't have any trouble keeping track of the sedan following them.

"We've got company."

"We do?"

"The gray sedan two cars back. They've been following us since we left the hotel, and they don't seem to care if we notice them or not. I'm not worried, just irritated."

She tried to see the sedan from her side-view mirror, and when that didn't work, she twisted in her seat to look out the back window. The seat belt cut into her neck.

"I don't see a sedan."

He pulled over into the middle lane and accelerated, and as soon as he did that, the sedan followed.

Her eyes grew huge. "I see them. There are two men." Turning to Alec, she said, "Why aren't we worried?"

"They're security guards."

"So now I've got security guards following me around the city? Even when I'm with you? Who do you suppose gave that order?"

"Your brother."

She settled back in the seat, adjusted her raincoat over her knees, and stared out the window. She didn't say another word for several minutes. Alec glanced over at her and saw the worry on her face. "What's on your mind?" he asked.

"I was just wondering why we haven't heard from him," she said. "Why hasn't he tried to contact me? It's been two weeks, Alec. Do you still think he will?"

He could hear her anxiety. "Yes, I do."

"But what happens if he waits?"

"Then we wait."

"How much time will the lieutenant let Detective Wincott and you and the others spend on this? You're all overworked, and I know there aren't enough of you to go around. If nothing happens, and you leave Chicago, and he goes into hiding . . ." She suddenly stopped, took a breath, and told herself to calm down. Alec wasn't clairvoyant. He couldn't possibly have all the answers.

"Listen, Regan. Wincott and Bradshaw haven't been twiddling their thumbs. They're working on this, okay?"

"Yes, okay," she said, feeling guilty now because she knew the detectives had been putting in long hours. "I'm sorry. It's just that, the more I know —"

"The less afraid you'll be."

"That too."

"What were you going to say?'

"The more control I'll have. Besides, I can't come up with a plan to help catch him unless I know all the facts, now can I?"

"I don't like the sound of that, and neither will Wincott. Don't you get in the middle of this."

"I am in the middle of it."

"I'm talking about the investigation. Don't muck it up with foolish plans . . ."

"You sound like you think I'm going to do something crazy."

She had one hand on the dashboard, getting ready to brace herself should he swerve or increase his speed.

"Would you like to drive?"

The question jarred her. "No, I wouldn't."

"I'm only going sixty."

"Did I criticize your driving?"

He reached across the console and pulled her hand away from the dash. "Try to relax," he said. "And no more talk about the investigation tonight. Okay?"

"Yes," she agreed. She leaned back and folded her hands in her lap. "About those security guards following us . . ."

"Yes?"

"I don't want them to follow us inside the club, and I'd rather no one knew that you were my bodyguard. The focus shouldn't be on me tonight, and I don't want a lot of questions."

The only way the focus wouldn't be on her was if she kept her coat on all evening and no one got a look at her dress. Actually, it was her body inside the dress, he silently corrected.

"I'll talk to the guards and make sure they keep a low profile."

"Thank you."

The clouds suddenly erupted, and within seconds, fat raindrops splattered the windshield. Alec turned on the wipers and said, "I think we're going to set a record for the most consecutive rain days."

"That's our exit."

"I know."

"Does Wincott know where Shields is hiding?"

"You'll have to ask him that question."

"Aiden wants me to hide too. I'm not going to, though. I'm not running away. I want to help catch him."

"Aiden's trying to look out for you," he said. "I've got two younger sisters, and I'd probably react the same way."

"He's bringing in reinforcements."

"Oh?"

"Spencer's on his way. He's probably

already at the hotel."

"Wasn't he coming to Chicago for that meeting you told me about?"

"Yes."

"But you think the two of them will try to gang up on you to get you to go into hiding?"

"Yes, but it won't work. Like I said, I'm not going anywhere. And if anyone is hiding, it's Aiden."

"Yeah?" He was trying not to smile. She sounded so disgruntled now. "Who's he hiding from?"

"Me."

"He's that scared of you, huh?"

"I wish."

He did laugh then. "I gather that's a no?"

"Aiden isn't afraid of anyone, least of all me. He isn't really hiding from me," she admitted. "He is driving me crazy, though. It seems that every time I turn around, there he is, and yet, he doesn't have time to even schedule a meeting. He keeps hiring more guards too. I'm bumping into them."

"He's worried about you, and that's why there are so many security guards around. Did you ever talk to him about having your car towed away?"

"Not yet, but I will."

"What about Walker? Is he going to gang up on you too?"

"No. He's pretty self-absorbed these days, and I'm glad of it. I can handle two, but three against one is more difficult."

They'd taken the exit and were slowing to a stop at a red light. The country club was a little over two miles away.

"You're tougher than you look."

She smiled. "I hope that's a compliment."

"It is," he said. "Families can be complicated. Trust me. I know."

"From some of the stories you've told me, you were pretty wild."

"I had my share of wild times."

With women? she wanted to ask.

"How come you're not married?"

He shrugged. "I don't have anything against marriage. My brothers Nick and Theo love being married. I just haven't had time for any kind of meaningful relationship."

"Women are like potato chips."

"I'm sorry?" He couldn't believe he'd heard her correctly. "Women are what?"

"Like potato chips," she repeated. "That's what a guy in college once told me."

"A boyfriend?"

She shook her head. "No, he was dating a friend of mine, and sleeping around on her."

"Did he tell you why he thought women were like potato chips?"

"Yes. He said he couldn't eat just one."

He thought that was hilarious. He'd heard a lot of lame reasons men gave women when they got caught cheating, but this one had to be the worst yet.

"It's not that funny," she said.

"Yeah, it is."

He turned the corner. The rain was coming down in torrents now. They followed a limo through the iron gates. There were gaslights outlining the half mile drive that curved through the palatial grounds to the clubhouse. Whoever had designed the club had wanted to impress, and he had certainly achieved that goal. The opulence of the three-story structure at the top of the rise was close to being an embarrassment of excess. Soft lights shone down on massive white pillars. The brick building reminded Alec of a southern plantation run amuck.

Chapter Thirty-one

The rain didn't let up. Alec handed his car keys to the valet and followed Regan up the stairs. He was one step behind her, and it occurred to her that he was making himself a target in order to protect her.

"Do you belong to this club?" he asked.

She shook her head. "It's not my kind of place."

The comment surprised him. "Not my kind of place either. It's too . . ."

"Pretentious?" she whispered.

"Yes."

Two men in red tailcoats opened the massive double doors as they approached. As Regan and Alec were walking inside, he took her arm and said, "I don't want you to go anywhere without me. Not even the ladies' room."

She turned to him. "Are you going to go in there with me?"

"No, but I'm making sure it's empty."

He took her coat, removed his own, and handed both to the coat check woman. His frown told Regan that he didn't approve of what she was wearing. She almost said something and then changed her mind. She draped the silk shawl around her shoulders and knotted it, and as soon as she did that, his frown eased.

He looked so dashing all dressed up in his tux. His bow tie was crooked, though, and a lock of his hair had fallen down on his forehead. Without a thought as to what she was doing, she stepped closer, adjusted his tie, and brushed his hair back in place.

She made the mistake of looking into his eyes. They wrinkled at the corners, and she knew he wanted to laugh at her. She could have stared at him all night. Time to get hold of yourself, she thought.

She stepped back. "I didn't mean to . . . you know."

"No, I don't know. You didn't mean to what?"

"To touch you," she whispered.

He grinned. "I like you touching me."

"I still shouldn't have . . ."

She was saved from having to continue the awkward conversation when she heard someone call her name. She whirled around, lost her balance, and fell back against Alec. He grabbed her around the waist and held her until she stopped wobbling. She shouldn't have worn such impossible high heels, she told herself.

He had to think she was a complete klutz. Fortunately, she didn't have to dwell on that depressing thought long. Cordie caught her attention. Regan smiled as her friend came rushing forward. As usual, she looked lovely. The sapphire blue dress had a long full skirt and a fitted bodice that showed off her perfect figure.

"Have you been waiting long?" Regan asked. She might as well have added, "Yo, I'm down here." Her friend was staring at Alec and having trouble keeping her mouth closed. Regan couldn't fault her.

"Stop staring," she whispered.

"I'm not staring."

She was, and she didn't seem inclined to stop. Regan nudged her. "I asked you if you had been waiting long. For heaven's sake, Cordie, look at me."

"What? Oh, no, I just got here."

Regan remembered her manners. She stepped to Alec's side and introduced the two. Cordie smiled as she shook his hand. "You don't look like a detective, at least not in that tuxedo." She glanced down at his waist and asked, "Are you carrying?"

"Carrying what?" Regan asked.

"A gun," she explained. "You know . . . packing."

Alec smiled. "You watch a lot of television, don't you?"

"Sorry to say I do," she said. "At least I do when I'm not grading papers. I lead a very boring life."

"No, you don't," Regan said. "Cordie's a woman of many talents. Do you know, she totally rebuilt the engine in her car?"

Alec thought she was joking. Cordelia was extremely feminine — very like Regan — and it was easier for him to picture her getting her nails painted at one of those fancy salons somewhere than changing the points and plugs in a car. Then the name clicked inside his head. Cordelia Kane as in Kane Automotive. "Your family owns a couple of auto repair shops around town, don't they?"

"More than a couple," Regan said. "They're nationwide."

She suddenly remembered she hadn't told Cordie the latest about her brother. "Aiden had my car towed away."

"No."

"Yes."

"Get it back," she said.

Regan shook her head. "He had it taken to a junkyard. I'm sure it's been stripped by now. Oh, and he bought me a BMW. Can you believe his gall?"

Alec would have laughed, but he knew Regan was serious, and angry. So was her friend.

"I can't believe I wasted an entire weekend putting in a brand-new radiator and shocks . . ."

"And a new muffler," Regan said.

"That's right, a new muffler. Where does he get off towing . . . ?" Cordie suddenly stopped ranting and took a deep breath. "It's getting crowded in here. We should probably go into the banquet."

Alec had been blocking Regan from anyone entering through the double doors, but he, too, wanted to get her inside the dining room and hopefully settled at an out-of-the-way table.

The two security guards who had followed them from the hotel walked into the foyer. They stopped just inside the door. Both were wearing their uniforms and were already getting noticed by the other arriving guests. Alec touched Regan's arm to get her attention, leaned down close to her ear, and said, "Stay here with your back to the wall. I'll be right back."

The second he was out of earshot, Cordie said, "Oh, wow."

Regan smiled. "Excuse me?"

"You heard me. Oh, wow. You didn't

tell me he was so . . ."

"So what?"

"So . . . everything. There's this raw, sexy appeal about him . . ."

"Really?"

"You haven't noticed?"

Regan laughed. "Of course I noticed."

Like Cordie, she was watching Alec as he walked over to the guards and spoke to them. Whatever he was saying was making the men nervous. They both began to fidget. One was comically tugging on his collar.

"Why are those men here?"

"The guards? Aiden hired them as extra security."

"They're not subtle, are they?"

"No, they aren't. I hope Alec sends them home." She turned to Cordie and said, "I would appreciate it if you didn't tell anyone that Alec's a detective. I don't want to field questions, and the focus should be on the hospital fund-raiser tonight."

"I won't say a word."

"Except Sophie, of course. You can tell her."

"Of course."

The three of them never kept secrets from one another. "About the detective . . ." Cordie began.

"Yes?"

"I'm thinking he's interested in you."

"Why would you think that? You've only spent two minutes with the man."

"Body language," she explained in a very matter-of-fact tone. "I know he's interested because of the way he looks at you. You're going to have to take my word on this, Regan. He's attracted to you, but then, come to think of it, most men are."

"They are not. Now, can we please change the subject."

"Not yet. You're gorgeous. You've got a face and body Sophie and I would die to have, and I swear that if you weren't my best friend, I'd have to hate you. Your brothers, especially Aiden, have done a real number on you to keep you in line."

"For heaven's sake," Regan said, exasperated. "No one's done a number on me."

Cordie didn't want to argue. "Will your brothers be here tonight?"

"Maybe," she said.

"So tell me. Is he single, married, or divorced?"

"Who?" she asked, just to provoke her friend.

"Oh, please. You know who I'm talking about. The hunky detective."

"He's single, but he's leaving Chicago in another week."

"For how long?"

"Forever," she said.

Cordie sighed. "You know what I'm thinking?"

Regan smiled. "I never know what you're thinking."

"I'm thinking you should take that blanket off and go after that man."

Regan took exception. "It isn't a blanket. It's a wrap." She self-consciously adjusted the knot she'd made to hold the shawl in place. "It wouldn't be right for me to *go after* him. He's on the job. He's . . . trapped with me."

The conversation ended when Cordie said, "Here he comes."

Regan noticed the guards, looking quite disgruntled, were leaving. "What did you say to them?" she asked.

"Not much."

"In other words, you aren't going to tell me?"

He smiled and completely ignored the question. "Shall we go inside the ballroom?"

"The doors aren't open yet," Cordie said. "That hallway leads to the ballroom, where we'll be dining. They're serving champagne and hors d'oeuvres in the reception. I'm going to go look for Sophie.

Want to come with me?"

Regan didn't answer her. She was watching a couple coming in the doorway. Her frown was immediate, and she was suddenly feeling sick to her stomach.

"What's wrong?" As Cordie asked the question, she turned around to see who Regan was watching. "Oh, I see."

The couple disappeared into the cloakroom. Alec caught a glimpse of them. "Who are they?"

"No one important."

Alec looked at Cordie to get an answer. She sighed and said, "The silver-haired man used to be married to Regan's mother, and the young woman having trouble keeping her dress on is his wife. They are, as Regan said, not important."

Alec touched Regan's shoulder. "I'd like to go into the ballroom. As Cordie said, it's getting crowded out here," he added.

Cordie took off down the hall to go to the reception, and by the time she reached the door, there were two men at her side.

Alec took Regan's hand. "I want to see where you will be sitting. Let's go."

She didn't argue. She didn't particularly want to stand in a crowded room and sip champagne.

An employee stepped forward to block

the doors and explained that they would have to wait until the room was officially opened, but the look Alec gave the man changed his mind, and he hastily stepped out of the way.

The ballroom was surprisingly large. To the left, the musicians were busy setting up their equipment on a wide square platform adjacent to the spacious dance floor. Straight ahead and to the right were round tables with white linen tablecloths. The cushioned chairs were covered with white linen slipcovers, and tied on the back of each chair was a blue satin bow with ribbon spilling to the floor. Long white tapered candles in sparkling silver candleholders were being lit by the waiters.

There were place settings for eight at each of the tables. Name cards, propped on silver cubes, sat directly behind each silver-rimmed dinner plate. Regan found their table near the front by the podium. One of the waiters was fiddling with the microphone, making sure it worked, but he stopped what he was doing and smiled at her.

She walked around the table to find out who else was seated there, oblivious of the appreciative looks she was getting. Alec didn't like the way the staff was looking at her, but he knew he couldn't do anything about it. He glared at one overzealous employee who started toward Regan and was pleased when the man did a hasty turnaround.

Regan was shaking her head. "What's the matter?" he asked.

"We're not sitting here."

"Okay," he said. "So who is?" He was standing beside her, keeping his eye on the doors.

"Aiden and his guest, Spencer and his guest, which means he's back in town, the administrator of the hospital and his wife, and my former stepfather, Emerson, and his wife, Cindy. No, we aren't going to sit here."

She was trying hard not to let Alec know how furious she was. She knew Aiden was responsible for letting the sleazebag join in. She understood his motives. Emerson had already gone to several attorneys trying to find a way to break the prenup, and Aiden was simply trying to keep him pacified. In Regan's opinion, her brother was only putting off the inevitable and being extremely disloyal to their mother's memory in the process.

There were bright spots of color on her cheeks. She was angry, all right. "Okay,"

Alec said calmly. "Where would you like to sit?"

"Anywhere but here."

Alec picked up her name card and his. He looked around, found a table near the back he liked because it was close to the wall, and walked toward it.

He traded names with a doctor and his wife. "This okay?"

"It's perfect." The frown eased from her brow.

She put her evening bag down on the seat of the chair and straightened just as the doors were officially opened. Sophie and her date were the first to walk inside. She waved to Regan and hurried over. She looked amazing. Regan watched Alec to judge his reaction to her friend. He'd taken the name cards of the doctor and his wife and placed them next to Aiden and his guest, and was on his way back to their table when Sophie caught his attention.

He seemed curious but not overly so. Men had a tendency to lose their train of thought around Sophie, but Alec seemed to be in full command of his senses. Odd, Regan thought. Definitely odd.

Sophie was wearing a new black Chanel gown and had diamond clips in her hair. Regan recognized her friend's date. He was

Jeffrey Oatley. His family owned Oatley Electronics, and Regan knew that Jeff and Sophie were both members of the same country club. He was a sweet, laid-back man who always looked as though he was about to burst out of his clothes. Everything he wore was two sizes too small.

"Alec, I'd like you to meet my dear friend, Sophie Rose," she said.

While she was introducing Jeff, she noticed Sophie was smiling at Alec. She, too, was obviously mesmerized by the man.

"Are you the bodyguard, or rather the detective, assigned to Regan? It's okay," she hastily added for Regan's benefit. "Cordie explained everything to me, and I assure you that I can keep a secret."

"Sophie's going to be a reporter," Regan said.

"What secret?" Jeff asked.

Alec answered. "Regan's dating a cop. That's the secret."

"What cop?"

"Me," Alec said. "She's dating me." He put his arm around her waist and pulled her in to his side.

Alec didn't let go of her. Regan wondered if he realized his arm was still around her. She liked it, though. She liked pretending that they were together too, and, Lord, how pathetic was that?

"Would you like for us to join you?" Sophie asked, and before Regan could answer, she turned to her date and said, "Will you go find our name cards, please?"

He immediately turned around to do what she asked. She grabbed his arm. "Wait a minute. Take all of these name cards and put them somewhere else. I'm sure there are empty seats, and if there aren't, ask the waiter to set up another table. I don't want to sit with strangers tonight. Oh, and, Jeff? Find Cordie's name too. She'll want to sit with us."

Regan leaned toward Alec and said, "Sophie and I have been friends since kindergarten, so I'm used to the way she bosses everyone around."

Sophie heard the comment and laughed. "Everyone but you and Cordie. It is true, though. I do tend to be bossy, especially with Jeff. He's my go-with guy."

"Go with?" Alec asked.

"We're just friends," she explained. "But when I want or need a date for some function, Jeff goes with me, and I do the same for him. It's a perfect arrangement when one or both of us is between relationships. Jeff was eager to come tonight, though, because of Regan."

"Why's that?" Alec asked.

"He's had a thing for her for years," she explained. "Shouldn't we sit down?" She motioned to a waiter, who immediately hurried over. "Would you please remove these three place settings? Thank you," she said as he began to gather up the silverware and the wineglasses. Sophie leaned around him to see Regan. "Cordie can sit next to Alec on his right, and you can sit on his left."

"She *is* bossy," Alec said.

Regan nodded. She was smiling until Sophie said, "Cordie's right. You really should take off the blanket. It hides your beautiful dress."

"It isn't a blanket. It's a wrap."

"No need to sound so defensive."

"I'm not being defensive," she argued in a voice even she knew sounded extremely defensive. "I'm simply telling you it's a wrap."

"Okay," Sophie said, and it was obvious that she was now trying to placate Regan. "And I'm simply suggesting to you that it's time to unwrap the wrap. Speaking of dresses, do you like mine?"

"Very much. Is it new?" Regan's tone was laced with suspicion.

"Sort of."

"What does 'sort of' mean?"

"I picked it up at the Chanel boutique a couple of weeks ago, but this is the first time I've worn it."

"How did you pay for it? With your salary —"

Sophie stood. "I had a relapse. Okay?"

"Oh, Sophie . . ."

"I'm going to help Jeff find Cordie's name card. He's wandering around in circles. When I get back, don't lecture me. I already feel guilty."

Alec stood when Sophie did, but as soon as she walked away, he sat down again and put his arm on the back of Regan's chair. The fringe from her wrap was draped over his hand, and when she shifted positions, his fingers brushed against her skin. She didn't move away, and neither did he.

"What kind of relapse was she talking about?" he asked.

"Sophie asked Cordie and me to help her stop taking money from her father."

"What's the big deal? If he wants to give her money and she needs it . . ."

Regan turned to look at him. "But she doesn't really need it. And she wants to be completely independent." She sighed. "Sophie loves her father very much, and she's extremely loyal to him."

"In other words, she's a typical daughter."

She smiled. Nothing about Sophie or her father was typical. "Yes," she said. "Recently she decided that it was up to her to try to rehabilitate him, and if that didn't work, then she's determined to get him to retire."

Alec literally jerked back. "Ah, hell. Rose isn't her middle name, is it? Man, I didn't put it together. I should have, but I didn't. She's Bobby Rose's daughter, isn't she?"

"Yes, she is."

He was stunned. The FBI had been trailing Bobby Rose for years, trying to get enough evidence to indict him. Bobby was considered by many to be the ultimate con artist, but because he only fleeced those men and women he considered to be bigger crooks than he was, the public had taken a real shine to him. High-stakes gamblers who had robbed their own companies and who had cleaned out their employees' pensions and then hung them and their families out to dry were Bobby's meat and potatoes. Bobby Rose loved targeting the greedy bastards, and that was all the more reason the public loved him. Unfortunately, the sad truth was that Bobby was never going to run out of marks.

Not only did the public adore him, other crooks looked up to Bobby as an idol. He was everything they hoped to become. Bobby lived somewhere in Florida, and in all the articles about him, there was never any mention of a family.

"Spencer told me that a lot of people think of Bobby Rose as a modern-day Robin Hood. He only steals from the rich —"

He interrupted her. "Yeah, well, he doesn't give the money to the poor, now does he? He keeps it."

Her back stiffened. "He does a lot of charitable work."

He gave her a look that suggested he thought she was nuts. "He's a criminal, Regan, and he should be behind bars."

"It's obvious you've made up your mind about him, and nothing I say will change your opinion, will it?" She sounded disgruntled.

"He's a criminal," he patiently repeated.

"If you're going to be judgmental . . ."

He was incredulous. "Have you forgotten what I do for a living?"

She turned away from him and stared at the crowd of people searching for their tables. "I'm through discussing Sophie's father with you."

"Oh, we've only just gotten started." He tugged on her wrap to make her look at him and asked, "Did you tell me Sophie works for a newspaper?"

It would have been petty not to answer. "Yes, she does. At her father's insistence she uses her mother's maiden name as her byline, but I think everyone at the paper knows who she is. Detective Wincott found out, and I assumed he told you."

Wincott was probably having a real good laugh about now. "No, he didn't tell me," he said. "It must have slipped his mind. What was it like for Sophie growing up with Bobby Rose for a father?"

"He's a very good father," she said. "He never missed a parent-teacher conference, and he always went to the plays and the tennis matches. He did his share of car pooling too."

"Were there parents who wouldn't let their kids hang around Sophie?"

"Yes."

"Did your family?"

"Forbid me to hang out with her? Sophie and Cordie and I had already become friends before Bobby Rose became so . . ."

"Notorious?"

"Famous," she corrected. "My mother was busy socializing and traveling. My grandmother was in charge of me, and when she became ill, Aiden took over. I don't think my grandmother knew who Sophie's father was, but Aiden knew, and he didn't tell her. My brother would never forbid me to be her friend. Sophie was always welcome in our home, but I wasn't allowed to go to hers." She smiled as she added, "I did, though, all the time."

He was teasing when he asked, "Did you ever get down in her basement? No one knows where Bobby Rose hides all his money. Maybe it's there."

She put her hand down on top of his. "Alec, Sophie is my friend."

He started to ask another question. She stopped him by squeezing his hand. "She's my friend."

Chapter Thirty-two

Alec hated black-tie affairs, and he didn't particularly like the country club scene either, but he didn't mind wearing the tuxedo tonight because of Regan. There was something about her that was so compelling, so vibrant, and yet there was a vulnerability too he found utterly charming. Sophie told them a sad story about a young man she knew, and when she was finished, Regan had tears in her eyes.

"It had a happy ending," Sophie said.

Embarrassed by her tears, Regan dabbed at her eyes with her napkin and laughed. "I'm a crybaby."

"That used to be her nickname," Sophie said.

"When I found out what some of the kids were calling me, I cried," she said. "But that was when I was in school. I got over it."

"Regan wears her heart on her sleeve."

Regan didn't argue. She picked up her glass of Perrier and lime and took a sip.

Alec loved watching her expressions. She was so refreshingly different. What she was feeling was right there for anyone to see.

She wasn't a game player, and she wasn't the least bit self-serving or self-involved. That, too, was a refreshing change from the other women he'd known.

Regan had a face that could grace the cover of a fashion magazine and an incredible body, but what he liked most about her was her loyalty to her friends. Well, maybe not most of all, he admitted. Her body was pretty damned great.

But she was still just a job. He had to remind himself of that fact every time he looked at that sweet mouth of hers.

Sophie excused herself to go search for her date. Alec sat down again, declined the wine the waiter was offering, and asked Regan, "Is that any good?" with a nod toward her nonalcoholic drink.

She handed the glass to him and watched him gulp it down. Smiling she said, "You were supposed to take a sip."

"I never sip. If I'm gonna drink something, I don't fool around," he said. "And that pretty much defines my philosophy of life."

"Don't sip, gulp?" When he nodded, she laughed. "You belonged to a fraternity when you were in college, didn't you?"

"Sure did," he said. "I ate a lot of potato chips too."

He put the empty glass down, ordered two more, one for Regan and one for himself, and then said, "Heads up."

"Excuse me?"

"Aiden's here."

She was still smiling when she turned and watched her brother walk into the ballroom. He didn't have a date, and he didn't notice Regan, but then she was all but hidden in the back corner. She watched him walk toward the podium, where Daniel O'Donnell, the administrator of Parkdale Hospital, stood waiting for him.

Sophie also saw Aiden as she was making her way back to their table. She hurried to intercept him, said something that made him smile, then stretched up and kissed him on the cheek.

Spencer walked in a minute later with Cordie at his side. He, too, was smiling. Her brother looked relaxed, she thought. Sleep-deprived, but relaxed. Jet lag would, no doubt, catch up with him tomorrow.

"The man with Cordie . . ."

"Spencer, right?"

"Yes, that's right."

"I see the family resemblance," he said. "But I also recognized him from a newspaper photo Henry showed me. You and your brothers were at a dedication. Henry told me he was going to have the photo framed because it was rare for all of you to be together."

She nodded. "That's true. It seems the only time we get together is when there's a funeral or a crisis."

"A what?"

"A crisis."

He leaned his elbows on the table and thought about what she'd just said.

Regan looked back at Spencer and said, "I should go say hello to my brother."

"*Two* brothers are here," he said.

She smiled. "Yes, but I'm only going to be nice to one of them."

He smiled. "Spoken like a true sister."

The knot in her wrap came undone, and when she pushed her chair back to stand, it fell to the floor.

He bolted to his feet. The dress showed off her attributes a little too well for his liking. No, that wasn't exactly true. He liked looking at her. He just didn't want anyone else to.

He was about to tell her to put the blanket back on when she turned to him. They stood just inches apart, her face up-turned to his. If he moved so much as a couple of inches, his mouth would be on top of hers. He stopped himself in time. It wasn't his place to tell her what she could or couldn't wear, no matter how much it bothered him. If he tried that on one of his sisters, she'd laugh right in his face. Then she'd give him hell.

Regan wasn't his sister, though. *She's a job, nothing more.* Those words became a chant inside his head, and yet he was having trouble accepting it.

"Alec? You were saying?"

"Stay in the room," he said gruffly. "I'll be watching, but stay in the room."

"Yes, of course."

Cordie was bringing Spencer to Regan. She met them halfway across the ballroom, hugged her brother, and welcomed him home.

Alec watched the reunion as he pulled out his cell phone. He dialed Wincott's cell number. The detective answered on the second ring.

Alec didn't waste time on pleasantries. "Check out the brothers."

"The ball that boring, huh?"

"I mean it. Check them out."

"We already have," he said. "And you're not supposed to have any involvement in the investigation."

It was almost impossible for Alec to back

off. He didn't want to jeopardize Wincott's future with the department, and he knew that if Lewis found out he was doing anything more than guarding Regan, he would make Wincott's life miserable.

"So what are you thinking?" Wincott asked.

"Maybe this guy is after the whole family, or maybe he's using Regan to get all the brothers back in Chicago. I know you've checked them out, but go deeper. There might be something there."

"Okay," he said. "We'll dig deeper."

"Look, I know you're overworked and understaffed. I'll call Gil and ask him to check out a couple of things."

"So you're not involved, but you are?"

"I really want to follow up on a hunch."

"That's fine with me . . . if Gil doesn't mind."

"Did anything come up on Regan?"

"Since you asked this morning? No. The people she turned down for grants were the only ones who had a grudge. Although, there were a couple of nutcases — you know, people who wanted money for weird inventions — but they checked out okay. Weird, but okay," he said. "I already told you we're looking at Peter Morris," he added. "Her friends checked out too. I guess by now you've figured out who Sophie Rose's father is."

"Thanks for telling me."

Wincott laughed. "I almost fell off the chair when I found out. It doesn't appear to make any difference to Regan or her brothers. They don't blame the daughter for the sins of her father."

"That's the way it should be."

"We've ruled Bobby Rose out. I'm getting another call."

Alec flipped the phone closed and put it back in his pocket. He stood with his back to the wall, his arms folded across his chest, watching the crowd.

Aiden had joined his brother and sister. Cordie seemed to be the only one interested in what he had to say. No, *interested* wasn't the right description, Alec thought. She looked enthralled. Regan, on the other hand, looked furious. Aiden was still talking when she shook her head, turned, and walked back to their table. Several men tried to engage her in conversation, but other than smiling at each one, she paid them no attention and continued on.

Alec pulled the chair out for her, but she didn't sit. She stood next to him and stared at the entrance.

Cordie had followed Regan, and she

smiled when Alec pulled her chair out for her. "Who are you looking for?" she asked Regan as she placed the napkin on her lap. She turned around to see who Regan was watching, and then said, "Oh, I see."

"See what?" Alec asked.

"Mr. and Mrs. Sleazebag just walked in," Cordie said.

Alec didn't comment, but he did track the couple as they made their way around the tables to get to their seats. Emerson's face was red, no doubt from alcohol, Alec thought. His wife was adjusting her bodice and fluffing her long platinum hair. An interesting couple, he decided, and he wondered what Wincott had found out about them.

Sophie and Jeff returned to the table, and Sophie craned her neck so she, too, could watch the couple. When they had taken their seats, she turned to Regan and said, "The whole family's here. Isn't that lovely?"

"Just super."

"Walker isn't here," Cordie pointed out.

"I was being sarcastic," Sophie said. She told Regan and Alec to sit down, for heaven's sake, and then added, "Aiden had no right to invite Emerson. He knows how Regan feels about him. I think it was terribly disloyal of him, and I told him so."

Cordie immediately rushed to Aiden's defense. "You can't know if he invited him or not."

"Of course I can know," Sophie countered. "Aiden told me he invited him," she rushed to add when Cordie looked as if she was going to argue.

"What did he say when you called him disloyal?" Cordie asked.

"He said it was cheaper than a lawsuit and for me to behave myself tonight," Sophie said. "He still treats me like I'm a ten-year-old."

Waiters appeared with the first course. The conversation turned to lighter topics during dinner, and Regan was thankful for that. Jeff told several humorous stories about a tennis competition he'd entered, and Regan tried to look interested. She wasn't hungry. Seeing Emerson had destroyed her appetite, but no one seemed to notice she was moving the food around her plate.

After dinner, but before the dancing began, Daniel O'Donnell stepped up to the podium and tapped on the microphone to get everyone's attention.

"Please tell me there aren't going to be a dozen or so boring speakers," Cordie said.

"Just one boring speaker," Regan replied.

"For a thousand dollars a plate, we shouldn't have to listen to anyone," Sophie said.

"Hush," Cordie whispered. "People can hear you."

A moment later, after the administrator had thanked everyone for attending, he introduced Regan. Cordie and Sophie both laughed.

"Keep it short and sweet," Sophie said.

"As opposed to long and boring?" Regan teased.

Deciding to wing it, she left the note cards in her purse. Alec stood when she did, but he didn't follow her. He watched the crowd and the doors. He did notice that every eye was on Regan as she made her way to the podium.

It took her all of thirty seconds to hook her audience and less than that to mesmerize them.

The hospital was located in the heart of the inner city, and Regan stressed the importance of keeping it open. There was a desperate need for money and for additional beds, which meant a drive to expand.

"And that's why you're here," she said.

They were smiling as she reeled them in.

Alec was amazed. She talked about money, and she got them to listen. She had her audience in the palm of her hand, and by the time she finished, Alec wanted to empty his savings account to help out. She was that good.

There was such passion in her voice and a determination to get the job done. It was a side of her Alec hadn't seen until tonight, and he was all the more impressed. The woman just kept getting better and better.

She received a standing ovation and was immediately surrounded by guests. Alec didn't like the crowd pressing in on her. He went to her, put his arm around her, and pulled her back so that her shoulders were pressed against his chest.

Alec spotted Emerson, drink in hand, tottering toward her with a scowl on his face. "Come on. Let's dance," he said.

"The music hasn't started yet."

"I'll hum."

He was treating her like a football he had tucked under his arm as he zigzagged his way to the dance floor. Fortunately, the music did start just as he pulled her into his arms.

"Alec?" she began.

"Yes?"

"Thank you."

He'd been looking over the crowd but glanced down and smiled. "You saw him coming?"

The top of her head bumped his chin when she nodded. Her fingers were tickling the back of his neck. He was trying hard not to show any reaction, but he couldn't help thinking how soft and right she felt in his arms. When she looked directly into his eyes, he began to imagine all sorts of things.

Man, did he need to get laid. Yeah, that was why she was having such a powerful effect on him. Lust. That's what it was. Plain old lust. And he needed to clear his head and stop thinking about how good she would feel in his arms in his bed with her legs . . .

"We won't have to stay much longer."

One of the waiters caught his attention. He was standing by the door holding an oval tray. He was staring at Regan. While Alec watched, another waiter tapped the man on his shoulder and got him moving again.

"I'm not in a hurry to leave."

"Who are you watching?" she asked.

The waiter carried the empty tray out of the room. "No one in particular."

"You're not bored to death?"

He smiled. "I'm still breathing, aren't I?"

The song ended. Men were moving in on Regan, but Alec managed to run interference and get her back to the table without stopping.

"You're being rude dragging me along. I'm supposed to be nice to these people so they'll give me some of their hard-earned money for the hospital expansion."

"Most of the people here didn't earn their money. They inherited it."

"Yes, but I still have to —"

He cut her off. "You can be nice sitting here," he said. He pulled out her chair and added, "You don't want Cordie to sit all by herself, do you?"

The chair hit the back of her knees. She didn't have a choice. She was sitting whether she wanted to or not.

"You have noticed Cordie isn't at the table. She's dancing."

"Yes, but she's coming back. You look cold," he remarked. He sat down next to her. "Why don't you put your blanket back on."

One eyelid dropped. "It isn't a blanket."

He draped the wrap around her shoulders, and his finger trailed down the side of her neck. She sat beside him for several minutes watching the couples on the dance floor, but every once in a while, she'd glance over at him. Had she imagined the touch, the shiver he'd evoked? Was she that starved for affection that a simple brush of his hand against her skin sent her into a spin?

Don't think about it, she told herself. Think about something else. Her friends. Yes, she'd think about them. Were they having a good time? Sophie looked as if she was. She and Jeff were having an animated conversation as they waltzed past, and Cordie, she noticed, was dancing with Aiden.

"What do you think of my friends?"

Alec was watching Cordie when he answered. "I like them."

She smiled as though he'd just complimented her. "When we were little, Cordie and I were certain that Sophie would be married before she turned twenty, but now we're not so sure she'll ever settle down. She's having too much fun. Cordie, on the other hand, is a true romantic. She says she's waiting for her one true love."

Alec nodded toward the dance floor. "Maybe she's already found him."

She leaned in to Alec's side while she looked over the crowd. When she found

Cordie, she burst into laughter. "She's dancing with Aiden, for heaven's sake."

"Yes, she is."

"Are you suggesting that Cordie and Aiden . . . ?" She laughed again. The possibility was ludicrous to her.

Alec wanted to tell her to watch her friend's face. The way that Cordie was looking at Aiden more than suggested that *she* at least had the hots for the guy. Alec didn't think Aiden had a clue, though, how Cordie felt.

"I could be wrong," he said, deciding to be diplomatic.

"You are wrong. Aiden thinks of Cordie as my friend. Nothing more. He watched her grow up because she was always at our house. And she thinks of him as my brother —"

"Yeah, I've got it. And nothing more, right?"

"That's right."

They continued to watch the dancing couples.

"Daniel's looking worried," Regan said.

"Who's Daniel?"

"Daniel O'Donnell."

She could tell he still didn't know whom she was talking about. "The hospital administrator. He's waiting for me to circulate and beg for money. Would you like to come with me?"

"No, I can watch you beg from here. Just stay in the room where I can see you."

He almost added, "And wear the tarp or whatever the thing is called," but stopped himself. He stood with his back to the wall and watched her walk away. She turned once and smiled at him. There was the dimple he'd been pretending not to notice since that first smile. He loved women with dimples, no matter where those dimples were.

His cell phone vibrated. He didn't look at the caller ID before answering.

"Buchanan."

Noah Clayborne was on the line. "I'm stuck in Seattle."

"What are you doing there?"

"Eating fish."

"So you're not coming to Chicago?"

"Probably not. Where are you? I hear music in the background."

"I'm at a country club, and you're hearing a band playing. I'm on duty," he explained.

"Doing what?"

He sighed and braced himself for the razzing to come. "Bodyguard duty."

"Huh. I guess that's better than a suspension. What'd you do wrong?"

"What makes you think I did anything wrong?"

Noah laughed. "You're kidding, right? You've been demoted to bodyguard. You did something wrong, all right."

"Yeah, I did. I made the lieutenant look bad."

Noah was nosy as usual. "How'd you do that?"

"I resigned," he said, and then added, "look, it's a long story. I'll tell you all about it over a beer sometime."

"Yeah, okay. So maybe I'll see you in Boston. I'll call to let you know."

"Wait a minute. I want to ask you something."

"What?"

"It's kind of an odd thing to ask, but I was just curious . . ."

"Curious about what?" he asked when Alec hesitated.

"Women."

"Huh. I sort of thought your father or one of your older brothers would have given you the sex talk, but if you —"

"Very funny," he snapped. "What I was wondering . . ."

"Yeah? Spit it out."

"You've been with a lot of women."

"I like women."

"And you've been in a few relationships, haven't you? You know what I'm talking about, don't you? A relationship that's lasted more than twenty-four hours, maybe even as long as a week? Short-term, but still a relationship."

"Yes, I have."

"Okay, so what I want to know is this. In any of those relationships, did you ever become possessive? Did it ever bother you that other guys were trying to hit on the woman you were with?"

"Ah, jeez. Who is she?"

"Just answer the question."

"No, I've never become possessive." There was laughter in his voice.

It wasn't the answer Alec wanted to hear, and he was sorry he'd asked the question because now Noah's curiosity was pricked.

"You're in a relationship with a woman, and you don't want any other man hitting on her. Did I get that right?"

He knew Noah was yanking his chain, but he still reacted. "No, damn it. That's not right. I'm not in a relationship."

"Huh."

"Huh, what?"

"You're not sleeping with her, but you're still feeling possessive."

Alec spotted Emerson heading toward Regan again. She was standing next to her brothers talking to the hospital administrator, who appeared to be hanging on her every word.

"Listen, I'd appreciate it if you didn't mention this conversation to Nick."

Noah laughed. "Yeah, like that's gonna happen. Your brother's my partner. I've got to tell him. We spend a lot of time on stakeouts together, and this is definitely stakeout conversation. Besides, how often do I get to make fun of one of his brothers?"

Alec could feel his temper rising. "There's nothing to tell." He pictured putting his hand through the phone and grabbing Noah by the neck and choking him. Odd, but that fantasy actually made him feel better. He was still sorry he'd brought up the topic, though, and he knew it was going to take a long time for Noah to forget about it.

"Listen, Alec. You better be careful, or you won't leave Chicago a single man. I know what I'm talking about. I saw it happen to Nick and Theo. And it was pretty painful to watch. Both of your brothers went through the juvenile don't-look, don't-touch, don't-even-think-about-it phase when they first met their wives."

"That's never going to happen to you, though, is it, Noah?"

"Hell, no."

Alec laughed, his good mood restored. He could almost hear the shudder in his friend's voice when he'd given the denial.

"Are you about finished with the girly talk?"

"Yeah."

Noah then moved on to a matter he considered far more important. He told Alec all about the fishing trip he and Father Tommy, another family friend, were setting up. "We're thinking Canada. You interested?"

"Sure, if I can get away."

Regan was now dancing with Sophie's date. What was his name? Oh, yeah. Jeff something or other. He was harmless, Alec thought. Emerson didn't look harmless, though. Anger radiated from his eyes as he watched Regan. He leaned against a pillar gulping down a tall drink while he waited for the music to end. He obviously wasn't through pestering her.

"Gotta go," he said and ended the call.

Emerson had just trapped Regan as she was leaving the dance floor. Alec started forward, then stopped. He decided not to interfere. She was a big girl. She could handle herself.

Regan's expression went stone-cold, but she didn't run from Emerson. She simply stood there as he rambled on and on. When she had had enough, she tried to walk away, but he grabbed hold of her arm just above the wrist and wouldn't let go. Her demeanor didn't change, but his sure did. She put her hand down on top of his, and from the look of shock and pain on the drunk's face, Alec surmised she'd bent a couple of his fingers back into an unnatural position.

Thatta girl. Alec was proud of her. Being raised by three older brothers did have some perks after all — even if those brothers were overbearing and intrusive.

Regan didn't come back to the table for a long time. She made the rounds, working the room, and she was fun to watch. The administrator followed in her wake to collect checks and pledges for more. People loved Regan. Most people, anyway. When Emerson's wife wasn't busy pushing her silicone breasts back into her leopard-print dress, she was glaring at her.

Every once in a while, Regan would turn toward Alec and smile at him. He thought maybe she was checking to make sure he was still there.

A good forty-five minutes passed before she stopped selling the hospital. She scanned the crowd until she found Aiden. It took her a while to get to him because men and women kept stopping her, some taking her hand as they spoke to her. When she finally reached her brother, he started talking before she had a chance to say anything, and whatever he was telling her didn't sit well. She looked stunned, but she was quick to recover. Her face was flushed, and she shook her head several times.

Then Spencer joined in, and it didn't take Alec any time at all to figure out that the two brothers were united on some issue, and she was disagreeing. Alec would have bet a hundred dollars that the issue under hot discussion was Emerson.

By the time Regan walked back to the table, she was trembling. He knew her reaction was due to anger, not fatigue. She was too furious to sit, and so she stood next to him and tried to calm down.

"Anything I can help with?" he asked.

"No, but thanks for offering."

"Then I suggest you take a couple of deep breaths and shake it off."

He didn't miss a trick. "You saw?"

"Yes."

"My brothers are so . . ."

He waited for the zinger only a sister could come up with.

"So what?" he asked, trying not to smile.

"Practical."

He blinked. She made practical sound like a sin. "And that's pretty awful, is it?"

"In this instance it is," she said. "And stop laughing at me."

Her hands were balled into fists and her spine was as rigid as one of the marble columns. He put his arm around her shoulders and gave them a gentle squeeze.

She turned to him, her back to the room, thinking to tell him that they didn't have to stay any longer, but the words got all tangled up. It was his fault. The way he was looking at her, with such warmth and obvious amusement . . . she'd never met anyone like him.

"Alec?"

"Yes?"

She took a step closer and whispered so she wouldn't be overheard. "I was wondering . . ."

He didn't say a word. He simply waited until she continued. She could feel herself blushing now.

"If we had met in a different place . . . at a different time . . . would you . . . ?"

She didn't go on. She didn't have to. He

nodded and quietly said, "Oh, yeah, I would."

Neither one of them said another word for several minutes. An old Roberta Flack song was playing in the background. She picked up her wrap, folded it, and draped it over her arm.

She looked into his eyes. "What are you thinking?" she asked before she could stop herself.

His smile could melt steel. "I'll tell you later."

"Tell me now."

He looked over the room again. She thought he'd dismissed the question until he said, "I'm on duty now."

"And?" she prodded.

He grinned. "I won't be later."

Chapter Thirty-three

It was more show than tell.

There was very little conversation on the way back to the hotel. After making certain they weren't being followed, Alec put the car on cruise control, settled back, and thought about his current situation. He was determined to figure out why he was having so much trouble keeping his professional and his personal life separate.

He knew what he should do. He should leave Regan the hell alone, tell the lieutenant he was through, and then pack up his things and get out of town. Yeah, that's what he should do.

He had the feeling he wasn't going to, though. She'd already gotten to him and was now messing with his mind. He wasn't sure how it had happened or what he could do about it, and not knowing was making him as anxious as a caged animal.

Next to her, however, he looked absolutely tranquil. Ever since they'd left the country club, she had been staring straight ahead and sitting ramrod straight. The woman was so stiff, he thought he could probably bounce a quarter off her.

Regan was trying very hard to look calm and cool. She didn't want Alec to know how nervous she was, and she was pretty sure she was doing a fair job of concealing it.

She'd never felt this way before, all twisted up in knots inside. Everything about him disrupted her concentration, the way he smiled, the way he moved, the way he looked at her. He'd probably used just that look on at least a hundred other women and most assuredly had gotten exactly what he wanted from them. As crazy as it was to admit, just sitting this close to him in the car was making her breathless.

Alec noticed she had folded her arms and she was frowning intently. Whatever she was thinking about wasn't pleasant.

"Is something wrong?"

Of course something's wrong. I've just realized I'm a complete idiot. "No, nothing."

"Okay," he said, going along with the lie. "Then what are you thinking about?"

"Just now?" She was stalling for time while she tried to come up with something mundane.

"No, a week ago Tuesday." He smiled. "Yes, just now."

"Physical attraction," she blurted.

"No kidding. I never would have guessed that."

She pretended indifference. "You asked. I answered."

"So, what about it?"

"I just realized that you can't control who you're attracted to," she said. "It can be . . . instantaneous. Yes, instantaneous." She nodded for emphasis.

It wasn't until he reached over and put his hand on top of hers that she realized she was digging her nails into her skin. She immediately stopped.

He pulled his hand back as he said, "You're just now figuring that out?"

She shifted positions and folded her hands on her lap. "I was just now thinking about it." Her tone was definitely defensive.

He wouldn't let her get away with that. "No, you said you just realized that sometimes —"

She interrupted. "Okay, maybe I was just now figuring it out. I haven't taken the time to think about it until now."

"The 'it' is physical attraction?"

From the laughter in his voice, she could tell he was having a good time.

"Oh, be quiet."

"You're easy to get riled up."

"Sometimes," she replied. "But I'm very good at concealing my feelings when I want to."

He laughed. "No, you're not. You're terrible at it."

She was floored he'd think such a thing. "I beg to differ. I've had years of experience," she said. "And if I didn't want you to know what I was thinking, then, trust me, you wouldn't."

Exasperated, he said, "I don't care how many years you've practiced, you still aren't any good at hiding anything. Your every emotion shows on your face."

She wasn't going to continue to argue with him. She certainly didn't need to have the last word. "You're wrong."

He changed the subject. "All those guys at that club tonight . . . ?"

"Yes?"

"Did you ever date any of them?"

"No."

"Are you dating anyone now?" he asked.

"No."

"Huh."

She smiled. "Huh, what?"

"I never would have guessed that."

"Are you dating anyone now?" she asked.

"No."

"Huh."

He began to laugh. "Huh, what?"

"I never would have guessed that." Then she added, "We should probably talk about something else."

"Why?"

"We just should."

"Okay," he said. "Have you ever been in a long-term relationship?"

"That isn't talking about something else."

"Have you?"

He changed lanes, checked the rearview mirror, and then glanced at her. "Are you going to answer or what?"

"I was . . . sort of in a relationship with a man named Dennis, but it ended several months ago."

"What's a 'sort of' relationship?"

"I wanted it to work. There wasn't any physical attraction, though, but I thought that in time there would be."

"You can't program something like that. It's either there, or it isn't."

She nodded but didn't comment. "We're the next exit."

"I know. Is that why you ended it?"

"How do you know *I* ended it?"

Because Dennis would be frickin' crazy to walk away from you. "Just a guess," he said.

"Yes, I ended it. He was interested in my money, not me. I was more angry than

443

hurt when I realized what a jerk he was. We never —"

"Never what?"

"The relationship hadn't become physical." She couldn't believe she'd told him that.

"Because there was no physical attraction."

"Exactly."

"Were there any hard feelings?"

"Maybe at first. He called often," she said. "But then he finally gave up and moved on. Last I heard, he was engaged."

"That was quick."

"She was an heiress."

He nodded. "Did you tell Wincott about Dennis?"

"Yes, I did."

Neither one of them said another word for several minutes. Regan was thinking about Alec and her reaction to him. It was dangerous, this attraction. He was doing his job, and when he was finished, he would leave. Simple as that. If she became too attached to him, she'd be miserable when he left.

Okay, think of all the reasons why she shouldn't get involved, no matter how outrageous. There was, of course, the obvious reason. Her heart would be broken.

Even to kiss him would be unethical, she decided, and maybe grounds for a sexual harassment lawsuit. She sighed. Heaven help her, she was beginning to think like Aiden. The possibility of litigation would always leap into his mind first. But it could happen, she told herself. After all, the man was stuck with her. She was the one in the position of power, wasn't she? And in a way, didn't he work for her? He had been ordered to protect her, and if she made any kind of sexual advances, he'd have every right to take her to court. She could just see it now. Her picture plastered all over the newspapers, and reporters with camera crews chasing her into the courthouse. It would be a nightmare.

By the time they'd reached the hotel, Regan had convinced herself that she was in complete control of her emotions. She had sorted it all out. Yes, she was definitely back in control.

Alec took her hand as they crossed the lobby. He nodded to the security guard stationed in front of the elevators. He'd already checked his credentials and knew who he was.

They were on their way up to her floor when she said, "I'm sorry I didn't introduce you to Spencer."

"That's okay. It didn't look like you were having a happy reunion."

"You noticed?"

"You mean you were hiding your emotions, and I wasn't supposed to notice?"

"Are you making fun of me?"

"A little."

The elevator stopped. Alec stepped out first. He nodded to the policeman facing the doors.

"Is it quiet tonight?"

"Yes, sir, it is."

"Good."

All of the rooms down her corridor were now vacant and were to remain that way until further notice. That was yet another security precaution Aiden had made without consulting her.

"That policeman looks familiar," she said. "But I haven't seen him here before, have I?"

"No," he answered. "This is his first night. You saw him in Lewis's office."

"That's right. You were defending him. He didn't get fired, did he?"

"No," he assured her. "He's taking a couple of shifts here for extra money."

She nodded and then asked, "Are you going to be here tomorrow?"

"Yes."

"You're sure? It's Sunday."

"I know."

"When are you going to pack?"

"Let me worry about that."

"I'll introduce you to Spencer tomorrow then. And you'll get to talk to Aiden again. Won't that be a treat? They'll both try to tell you how to do your job."

He shrugged. "That won't bother me. So, I'm gonna be seeing both of them?"

"Oh, yes. Tonight, you see, was round one. They'll try again tomorrow."

"Try what again?"

"To get me to agree to give Emerson a 'go away' settlement. I won't agree, though, no matter how practical it is."

"Are you telling me they blindsided you during that party tonight?"

She nodded. "Of course they did. They knew I wouldn't make a scene."

He smiled. "And you've made a lot of scenes in the past?"

"When I was younger."

They'd turned the corner and were standing in front of her door. She tried to tell him thank you and good night in the hall. He looked exasperated with her, took the key out of her hand, and unlocked the door.

"As many times as we've done this, you

still don't have it down?"

She didn't answer. Alec went in first, as was the routine. She followed and shut the door, then waited until he had checked the bedroom, the closet, and the bath.

"All clear."

He was removing his tie as he walked into the parlor. She'd already taken off her coat and draped it over the arm of a chair. She dropped her wrap and her purse on top. She was blocking the door but couldn't make herself move.

She cleared her throat. "Thank you for going with me tonight." The suite seemed to be getting smaller and smaller the closer he came. He smiled, and her knees began to wobble. "I really appreciate it." She sounded as if she had a bad case of laryngitis now. If he would only stop looking at her and give her time to unscramble her thoughts, she might be able to move out of his way and let him leave.

"Regan, I was doing my job." He tucked the bow tie into his pocket and unbuttoned the top two buttons of his shirt. "There, that's better. Now I can breathe. So here's the thing." He walked over to her, reached around her to slip the dead bolt in place, and then placed both hands on the door on either side of her face, trapping her. Her shoulders were pressed against the door.

Don't think about it, she told herself. Just don't think about it. God, he smelled good. She'd never realized how erotic Dial soap could be.

Okay, she was definitely losing it, she thought. If she could just make herself stop staring at him, but those eyes, oh, Lord, those incredible, gorgeous, seductive eyes.

What had he just said? Something about the thing? "What thing?" she whispered.

He knew he was rattling her. He leaned a little closer, but he still wasn't touching her. "Guess what?"

His voice was husky and low. She had goose bumps all over her arms. "What?"

He leaned closer yet still wasn't touching her. "I'm not on duty now."

Alec moved back an inch, then went completely still, and waited. If she showed the least hesitation, he would walk away, and that would be that. He just hoped to God she wanted him to stay.

It took a couple of seconds, but then Regan understood why he had stopped. It was up to her now.

She slowly lifted her hair away from that spot just below her left earlobe that was so very sensitive. Then she angled her head to the side. And waited. If this were a tennis match, the ball was now in his court.

She took a breath and held it. And closed her eyes. She felt his warm sweet breath against her ear a scant second before his mouth touched her skin. Shivers cascaded down her limbs. A simple little kiss and her heart started racing. He kissed his way down the side of her neck. His mouth was hot, yes, definitely hot.

She wondered how she would react if he kissed her on the mouth. She'd probably turn to mush. It was time to stop fooling around. She was definitely going to send him home before she did anything she knew she would regret in the morning.

She put her hands flat on his chest and whispered, "Alec?"

He immediately stepped back. He didn't say a word. He simply stared into her eyes and waited.

She couldn't blame anyone but herself for what happened next. She grabbed the labels of his jacket and jerked him toward her. Her mouth was but an inch away from his when she said, "Don't sue me."

Chapter Thirty-four

She wasn't messing around.

She didn't give him time to ask her to explain. Clutching those lapels in a death grip, she stretched up on tiptoes and kissed him, long and hard, frantically and passionately, just the way she had fantasized. One absolutely perfect kiss, she told herself, one powerful, all-consuming kiss that would surely satisfy her unreasonable craving. Then she would let go of him, unlock the door, and send him home.

It was a good plan, really it was. It would have worked too if he had cooperated and remained passive. He didn't cooperate, though. He participated. And then he took over. His arms suddenly wrapped around her, and he held her tight as his mouth slanted over hers with amazing control. After about five seconds it became apparent to her that he had far more experience at this sort of thing than she did. The man made kissing an art form. His hands slid down her back. His mouth never left hers as he lifted her up against him. Oh, no, he definitely wasn't remaining passive.

She probably should have spelled out the plan ahead of time, she supposed, and that was one of the last coherent, though admittedly idiotic, thoughts she was able to hold onto while he kissed her senseless. Her hands were now around his neck — had she moved them there or had he? — and her fingers were tugging on his hair.

He didn't force her to part her lips. She did that all on her own. She didn't push him away when his tongue slipped inside. She gave as good as she was getting, and then some.

When he finally ended the kiss, she was shivering all over. She clung to him because she knew that if she let go, her legs wouldn't support her. His hands were around her waist and she thought maybe he was holding her up, but she couldn't be sure.

Neither one of them seemed inclined to let go. She wanted a little bit more, just one more kiss, she thought, before she lost her nerve, and reason rushed in.

He must have wanted the same thing, because he tilted her head back and kissed her again. Though it didn't seem possible, this kiss was even better. And hotter. He was a master of seduction and so smooth he scared her. She tightened her hold and tried to get closer to him. It was a scorching kiss that made her burn. She had never felt this way before. Never had a kiss affected her so passionately.

Alec pulled back, let out a ragged breath, and tried without success to move away. He couldn't make himself let go of her. Hell, he just didn't want to. His head dropped to the crook of her neck, and he took a couple of deep breaths, trying hard to recover. He loved the way she felt in his arms. He loved her scent, and he loved the taste of her. He was having real trouble getting it together. How could a couple of kisses shake him like this?

He said out loud what he was thinking. "Damn, Regan." His voice was as rough as gravel.

"Was that a good 'damn' or a bad one?" she panted.

He had to think about it before he answered. He lifted his head and looked into her eyes, saw the passion he'd ignited there, and felt tremendous satisfaction. And desire, he acknowledged, for a whole lot more.

"It was a good 'damn.' Too good." He was picturing her naked underneath him when he added, "We should probably stop while we —"

She put her index finger over his mouth to silence him. "Or . . ." She dragged the word out.

He grabbed her hand and placed it flat against his chest. "Or what?" A hint of a smile softened his expression.

Don't lose your nerve, don't lose your nerve, she silently chanted. She took a breath and whispered, "Or we could not stop."

His hands moved to her shoulders and even as he was shaking his head at her, he was noticing how smooth and warm and soft her skin was.

"You do know what kissing will lead to, don't you?"

It was a stupid question, and he didn't expect or wait for an answer. "A heap of misery, that's what. I'm not a machine, sweetheart. I can't just turn it on and off. You know I want you. I'm burning up with the need to —" He suddenly stopped, took a deep breath, and said, "But you also need to know that I don't want what comes with it."

Did he realize he was shaking her? She didn't think so. He wasn't hurting her. In fact, his touch was surprisingly gentle and sweet. He wanted her. He'd said those very words to her, and he couldn't take them back. She was thrilled, and yet frustrated, because he obviously wasn't happy about it. The look on his face was so intense and angry, and intimidating, she suddenly felt as though she'd just poked a lion.

She pushed his hands away. "Tell me, Alec, what comes with it?"

He was glaring at her now. "I'm leaving Chicago, remember? I've made that clear, haven't I? I'm packing up and getting out of here. Understand that?"

"Yes, I understand."

"Okay then."

"Okay, what?"

Alec gritted his teeth. He guessed he was going to have to spell it out for her. "The last thing I need or want is to leave a mess behind."

Whoa. She didn't like hearing that. Her eyes turned a darker blue, and her face became flushed. She was angry, all right, but he wasn't going to take the words back.

"And I'm the mess?"

He threaded his fingers through his hair to keep himself from grabbing her and kissing her until she wanted him as much as he wanted her. He shook his head. Bad plan, he told himself. He wasn't going to give in to his desire. No way. He could be as tough as steel when he needed to, and he was always in control.

"What I'm trying to tell you is . . . ."

"I'm a mess."

"Okay, that's it. I'm through trying to be diplomatic about this."

She blinked. "Telling me I'm a mess is being diplomatic?"

"Damn right, and you are. A mess, that is. And that 'damn' wasn't a good one."

He ripped off the jacket of his tux and tossed it on the chair. "It's hotter than hell in here."

He began to roll up his shirtsleeves to keep his hands busy. Better to tear his clothes than hers. That skinny little nothing of a dress she was wearing was so amazingly perfect on her. He didn't want to ruin it, but he didn't want her wearing it with any other man either, and how could he justify that backward reasoning?

She couldn't hold his stare long. She focused on his chin and said, "I know I put you on the spot. It's just that this is the first time I've ever tried to . . . you know . . . and I'm apparently causing you extreme anxiety. I'm just not any good at it. I realize my mistake. I just didn't put enough thought into it."

"Into what?"

He couldn't be that dense. No one could. Was he deliberately toying with her?

"Into what?" he repeated when she didn't answer.

Seducing you, you idiot. That's what she wanted to say. She didn't, though. Some inhibitions were just too firmly entrenched to get past. Besides, Alec was right. It would become messy, and she had the feeling she'd be the one all messed up when he left.

"You're right," she said. "Becoming involved, even for one night, would make things . . . awkward."

He didn't look relieved. She edged around him, flipped off her heels, and continued on to the French doors. Alec had left one open when he'd checked the bedroom. She pushed the other door back and then turned around to tell him good night.

He stared at the king-sized bed for a long minute. He felt a tightness gathering in his chest, and his mouth was suddenly dry. Every possible fantasy about her bombarded him. Hell, it was already messy.

And he wasn't going anywhere.

Chapter Thirty-five

From the moment Alec had bumped into her on the street and heard that wonderful laugh, he had become hers for the taking. He never had a chance. He understood that now. No reason to keep fighting the attraction, he decided as he pulled away from the door. He made sure everything was locked up tight, then reached over and turned the lamp off.

He was unbuttoning his shirt as he headed toward her. Light from the lamp on the bedside table spilled across her shoulders. Her skin was golden, and she was, without a doubt, absolutely breathtaking.

And nervous as hell. Her eyes were huge, but she didn't look away. She took a step toward him and then stopped. His gaze swept down her body. He noticed her hands were clenched at her sides, and her toes were curled into the carpet as she watched him come toward her.

"Just remember," he whispered gruffly as he reached her. "You started this."

He pulled her close, kissed her forehead,

and then let go. Regan knew he was giving her yet another chance to change her mind, one last chance perhaps to tell him to leave.

Like that was gonna happen.

Alec held his breath while he waited for her to make up her mind. She put her arms around his neck and smiled up at him with that tantalizing dimple just above the corner of her mouth. Nope, he never had a chance.

"Just *you* remember," she said, "that I started this."

She kissed his chin, then moved lower and kissed the pulse beating rapidly at the base of his neck. He must have liked what she was doing because he pulled her tight against him, and so she did it again.

And then he took over. He tilted her head back with a kiss that didn't leave any doubt how much he wanted her. He lifted her off the ground as he ravaged her mouth.

They were suddenly frantic to get their clothes off. His hands shook as he reached for the zipper at the back of her dress. It was awkward because he couldn't stop kissing her long enough to pay attention to what he was doing, and she was trying to remove his shirt at the same time.

She'd gotten a couple of his buttons undone, and was tugging his shirt from his waistband when she accidentally touched his gun and holster. She reacted as though she'd just touched fire. Flinching, she jerked back, but Alec was still quicker. He had her hand flat against his chest before she could pull away from him.

"Could you . . ." she whispered. She was trying to ask him to remove the gun but couldn't get the words out. He was distracting her by nibbling on her earlobe. ". . . get rid of . . ."

"It's okay," he answered.

She sighed. Her heart was racing, and she was trying to catch her breath. Kissing had never caused such a reaction before. Granted, she hadn't kissed all that many men, but enough to know that kissing Alec was completely different. Maybe because she was already emotionally invested. Everything about him aroused her. She needed to slow down so that she could savor every single minute of this night with him, but at the same time, she wanted him to hurry up and take his clothes off.

He made her step back so he could pull his shirt over his head. His chest was all muscle, swirling dark hair, and bronzed skin.

He was beautiful. He pulled her back into his arms, and she felt his hot skin against hers. It wasn't enough. She wrapped her hands around his neck and tugged on his hair to get him to kiss her again.

The kiss was hot and wet. She felt like she was melting against him.

He removed his gun and holster, and backing her to the side of the bed, he put the weapon on her nightstand and then forced himself to stop kissing her long enough to get her clothes off.

That was the goal anyway, but the dress wasn't cooperating. The zipper got stuck and wouldn't budge, no matter how much he tugged on it. He thought maybe he'd jammed it. He clenched his jaw and tried again. He was usually a hell of a lot smoother undressing women, but tonight was different because he was with Regan. He had never felt this kind of desperation before. He wanted to wrap her in his arms and never let go.

He tried to concentrate on the task at hand, but she was making it difficult. She was kissing his neck again and stroking his back. It felt so good he didn't want her to stop.

"Turn around," he whispered as he

pulled her hands away and forced her to do as he'd asked. Then he tried again to get her dress unzipped.

She tried to help, but her hands just got in his way. "How much do you like this dress? The thing . . . it's stuck."

"The thing?"

"The zipper." He was smiling now because she sounded as rattled as he did.

"I hate this dress," she blurted out.

She sure looked hot in it, but if he had to, he was going to tear it to shreds to get to her. The zipper finally gave and slid down . . . all the way to the base of her spine.

She wasn't wearing a bra. He noticed that right away. Then he noticed how flawless her back was. He slowly trailed his fingers down the opening until he reached a tiny wisp of black lace.

He didn't know which turned him on more. Her indrawn breath when he'd touched her or seeing that little bit of lace.

"You're beautiful," he whispered.

Regan reached up to pull the straps over her arms but suddenly froze when his hands slid inside her dress and began to caress her skin.

His hands slowly circled her. She started to turn in his arms, but he wouldn't let her, and when at last he touched her breasts, she made a tiny gasp in the back of her throat and fell back against him. Trembling with desire, she didn't know how much of this exquisite torture she would withstand without coming apart.

Her response drove Alec crazy. His head dropped down to the side of her neck, and his breathing became harsh. He managed to let go of her long enough to get undressed. Her dress fell to the floor, and she gracefully stepped out of it and reached for the covers. She pulled them back and then began to pull the clips from her hair. Alec's shoes and socks went flying in one direction and her clips in another.

He knew it was only a matter of minutes before he lost all control. He wanted her ready before he did that.

"We've got to slow down."

He meant what he said, but then she turned around and those perfect breasts rubbed against his chest. Slowing down didn't seem all that important any longer.

They fell together onto the bed. He cradled her in his arms as he rolled her onto her back and nudged her thighs apart with his knee. He braced his weight so he wouldn't crush her. Then he growled low in his throat with sheer male satisfaction because one of his fantasies about her was finally coming true. He had her right where he wanted her.

She looked disheveled and thoroughly aroused. Her hair was spread on the pillow, framing her flushed face; her eyes were dark with passion, and her lips were swollen from his kisses. He knew it was a primitive, barbaric response on his part, but he was still arrogantly pleased that he had put his mark on her. He'd never felt this way about any other woman. What was next? he wondered. Would he start dragging a club and carrying her over his shoulder? Would he start shouting like Tarzan?

He shook his head when she tried to pull him down to kiss her. He rolled to his side and took his time looking at her perfect body.

"I've been thinking about this a long time." He slowly trailed his fingertips down her neck, then lower to the valley between her breasts, smiling over the goose bumps he left behind. She tried to grab his hand when he reached her navel. He wouldn't be stopped, though.

And he wouldn't be rushed. Ever so slowly he removed her lace panties, taking his time, savoring every inch of golden skin he touched.

She battled her shyness, but she didn't cover herself. She watched his face as he stroked her. His jaw was clenched tight, and sweat had broken out on his forehead. He seemed to be on the verge of losing his control.

But then so was she. Her legs moved restlessly against him. He was tormenting her, making her crazed because he wouldn't let her touch him. His hand moved between her thighs. She almost came off the bed then. His touch was magical and demanding.

She couldn't remain passive any longer. She pulled her hand away from his and reached up to stroke the side of his face. Her fingers slowly traced his mouth, then moved lower to caress his neck and shoulders. His body was absolutely perfect. His skin was hot, and she could feel the power of those hard muscles in his upper arms. The crisp dark hair on his chest tickled her fingertips.

She took her time, for she was determined to drive him out of his mind, but he kept distracting her. He was stroking her breasts as he nibbled her neck.

She closed her eyes, arched her neck back, and then trailed her fingers down his stomach. The muscles in his abdomen flexed in response, and he growled low in his throat.

She knew her touch pleased him, but she wanted more. Ever so slowly her fingertips circled his navel and then moved lower. Her hand slid down between his thighs. His deep indrawn breath told her how much he liked what she was doing to him.

She became more demanding. She wrapped her hand around him . . . and sent him right over the edge. He grabbed her hand, rolled on top of her, and kissed her passionately. His tongue rubbed against hers as his hands caressed her. He moved lower, and when he began to kiss her breasts, she arched up against him and let out a ragged sigh. He told her he was going to kiss every inch of her body, and then he set about proving it. He tickled her navel with his tongue, then moved lower still until he was touching the very heat of her.

The pleasure was exquisite, consuming. Her nails dug into his shoulder blades and she cried out.

Alec's control was in tatters now, and he was desperate to be inside her.

"Alec . . ."

"It's okay. I just need to protect you."

He reached down and grabbed his trousers. Regan rolled on top of him and was fervently kissing his shoulders while he fumbled in the back pocket for his wallet. He found what he was searching for and gently rolled back until she scooted off him.

When he was ready, he grabbed her hands, stretched her arms high above her head, and held her there. And then he once again began to make love to her with his mouth, his tongue, and his fingers.

The first tremors of ecstasy caught her unaware. It should have ended there, but it didn't. The pleasure was gathering, building, so intense she almost couldn't bear it. Terrified of what was happening, she struggled to stop it.

"It's okay," he whispered as he continued to stroke her. "Just hold me and let it happen. It's okay, Regan." He moved between her thighs, and with one swift plunge, he was inside her, deep inside. He squeezed his eyes shut and clenched his jaw tight for pleasure was almost too much to bear. She cried out and arched up against him, then drew her knees up and wrapped her legs around him.

His control snapped. She felt so wonderful he couldn't make himself slow the pace. Her passion more than equaled his, and her response to his touch was wild, uninhibited.

She lifted her hips to meet each hard thrust, and when at last he climaxed inside her, she was there with him, screaming his name as she came apart.

She thought she just might die from the sheer ecstasy shimmering through her. Alec collapsed on top of her and buried his head in the crook of her neck. It took him several minutes to calm his labored breathing.

It had never been this good, no, not good, *perfect* before. She had overwhelmed him, and he was staggered by his need for her.

He slowly regained enough strength to move. He lifted up and looked into her eyes. "You okay?" His voice was no more than a raspy whisper.

She was still reeling from what had just happened. She'd read about it. She'd heard about it, but until tonight, she had never experienced it.

Amazing, she thought. Simply amazing. And beautiful. There weren't enough words to describe what had happened to her. She still felt a warm glow all over. Could he feel her heart pounding against his? Did he have any idea what he had done to her? Had he experienced the same splendor? Or was it different for a man? The wonder of their lovemaking stunned her, and she couldn't stop trembling.

"Regan?"

"Yes, I'm okay." That had to be a gross understatement.

He kissed her once hard then rolled away from her and went into the bathroom.

His abrupt departure startled her. She didn't want him to leave, not just yet anyway. She wanted him to hold her in his arms and whisper all the romantic words she longed to hear.

She could feel the tears gathering in her eyes. Oh, God, not now. Don't let me cry now. She took a deep breath, groaned, and then pulled the sheet up and rolled onto her stomach. His scent was on the pillow. She had the urge to pick up that pillow and bury her head under it. She couldn't believe how vulnerable and self-conscious she was feeling. What was the matter with her? She had started this. What had she expected? For him to drop down on his knees and tell her how much he loved her? That was the stuff of fairy tales.

A tear spilled out on her cheek. She impatiently wiped it away. Tonight was driven by lust, not love . . . for him, anyway. She groaned again. She wasn't going to regret tonight. Her heart was too fragile to ever let it happen again, but she wouldn't be sorry.

She didn't hear Alec walk back into the bedroom. She felt him when he sat down on the bed beside her. "Move over," he said.

She rolled onto her side to face him just as he tried to yank the sheet down. She held tight. "I thought you were getting dressed."

"You didn't notice my clothes are all over the floor?"

"No, I didn't notice."

They were involved in a tug-of-war with the sheet. He won. He stretched out beside her and pulled her to him. "I should go." He began to nuzzle her neck. "Yeah, I should go. How come you smell so good?"

"I bathe."

He laughed. Then he pinched her backside, and she yelped.

"How come you're so soft?"

She kissed his neck before answering. "I'm a girl."

"Yeah, I noticed."

She couldn't stop touching him. She loved the feel of his hard muscles beneath her fingertips. They glided over his shoulders and his chest. His body was warm and hairy and sexy. She wrapped her arms around his waist and decided she was never going to let go. He was going to have to peel her off of him. That image made her smile.

"It was better than my fantasy," he said.

"You've thought about it?"

"Oh, yeah. You did too."

She didn't deny it. "Yes."

"Was it as good as your fantasy?"

Her voice dropped to a whisper. "It was . . . so-so."

He laughed. Then he pushed her onto her back and leaned over her. "So-so?" he repeated.

He looked a little worried. She realized then that there was a thread of insecurity hidden under all those layers of arrogance. She was stunned. How could he not know how much pleasure he had given her?

She cupped the side of his face. "It was perfect."

He leaned down and kissed her. He thought it would be a see-you-later kind of kiss, but as soon as his mouth touched hers, everything changed. His tongue rubbed erotically against hers. He kept telling himself he just wanted a little bit more and he'd be satisfied. How come he couldn't get enough of her?

She moved restlessly against him. "Alec?" she whispered.

"You want to go again?"

Her eyes widened. She pushed his shoulders. "Go again? What kind of pillow talk is that?"

She honestly didn't know if she wanted to yell at him or laugh.

Then he grinned and laughter won out. "I can do pillow talk," he boasted.

"Prove it."

He got sidetracked by the devilish way her lips curled up. The dimple was interfering with his thought process too, and so he looked into her eyes. It seemed to hit him all at once, the reality of what had just happened. This beautiful, sweet, perfect creature had taken him to her bed.

She nudged him. "I'm waiting," she whispered, and then she batted her eyelashes at him.

He laughed again. "Okay. Here's what I think we ought to do." And then he explained in the most graphic detail how he wanted to make love to her and what he expected in return.

By the time he'd finished, her cheeks were bright pink. "What kind of women have you been hanging out with?" she asked. She tried to sound shocked.

"Gymnasts, acrobats. Why do you ask?" His hands moved down to her hips.

"Alec, what are you doing?"

"It's called multitasking. I'm talking and touching at the same time." He slowly moved down her body, and his mouth and tongue were driving her wild. "We could try something new," he said. He kissed the valley between her breasts and then whispered, "But why mess with perfection?'

Chapter Thirty-six

Alec wouldn't spend the night. She tried to entice him, but she couldn't get him to change his mind. He was far more concerned about protecting her good name than she was. She put on a blue silk robe that didn't quite reach her knees and sat on the side of the bed while Alec got dressed.

Her legs distracted him from what he was doing. When he realized where his thoughts were taking him, he turned and walked into the living room.

"What'd I do with my phone?"

She followed him. "It's in your coat pocket."

He turned around to tell her good night. She stepped closer and buttoned his shirt for him while he clipped on his holster and flipped the leather snap in place over his gun.

She stretched up on tiptoes and kissed him just below the jaw. "Sleep over," she whispered.

"No."

His harsh tone didn't bother her because

he was kissing the side of her neck while he refused her.

"Don't you want to?"

"Of course I want to," he said. "And if the circumstances were different, I would."

His hands slid inside her robe. He couldn't get enough of her. Not good, he told himself. He pulled his hands back. "The whole world is watching you, and I don't want anyone talking . . ."

"The whole world? Surely not."

"You've got the police department, the security team, the hotel staff, and your brothers watching your every move. Did you forget there's a policeman standing outside your door? I don't want anyone speculating about you or gossiping or teasing . . ." She was kissing his neck and tormenting him with her tongue. "Stop that."

After giving the order, he put his hands on her shoulders with the intent of making her step back. He pulled her up against him instead. His chin dropped down on her head.

"Am I the only one worried about your reputation?"

"Apparently so."

He laughed. "Damn, you're sweet."

He tilted her chin up and kissed her. If

she hadn't been so hot, he might have been able to give her a quick good-bye kiss. Regan wasn't just sweet and sexy and hot, though. She was enthusiastic and demanding. She could turn him into Jell-O if she kept kissing without a hint of reservation. The little whimper she made in the back of her throat triggered a primitive response.

When he ended the kiss, she collapsed against him.

What had happened to his self-restraint? His discipline? Regan could turn him on faster than he could snap his fingers. Man oh man, she was getting to him, and he had to somehow put a stop to it. He was leaving, and nothing was going to change his mind.

"Listen, Regan. This can't happen again."

He waited for an argument. He expected her to be upset. Their lovemaking had been pretty incredible, and he had the scratches on his shoulders where her nails had dug in to prove that it was perfect for her too. Yeah, of course she would argue.

"Yes, I know."

"What?"

"I agree," she said. "It can't happen again."

A pang of disappointment went through him. "I've got to get out of here. Lock the door after me."

His hand cupped the back of her neck and he jerked her close so he could kiss her again.

And then he was gone. Regan flipped the dead bolt in place and fell back against the door. Alec had clearly worn her out. She was still trembling. She dropped her robe on her way back to bed. The sheets were still warm from the heat of their bodies. She wrapped herself in them and closed her eyes.

She was determined not to think about the future, but that was easier said than done. Tears streamed down her face. What an idiot she was. She was falling in love with him. No, she wasn't falling, she was already in love with him. She would never have been able to let go the way she did tonight if she hadn't loved him. She knew exactly when she realized it too. She and Henry had been sitting in the hotel bar watching as Kevin poured his heart out to Alec, and the compassion she'd seen in Alec's eyes had been her undoing. Oh, yes, she'd known it for a while; she'd just been too stupid to admit it.

Besides his compassion, there were so

many things she loved about him. He was a man of honor and integrity. She'd figured that out after spending an hour with him. He was also dedicated to his job. He was fiercely loyal to those he cared about, and he had the most wonderful sense of humor.

He did have flaws, but at the moment she could not remember any. She let out a loud groan. Don't think about the future, she told herself. Don't think about the day he leaves.

She couldn't turn her mind off, and the more she told herself not to think about him, the more she did. Regan buried her face in the pillow and cried herself to sleep.

Chapter Thirty-seven

It was a new day and Regan had a new attitude. While she showered and dressed, she gave herself a lecture. She was a big girl; she could handle a broken heart. Sure she could. She would survive when Alec left, and she vowed he would never know how she felt about him.

Alec wasn't outside her door. She'd already looked through the peephole. The same young policeman who'd come on duty when she and Alec had left for the country club last night was waiting for her. She hurried because she knew the policeman had to be exhausted. She'd just pulled on her jeans and slipped into her sandals when her phone rang. Spencer was on the line. He told her he was in her office, but she'd already guessed that because she could hear the television blaring in the background.

"Want me to come up there after the game, or do you want to come down here?"

She didn't ask what game because there was always some game playing. "I'll be right down," she promised.

"Aiden's here."

"Is that a warning?"

"Maybe."

"Yeah, well, you need to warn him. Time has not softened my attitude, Spencer. I'm still out for blood."

Spencer laughed. "I can't wait to see that."

The second she hung up the phone, she started sneezing. Maybe she was allergic to her brothers. The ridiculous thought made her laugh. She went back into the bathroom, took her allergy medicine, then grabbed her keys, stuffed them into her pocket, and opened the door.

The policeman escorted her to her office. She tried to coax him into coming inside and relaxing on the sofa, but he refused. He'd been told to stand guard in the hall, and that's what he was going to do.

She noticed the stack of mail on Henry's desk as she walked past, but she didn't take time to go through it. Henry would get to it tomorrow, and he'd let her know if there was anything that required her attention.

Aiden was standing behind her desk using her phone. He smiled and nodded when he saw her and then picked up a paper from a folder he'd spread open and began to read to whoever was on the line. He was wearing what he considered weekend or casual attire: a pair of khaki pants and a polo knit shirt. Aiden worked out, and he had the muscles in his upper arms to prove it. He looked tired, though, but then he always did. Building an empire apparently required putting in a twenty-four-hour day.

Spencer, on the other hand, didn't look jet-lagged or tired at all. He was sitting on her sofa and was hunched over another file folder he'd spread on her coffee table.

"Hey, you," she called out.

Spencer quickly stood and then stretched his arms over his shoulders. His clothing really was casual, an old pair of jeans and a well-worn blue rugby shirt.

She crossed the office and hugged him. "I didn't get to tell you last night how happy I am that you're home."

"Me too," he said. "Unfortunately, I won't be here long."

She stepped back. "How long?"

"That depends."

Aiden distracted her when he came up behind her and put his arm around her shoulder.

"Are you doing okay?" he asked.

"Yes," she answered. She folded her arms across her chest and asked, "Are you ready to talk?"

"About what?"

"Oh, please."

"The stress is getting to you, isn't it?" Spencer said.

Before she could answer, Spencer turned to Aiden and said, "I talked to a man with the police, a guy named Lewis, and he told me the investigation was progressing nicely."

"Lewis doesn't know what he's talking about," Aiden said. "But the detective Lewis put in charge is good. Talk to him," he suggested. "His name is John Wincott."

"Don't pester him," Regan said. "Let him do his job."

Her brothers stood side by side facing her, and as she looked from one to the other, she suddenly realized how handsome they were. She'd never really noticed how much they looked alike. They also shared some of the same mannerisms. Like the frowns they were giving her now. Those were definitely identical.

"They don't have anything yet, do they?" Spencer asked.

Aiden answered. "Talk to Wincott."

Spencer rubbed the back of his neck. "Okay, I will. Maybe we ought to hire more security, just until we leave."

Regan shook her head. "I'm tripping over security guards now. I don't want you to hire more men. I mean it, Aiden. Promise me."

"I'm going to do what I think is necessary to keep you safe."

Spencer agreed. "You're our little sister, and if we don't look out for you, who will?"

"We know that under normal circumstances you can take care of yourself, but this isn't a normal circumstance," added Aiden.

"I think he should hire more guards. For God's sake, there's a killer out there just waiting for the opportunity, and that's why Aiden and I . . ." Spencer paused.

"Yes?"

"We both thought you would be safe in Melbourne."

They were doing it again, she realized. Ganging up on her. She couldn't blame them. The tactic had always worked on her. They were used to wearing her down until she agreed to whatever it was they wanted. She wasn't upset. In the past, she had always caved. But those days were over. Her brothers just didn't know it yet.

She couldn't wait to enlighten them.

"You think I'll be safer in Melbourne?"

"Yes," Spencer said. "We'll fly back together, and we'll find a nice, safe, secluded place for you to stay."

She smiled. "And it will be safe because killers don't get on planes. Is that what you think?"

"No need to be sarcastic, Regan," Spencer said.

"Spence, why don't you tell it like it is? You've already found that nice, safe, secluded place, haven't you?"

"As a matter of fact, I have."

"I'm not going."

Before he could argue, she turned to Aiden. "What made you think you had the right to get rid of my car?"

"Didn't he buy you a BMW?"

"Stay out of this, Spencer."

"The only reason you kept that piece of junk was to irritate me. Isn't that right?" Aiden asked. Before she could answer, he plunged ahead. "If you had had a new car when you left that seminar, you could have pushed the panic button on the key, and maybe, just maybe, someone would have come to your aid when that maniac was chasing you."

"When I think what could have happened to you," Spencer said with a disapproving shake of his head. "You've got to know how important you are to us."

"Running from him . . . look what you did to your knee," Aiden said.

"Are you suggesting I shouldn't have run?"

"Don't be a smart . . ." Spencer started and then stopped.

"You had surgery," Aiden reminded her. "And when did we find out about it?"

"After the fact," Spencer answered. He was getting angry now. "You should have told us."

"It was a minor surgery," she said.

She walked over to the desk and leaned against it. "I didn't want it to become a big production. I didn't even tell Cordie or Sophie."

"We're your family," Spencer said. "You should have told us."

"Look, Regan, I know you want to be independent, but you take it to the extreme."

Spencer dropped down on the sofa, but Aiden continued to stand. He looked as if he wanted to tell her something but wasn't sure how.

She sighed. Now she was trying to read his mind. "About the car . . ." she began.

"We're finished talking about the car," Aiden said.

There was a time she would have backed down. Not today. "No, we aren't. I'm only just getting started. I'll admit that I was being childish. I kept the car because I knew it irritated you, so, yes, Aiden, you were right about that. However, I don't agree with or like what you did. You should have asked me before you had my car towed away."

"You would have said no."

"Aiden, you had no right —" she began.

"I agree with Aiden," Spencer said.

She glared at him. "When don't you agree with him?"

He looked shocked. He wasn't used to her arguing with him. "When I don't agree with Aiden, I tell him I don't agree."

"It's done," Aiden said. "Let it go."

"We've got some important things to discuss," Spencer added. "And I want to get to them."

"Maybe we should go into the board-room," Alec suggested as he gathered the papers and slipped them back into the file folder.

"Do you want to have the annual meeting now? Are you prepared?"

Spencer stood and walked forward.

"Actually Aiden and I already did that."

She was furious. "When?"

"Early this morning. You've got so much on your mind that we didn't think you would want to be bothered," Spencer said. "Everything we went over is in that black binder on your desk. Take your time looking it over."

She didn't say a word, but she was so angry with the two of them she thought steam might be coming out of her ears.

"Okay," she said quietly.

Spencer looked relieved. Then she asked, "Did you allocate funds?"

"Yes."

"What's my budget?"

"Same as last year."

"No."

"What do you mean, no?" Spencer asked. "It's done."

"No, it isn't done. We're going to talk about this. I want to triple my budget."

She was looking at Aiden when she very calmly stated what she wanted. He shook his head. "That's out of the question. We've already slotted money for most of the charities in the city because you wanted us to —"

"And because it was the right thing to do," she interjected.

"Yes," he agreed. "But we can't do any more than that, at least not this fiscal year."

"We have to think about the bottom line," Spencer said. "We're trying to make a profit."

"You are making a profit, Spencer."

"The budget's set," he said. "And we've got a new hotel going up."

"Yes, I know," she said. "In Melbourne."

"Yes, in Melbourne," he agreed. "But we're just now finalizing plans for another one."

"Oh? Where?"

"Sydney."

"I didn't know that."

"Now you do," Spencer said. "We're hoping to break ground within six months. We're on a tight schedule, and we're really moving ahead on this one."

"And did Walker vote for this?"

"Of course he did. You know Walker. As long as we don't interfere with his racing, we can pretty much do what we want."

She picked up a pencil and began to twirl it between her fingers like a baton.

"I'm not a real important part of this organization, am I? Did either of you ever think to talk to me about this expansion?"

"No," Spencer said. "You've been under tremendous stress."

"Yes, right. Stress."

"What's gotten into you?" Spencer said. "I've never seen you so antagonistic."

"I've been doing a lot of thinking."

She waited for one of them to ask her what she had been thinking about, but neither one of them did. She wasn't really sure Aiden was even paying attention to the conversation. He seemed far more interested in the paper he was reading. The pencil twirling got away from her, and the pencil went flying. It landed at Aiden's feet. Regan immediately reached for another one.

As she turned, she spotted Henry. He was standing at his desk. What was he doing here on Sunday? He should be out, having some fun, she thought. And who was he talking to? She couldn't quite see.

"Why are you so nervous today?" Spencer asked.

"Why do you think I'm nervous?"

In answer, he looked at her hard. Her pencil was going at Mach four speed. She made herself stop.

Aiden picked up the pencil from the floor, handed it to her, and then pulled out the chair behind her desk and sat down. He opened the folder and said, "Regan, you need to look over these contracts Sam sent over."

"For the new hotel?" she asked.

"Yes."

"If our attorney sent over contracts, you two must have known about the expansion a long time ago. Odd that you never mentioned it to me."

"Would you have been interested?" Spencer asked.

"Yes, I would."

He didn't believe her. "There's a basic difference between our philosophies," he said. "Aiden and I try to make money, and you try to give it all away."

She smiled. "Not all, Spencer. Just some."

Her brother walked over to the credenza and poured himself a glass of water.

"I don't know how it happened," he said. "We grew up in the same house."

"I knew I was different and I tried to be more like you, but I didn't become a capitalist."

"Right."

"That's what I've been thinking about," she said. "And I've come to some startling realizations."

"Like what?"

"I've always thought I had to earn your love. Silly, huh? I worried that if I didn't please you and Aiden, that you would stop loving me."

"Where did you get that crazy idea?" Spencer asked.

Aiden answered the question. "Mother. When she was there, withholding affection was her way of manipulating us into doing what she wanted."

Regan turned to Aiden. "She did that to you?"

He nodded. "She did it to all of us."

"You don't think we're doing that to you, do you, Regan?" Spencer asked.

She sighed. "All I'm trying to say is that I've spent my life trying to please you, and it's wearing me out. I grew up worrying that you'd stop loving me . . . but I don't feel that way any longer. I'm your sister, and as far as I'm concerned, you have to love me no matter how angry I make you."

Aiden nodded. "Good. I'm glad you worked that out. Now will you look at these papers? I've got to get going."

She turned to him. "I'm not finished yet. Aiden, I'm sorry you got stuck with the job of being my parent, and I'm sorry you and Spencer had to carry such a burden. I can't change the fact that our mother didn't like being a mother, but I want you to know how thankful I am that I had you."

Tears gathered in her eyes. Spencer noticed. "Ah, no. You're getting all emotional on us, aren't you?"

"Yes, I am."

"You know we love you," Spencer said.

"Yes."

"Okay then. Let's move on."

Like Aiden, Spencer was uncomfortable showing any kind of emotion. "Okay," she agreed. "About the meeting . . ."

"Yes?"

"Besides setting the budget for next year and agreeing to start another hotel, what else did you boys decide?"

"That's about it."

She started to reach for the papers Aiden wanted her to read, but Spencer stopped her when he said, "Actually, there was one other matter we discussed."

She turned back. "Yes?"

"We talked to Sam about it, and he agreed," he said. "I know you aren't going to like this, but we decided to pay Emerson nuisance money to get rid of him."

She jerked away from the desk. "No," she said in a near shout.

"It was either that or give him the house," Spencer said. "And you know what that property is worth. Emerson's agreed to get out by the end of next week. Then he'll get a check."

She shook her head. "No."

"Regan, it's a done deal," Aiden said.

"How can you do this?" she cried out. "My God, he was cheating on our mother when he married her."

Aiden was suddenly angry. He stood, planted his hands on the desktop, and said, "And what do you think she was doing?"

She didn't understand. "She was getting her heart broken."

"Yeah, right." The derision in Spencer's tone infuriated her.

"What does that mean?"

"Jeez, Regan, grow up. Our mother was doing the same thing Emerson was. She was never faithful."

She shook her head. "You can't know that."

"Oh yes, I can," Spencer said.

"All those trips she took," Aiden said. "Did you think she went alone?"

"Come on, Regan. You had to have known what was going on."

She and Spencer were suddenly shouting at each other while Aiden patiently waited for the argument to end. Spencer accused her of living in pretend land, and she finally conceded that she had wondered how her mother could fall in and out of love so easily.

"Love?" Spencer scoffed at the notion. "Love didn't have anything to do with it."

"Mother always wanted what she couldn't have."

It suddenly dawned on her that she was screaming, giving both of them hell, and they were still there. No one was walking out on her. Aiden looked as if he wanted to put a gag in her mouth, but she wasn't intimidated . . . or worried.

"You need to grow up," Spencer said, his tone calmer now. "And face facts."

"Acknowledging that our mother was a slut is growing up?"

He shrugged. "It's facing reality."

"All right," she said. "You both believe that since Mother slept around, it's okay that Emerson did? Isn't anyone faithful anymore? Don't wedding vows mean anything, like now and forever?"

"Apparently not," Spencer shouted.

"Don't be so dramatic," Aiden snapped. "We're getting rid of a problem."

"The cheapest way we know how," Spencer said. He shoved his hands in his pockets and frowned at her.

"And nothing I say will change your minds?"

Both of her brothers shook their heads. Then Spencer said, "Sorry, Regan, but we've got to play hardball on this one."

She smiled. "Okay."

Then they smiled . . . until she walked to the door.

"Wait," Spencer called out. "You forgot to sign the papers."

She pushed the doors open as she turned back. "You need my signature to go forward, and you know what? I need you to triple my budget for next year. When that happens, I'll sign. And that, boys, is playing hardball."

Chapter Thirty-eight

"I've never heard you lose it like that before." Henry made the comment, and from the look on his face, it was apparent he was impressed.

"I didn't lose it. I simply stated my position."

Henry spotted Spencer walking toward them, and so he lowered his voice to a whisper. "Yes, but you were shouting when you were stating your position. Honest, I've never ever heard you raise your voice. Come to think of it, I've never heard Aiden or Spencer raise their voices either," he said. "Except during football games. Spencer yells at the television then."

Henry hadn't included her brother Walker, but then why would he? He barely knew him. Walker was never around. Henry had met him a couple of years ago, while he was still training, but he'd only seen him once since, at the dedication in Conrad Park that they had all attended.

Spencer turned her attention when he walked past her. He tugged on a strand of her hair and nodded to Henry.

Aiden came out of her office a minute later. He stopped to talk to Henry. He noticed the article and the photo Henry had framed and hung on the wall.

"That's nice," he said. He started to walk away, then changed his mind. "You're doing an excellent job here. Paul Greenfield, my senior manager, keeps me informed," he explained. "If you ever want a job making money instead of giving it away, come work for me."

Henry smiled. "Thank you, sir, but I'm good here. Besides, someday this is all going to be mine."

Aiden laughed. "The hotel, or this office?"

"Stop recruiting him," Regan said.

Aiden ignored her. "If this is really what you want . . ."

"It is, sir. Besides, I could never work with . . ."

"The dragon? Isn't that what you call Emily?"

Henry didn't seem embarrassed or look the least contrite. "Most of the time that's what I call her, but I've also got a couple of other names for her."

"Yes. I've heard about those too."

"I appreciate your offer," he said. "But I love what I'm doing, and like I said, I could never work with Emily."

"Apparently no one can." He was looking at Regan when he made that remark.

She didn't ask him what, if anything, he planned to do about his assistant because he might use that as a bargaining chip to get her to sign the papers. She was happy, though, to know that he was aware he had a problem.

Her brother nudged her shoulder as he walked by. "I left the papers on your desk. Sign them."

"Triple my budget and I will."

"That's not going to happen."

As soon as Aiden was out of earshot, Henry whispered, "He's never going to go for triple. That was reaching."

"I know he won't. So we'll negotiate, and we'll get double, which is what we want."

Henry shook his head. "Aiden's got to know what you're up to."

"Of course he knows," she said. "But he'll still give in to us. At least I hope he will."

"He acts like he doesn't care about the job we do, but he does care, doesn't he? It's not just about a tax write-off."

"No, he cares, and so does Spencer.

They're just so busy building their empire, they don't have time for anything else." She glanced around the office. "Henry, who were you talking to when I was inside with Spencer and Aiden?"

"Alec."

"Alec was here?"

Her reaction to the news was bizarre. She could feel herself blushing, and she hoped Henry wouldn't notice. She tried to sound nonchalant when she asked, "Did Alec happen to overhear any of the conversation?"

Henry smiled. "Are you asking me if he heard you and Spencer shouting?"

So much for trying to act nonchalant. "Yes, that's exactly what I'm asking."

"I know he heard some of it because he started laughing," he said. "But I don't remember how much. Why? Is that important?"

She shook her head and then decided to change the subject. "You know what? I should have talked to Aiden about Emily. He needs to know how much trouble she's causing, and I want him to know I don't like the way she blames you for her mistakes."

"You heard Aiden. He's going to do something about her. I hope he follows

Cordie's suggestion."

"And that was?"

"Fire her ass."

Regan tried not to laugh. "Those were her exact words, weren't they?"

"Yes."

"Shame on her, corrupting a young, impressionable boy."

Henry laughed. "I've heard worse."

Regan went back into her office and closed the doors. She was feeling horribly nervous and thought she would hide until she had rehearsed what she was going to say to Alec about last night. Maybe he wouldn't bring it up. Then again, maybe he would, and she wanted to be prepared.

She knew she was being foolish. What happened last night wouldn't happen again; they had agreed on that, and Alec surely wouldn't mention it today. Besides, he was on duty. He probably wouldn't even be thinking about it.

"I can do this," she whispered.

She took a deep breath, straightened her shoulders, and opened the door again. She was going to find Alec and say hello. The sooner she got through the awkwardness of seeing him for the first time after . . . oh, God, she was doing it again. Getting all flustered and panicky. If this is what love felt like, she didn't want any part of it. She certainly didn't want the broken heart she knew was coming either, but she couldn't do anything about that now, could she? She had no one to blame for that misery but herself.

She walked past Henry and said, "Go have some fun. It's Sunday. The mail will be here tomorrow."

"I'm leaving," he promised. "I just want to do a little catch-up. I won't stay long."

Time to get the moment over with, she thought as she walked out into the hall. She stopped short. Aiden and Alec were standing in front of Aiden's office at the end of the hallway. Aiden was doing most of the talking, and Alec was nodding every now and then. She stood there a long minute, waiting until they finished their conversation. She assumed Aiden wanted the latest update on the investigation.

They both noticed her at the same time. Aiden nodded, then walked around the corner to the elevators. Alec started toward her.

He looked wonderful. And sloppy, of course, but comfortable sloppy. He had a five o'clock shadow, so he hadn't bothered to shave this morning. And did he ever comb his hair? No man should be this sexy.

She swallowed and tried to block out the memories of last night. What was it she was going to say to him when she saw him? What had she come up with? She couldn't remember. She had to look over his shoulder in order to concentrate.

"I thought you weren't coming in today."

Good. That worked. She'd sounded quite normal, and she was sure nothing of what she was feeling was showing in her face.

"I told you I was."

She nodded. Okay. The awkward moment was over. They were now having a normal conversation. She began to relax. Definitely okay. He wasn't going to say anything about last night, and neither was she. She could stop worrying.

"Regan?"

"Yes?"

"Did it feel good?"

She was mortified. She knew her mouth dropped open. The question so shocked her. She couldn't believe what he'd just asked, and so she made him repeat it.

"I asked you if it felt good."

In seconds her face was burning with embarrassment. "Alec, I think it would be best if we didn't discuss last night."

He laughed. "I was asking if it felt good

to stand up for yourself with your brothers."

"Oh." Instantly flustered, she said, "Yes, of course it felt . . . wait a minute. You did that on purpose, didn't you?"

He pretended not to know what she was talking about. "Did what?"

"Phrasing the question the way you did, asking if it felt good but not explaining . . . oh, never mind."

He loved how easily he could embarrass her. "So did it?"

She sighed. "Yes. I think maybe fighting with my brothers occasionally is a nice outlet for all my pent-up nervous energy."

He shook his head. "I think maybe we found a better outlet last night." He grinned as he added, "and I'm not going to ask you if that felt good. I know it did."

His arrogance was totally out of control, and he certainly didn't seem to need any confirmation from her. But then, why would he? Last night had been incredible. He didn't need her to tell him so. He was there, after all. Oh, boy, was he.

She really needed to think about something else . . . anything else. She wanted to kiss him. She stepped back instead. "I think we should change the subject."

"Yes, okay."

"And please, stop looking at me that way," she whispered.

"What way?"

"Like you'd like to find the nearest closet."

"I wasn't thinking closet. I was thinking —"

She interrupted. "We are finished talking about this." She folded her arms across her waist. "Okay?"

Before he could argue, she asked, "What were you and Aiden talking about?"

"I asked him if there were any grudges against your family, any disgruntled employees, any threats, lawsuits, et cetera. He said he'd already talked to Wincott about that, but he'd set it up for us to talk to your family attorney. I'm just trying to cover all the angles, and I want to know what the legal problems have been."

"With my brothers?"

"And you."

"Oh." She was taken aback by that admission. "I doubt you'll find anything."

"I'm still going to talk to Sam."

"Yes, of course."

"Are you hungry? You want to get something to eat?"

The abrupt change in subjects jarred her. "Yes . . . okay."

She walked around him and headed for the elevators. He caught up with her in two strides. "By the way, the answer is yes."

She glanced up at him. "What was the question?"

"You asked your brothers if anyone was ever faithful, and I'm telling you yes, some are."

She reached to push the button for the elevator. He grabbed her hand and forced her to look at him. "I've got a lot of examples," he said softly. "But there's only one you need to know about."

"Oh? Who?"

"Me."

She didn't know how to respond. "Why are you telling me this?"

He shrugged. "I don't know. I just thought you ought to know that I'd be faithful."

"If you ever married."

"That's right," he replied. "If."

The conversation was cut short when his cell phone rang. Henry was calling, and he sounded frantic.

"Where are you?"

"Right down the hall. What's going on?"

"You've got to get back here right away. You've got to see this."

Alec had already turned around and was

pulling Regan along as he strode back to the offices.

"What's wrong?"

He didn't need to answer her because Henry was standing in the doorway, and as soon as he spotted Alec and Regan coming around the corner, he blurted, "I opened this letter. It's on our hotel stationery, and it came in one of our envelopes. You know what that means? He was here. He was in the hotel."

Alec let go of her hand and went to the desk. She touched Henry's arm and said, "Take a deep breath."

"Regan, he was here."

She nodded. "Yes, I heard you. And he sent a letter?" she asked, but she was already walking over to his desk.

She leaned against Alec and looked at the sheet of stationery Henry had put on the blotter. He'd placed a long silver letter opener on the edge of the paper to keep it from folding up again.

It wasn't a letter, though. It was another murder list. This one had a different heading. *"Our Murder List"* was written on top of the paper, and the *Our* was underlined several times. The killer had handprinted this one. All of the names on the list were there, but lines had been drawn through Ms. Patsy's name and Detective Sweeney's. There were question marks next to Shields's name and the references to the two bodyguards.

Another name had been added to the list. Haley Cross. On the bottom, just below her name, he'd written, *"You owe me for this one too."*

Alec was on his cell phone dialing Wincott. While he was waiting for the detective to answer, he asked Regan, "Did you know this woman?"

She didn't pick up on the fact that he'd asked about the woman in the past tense.

"No," she said. "Alec, we have to warn her. Oh, dear God, the police need to find her before . . ."

Henry pointed to the paper. His voice was shaking when he said, "There's a line through her name, Regan, like he's already . . . you know . . . killed her."

"Henry, we cannot assume just because he's put a line through her name that she's dead. He might not have . . . Oh, God." She could feel the panic building inside. "There has to be time to save her."

Wincott answered the phone, and Alec let go of Regan and walked toward the hallway as he explained what Henry had found.

Regan was feeling sick to her stomach. She leaned against Henry's desk and stared at the wall. "I don't understand," she whispered. "Why would he send me this? And what in God's name does he mean by 'Our Murder List'?"

"Haley Cross. I swear I've heard that name before, but I can't remember where."

Alec ended the call and walked back into the office. "Wincott and Bradshaw are on their way over."

"On Sunday?" Henry realized how foolish the question was as soon as the words were out of his mouth.

"John was at work, but Bradshaw was home."

"Are they going to look for the woman? Are they . . ."

Alec put his arm around her. "It's too late."

She jerked away. His quick acceptance that the girl was dead infuriated her. "You can't know that. If they could just warn her . . . if they could find her and . . ."

Alec rubbed the knot in the back of his neck while he watched her pace. "They know where she is."

"Where?"

"In the morgue."

"Oh, God."

She sagged against Alec, bowed her head, and closed her eyes. He wrapped his arms around her and held her close. Henry had all but fallen into his chair.

"How did he kill her?" he asked.

Alec was staring at the article on the wall behind Henry's head. It all suddenly clicked. He didn't answer Henry's question, but said, "She was running on the path in —"

"Conrad Park," Henry blurted. "That's where I read the name. Regan, don't you remember? I told you about it. At least I think I told you."

Alec walked over to read the article again. "You're quoted here as saying you run there at least three nights a week."

"Yes, I did."

"But then the track was finished upstairs," Henry said.

Alec got Wincott on the phone again. "Where are you?"

"Getting out of the car in front of the hotel."

"What was the physical description of Haley Cross?"

"I've got some copies of the file with me, and I've got her photo. Hang on, Alec, I'll be right there."

Alec was too impatient to sit and wait.

He paced the hall instead. When Wincott jogged around the corner waving the file folder, Alec said, "Would you mistake Haley Cross for Regan?"

"Oh, come on. I wouldn't mistake any woman for her." He stopped, opened the folder, and held up Haley Cross's photo. "Maybe from behind . . . the long hair, approximate height and weight. I guess it's possible."

"What's possible?" Regan asked. She was standing in the doorway, but she stepped back when Wincott and Alec walked in.

Wincott answered her. "Mistaken identity," he said. "Where's the letter?"

A couple of seconds later, he and Alec were staring at the list again.

Wincott read the list and the note out loud. " 'You owe me for this one too'? So he's making Regan take some of the responsibility, isn't he?" Wincott said. "That's what I think the note implies."

"So, make the leap, John."

"Okay," Wincott answered. "He thinks Regan should have been there instead of Haley."

Alec nodded. Then Wincott asked, "You think he was waiting in the park for Regan?"

"If he read the article in the paper,

wouldn't he assume she still runs there?"

"Are you saying he killed that woman by mistake?" Regan asked.

Alec turned to her. "Yes. I think he went there to kill you."

Chapter Thirty-nine

The police had withheld important details about Haley Cross's murder, and neither Alec nor Wincott wanted Regan to know what those details were. She was already scared, and the autopsy report alone was enough to make a hardened cop shudder.

Still, there was the possibility that one of those details might trigger a memory that could help them.

Wincott leaned against the office window, one ankle crossed over the other, with a bottle of water in one hand and the autopsy report in the other. Alec sat next to her on the sofa. Regan couldn't understand how the two of them could look so relaxed while they took turns relating some of the horrific facts of the poor girl's murder. When Alec told her what the killer had done to her legs, Regan became nauseous and could feel the blood rushing from her head.

Alec noticed the way she was gripping her hands together in her lap, a telltale sign that she was having trouble, and there were tears in her eyes, but she kept it together.

He was proud of her, and had they been alone, he would have put his arms around her and told her so.

"You okay, Regan? You want to take a minute?" Wincott asked.

"No, I'm fine," she said.

Alec opened the folder Wincott had dropped on the table and handed Regan the photo of Haley Cross. Regan was surprised at how peaceful the woman looked in death.

"Do you know her?"

She shook her head. "Was she a student at the university?"

"No," Alec answered. "She'd already graduated."

"She lived close to the campus," Wincott explained. "And according to her friends, she regularly ran the park path."

"Did she live alone?"

"No," Wincott said. "She lived with a boyfriend. He was out of town on business the night she was murdered. Evidently she had told him she might go home to visit her parents while he was gone, so he returned to Chicago, and several days passed before anyone knew she was missing."

Regan took a couple of deep breaths before looking at the photo again. "I don't understand. Why would he do that to her legs? Why . . . ?"

When she suddenly stopped, Wincott said, "The coroner said her death was due to a blow to the head. Evidently this sicko went for the legs after she was already dead."

"She fought him," Alec said. "There was skin under her fingernails, so they have DNA." He took the photo from Regan and put it back in the folder.

Regan thought he looked worried about her, and so she gave him a quick smile to let him know she was okay as she stood and went to the credenza to get some water.

"Alec?" She held up the icy bottle.

"Yeah, sure."

She handed him the water, got another one for herself, and then circled the sofa to go to her desk. Lord, she was feeling old and worn-out all of a sudden. She pulled her chair out and sat down. Maybe going to Melbourne with Spencer wasn't such a bad idea after all. The change of scenery might do her some good. She sighed then. Even as the thought came into her mind, she rejected it. She wasn't going to run away, and if she went to Melbourne, that's exactly what she would be doing.

She thought about calling Sophie and Cordie. Talking to her friends always made her feel better, but if she let them see how upset she was, they'd become even more worried about her than they already were. And if the subject turned to Alec — which of course it would — she would definitely lose it. Turning into a crybaby for a little while was all right when she was with her friends, but not here, and not now.

Alec watched Regan from the sofa. Her eyes were sad and distant. She was pale and her brow was furrowed.

Lyle Bradshaw walked into the office. He looked as though he was on his way to a wedding, all dressed up in a dark pinstriped suit and a white shirt with French cuffs. His bold red tie provided the only spot of color. As usual, not a hair was out of place. In comparison, Alec looked as though he was getting ready to clean a garage.

Wincott observed from the other side of the room. Lyle was looking at Regan, and Alec was looking at Lyle looking at Regan, and from the expression on Alec's face, he wasn't happy.

"The letter and the envelope are on Henry's desk," Wincott said to break the staring contest.

"We aren't going to find any of his fingerprints." He made the comment on his way to the desk.

"You still have to bag it and get it to the lab," Alec snapped.

Lyle didn't seem to notice Alec's hostile tone. Wincott did. He diffused the situation by taking the two men into the outer office to discuss the new developments in the case.

As soon as she was alone, Regan switched on her computer and tried to answer a few of her e-mails. Anything to keep her mind occupied.

Henry poked his head in the door to say good-bye. She suggested he take Monday off, but he wouldn't hear of it. "What if another letter comes, or something else happens? I want to be here . . . you know, in case you need me."

He was such a sweetheart. "Okay," she said. "But sleep in and come in late."

"I'll try," he promised. He turned to leave and then said, "We can't tell anyone about the new list or about the woman."

"I know that."

"I was kind of surprised with everything happening and so many people involved that someone hasn't leaked the story to the papers."

"I don't think any of the security force knows the particulars," she said.

"Sophie would kill both of us if another newspaper broke this story. Okay, I'm leaving. See you tomorrow."

"Henry, be careful."

The door had barely closed behind him before it was flung open again, and Aiden came rushing into the room.

"Spencer and I just heard about the letter. Alec told me about the woman who was murdered. My God, Regan, that could have been you."

"Yes, I know," she said softly.

"Listen, Spencer and I aren't going anywhere until this lunatic is caught. Maybe I should call Walker and tell him to come home."

"Oh, please, don't do that. You know how he attracts attention. The press will be following him around, and if any of those reporters get wind of this . . ."

"All right," he said.

"Make him stay away," she insisted. "I wish you and Spencer would get as far away from me as possible, and I wish you'd take Cordie and Sophie and Henry with you. None of you is safe as long as you're around me. If anything ever happened to you or . . ." Her voice broke.

"I'm not going anywhere," he repeated. "And you need to stop worrying about us. You've got enough to think about, and you've got to stay strong."

"I'm doing okay, and you don't have to worry. I'm not going to crumble."

They continued to talk for several more minutes. Aiden paced around the room until he calmed down. He seemed to need her reassurance that she was well protected, that Alec and John would catch the lunatic, and that she would be okay.

He was walking toward the door when she said, "A long time ago, you taught me that Madisons face problems, and it's time I face some of mine."

"The police should handle . . ."

"I'm talking about our family and our business, Aiden."

He turned around and walked back to her desk. "Okay. It's time you face what problems?"

"Letting you and Spencer make decisions for me. That has to stop. What I do with the family funds is every bit as important as what you do. Investing those funds to make the world better is actually more important."

He leaned against the desk and folded

his arms across his chest. He knew she was right.

"And one more thing . . ." she said. "Giving back to the community, taking on projects that make a difference . . . when you see where the money goes, it's a reminder of why we're here. The way I see it, it's my job to help you boys stay on track." She smiled as she added, "You might say I humanize you."

He conceded. "Okay, we'll increase your budget for next year. I can convince Spencer and Walker to double it."

"That's good to hear," she said. "And I'll do something for you. I'll stop fighting you on a settlement for Emerson."

He headed for the door. "Emily's taking a week off," he said. "When she gets back, she'll be looking for another position."

Regan tried not to cheer. Aiden paused at the door and asked, "Is there anything else you want to talk about?"

"That's it for now," she said.

She wanted to tell him about Alec, to pour her heart out to her brother, but she didn't. Why would she? It was just one night. Alec was making that perfectly clear. Just five more days and she'd never see him again . . . unless they caught the lunatic before then.

Regan tried to fill those days with work to keep her mind occupied. Since their projects for the season had been completed, she and Henry continued to clean out old files and reorganize the office.

Each day, Alec came on duty as usual, but things weren't the same as they had been. He was cordial and friendly, but he was keeping his distance. There was no more teasing, and he avoided any situation where they would get close to each other. When a discussion became too personal, he changed the subject. He was acting as though nothing out of the ordinary had happened between them. Did he already regret their night together? If she'd had the nerve, she would have asked him that very question.

Regan wasn't sure if she had caught a virus or if the stress had made her sick, but she started throwing up one evening after Alec walked her to her suite. She had a horrible night. By noon the following day, she was feeling better.

She met Aiden late that afternoon to give him the signed contracts. He was waiting at a corner table in the atrium. Regan ordered iced tea and sipped it while she half listened to him talk about the new hotel.

"Are you paying attention?"

"Not really."

"Are you still sick?" He sounded suspicious, as though she were trying to pull a fast one by getting out of bed too soon.

"No, I'm fine."

"According to Alec, you sure didn't look fine last night."

"Excuse me? How would he know what I looked like?"

Aiden shrugged. "He heard you were sick. I'm not sure who told him," he said, "but he came back to the hotel, and he spent the night."

"In the hotel? Alec stayed in the hotel?"

"Didn't I just say he did? He stayed in your suite. He slept on the sofa."

She was astonished. And all she could think about was how horrible she'd looked with her hair hanging in her eyes and her pasty complexion. Had he been there when she was throwing up? Lovely, she thought.

"Aiden, why did you let him see me looking half dead?"

He smiled. "I didn't have much to say about it."

She decided to change the subject. "I ran into Paul. He told me he's cutting back on his hours."

Aiden nodded. "He's tired of so much

traveling, and he needs to be home more with his family."

"So you're okay with his decision?"

"Yes. I told him he can have any job he wants. We don't want to lose him."

She was handing the contracts to Aiden when she looked up and saw Alec walking toward her. He stopped to talk to the officer assigned to her for the day to get a report. She didn't want him to catch her staring at him, and so she hastily turned around.

Now Aiden was watching her. His cell phone rang, but he ignored it.

"You should answer that."

He picked up the phone, turned the power off, and then tucked it into his pocket.

"Did you want to tell me something?" he prodded.

She bowed her head. "I did something stupid." She made the confession in a whisper.

"What did you do?"

I fell in love. And how stupid was that? She didn't say what she was thinking, though. "I'm tired, that's all. I need a vacation."

Her brother was far more astute than she realized. He looked at Alec who couldn't seem to take his eyes off Regan, and then he looked at Regan again.

The two of them looked miserable.

"He told me he's going into the FBI."

Startled, she looked up. Aiden was smiling. She didn't pretend not to know whom he was talking about. "Yes, he is. And what is so amusing?" she asked, frowning.

"I was wondering how Alec will feel when Walker hires someone to do a background check on him."

Her eyes widened. "He wouldn't . . ."

Aiden shrugged. "He hired someone to check out Dennis, and you weren't serious about him."

"Aiden, he's leaving."

"Yes, I know." He stood then and said, "Here he comes."

She practically overturned her chair when she bolted to her feet, and if Aiden hadn't grabbed her glass, it would have crashed to the floor.

She took a breath, slapped a smile on her face, and turned around. He was at it again, she thought, looking even more handsome than the last time she'd seen him. The man could clean up when he wanted to. He'd already proven that last Saturday night when he'd worn a tuxedo. He had on a navy blue blazer and khaki pants, and he was wearing loafers, not beat-up tennis shoes.

She couldn't believe how rattled she was, and he hadn't said a word to her.

Alec nodded to Aiden and smiled at her. "You're looking better today." She guessed the pleasantries were over when he turned to Aiden, abruptly dismissing her. "Your attorney hasn't called Gil Hutton back yet. He told me he's left two messages for him. I think maybe you need to talk to him again."

"I'll get right on it," he promised. "Sam was on vacation, but I was sure he'd be back by now."

Regan decided to go up to her office. Aiden and Alec followed behind. "I want Gil to hear from him by tomorrow afternoon. If he doesn't, I'm going over to his office and look through those files myself."

"He'll call."

Regan was holding the elevator for them. Alec stood in front of her on the way up to the third floor.

"I talked to Lieutenant Lewis this morning," Aiden said.

"That had to be fun," Alec commented. "You'd better not mention my name, or it could be bad for Detective Wincott."

"What does that mean?"

Alec explained. "It means that Lewis would ruin his chances for promotion if he found out I'm helping him."

Aiden nodded. "He's not going to find out from any of us, and certainly not from Sam."

"So I guess the lieutenant doesn't like you," Regan said.

When he didn't answer her, she poked him in the back.

He flashed a grin, then reached behind him and grabbed her hand. When he realized what he'd done, he immediately let go.

Aiden pretended he didn't notice. "From what I understand, they really don't have any leads. He told me they're looking at Peter Morris."

"That could be another dead end," Regan said.

"They're not just looking at him," Alec said. "They're looking for him."

"He's hiding?" Regan asked.

"Yes, but he can't hide forever," Alec said. "He'll surface, and then they'll get him."

"But that could take forever."

As it turned out, Morris was apprehended one hour later.

Chapter Forty

Peter Morris made two mistakes and both of them were doozies.

His first mistake was to give in to temptation. He walked into a bar in downtown Chicago and started drinking hard liquor, and lots of it, which not only impaired his judgment but also gave him a false sense of security. The more he guzzled down, the more convinced he became that he was safe, and for the moment, untouchable.

The second mistake he made was to call Regan Madison. It took him several tries, and by the time he finally got through to her, he had worked himself into a froth.

Regan had told the operator to hold her calls and that she would be back in her office by three. Time got away from her, though, and when she and Alec reached her door, Detective Wincott was waiting. She assumed he was there to talk to her.

"Is there news?"

He shook his head. "I'm just here to pick up Alec. We've got a thing to go to. Sort of a going-away party for Alec," he explained.

She noticed a policeman standing down

the hall. Her phone rang. Wincott was turning to leave, but Alec lingered. She picked up the extension on Henry's desk and answered. "Regan Madison."

"This is your last chance to do the right thing."

The anger shocked her. The words were slurred, but she still understood what he had said.

Alec saw the change in her expression, motioned to Wincott, and then went running to the phone in her office so he could listen in.

"Who is this?" she demanded.

"Peter Morris," he answered. "Remember me?"

"Yes, I remember you."

Wincott was moving away as he flipped his cell phone open.

"You're a liar." Morris drew the words in a long whisper.

If Morris wasn't drunk, he was certainly well on his way, she thought. She could hear glasses clinking, music pulsating, and voices mumbling in the background. She was sure he was calling her from a bar.

"I'm not lying. I remember you."

"I meant what I said. This is your last chance."

His voice was chilling now. She heard

him swallow, then the sound of ice striking the glass again.

"My last chance?" she repeated.

"To save yourself."

"I don't understand."

"I'm not going to keep chasing you. It took me precious weeks to get past your assistant and finally talk to you, and what good did it do me? You wouldn't listen. You already had your mind made up. I told you that if we could only get together, sit down and talk, I could convince you. If you had just stopped and listened to me, none of this would have happened. You could have stopped it."

"Stopped what?"

"You know what."

She decided to pretend she knew what he was talking about. "All right. Tell me how I could have stopped it."

She looked at Alec. He nodded to her.

"I tried to get to you, but you left."

"When? Where?"

"At Liam House."

She nearly dropped the phone. Her breath caught in her throat. "You were there?"

"I just said I was."

"Did you follow me?"

"No."

"Then how did you know . . . ?"

Impatient, he answered. "She told me."

"Who? Who told you?"

"Emily. She said her name was Emily when she answered the phone. She told me where you were."

She was so stunned she fell back against the desk.

"Do you know how long I stood out there in the rain waiting for you to come outside?"

"No, I don't know how long you waited."

"I want the money," he snarled. "And you owe me, now don't you?"

"Why do I owe you?"

He didn't answer her but said, "It's gone too far. If you don't give me the money, you'll be sorry. You get it ready. You hear me? I want cash, not a check. We'll meet tomorrow. I'll let you know when and where."

"And if I don't have the money ready when you call?"

"Someone's going to get hurt." His words trailed off into a slurred mumble.

Regan heard a crash, and then the line went dead. Alec was suddenly there by her side. She started to speak, but he put his hand up for silence and then nodded toward Wincott.

The detective had his back to them as he was talking on his cell phone, but when he turned around he had a big grin on his face.

"We got him."

Chapter Forty-one

It was almost too easy. While Peter Morris was shouting threats over the phone and sloshing his drink down his shirt, two policemen walked up behind him and grabbed him.

Morris wasn't too drunk to lawyer up. As soon as he was handcuffed and read his rights, he started screaming for an attorney.

He did a lot of talking about not talking to anyone about anything. A confession would have been nice, but they really didn't need it. The evidence nailed him. Morris, as it turned out, was a collector. Hidden behind a block of insulation in the attic of the run-down house he rented was a mildewed shoe box tied with a bright pink ribbon, and inside that box were his trophies, a bloody hammer with a workman's initials burned into the handle, Haley Cross's driver's license, and Detective Benjamin Sweeney's wallet.

Lieutenant Lewis was ecstatic. As far as he was concerned, it was an open-and-shut case. After hearing about the evidence, he insisted that he be the one to call Aiden and give him the good news.

Wincott drove back to the hotel to tell Regan what they'd found in Morris's house. He called Alec and asked him to meet him in the lobby.

Alec was in a mood. He had wanted to sit in on the interrogation with Morris and his attorney, but Lewis wouldn't let him get near him. Wincott didn't think it was such a good idea either, considering Alec's frame of mind.

Wincott was waiting for Alec in front of the elevators. "Are you finished packing, or have you even started yet?" he asked when he spotted Alec striding toward him.

"He didn't confess, did he?"

"So I guess that's a no on the packing?"

"Answer me, John," he snapped.

"No, he didn't confess. Swears he's innocent. It was shocking. I've never heard any suspect say that."

Alec ignored the smart-ass remark. The elevator doors opened, and he stepped back to let Wincott go in first.

"Where are all the security guards? I haven't seen a single one since I walked into this building."

"The extra men who were sent over from the security company are probably on other jobs now, and the regulars are just being more discreet. You know, blending in. Now that we've got our man — and we do have the right man — the hotel's security staff doesn't need to have such a loud presence."

The doors opened on Regan's floor. "I don't like this," Alec muttered.

"I know. You wanted a confession, didn't you? But you know what? If he had confessed, you still wouldn't believe he was the right man for this."

Alec shrugged. "You could have gotten me in there. All I wanted was to ask a couple of questions."

Wincott shook his head. "We're doing everything by the book, and that means no one is going to touch him."

"And you think I would?"

Wincott smiled. "Of course you would. You'd have his face smashed into a wall the second he said her name. Face it, Alec. You're too involved in this . . . personally involved."

Alec didn't like hearing that. "If I'm so damned personally involved, why did you ask me to meet you here?"

"Because I figured what you need is closure."

Alec looked incredulous. "Closure?

You've got to be kidding me."

"I thought to myself that maybe, if you heard me telling Regan about all the evidence we had and the motive and opportunity, well then, you'd be able to close the door on this investigation and move on."

"It was too easy."

"Sometimes that's just how it ends up. Easy."

"The evidence . . ."

"I know. Someone else could have planted the evidence in Morris's attic. That's what you were going to say, right?"

"That's right."

"Morris is good for this. Physically he's big enough and strong enough to lift Sweeney and hang him the way he did, and he fits the description Regan gave us."

Alec knocked on her door. "Hundreds of men fit that description."

She opened the door, and in a flash, Alec took it all in. She was barefoot and wearing running shorts and a top that didn't quite cover her navel. She looked really good.

Wincott nodded to her and walked past.

"I just heard the news," she said.

"Who told you?" Alec asked. For the first time in the last three weeks, he didn't head for the comfortable sofa.

She closed the door. "Lieutenant Lewis

called and told me, and then Aiden called. Why aren't you smiling, Alec? Aren't you happy about this?"

"He thinks it's too easy," Wincott said. He sat down in the easy chair and leaned forward.

Alec stood in the middle of the room with his hands in his pockets and frowned at him. "Listen, the results of the DNA aren't in, I say we keep up the protection."

"You aren't convinced that Peter Morris is the man who killed . . . ?"

She stopped when he shook his head. "No, I'm not convinced."

"He doesn't want to be convinced."

"What's that supposed to mean?" Alec asked.

"It means it's crunch time." He gave a barely perceptible nod toward Regan.

Alec's jaw was clenched tight as he glared at Wincott.

Regan wasn't certain what was going on. "John, do you think we have the right man?"

"Yes, I do. Evidence doesn't lie."

"Unless it's planted."

"A strand of Morris's hair was found embedded in the hammer."

"Do you know how easy it would have been to plant that evidence? All someone had to do was take a hair from his brush," he said as he slowly paced.

"He had a motive," Wincott told Regan. "He owed the wrong people a lot of money, and he was counting on the grant to bail him out. When you turned him down, he went after you. He admitted he went to Liam House and waited for you. The evidence is going to bury him. Morris was desperate . . . and losing it. He picked up Regan's cell phone and that folder with her murder list and thought that maybe if he did something nice for her . . ."

"I'd give him the money? My God . . ."

Wincott nodded. "I had a nice long talk with Emily Milan. She admitted she told Morris where you were."

"Did she know she was talking to Peter Morris?" Regan asked.

"Yes, but she claims she had no idea what he wanted," Wincott answered. "She also admitted she'd gotten into your computer so she could read all your e-mails. She said she only did it so she could keep current."

"I'm amazed she'd own up to that. She's the one who printed the picture of Sweeney and put it on Aiden's desk. She also forwarded it to your other brothers."

Wincott smiled. "The pair of handcuffs I pulled out made her real chatty. She suddenly wanted to cooperate."

"Where is she now?" Alec asked.

"She was fired, of course," Wincott said. "And security escorted her out of the hotel. I doubt she'll be asking for a recommendation."

"Are you still convinced he killed Haley Cross because he thought it was me?"

"Yes," Wincott said. "Like I said before, it was rainy and dark, and Cross was about your height, maybe a little taller, and had dark hair like yours. If he came up behind her, it would be an easy mistake to think she was you. And you let Morris know where you would be," he said. "You know, that article and photo from the paper Henry cut out and framed?"

She nodded. She knew where John was headed.

"At the dedication, you said that you ran the jogging path every Monday, Wednesday, and Friday. We believe Morris read the article and went to Conrad Park to wait for you. I don't think he went there to kill you. I think it just got out of hand. He probably wanted to convince you to give him the grant. He must have been shocked when he realized he'd grabbed the wrong woman. Maybe that's what triggered his rage."

"You told me she fought him."

"Yes," Wincott said. "One of the workmen left his hammer. Morris saw it, picked it up, and killed her." He looked at Alec when he added, "But it's finished now. When the DNA results come back, we'll have enough to put Morris away for three lifetimes."

He stood and offered Regan his hand.

"John, I can't thank you enough," she said.

"Things should wrap up fairly quickly. The prosecutor's office will be in touch with you and let you know where things will go from here." He glanced at Alec. "I should be going."

Alec didn't follow him. He pushed the door shut so he could have a moment of privacy with her. He needed to say good-bye.

"Listen, Regan . . ." he began, and then stopped. He was suddenly tongue-tied.

"Yes?" She looked into his eyes and waited.

"You knew I was going to leave."

"Yes, I did."

"Okay then. I'm going home to pack up, and then I'm driving to Boston."

"To see your family?"

He nodded. He sounded resolute when

he muttered, "That's right."

"And then the FBI."

"Right again. I'm moving forward."

Did he know he was breaking her heart? "I understand."

"Look . . . I shouldn't have . . ."

She wouldn't let him finish. If he told her that he shouldn't have made love to her, she didn't know what she would do. "I don't have any regrets. You should go home now and pack."

He leaned down and kissed her forehead. "Yeah, I should."

She opened the door. "Remember, Alec, you're moving forward."

"That's right. I am."

"Then go."

"If you're ever in Boston . . ."

Chapter Forty-two

Sometimes extraordinary things can happen on the most ordinary of days.

When Eric Gage opened his eyes early Saturday morning, he knew that today was going to be extraordinary. He couldn't explain why, not yet anyway, but he believed that as the day progressed, he would come to understand.

Eric had learned not to question.

The answer came much quicker than he had anticipated. He got out of bed, put on his robe, and shuffled into the kitchen. He was standing at the sink pouring himself a glass of orange juice when he heard it. A whisper from behind. A hiss really, and though he tried, he couldn't quite make out what the hiss was trying to tell him.

He didn't look behind him. He didn't need to, for he knew who was there in the kitchen with him. He closed his eyes and waited for the whisper to come again. Five minutes passed, then five more, and still the only sound he heard was the thunder of his heartbeat.

He began to doubt. Maybe he had imagined it. He decided to get on with his day and his chores. By six a.m. he had dressed in his old work clothes and had driven to his neighborhood QuikTrip to buy an extra-large cup of coffee.

By seven-thirty he had cleaned out the garage — a ritual he completed every Saturday — and had eaten his breakfast and prepared a tray for Nina. Then he showered and dressed in a brand-new black running suit with a narrow, white stripe down the outside of each leg. The lightweight jacket had a white cloverleaf logo on the breast pocket. The zippered pockets were the reason he'd purchased it.

There were two loaded guns in the bureau drawer. He put one in his right pocket. When he zipped the pocket closed, it was impossible to tell what was inside. He looked at himself in the mirror just to make sure. He worried he might need extra rounds, and so he opened the drawer and pulled out two more magazines and slipped those into his other pocket. He carried the second gun into the kitchen and laid it in the center of the table.

He was ready now, but ready for what?

The familiar and terrifying anxiety was building inside him. His hands became stiff and icy cold, and he had trouble drawing a deep breath. He knew what was happening. The demon was taking control.

He tried to stop it. He sat down at the kitchen table and began to rock back and forth, back and forth, but he couldn't sit long. He jumped up. Maybe it wasn't too late to change the future . . . maybe, he thought, there could be a new beginning. The burst of optimism was gone in an instant. He was walking toward the back hall when he heard it again. The whisper was right behind him. He couldn't escape. He knew that now.

"It's time."

"No," he cried out.

"You know what you must do."

He bowed his head and began to weep. "No, no, I can't . . ."

The whisper turned into a scream. "You will do this."

He stubbornly clung to the last threads of sanity. He squeezed his eyes shut and covered his ears in a weak attempt to block the terror from consuming him. "No, please, no, no," he sobbed.

The rebellion was short-lived, and the demon won.

"Turn around and look at me. Open your eyes and look."

He did as he was told, his movements

wooden now. His acquiescence complete.

He stood there rigid as he waited for the demon's next command. It wasn't long in coming.

Nina's eyes bored into his. "Kill her for me."

Chapter Forty-three

Alec was trying to squeeze another suitcase into the trunk of his car when a bright red 1968 Mustang convertible in mint condition came roaring around the corner. Gil was behind the wheel. The top was down; the radio was blaring, and the five or six thin strands of hair on his head were blowing in the breeze.

He pulled up alongside Alec's car, double-parked, and turned the radio and the motor off.

"Have you handed in your badge yet?" he shouted as he smoothed his hair down with the palm of his hand.

"Not yet," Alec called back. He shut the trunk and walked around to the passenger side of Gil's car. "I'm surprised you didn't know that."

"I did know that," he said. "But things have a way of changing, and I was hoping you might change your mind."

"It's the FBI, Gil."

"You gave your word, huh?"

Alec shrugged. "Something like that."

"You're putting suitcases in your car.

You've got to be leaving soon."

Alec had the day off and was trying to cram as many things as he could into it so he wouldn't have time to think about Regan. He wasn't going to admit that to Gil, though. It would be all over Chicago by noon if he did, and so he said, "I'm just getting a head start."

"What about your furniture and the other stuff in your apartment?"

"I'm taking my clothes and a couple of other things I want to keep, but the rest of the stuff is going to a friend."

"What friend?"

Gil was as intrusive as ever, but Alec didn't mind as long as the questions didn't become too personal. "His name's Henry. He's moving into my apartment next week. You don't know him."

"He works for Regan Madison, right?"

Alec laughed. "Is there anything you don't know?"

"Yeah. Next week's lottery numbers." He looked up at the sky as he added, "And I don't know if I'm going to make it home before the rain starts up again."

"Was there a particular reason you stopped by?"

"I don't have a cell phone."

Alec nodded. "I know."

"I don't like them," he said. "Needless expense now that I'm retired. If I did a lot of traveling, then it would make sense, but these days I rarely leave the neighborhood. I can walk to my favorite bars and restaurants. Finnegan's is just a block away from my house."

"I'm not going to argue with you. If you don't want to carry a cell phone, then don't."

"I tried calling your apartment, but you didn't answer. Guess you were out here."

"Guess I was."

"I could have called your cell phone, but the rain had stopped, and so I decided to drive over to say hello. I heard Wincott and Bradshaw arrested Sweeney's murderer."

"That's right."

"I also heard you were giving them trouble. You thought maybe they had the wrong man. Is that true?"

"Yes, I did give them some trouble, but it didn't make any difference. They're convinced Morris is their man."

"The evidence backs them up."

Alec nodded. Then Gil said, "I heard Wincott thought you were too close to it, if you know what I mean."

"No, Gil. Explain it." Now he was getting irritated.

Gil didn't seem to notice. "You know, personally involved. So, were you?"

Alec didn't answer. "Why all the questions?"

"I'm getting to it," he said. "When I heard about the arrest and all the evidence they had, I thought that maybe you didn't want me to keep looking into the Madisons' backgrounds, but then I thought, if Alec wanted me to stop looking, he would have called and told me so. You didn't forget, did you?"

"No, I didn't forget."

"There's nothing in her background to raise a flag, but I figured you already knew that."

Alec nodded. "Yes, I did. What about the brothers?"

"None of them have a criminal record, and none of them have ever been arrested."

"I already know that, Gil."

"Walker's had some trouble. He's the most well-known in the family because he's a big-time race car driver. I hear he's good too. Anyway, people know he's got money. He doesn't keep a low profile like the others, and you know how some people are. They see it; they want it. The money, I mean."

"You said he had some trouble?"

"He's had his share of fender benders, but there were only two bad accidents, one with fatalities. Walker wasn't responsible for either one, though. He was luckier than some of the others because he walked away from both without a scratch. Now, the first accident happened up in Wisconsin. I couldn't find anything there."

"What about the other one?"

"That was the real bad one. It happened down in Florida, but the man who the witnesses say caused the accident died at the scene. His insurance company settled with the families. Like the accident in Wisconsin, lots of people with injuries, some real, some bogus."

"But Walker wasn't responsible for that one either?"

"No," Gil said. "I'm waiting to hear back from the officer who was first on the scene. Maybe he can tell me something I don't already know. After I talk to him, I'll hunt you down . . . unless you want me to stop now. Do you?"

Alec's answer was immediate. "No, don't stop. Keep looking."

Gil took off a minute later, and Alec went back inside to finish up, but his mind wasn't on what he was doing. He kept thinking about Regan. Was he having trouble letting go? Was that why he wanted Gil to keep searching? Maybe if he had had an active role in the investigation, he wouldn't feel so frustrated now.

He picked up a box and carried it down to the car. Why couldn't he accept that they had arrested the right man? He sighed and shook his head. He knew why. Because it was just too frickin' easy.

Chapter Forty-four

Sunday turned out to be a miserable day for a race. The weather had gone from chilly and damp to beastly hot and damp. The air was as thick and humid as a rain forest.

Sophie, Cordie, and Regan had been in the park for well over an hour, but had spent most of that time huddled together in a shelter, squeezed in like sardines with at least fifty other people while the rain poured down. There wasn't any privacy, and it was too crowded to talk anyway.

As soon as the rain let up, they got into line to sign in and pick up their numbers.

Sophie had already told them her good news, but Cordie and Regan wanted to hear all the details again. Besides, they knew Sophie was dying to rehash her victory.

"Come on, Sophie. Start at the beginning," Regan said.

She didn't have to be coaxed. "Okay. So after my article — my exceptionally well-written article — was in the paper, women started coming out of the woodwork. All of them are begging for a chance to testify against Shields. Unfortunately, we'll never know if he had anything to do with Mary Coolidge's death. There's no hard evidence, but the prosecutor told me she has enough to put him in prison for a long time. She's going after the bodyguards too and thinks she can convince a jury that they were coconspirators in extortion and fraud."

"What about the money?" Cordie asked.

"After Shields is found guilty, and he will be," she said, "Mary's daughter will be getting what's left of her mother's money."

"I'll bet she'd rather have her mother back," Cordie said.

Regan patted Sophie on the shoulder. "Sophie, we're so proud of you."

"And we're proud of you too, Regan," Cordie said. "Sophie and I haven't slept for weeks worrying about you. You kept it together, though."

"Not always," Regan said.

"Now that the police have arrested the man who killed the detective and Haley Cross, are you able to get back to normal and breathe again?"

"How can things ever be normal? Because of me, two people are dead."

"You can't blame yourself for Morris's actions. He's obviously very disturbed.

There was no way for anyone to predict that he would become violent."

"Cordie's right," Sophie said.

"We've heard all about the man they arrested, and we've heard all about the evidence and how they found it, but you haven't said a word about Alec. Do you miss having him around?"

Regan didn't answer. She didn't really need to. Tears were already gathering in her eyes.

Cordie handed her a tissue. "What happened?"

She finally told them about the last time she'd seen Alec and how he'd said goodbye to her. When she finished, her friends were speechless for a good ten seconds or more. Then both of them exploded.

"He said *what?*" Sophie all but shouted the question.

" 'If you're ever in Boston,' " Regan repeated.

Cordie was furious. "And that's it? He didn't say anything else?"

"Like what? Thanks for a good time?" She was crying now and strangers were noticing. One woman actually moved closer, no doubt so she could listen in on the conversation. She was staring too. Regan turned her back on the nosy woman. She was embarrassed she couldn't control her emotions. "My allergies are acting up today."

Neither Cordie nor Sophie believed that nonsense — she was crying because her heart was broken.

Cordie handed her another tissue. "It's going to be okay."

The lie only made things worse. "I did the most horrible thing."

Cordie and Sophie stepped closer. "What'd you do?" Cordie whispered.

"I fell in love with him."

"We sort of thought you had," Cordie said sympathetically.

"Did you tell him?" Sophie asked.

"No."

"It's just as well."

The woman standing behind Regan was nodding in obvious agreement. Sophie decided to ignore her. "Since he's leaving . . ."

"Come on, it's our turn," Cordie said.

The line had been moving at a quick pace, and they had finally reached the sign-in table. A couple of minutes later they were helping one another pin their numbers on the back of their T-shirts.

Dark clouds were hanging over them as they made their way to the starting area.

The streets surrounding the route were blocked off, and policemen were directing traffic.

The park was green and lush, the shrubs and bushes all overgrown, much like a wilderness, but paths had been cut out of the woods for biking and jogging. Several men and women were sitting on top of a stone wall alongside the trail while they waited for the race to start.

Cordie was still fuming. "I can't believe he said that. Are you sure, Regan? 'If you're ever in Boston'? That's how he said good-bye? Those were his exact words?" Too late, she realized she'd inadvertently opened the floodgates again.

"Yes," Regan said through her tears.

"I can't believe you didn't tell him to stick it —"

"Cordie, for heaven's sake," Sophie said.

"I really don't want to talk about Alec anymore." Regan sniffed.

"Okay," Sophie said.

"Not another word about him," Cordie promised.

"He isn't my type anyway. He's all wrong for me."

"All wrong," Sophie agreed.

"Why is he all wrong?" Cordie asked.

"He's a slob. That's why. The man's

never quite put together."

"He sure looked put together in that tuxedo at the country club," Sophie commented.

"Not helping," Cordie whispered.

"Yes, he can pull it together when he wants to, but he prefers being a slob. He's always forgetting to shave, and he never combs his hair."

Tears were streaming down her face as she complained about him. She impatiently wiped them away and said, "How sad am I that I can only come up with superficial, unimportant criticisms that are really kind of sexy and endearing anyway? The truth is, I like that he doesn't have everything tucked in all the time."

Cordie handed her yet another tissue. Regan thanked her and then said, "Alec has all the qualities that matter, like honor and integrity. He's strong and brave . . ." She paused to dab at her eyes and then added, "He's just about perfect."

"No, he's not," Cordie said. "If he were so perfect, why would he walk away from the best thing that will ever happen to him?"

"I don't want to talk about him. I mean it. Not another word."

"Okay," Sophie said. "We'll talk about something else."

"If he can move forward, I certainly can," Regan said. "In fact, that's exactly what I'm going to do. Move forward."

"That's great," Cordie said.

"Could we please change the subject?"

"We better," Cordie said. "I'm out of tissues."

"And I'm finished crying over him."

"That's good to hear," Sophie said.

"I think we should celebrate your promotion," Regan told Sophie.

"Let's do dinner next week," Cordie suggested. "But before Thursday. I'm starting a new diet then."

"Why Thursday?"

"It's the day I chose, and I've circled it on my calendar. I'm psyching myself up. I start Thursday, no matter what."

"Maybe we could do it Wednesday night," Regan said.

"The flag's going up," Sophie said. "That's the five-minute signal. I'm going to push my way up front. Are you going to run?" she asked Regan.

"No, I'm walking. One mile up and one mile back, and then I'm done."

"What about you, Cordie?"

"I'm doing a one-mile combo. Walk and crawl."

"I've decided I'm going to run, not

walk," Sophie said. "And I'm going the distance too. All six miles."

Regan smiled and Cordie began to laugh. Their reaction didn't sit well with Sophie.

"You don't think I can do it, do you?"

"No, I don't think you can," Cordie said.

"I know you can't," Regan said. "Sophie, you're not a runner."

"I am now. Let's meet at the finish line. See you there."

They watched her squeeze her way through the throng oblivious of the glares as she pushed ahead.

"I'll bet you ten dollars she doesn't make it farther than a mile."

"Half a mile and she's finished," Regan said.

"Hey, look. That new frozen custard shop is open. See? Across the street. Maybe after, we could stop in." And then she, too, blended into the crowd.

Regan had looked across the street when Cordie pointed out the custard shop, but her attention turned to a couple walking out the door. Both of them had ice-cream cones. They were holding hands as they strolled along. The woman was around nineteen or twenty, and the man she was with was at least fifty.

"Another sleazebag," Regan muttered.

Her reaction was instantaneous. She felt disgust. Then she shook her head. Aiden was right. She really did need to get over this ridiculous obsession. Until she walked in their shoes, she couldn't possibly know what their situation was or what was in their hearts.

Yes, it was definitely time for a change of attitude. She would start working on that right away. And yet, despite the best intentions, she couldn't make herself stop watching the couple as they made their way across the street.

And that's why she noticed him. He was a big, muscular man, and he was coming up fast behind the couple. He knocked the older man off his feet as he ran past. The young woman shouted something, but the runner never looked back. He was dressed for the race in a black running suit, but with the heat and the humidity, she thought it was odd that he was wearing a jacket. She also noticed he was carrying a pair of binoculars. The man quickly disappeared into the crowd.

She jumped when the starting gun fired, then turned and joined the people moving onto the trail. She stayed at the back of the crowd and tried to avoid elbows as she walked along.

The rude man with the binoculars was nowhere in sight. She didn't give him another thought. She wouldn't let herself think about Alec either, but that was easier said than done.

Chapter Forty-five

Alec had kept her keys. Now, why had he done that? It wasn't like him to be so forgetful and not realize he had them in his pocket. Maybe he'd kept them so he would have an excuse to go back to the hotel. That's what the shrinks would tell him. His subconscious wanted to see her again.

And so did the rest of him.

Alec stayed up half the night thinking about his future. About three in the morning he finally figured it all out. His future was with Regan . . . if she would have him. "Moving forward" took on a whole new meaning to him now. He didn't want to go anywhere without her.

He made a couple of decisions about the job too, and he felt pretty good about them, but he fell asleep thinking about Regan and wondering how he would ever be able to convince her to love him.

The next morning, after he showered, he decided he ought to get cleaned up before he went to the hotel. He shaved and then put on a clean pair of jeans that only had a couple of holes below his knees. He opened one of the packed boxes and found a clean, though wrinkled, short-sleeve T-shirt and even took the time to tuck it in.

He happened to glance in the mirror while he was putting his gun in his holster and realized he should have gotten a haircut. His hair was sticking up all over the place. He shrugged. It was too late to do anything about it now anyway.

It was raining when he drove to the hotel. He was walking into the lobby when Gil caught up with him.

"What are you doing here?"

"Didn't you hear me honking at you when you were crossing Michigan? I got caught at the light," Gil panted.

"Sorry, I didn't hear you."

"Alec, I might have something for you." He glanced around and then said, "Maybe we ought to find someplace private."

"I was just going up to Regan's office. We can talk there."

He used Regan's key to get up to the third floor. Gil started explaining as soon as the elevator doors closed. "I finally heard back from that patrolman down in Florida, and he had some interesting news."

The doors opened on the third floor, and both of them stepped into the corridor. It was empty and as quiet as a confessional on Friday night.

"So what did he tell you?"

"The accident happened over a year ago, closer to two," he said. "And it was bad, just like I told you. A five-car pileup. I was worried the patrolman wouldn't remember much about it, but he told me it was so gruesome he'll take the memory to his grave.

"There was this ten-mile stretch of two-lane highway outside of Tampa. Walker Madison was driving a sports car, and the engine had a lot of power. Evidently he was passing this truck, and this late-model sedan pulls out behind him and follows him. A guy named Gage, Eric Gage, was driving, and his wife was in the passenger seat. Walker gets around the truck and back into his lane without any trouble at all, but Gage's sedan didn't quite make it. There are some conflicting reports. The patrolman said one witness swore the truck driver wouldn't let the sedan in, that he deliberately sped up. There was another possibility that the sedan clipped the truck trying to get back in. Anyway, there was a terrible crash," he explained.

Alec noticed Gil was talking faster and faster now, and his face was getting red. A knot was forming in Alec's gut. He had a really bad feeling about what he was going to hear. "Go on," he urged.

"The truck lost control, spun, and flipped. The sedan was totaled, but the driver, this Eric Gage, didn't get so much as a bruise. His wife wasn't so lucky. The patrolman said they had to pry her out of the passenger seat. He said it looked like the car had folded in on her. Sometimes he says he can still hear the screams. The wife was unconscious and barely hanging on by a thread. It was the husband who was screaming. The patrolman said he went crazy, pulling at his hair and sobbing that he should have let her drive like she wanted, and it should have been him in that seat. He got more and more out of control the longer it took to get his wife out of the car. The paramedics had to sedate him, and because of his size, it took three men to strap him down to the gurney. He was out of his head, all right," Gil said. "And do you know what the patrolman told me he was trying to do?"

"What?"

"Get across that highway to Walker. He wanted to kill him. He was ranting about how Walker had been driving too fast, and that was why the truck veered."

"But that wasn't true?"

"Not according to the witnesses. The truck driver's insurance company settled with the families."

"How bad was Gage's wife?"

Gil was pulling slips of paper out of his pockets. He unfolded one and nodded. "Her name was Nina, and she was all broken up, but her legs got the worst of it. The bones were crushed."

"Ah, hell," he whispered. "I knew it was too easy."

He thought of Haley Cross and how her legs had been crushed with a hammer, and he knew it wasn't a coincidence. He sprinted to Regan's office. He just wanted to see her, to know she was okay. Then he could calm down and call Wincott.

Gil was chasing him. "Wait. Don't you want to know where Eric Gage is now?"

"He's here, isn't he, Gil? He's in Chicago."

Gil nodded. Then he thrust the slip of paper at Alec. "Here's his address."

Alec grabbed the paper, opened the door, and rushed into her office. It was empty. Panic like he'd never felt before bore down on him. He was reaching for the phone when he heard the fax machine humming.

He knew what it was before he looked. He dropped the phone and ran to the fax machine. He grabbed the paper before it slid into the tray. It was another murder list, but the heading was different. *"My Murder List,"* he'd written, and underneath there was just one name. *"Regan Madison."*

Chapter Forty-six

Regan walked at a fast clip at the beginning and then slowed down. The crowd thinned out. She was so lost in thought she didn't realize everyone had passed her until she reached the second-mile marker. She'd already gone farther than she'd intended. It started to drizzle, and she was hot and sticky. The die-hard runners were probably crossing the finish line by now, she thought.

She wasn't sure where she was. She didn't want to turn around and walk another two miles back to the starting line, and she didn't want to keep going to the finish line because that was another three-and-a-half-mile trek. She knew she'd run into a volunteer if she turned around and started back, and so she did just that. She really should have paid attention to all the signs and arrows the staff had placed along the route, but she'd been too busy feeling sorry for herself. And thinking about Alec, of course. Why didn't he know she was the best thing that would ever happen to him? No other woman would ever love him as passionately as she did.

He didn't love her, though. He wouldn't have stayed around as long as he did if it hadn't been for his job. It was all over and done with now, and she needed to stop crying over him. She was probably dehydrated from all the tears she'd already shed. The only good thing to come out of all of this was that her pride was still intact. Alec would never know that he had broken her heart. He would feel bad about it if he ever found out, and the last thing she needed or wanted was for him to feel sorry for her.

Tears blurred her vision. She was thoroughly disgusted with herself. "For the love of God, get it together," she whispered. And stop thinking about him.

She was thirsty and decided to focus on that. She wanted water, but anything cold and icy would do. She increased her pace as she walked along, but slowed when she saw a volunteer riding his bicycle toward her.

She waved to him and asked if he knew of a shortcut to get back to the starting line.

"Didn't you see the signs? There's a path that cuts through the park. Just around the curve behind me," he said. He smiled then. "Lots of the walkers have quit already."

She didn't much like his smug, condescending attitude. He'd certainly put her on the defensive. He rode on before she could explain that she wasn't a quitter. She had planned to walk only two miles, and that's exactly what she had done. In fact, she'd gone farther.

She shook her head then, for it finally dawned on her that she didn't need to defend her actions to anyone, and what did she care what the volunteer thought about her? She saw that the biker had stopped again, and she guessed someone else was asking him if there was a shortcut through this maze.

She walked around the corner and spotted a trail angling to the south, but there was another one that branched off it twenty yards ahead. If it didn't meander, it would take her directly to the parking lot beyond the starting line. She took it, but it didn't really go anywhere, and she ended up circling halfway back to where she'd started. She tripped over something, looked down, and saw that her shoelace was untied. The stone wall was on her right. A huge oak tree, at least seventy-five years old, butted up against it. Its gigantic branches, covered with leaves, draped down over the wall, and she noticed someone had carved initials in the trunk. She leaned against it, swung her foot up on the edge of the wall, and tied her shoelace, and then straightened and leaned forward to see what was on the other side.

A steep, narrow ravine sloped down a good forty feet to a wooded area with a stream running through it. Jagged rocks jutted out on one side of the drop, but across the stream, there were trees with thick gnarled branches that looked as though they were growing into the side of the hill.

It was drizzling again, and a fine mist was hanging like a puff of smoke between the trees. There wasn't any breeze, and the air was stifling. It was suddenly so quiet, so still, she felt almost disconnected from the world around her.

Her gaze moved upward. That's when she saw him. There, standing between the trees was the man in the black running suit. He was directly across the ravine, and he stood as still as a statue. He was waiting for her to find him. She was so shocked to see him there, she flinched. He nearly gave her heart failure. What was he doing?

Surely no more than three or four seconds passed as they stared at each other. His face was completely devoid of any expression. She kept her eyes locked on him as she slowly backed away from the wall. He suddenly tilted his head ever so slightly and shouted something to her. Just one word, she thought, but she couldn't make it out.

His face changed then, and, oh, God, she suddenly knew who he was and where she had seen him before. Terror crushed down on her. He mouthed the word again, much slower this time, clearly enunciating, and then he motioned with his hand, and she finally understood.

Run. He was telling her to run.

Chapter Forty-seven

Eric Gage only needed a minute alone with her. That was more than enough time to do what he intended. He almost wished she would get away, and yet he knew he couldn't let her escape. He had to kill her.

Walker Madison had put his sweet, innocent Nina through hell, but Eric wouldn't make Regan Madison suffer the way his wife had. No, the kill would be quick. And justice would at last be served.

The demon would burn with rage, but it would end today. Eric was determined. It would end with Regan's death.

Still, he wanted to give her a fighting chance. That was the fair thing to do. Wasn't that why he hadn't killed her when she'd been standing at the wall looking at the trees? He'd let a perfect opportunity slip by. She was sweet and innocent like his Nina, and he hoped, before she took her last breath, that he could help her know, help her understand why she had to die. He would tell her, just as he had told Nina, that none of this was her fault.

Run, Regan. Try to save yourself.

Regan didn't move. Like a deer caught in the headlights of a car, she froze with terror as she stared in shocked disbelief across the ravine at the crazed man. She didn't see the gun in his hand until he was lifting it up. He fired twice in rapid succession before she even had time to turn. The first bullet scraped the top of the stone wall and sent bits of rock flying up in her face. One fragment nicked her right cheek. The second bullet ripped a piece of bark off the oak just inches away from her. The noise from the gun blast was horrific and felt like a fist slamming against her eardrums.

She flew into the trees. She dared a quick look back and saw him circling the ravine. He was running so fast he looked like a blur.

She didn't dare take time to look back again. Faster, faster, she had to run faster.

Her mind couldn't make sense out of what was happening. She desperately tried to concentrate. She remembered the broken path wound back around to the ravine. She didn't want to go back that way; she wanted to get to the street, but her sense of direction was all screwed up, and she wasn't sure which way to turn.

She was running flat out through the

trees, staying off the path, her head down as she raced ahead.

He fired again. The bullet grazed her thigh. It burned, but the pain didn't slow her down. It shocked her, though, that he was that close. She'd thought she'd put some distance between them, yet she could feel him closing in.

She had to run faster. He fired again. The bullet tunneled into the ground in front of her, and a clump of mud splattered her legs. She could feel the scream building in her throat, but she didn't make a sound as she began to cut back and forth through the trees and the brush so she wouldn't be such an easy target.

Where in God's name were all the runners? Was the race over? Had they all gone home? She had the insane urge to look at her watch to find out what time it was. Had she veered that far off the beaten path? Hadn't anyone heard the gunshots? My God, it sounded like cannon fire to her.

She thought she heard someone shouting her name, but she couldn't tell where the sound was coming from. Had she just imagined it, or had someone really called out to her? Maybe Sophie and Cordie were looking for her. Dear God, she hoped not.

She kept running through the woods, the wild brush scraping her legs. If she could just make it to a street, she could get help. Faster, faster, she chanted. She didn't have to look behind her to know he was gaining on her. She could hear him crashing through the brush.

No. Wait. The sound wasn't coming from behind now. She strained to listen. It was difficult to pinpoint exactly where it was because her own heartbeat was roaring in her ears.

Run, run. She had to keep running. There it was again . . . branches snapping back, but the noise was coming from her right now. Oh, God, he was parallel to her. She understood what he was doing then. He was working his way around to get in front of her.

And then he would stop and wait, and she would turn right into his arms. It was a game to him. All this time she'd thought she was staying ahead of him, outrunning him, and he'd been leisurely toying with her.

She barely slowed as she changed directions. Even in her panic and near hysteria, she was careful not to twist her knee or pivot. She'd drop then, and he'd have her. She leapt over a thorny, dried-up bush and kept going. Then she changed directions again . . . and again.

Where was everyone? Should she scream in hopes that someone would hear her? No, she shouldn't do that. Even though she was pretty sure the maniac knew exactly where she was, she couldn't be positive, and she wasn't about to give him any help.

She couldn't keep up this pace much longer. The muscles in her legs were on fire. In another minute or two, they would give out on her and she would collapse.

Oh, God, it was hopeless. No, no, don't think that way. Don't give up. Run, just keep running. Her legs were shaking now and burning with pain. The muscle spasm in her calf made her want to cry out, but she kept going. She would not give in. There was too much to live for, and she wasn't going to let a maniac snatch her future away.

What she needed was a plan to buy her some time. Okay, okay, what could she do? Think . . . He had a gun. She didn't. He was obviously in much better shape, and he was stronger. He was also faster.

But she could have one advantage. She could be smarter.

And then it came to her, and she knew

exactly what she was going to do. Her plan hinged on her finding her way back to the ravine. She had to keep running. She broke through the bushes onto the path and saw the wall directly ahead of her. Which way should she turn?

The maniac made that decision for her. He was on her left now, and so she ran in the opposite direction. She didn't dare stay on the open path, though, and so she raced in and out of the trees, keeping the wall in sight.

There. There it was. She could see it up ahead, that huge oak with the branches hanging out over the wall. That had to be the spot she was looking for.

She broke through the brush again. Do it. She had to do it. He was coming up fast, but she didn't think he could see her yet. She wiped her hands down her sides, and with one final burst of speed, she raced down the path and vaulted over the wall.

Chapter Forty-eight

Eric reached the path and stopped. Where was she? Which way had she gone? He tilted his head and listened, but he didn't hear a sound. She had vanished.

His disappointment was severe. She had turned the chase into a game of hide-and-seek. He couldn't hear her, but in the distance someone was shouting her name, and whoever he was, Gage thought he was getting closer.

Gage knew he had to hurry. He didn't have time for this silly game. She was being foolish. She had to know he was going to find her and kill her. Why was she fighting the inevitable?

He could feel his anger gathering inside him, and with it came a tremendous sadness, for he knew that when he did find her, he would be in a rage, and she would suffer his wrath before she drew her last breath. If she didn't show herself soon, there wouldn't even be time for him to explain, to help her understand why she had to die.

He realized then he'd made a mistake. He should have killed her right away. He shouldn't have let her run. But he'd wanted her to feel that she had some say in her fate. His Nina hadn't known what was coming. She'd been asleep, curled up in a little ball in the passenger seat, using her jacket for a pillow against the window, oblivious of what was happening. The truck flipping and rolling, the cab sliding down the center of the highway with fiery sparks shooting out on both sides like electrified cables, coming closer and closer. It had all happened in an instant, but in his mind's eye, it had taken an eternity to strike . . . and destroy their lives forever.

Another shout came from behind, jarring him. He realized then that the sound was fainter than before.

Gage thought he heard the crunch of gravel underfoot. The sound was coming from up the path, and he bolted in that direction. He rounded the curve and stopped. He recognized where he was now. Full circle, he thought. She'd taken him back to the very spot where she had stood when he'd first fired at her. Yes, she'd stood right there next to that old tree.

He had watched her stare down into the ravine, the palms of her hands flat on top of the stone as she leaned over. She'd looked across the ravine . . . and then she'd found him, waiting so patiently for her to look up and see him standing between the trees. Oh, yes, this was the very same spot.

But where was Regan hiding? He stood perfectly still and listened. He couldn't hear her. He turned around and looked behind him? Nothing there. Ah . . . there it was. A hint. He could hear what sounded like rocks cascading down the ravine.

She'd jumped over the wall and was hiding down below. Clever girl, he thought, but not too clever. He rushed to the wall and looked over. Small stones were skipping over the larger ones. She was down there all right, but where?

He thought he saw something move to the right behind some dead, rotting branches. His reaction was instantaneous. He fired twice, hoping to hit her or spook her into showing herself.

The blast from the gunshots reverberated through the trees, and more rocks showered down the incline. He knew the police had heard the noise and would be closing in on him. It was too late to do anything about that now.

He heard someone shout her name again, knew someone was coming. Gage leaned against the wall, turned, and aimed. Then he waited.

Chapter Forty-nine

Alec heard the shots as his car skidded to a stop. He threw the gear into park and didn't bother to turn the motor off. He was out on the pavement and running, ignoring the crowd and barriers he knocked down as he raced forward.

Behind him, John Wincott's car, with sirens blaring, careened to a halt in the parking lot.

Alec spotted Sophie and Cordie across the lot at the same instant they saw him. Cordie ran to intercept him while Sophie shouted, "We can't find Regan. The police won't let us look for her, and then there were gunshots . . ."

Alec grabbed Cordie. "Where did you last see her?"

"At the starting line. She was going to walk two miles so that would be a mile on the path and then a mile back."

A shot sounded, and before Cordie could say another word, Alec's expression changed and he was gone.

She had never seen that look on anyone's face before, and it terrified her. She knew that when Alec caught up with whoever was firing those shots, he would kill him.

Alec was crazed. If anything happened to Regan, if he got there too late . . . if one of those bullets had already struck her down . . . No, there was still time to get to her. There had to be. The son of a bitch was going to die and die hard. If he touched one hair on her head, Alec would flay him alive.

Where in God's name was she? Did Gage already have her? Alec shouted Regan's name.

Wincott was behind him. Alec could hear him panting as he tried to catch up. He was shouting too.

"Wait, Alec. Don't go nuts. Let me get ahead of you. Don't give the bastard a shot. You're no good to her dead."

Alec ignored him. He couldn't think about anything but getting to her.

Two more shots were fired. Alec raced toward the sound.

Chapter Fifty

Gage was becoming frustrated. He leaned over the wall and looked down again. She wasn't as easy to kill as he had anticipated. The ingrate. After all the trouble he had gone to for her. She'd made that list, and he'd played along, hadn't he? She'd even told him what to do about Peter Morris — she'd given him the idea anyway — with those notes she'd written on her folder. Yes, he'd played along. He'd given her what she wanted. He had taken a risk for her by not letting the demon know what he was doing. He had thought to do a kindness for her, to make her happy, because none of this was her fault and he felt she deserved a little happiness and joy before she died.

She wasn't appreciative. And that infuriated him. He could feel rage taking control. What a mess he had made of this. No, no, he mustn't blame himself. This wasn't his fault. He hadn't done anything wrong. She had. She was the slippery one. She was responsible for this mess, not him. Oh, he knew what she was doing. She wanted him to blame himself just like he had after the accident, but the demon had helped him understand that it was all Walker Madison's fault.

Gage could still see Walker clearly in his mind's eye, the celebrity standing across the highway, his hands in his pockets, his expression solemn. He was surrounded by men and women, adoring fans who were all wanting a tiny piece of his attention while the paramedics peeled his Nina's broken body from the wreckage.

The truck driver had died at the scene, and the police had placed the blame on him, but what good was it to rage against a dead man? No, Walker was responsible.

A voice jarred him. Someone was shouting Regan's name again, an anguished cry he didn't understand. Then it came again, much closer this time. He didn't have time to swing over the wall and slide down into the pit to find her. Regan would have to wait a little longer. He straightened, leveled his gun on the path where he heard the pounding footsteps, ready now to kill again.

Alec broke through the trees with his gun drawn.

Gage had a clear shot at him. Suddenly a scream of warning came from the branch above him, and he looked up a scant second before Regan slammed both feet into the side of his head. She landed hard on top of him, rolled, and tried to crawl away, but he was as quick as a snake and latched onto her ankle. He was dragging her back as he swung the gun around.

Alec dove to the ground, waiting for a clear shot, and the second she scrambled to get away from Gage, Alec pulled the trigger. It was a clean kill, one bullet into his skull, but Alec wasn't taking any chances. He kept his gun trained on him as he ran forward and kicked the gun out of Gage's hand.

Alec dropped to his knees. It took him two tries to holster his gun. He grasped her shoulders in both hands. "Are you okay, Regan? Are you okay?"

She became hysterical. "Make him let go of me. Get his hand away from me. Make him let go."

Alec ripped Gage's hand away from her ankle. Then he stood and pulled her to her feet. He was checking her over as he asked once again, "You're okay, aren't you?"

He sounded frantic, but he couldn't help it. He'd come so close to losing her. Now that he had her in his arms, he couldn't make himself let go. He held her tight.

"I'm fine," she told him. Her voice was

surprisingly calm. Running that long and that hard had taken its toll, though. She was amazed her legs could support her. Her muscles felt like rubber.

She was thankful for his strength. She was trembling almost uncontrollably, and just when she thought she was getting over the trauma, she started crying. Alec didn't seem to mind that she was sobbing all over his T-shirt while she was trying to tell him how scared she had been for him.

"You could have died," she cried. "He was waiting for you. I knew it was you because you were shouting my name. Alec, he was going to shoot you. You could have been killed. Do you know how close you came?"

He was stunned. Gage had chased her, shot at her God only knows how many times, and she had worried about him. He wanted to kiss her and tell her he loved her, but she was going to have to finish crying first.

Wincott was standing by Gage's feet staring at Alec.

"Did you see her?" Alec asked.

Wincott nodded. "I did. She came down out of that tree like a shooting star. Shocked the hell out of me. Sure surprised Gage too. She saved your life, Alec.

He had you in his sights."

"I know she did." Alec tightened his hold on her. "I'm going to get her out of here."

"There should be at least one ambulance waiting in the parking lot. I'll catch up with you after I get the crime scene crew in here."

Regan pulled away from Alec. "What are the ambulances waiting for?"

Wincott answered. "They're prepared for just about anything. One of the paramedics will clean up those cuts for you."

Alec put his arm around her and started walking.

She leaned against him. "Alec," she whispered.

"Yes?"

She sounded bewildered when she asked, "Who was that man, and why was he trying to kill me?"

Chapter Fifty-one

Nina Gage watched the news bulletin on the television. She saw her husband being placed in the ambulance by the paramedics and the police. They weren't in a hurry. A sheet covered the body, but Nina knew the unidentified male was Eric. They knew who he was too but were withholding that information until the next of kin was notified. They would be knocking on her door any minute now.

She felt no sorrow or pity for Eric. Had he failed or had he succeeded? That was all that mattered.

She waited to see another body. The TV camera scanned the parking lot, and she saw her. Regan Madison was alive. For a split second, Regan turned and looked into the camera's lens, her eyes, like daggers, piercing Nina's heart. A low, keening sound in Nina's throat erupted into a scream.

She heard someone knocking on her front door.

She picked up the gun Eric had so thoughtfully left for her and pressed the barrel to her temple.

Chapter Fifty-two

She wasn't kidding about being a crybaby. Every time Alec thought she was finished, she started in again. He wasn't concerned. He knew that crying was her way of getting rid of all the tension inside her. She had been through hell today and had shown remarkable courage and strength and grace, but now that it was over and she was safe, she could let it all out.

Alec sat next to her on the sofa in her suite, and had they been alone, he would have lifted her onto his lap and cradled her in his arms. They weren't alone, though. The room was crowded with family and friends.

Aiden and Spencer were sitting in easy chairs, leaning forward as they listened to John Wincott explain once again how their brother Walker had unknowingly triggered Gage's obsession for revenge.

Sophie and Cordie, looking as if they were about to burst into tears themselves, sat in straight-back chairs by the French doors leading to the bedroom.

Regan was dabbing at the corners of her

eyes and trying to pay attention to the conversation, but Alec kept distracting her. He had taken hold of her hand. She pulled it away. He grabbed it again. When she looked up at him, he winked at her. She was confused. He shouldn't be teasing her. Had he forgotten he was leaving? Maybe she should remind him.

She didn't know how she was going to get through another good-bye. Just thinking about it made the tears flow again. John Wincott leaned forward to hand her another tissue from the box he'd placed on the coffee table and said, "Are you going to be okay?"

"Yes," she assured him. "It's just what I need to do sometimes."

Wincott glanced around the room. Her brothers and her friends were obviously used to the tears because they all nodded. Alec didn't seem fazed either. Wincott smiled then. In the crisis, she'd been incredible, and if she wanted to cry now, it was fine with him.

"I do this a lot," she admitted.

Everyone nodded again. Even Alec. She decided to ignore him and turned to ask Cordie a question, but he distracted her again. Before she realized what he was going to do, he'd put his arm around her and pulled her in to his side.

Regan noticed that neither one of her brothers looked the least bit surprised. Sophie and Cordie, on the other hand, looked astonished.

"So that's some good news, isn't it, Regan?" John had asked the question.

"I'm sorry," she said. "I wasn't paying attention."

"It's been a long day. I was talking about Peter Morris and saying that the murder charges were dropped, of course, but he had already confessed to stealing that grant money and gambling it away. If the judge throws that confession out, they'll still get him for embezzlement. Seems Morris was dipping into the center's bank accounts. He's going to be doing some hard time."

"That's good to hear," Spencer said.

Regan agreed. Both of her brothers were calmer now. When they had arrived at the park, they were half out of their minds with worry. Regan was sitting in the back of an ambulance with Cordie and Sophie while the paramedic cleaned her cuts. Regan had never seen Aiden or Spencer carry on so. It was another revelation. Aiden was actually shouting at a detective. Spencer had tried to punch out one of the TV cameramen when he tried to climb into the ambulance to get a close-up of her. Spencer needn't have bothered. Alec wouldn't let the man get near her. He reined in Aiden too and got him to calm down.

"We still haven't been able to get hold of Walker," Spencer said.

"Do you think he'll remember the accident?" Sophie asked.

Regan frowned. "Of course he'll remember."

"He didn't cause it." Wincott repeated what he had already told them. "According to the patrolman's notes, he cited the truck driver and Gage for reckless driving."

"Then Gage did have a hand in the accident," Cordie said.

"That's right," Wincott said.

"Why did the truck driver's insurance company settle then?" she asked.

Alec answered. "There was an eyewitness who swore the truck driver deliberately increased his speed so Gage couldn't get back in when he was passing him. I'm sure the insurance company didn't want a long legal battle. It was cheaper to settle."

Regan looked at Aiden. "And more practical." She was thinking about Emerson and how they had decided to give him a small settlement to get rid of him.

"Gage shouldn't have tried to pass that

truck," Sophie said.

No one disagreed with her. Then Alec said, "I don't think Gage could accept responsibility for any of it."

"Walker got around the truck without any trouble, but Gage couldn't, and maybe that's what set him off."

"You should have seen that bedroom upstairs in their house. It was Eric's private domain because Nina couldn't climb the stairs. He had all sorts of interesting things sitting around."

"Like what?" Sophie asked.

"Nina's medical records from the hospital and the rehab facility. Among some of the papers were bills for Eric Gage from a psychiatric hospital."

"How did he get medical files?" Sophie asked.

"He must have stolen them," Cordie said. "But why?"

"Maybe she wanted him to steal them," Wincott answered. "He was the unstable one in that marriage. She wasn't, though."

"How do you know that?" Regan asked.

"Bradshaw went through her records and read me some of the comments the doctors and the therapists had written about Nina and her progress. She was an extremely difficult patient," he said. "And that's putting it mildly. She didn't want to get better; she wanted to get even. I think she pushed and pushed until Eric did what she wanted. Nina Gage was a bitter, broken woman."

"I think Eric was real conflicted about killing you," Wincott told Regan.

"He sure didn't act conflicted when he was chasing her through that park and shooting at her." Alec got angry thinking about it.

"He found your murder list, and maybe he was trying to fulfill your last wishes before he . . . you know," Cordie said.

"What a sick bastard," Aiden remarked.

"I'm with you on that," Alec said.

"Do you suppose he wanted someone to stop him?" Regan asked. "And that's why he sent the e-mail and the faxes? He knew the police would get involved."

Wincott flipped his notepad closed, put it in his pocket, and said, "At first he did, but then Gage set Morris up to get us away from you, so he must have changed his mind. It appears to have been a game to him. Nina was the controller in their marriage, and Eric was eaten up with guilt. He did whatever she wanted him to do."

"And they blamed my brother for their misery," Regan said.

"She knew exactly what she was doing. As soon as she was strong enough, they packed up everything they owned and moved here, to Walker's hometown. It's my belief that Walker was their first target, and Eric was waiting for an opportunity to kill him."

Alec nodded. "But plans have a way of changing."

"There were photos on Gage's kitchen table, and a clipping file on Walker. They were keeping track of where he was," Wincott said. "And you know what else was on that table? About twenty copies of a photo of all of you that was in the newspaper. I think that's when their plans changed. Imagine how she must have felt every time she looked at your smiling faces. In that picture, Walker is standing behind Regan, sort of looking down at her, and he's got his hand on her shoulder. He's looking so proud of her and happy, and that must have sent the Gages into orbit."

"They wanted to make Walker suffer before Eric killed him," Alec said. "They had a real hate going on."

Regan shivered. "The accident turned them into monsters."

"Sweetheart, I don't think they were real nice people before the accident."

"You almost have to pity them," Regan said.

"The hell with that. He tried to kill you. If I could, I'd shoot him again."

Wincott stood and stretched. "That's about it."

Sophie also stood. "I'm going home. You scared me to death today, Regan. I swear it's going to take me a week of shopping to get over it."

"Am I supposed to apologize?"

Sophie grinned. "If you want to."

"Sophie, you have to drive me home," Cordie said. "And if Regan apologizes to anyone, it should be me. I didn't want to walk in that race anyway. If you'll remember, I suggested we go to the frozen custard shop."

"No, we were supposed to meet there after the race," Sophie said.

They were arguing as they walked out of the suite. Wincott said good-bye, shook hands with her brothers, and also left. Alec followed him.

"Hey, John, hold up. I want to run something by you."

Aiden and Spencer also headed for the door. "Are you going to be okay tonight?" Spencer asked Regan.

"I'll be fine."

She walked over to Aiden and nudged him in his back as he was walking out the door. "You want to hear something funny?"

"I could use a laugh about now."

"You know that little problem I had?"

"Which little problem?" He made it sound as though she had too many problems for him to keep track of.

"The problem with sleazebags."

"You mean old men marrying young women?"

"Yes."

"I remember telling you to get over it."

"I did get over it, but that's how I noticed Eric Gage. There was this older man with this very young woman walking across the street. I, of course, homed right in on them. Old habits die hard," she explained. "And I was thinking that I shouldn't react with such disgust, just because . . . well, let's face it, he was a sleazebag."

"Oh, yes, I can tell you've gotten over your problem."

"If I didn't have that problem, I wouldn't have noticed him. That's all I'm trying to say."

"And did noticing him in any way affect what happened later?"

She knew where he was headed and was

sorry she'd started the conversation.

"Never mind."

He laughed. "You know what, Regan?"

"What?"

He tweaked her nose just to aggravate her and said, "We love you. You know that, don't you?"

She nodded and became teary-eyed again. "Does that mean you'll triple my budget next year?"

"No, it means we love you. But nice try."

Alec had walked with Wincott to the elevator and was on his way back to the suite when Aiden stopped him. Spencer was in the doorway talking to Regan.

Neither Aiden nor Alec minced words.

"What's going on with my sister?"

"I'm going to marry her."

"You are?"

Alec nodded. "It's going to take some time for me to convince her, but I'll eventually wear her down."

Aiden obviously approved. He shook Alec's hand, looked at Regan, and said, "I don't think it will take too long."

Spencer joined them, and Alec told him his intentions. Spencer was more protective and reserved. "If you ever make my sister cry . . ." He suddenly stopped. He glanced at Regan just as she wiped a tear away from her cheek and said, "Never mind."

Regan waited for Alec. She stood in the doorway and watched him walk toward her.

He thought she looked as if she wanted to give him hell.

"I want to thank you for your help today," she said.

He smiled. "Okay."

"You saved my life."

"You saved mine."

"Then we're even."

She stepped back and had every intention of shutting the door in his face just to let him know how upset she was, but his next question stopped her.

"How come you're so cranky?"

She swung the door wide and stepped forward again. "I am not cranky. I assume you'll be going on your way now . . . you know, *going forward*," she stressed. "And I want to wish you good luck with your career."

"Really."

"Yes."

He started to reach for her, but she put her hand up and shook her head.

"I am not going to let you break my heart again. You listen to me, Alec. You can't tell me you're leaving and then come back and put your arms around me and . . . you just can't." She was just warming up. She folded her arms across her chest. "You're moving forward, remember. That's what you told me. So go ahead, Alec. Go forward, right out the door."

She was ready for a fight, but he didn't play fair.

"I love you, Regan."

She blinked. "No."

His grin was adorable. "Yeah, I do. I love you."

She wouldn't believe him. "But 'If I'm ever in Boston' . . . you said, 'If I'm ever in Boston' . . ."

"I'm not going anywhere without you."

She was determined to make him squirm a little before she forgave him. But her heart belonged to him.

She stepped back and said, "If you're ever in Chicago . . ."

She tried to shut the door. His foot got in the way. He was laughing when he backed her up and then shut the door behind him.

"Maybe you didn't notice . . ."

Oh, but she loved him. "Yes?"

"I'm already here."

Epilogue

Alec was taking Regan home to meet his family. She was nervous and worried they might not like her. He thought that was the craziest thing he'd ever heard. He couldn't imagine why she was feeling so insecure, but he did his best to reassure her as they walked side by side through the airport.

They were an odd-looking couple. Alec had let his hair and his beard grow for an undercover assignment he'd just completed for the Bureau, and he hadn't had time to shave and get a haircut. He'd showered and put on his comfortable off-duty uniform, a T-shirt and worn-out jeans.

Regan was picture-perfect. She wore a pink blouse, a short khaki skirt, and sandals. Her only jewelry was a pair of tiny diamond studs and her engagement ring.

She looked like a cover girl. He looked like a serial killer.

Men tried to make eye contact with her, and women tried not to scream when they looked at him.

They were seated in the last row of first class, which afforded them a little privacy, and as soon as the seat belt light went off, he leaned across the armrest and kissed her. He took his time, deliberately trying to fluster her. Then he told her how much he loved her.

"You know what people are thinking when they see us together?"

"Yes," she whispered. "They're thinking how lucky I am."

"That's right. That's exactly what they're thinking."

She rolled her eyes. "You'd better remove that earring before your brothers see it. From what you've told me about them, they'll be merciless ribbing you."

"I'll let them have some fun. Then I'll take it off."

"Did you have a chance to read Sophie's follow-up article about Shields yet?"

"Yes, I did. She did a great job."

"She's very talented. Does that surprise you?"

He stretched his legs out, adjusted his seat, and took hold of her hand. "Sweetheart, after finding out that she's Bobby Rose's daughter, nothing she does will surprise me. Tell me how you met Cordie and Sophie. I know you became friends in school . . ."

"Spencer told you about the bully, didn't he?"

"No, he said to make you tell me."

"It all started with a pair of barrettes," she began, and then she told him the story of Morgan the Bully. Alec thought it was hilarious that Regan had thrown up on the girl.

"Did she leave you and your friends alone after that?"

She nodded. "I haven't seen her in years."

"I wonder what happened to her."

"Oh, I know what happened. She went into politics. She's a senator now."

He laughed again, sure she was joking.

She loved the way he laughed. She loved just about everything about him. He had walked into her office and forever changed her life.

The man of her dreams was falling asleep. "Alec?"

"Hmm?"

"When are you going to show me Nick's town house?"

"It's our town house now," he corrected. "We could go over tomorrow if you want, and if you don't like it, we'll put it on the market and look for something else."

"I'll like it."

"It's got enough bedrooms for your friends. I know you're going to miss them."

She would miss seeing them, but she knew she'd continue to talk to them every day.

"I'll be going back and forth for a couple of months, until Paul and Henry don't need me anymore."

"How did Henry take the news that you'll be working out of the Boston hotel?"

"Same way your friend took the news when you told him you were going into the FBI."

"So he cried like a baby too, huh?"

"I forgot to tell you the news. Your computer tech is now working for the Hamilton."

"Melissa took the job?"

Regan smiled. "Aiden didn't know what to make of her. She told him she wanted to replace all of our 'piece of junk' computers."

" 'Junk'? She said 'junk'?"

"She's working on her language skills."

Regan was telling him about the improvements she was going to make in the office she was setting up at the hotel in Boston. She stopped when she realized Alec had fallen asleep.

She kissed his cheek. "I love you, Alec."

Now and forever.

About the Author

Julie Garwood is the author of many *New York Times* bestsellers, including *Killjoy*, *Mercy*, *Heartbreaker*, *Ransom*, and *Come the Spring*. There are more than thirty-two million copies of her books in print.